# "5 of 5 stars!"

"The trilogy follows Steve, and his two best friends Angie and Geo (nicknames of course)...starting with a job at Homeland Security, taking out a terrorist cell trying to infiltrate the U.S. through Port Everglades, FL. Along the way, Steve finds love, and in that love, a sense of peace and calm within himself. But no one expects WHO that love comes from. Family, friends, and the support of everyone, give Steve aka Chic, something to fight for.

"Book 2 starts with Steve newly married, living in Italy, and planning a trip back home to the United States to visit his family, who are quickly adding to the family ranks. The morning starts off nice enough, but a colonel has other ideas. This time, he just wants Steve to be a consultant. But everyone knows it's not that simple.

"Book 3 (still with Steve, Angie and Geo, and family) is about twins who have been recruited by Al-Qaida to infiltrate the United States. And guess who gets "tagged" to help hunt them, and the rest of the cell down, and stop them? Yep, the good old boys from Florida!

"Now that the formal stuff is out of the way, let me say, I couldn't stop reading. I was constantly wanting to know what happens next. And a little more, and a little more, before you know it, you are done. The characters are heart warming, lovable and memorable. I felt like I knew them, and wanted the best for them. Amazingly written. From the descriptions, to the dialogues, it was believable and real. Nothing felt forced at all. 5 of 5 stars."

—Heather Badgwell of *Heather's Book Reviews*

# The Trihedral of Chaos

by Frank A. Ruffolo

THE TRIHEDRAL of CHAOS by Frank A. Ruffolo
www.frankaruffolo.com

First Edition, June 2012



Author Services by Pedernales Publishing, LLC.
www.pedernalespublishing.com



ISBN: 978-0-9836803-3-8

Printed in the United States of America

*for Christine, Michael, and Alicia*

# INTRODUCTION

Steve Ciccone, an ex-Vietnam War sniper, ex-police SWAT team member, is thrust into the difficult job of protecting his country against foreign and domestic terrorists. Currently in semi-retirement and working as a sky marshal for Homeland Security, he is chosen by the President of the United States to take charge of the Federal Security Agency, the FSA, an agency the president created to permit him to deploy the U.S. military within the borders of the United States.

As Steve struggles to heal from the sudden death of his wife, he encounters Diane Summers, a beautiful movie star, who captures his heart. He must reconcile his love of country with his love for Diane and a simple life, as he works closely with his FSA team to keep the country ever vigilant against chaos. Steve advances from commanding a team, to being pulled out of retirement to help a team, and finally to volunteering to assist an old friend to protect and defend the country he loves.

Will he be successful? Only time will tell.

The vigilance of good persons among us must be 100 percent at all times in order to ensure the safety of the citizens of the United States, but terrorists need only be successful once in order to create death and chaos.

Now enter The Trihedral of Chaos.

Book One
**Trihedral of Chaos**
Trilogy

# The Crescent Star

by Frank A. Ruffolo

# CHAPTER ONE

Soon after dawn on September 9, 2011, a target is sighted through a Barrett .50 caliber rifle, 2,700 yards down range on the weapons testing site at Eglin Air Force Base. Acquiring a target at that distance is almost the limit of accuracy recommended for this sniper rifle. Not many snipers can pull off this shot, but Chic and his spotter, Angie, have done this before.

Steve "Chic" Ciccone, a recipient of the Bronze Star, and Frank "Angie" Angelo, learned their trade during the Vietnam War. They served in Vietnam together, and then after they were discharged, they worked on the same SWAT (Special Weapons and Tactics) team for the New York City Police Department.

Steve is currently a consultant for the Fort Lauderdale Police Department while working part time as a sky marshal for Homeland Security. Widowed for almost two years, he is waiting for a cash settlement related to his wife's death from a horrible car accident. He has two married sons.

Frank never married and has no living family. Frank owns Duke's Saloon in Pembroke Pines, which is southwest of Fort Lauderdale. The saloon was named after John Wayne, the late, great actor, and Frank has decorated his establishment with John Wayne memorabilia. Anytime during the day or night, there is a John Wayne movie playing on a widescreen TV for the entertainment of his patrons.

Steve and Frank have been best friends since the war, and no matter what their schedules might be, they always make time to go to Eglin just for the hell of it.

It is a quiet morning with very little wind. Angie whispers to Chic to guide his shot.

"It will take about a second for the cartridge to reach the target. You need to compensate for the distance the projectile will be sucked to the earth by gravity."

Chic chuckles, "Ang, been doin' this too long to forget."

Chic sights his target through the scope, aiming high to compensate for the bullet's drop. He squeezes the trigger slowly and the rifle roars to life. Angie looks through his range finder, a sophisticated binocular with distances displayed, and gives Chic the results.

"Okay, the shot was about 1.5 inches high and dead on center."

Chic chambers another round and sights his target again, slightly adjusting his aim. As the next shot rings out, it muffles the sound of a black suburban pulling up behind them.

Their day is about to change.

# CHAPTER TWO

**September 9, 2011**

Dawn in Los Angeles:

Diane Summers is sleeping in her Beverly Hills mansion. Her personal assistant, Tammy Young, knocks on her closed bedroom door, trying to wake her up. There is no response.

Tammy realizes that if Diane does not wake up soon, she will be late for an important date with destiny. Tammy opens the door, turns on the lights and enters the bedroom, hoping this will awaken her boss.

It does not.

As Tammy frantically tries to wake the sleeping diva, she shakes the bed and says, "Miss Summers, you need to get up! You have an appointment at MGM Studios at eight o'clock this morning!"

Diane Summers is a three-time Academy Award winner; however, her last award was in 1990. Today, she will be briefed on a new movie that will be shot in South Florida. Diane needs this opportunity to get back in the limelight. She has already read the script's first draft and needs this job to boost her self-confidence.

Half asleep and annoyed, Diane retorts, "Tammy, it's too early for this. Reschedule it." She covers herself with the bed blanket.

Tammy is now very frustrated, and replies, "I cannot, and it's set in stone. You need to go; you haven't had work in years! The public will forget about you. *Please* get up!"

Diane is still a looker, but she needs this job to resurrect her career. She knows it, and drags herself into the shower. As she soaks in the stream of hot water, she realizes that this movie may be her last chance in Hollywood. Actresses are getting younger and roles are getting sexier.

After she steps out of the shower and wipes the condensation from the mirror, she notices once again that her youth is starting to fade. Surgeons have kept her fresh, but she's no Scarlett Johansson. She meticulously applies her makeup, covering up several new freckles and age lines that seemed to suddenly appear overnight. Trying to decide what to wear to the meeting, she searches for her favorite sexy black dress in the changing room closet, larger than most studio apartments. As she puts it on in front of the triple, full length mirror, she comments approvingly, "Damn! I still look pretty good for a chic in her fifties!"

Ready to tackle Hollywood, she runs down the stairs and kisses Tammy goodbye. As she walks through the front door toward her 500 SEL, she calls back to Tammy, "Wish me luck!"

Little does she know that she will be flying to Fort Lauderdale in forty-eight hours.

Her life is about to change.

# CHAPTER THREE

**September 9, 2001**

Moscow, shortly after dawn:

Scientist Sergei Andropov leaves his home and heads unsteadily toward Red Square. He is single, active in the local club scene, and vodka lost its kick a long time ago. His life is spiraling downward. He quickly moved from alcohol to marijuana, and then went on to heroin. Now he needs more money for his heroin addiction.

Sergei works with the research team at a spent nuclear material reclamation facility. His team is responsible for making the highly radioactive material inert so disposal and storage is safer. Sergei's job offers him access to spent uranium 235, which has a half-life of over two hundred years. If an area was contaminated with this material, it would be uninhabitable for generations. However, there is much interest in acquiring this material around the world, with a lot of money available for the person with the goods.

There is a chill in the air, and winter is coming soon. All those global warming activists were dead wrong, as the earth has actually cooled down. They are predicting an early frost, with snow by the end of the month.

Sergei is meeting a man from Dubai at a local Moscow café to work out the details of the purchase and transfer of uranium 235. He does not care about the early winter. With the money he will receive from this deal, he plans to take a long trip to sunny Havana.

After a short drive into downtown Moscow, Sergei parks his car and walks two blocks to the café.

The world is about to change.

# CHAPTER FOUR

At the firing range, two men emerge from the black Suburban and approach Steve and Angie. They flash Secret Service ID's.

"Steve Cicone, we represent President Baruch. He would like to see you at the White House. We have come to escort you there."

Steve and Angie, both pissed off, jump to their feet.

Steve responds, "Why in the hell does he want to see me? I didn't even vote for him!"

The first agent replies, "Some special assignment. He'll fill you in."

"If he wants me, he gets Angie, too, and another *compadre* from South Florida."

Angie chimes in, "Don't get me involved in this shit!"

Steve continues, "The three of us are a package deal for any 'special' assignment, but first we need to drive back down to Fort Lauderdale. We can leave here tomorrow morning."

The second agent states firmly, "We will fly you down to Washington on the next commercial flight. You will leave for D.C. this afternoon…alone."

Steve pauses, and then says, "All right. I'll go to D.C., but he gets all three of us, if he wants me."

"Bullshit!" exclaims Angie. "And wait 'till Geo hears about this!"

Coolly, Steve replies, "Calm down. How bad could this be?"

"If Baruch's involved, we're in deep shit."

Steve breaks down his weapon while Angie helps him load it into the agents' SUV. He climbs into the black Suburban with Angie, and the Secret Service agents drive them to Angie's car. Steve transfers his gear into Angie's car and says goodbye to his friend. He then climbs back into the black Suburban with the agents, and they drive off.

Angie is now alone, and has a long drive back to South Florida. He wants to tell Geo what happened, but decides to leave that to Steve.

Geo is George Jackson, a Red Beret from the Vietnam War, and a munitions expert. He retired from New York City's bomb squad and moved to South Florida with Steve and Frank. He now works part time for the TSA at Fort Lauderdale-Hollywood International Airport and helps Angie at Duke's Saloon. Three times divorced with no kids, he is currently dating a waitress who works for Angie at the saloon, and is thirty years his junior. He will not be retiring anytime soon. He has too much alimony to pay.

# CHAPTER FIVE

Diane Summers sits in the lobby of Rex Fishman's office and waits. Rex is an executive producer for MGM Studios.

When he finally comes out of his office, he greets her with a kiss on the cheek.

"Diane! It's so nice to see you! Come in. Please sit down."

Rex gets right to the point.

"This project will be shot on location in the Miami-Fort Lauderdale area. We sent all the details to your agent. We need you to fly down to Florida right away. The tickets are being sent to your house as we speak. We set up a suite for you at Ventura Country Club, not far from Fort Lauderdale. You can relax there and meet with the director and fellow cast members. If all goes well, we will begin shooting within four weeks."

He hands Diane the final script.

"This is the final version. Not much different from the script you already read. Do you have any questions?"

Diane, a little surprised by the quick trip to Florida, replies, "This is so sudden. I have my staff to worry about..." She is cut off in mid-sentence.

"Diane, everything has been taken care of. Talk to your agent, he has everything under control. Besides, you'll have a nice, relaxing time at the country club; everything is being paid by MGM. Look, I have to run. Everything will be handled for you. Have fun in Florida!"

Rex rushes out with a kiss and leaves her stunned, but happy. This could put her in the limelight again!

Halfway around the world, the meeting is taking place at the café in Moscow.

Sergei has an appointment with Mahmoud Attan, Vice President of Interplex LTD, a large corporation based in Dubai. Interplex manages seaports across the world and has just taken over operation of Port Everglades in Fort Lauderdale, Florida. Mr. Attan is also an agent for al-Qaida, and is arranging to obtain uranium 235 from Sergei Andropov.

"Mr. Andropov, do you have the merchandise we seek?"

"No, but I can get it at any time. Security is very lax. Do you have what *I* want?"

"I assure you, your fee is already in my possession."

They order tea from the waiter and Sergei demands that Mahmoud pay the tab. The deal is now set. Once Mahmoud has possession of the uranium, it will be transferred to an al-Qaida operative, who will then transport it to Port Everglades. The uranium's ultimate destination is the inner workings of a dirty bomb, which al-Qaida plans to explode outside the Capitol in Washington, D.C.

Sergei arranges to hand Mahmoud the package of uranium in Gorky Park within forty-eight hours. Mahmoud watches him leave. He smiles and finishes his tea.

After Sergei leaves the café, he stops at an ATM on his way home to withdraw some cash. He needs money for more heroin.

# CHAPTER SIX

As Steve takes his seat aboard the plane to Washington, his mind races between his impending meeting with the president and Julie, his late wife. Julie died suddenly and horribly in an automobile accident eighteen months ago. She was hit broadside by an FPX truck. The driver ran a red light and was arrested for DUI, driving under the influence.

Steve is about to receive a very large settlement from the insurance company for the accident. Neither FPX nor the Teamsters Union wants a long jury trial, since this was not the first DUI offense by this driver. After his first offense, the union had forced FPX to send the driver to rehab so he could retain his license. A jury trial would have shown negligence by FPX and the union, and that was something they both wanted to avoid at any cost. The large settlement is little consolation to Steve, however. He loved Julie very much and they had planned to retire together soon and move to a small villa on the Amalfi Coast of Italy.

His thoughts are interrupted by the flight attendant, who is whispering to him.

"Steve, are you working with us today?"

The flight attendant's name is Kathy. Because Steve is a sky marshal, she is questioning his presence on her airplane.

Steve replies, "Hi, Kathy. Not today. I'm on personal business."

Kathy smiles, "If there's anything you need, let me know, I'll get it for you." She leans over and whispers into his ear, "Even if I have to get it out of first class." She gives him a slight peck on the cheek.

Kathy is a flirt. Steve never paid attention to her attempts at seduction before, but he noticed her as soon as he boarded the plane today, and he's feeling a little conflicted. He still holds a large place in his heart for Julie, but he's enjoying Kathy's attention.

One hour into the flight, Steve is still wondering what President Baruch could want from him. Even though he's not officially on duty today, his eyes sweep over the other passengers while he ponders his future. As he scans the passengers, he notices that one of them is acting peculiar. He presses the call button for a flight attendant, and Kathy responds.

Steve rises from his seat and asks Kathy to accompany him to the back of the plane.

Steve asks, "Kathy, what is going on with the guy in the first row, next to the window? He looks nervous and agitated. He's sweating profusely, and its damn cold in here."

Kathy answers, "He must have been drinking before he got on, and he had a couple after we took off."

Steve replies, "I'll keep watch. Don't give him any more."

Kathy walks to the front of the airplane and Steve returns to his seat. The drunken passenger passes out and Steve notices that he's slumped in his seat. He leaves his seat again and makes his way to the galley.

"Kathy, let's check our friend in the first row."

When they approach the drunken passenger, Steve assesses the situation.

"I think he's sleeping it off, but you'd better notify the ground marshals when you land. They'll help you with him."

After the plane lands, ground marshals assist the

drunken passenger off the plane as Steve deplanes with the rest of the passengers.

Meanwhile, Angie's long drive back to South Florida from Eglin AFB has finally ended at Duke's Saloon. As he walks into the saloon, his friend, Geo, is tending bar and looks up when the door opens. He sets up a beer for Angie and asks, "Where's Chic?"

Angie hides a sneer. "He had some personal business. He'll tell you about it later."

Geo walks around the bar and sits down to share a beer with Angie while they watch the sports channel on a widescreen TV. During a commercial break, a news story expands on rumors that Daniella Patterson, a female driver on the Indy Racing League, is planning to drive at Homestead-Miami Speedway in the last NASCAR Sprint Race of the season. The story speculates that next season she will switch from the Nationwide series to NASCAR and then leave the Indy racing circuit to compete for the Sprint Cup full time.

As Steve carries his flight bag through the airport, he is greeted by the two Secret Service agents from Eglin, who were waiting for his flight to arrive.

"Mr. Cicone, please come with us."

Steve wonders how they arrived in D.C. before he did, but he follows them into another black Suburban and they speed away toward Pennsylvania Avenue.

When they arrive at the White House, Steve is met by one of the President's staff members and is directed to the Oval Office. He is left outside the door as the staffer enters and closes the door behind him. He waits for what feels like an hour, and is then ushered in.

President Baruch is standing, waiting to greet him. The President is taller than he looks on TV. He reaches out, takes Steve's hand in a firm handshake, and says, "Steve, welcome to my office. How was your flight?"

He directs Steve to a couple of chairs placed in front of his desk, where they both sit down.

Steve replies, "Thank you for having me here, Mr. President. My flight wasn't bad at all. But why did you ask for me?"

"As you are well aware, the United States is being threatened every day by terrorists inside and outside our borders. Before I was elected, I pledged to establish a private security force here at home to bridge the gap between our military and local enforcement agencies. However, the bad economy I inherited delayed that deployment. I would like to make good on my pledge now, and I want you to head up the Fort Lauderdale Bureau of this new security force. Your experience in the military and in law enforcement makes you the perfect candidate."

Steve replies, "Mr. President, I am currently working for Homeland Security, so I guess this would be a reassignment. As a condition of my accepting this role, I would like to bring two other persons on board with me. As I told your agents, I'm a package deal."

President Baruch responds, "If you take this assignment, it's your call. You can do whatever you think is best."

"Thank you, Mr. President. It would be an honor to serve my country."

"Good, good," the President replies. "Now here's our problem. We are quite concerned that a company from Dubai has recently purchased Port Everglades in Fort Lauderdale, Florida. We have been watching that company and have reason to believe they may be harboring terrorists, however, we can't prove it. Colonel Johnson, chief of the FSA, the

Federal Security Agency, is a member of my staff, and he will be your liaison between the Pentagon and my office. He will brief you on what we know. I have been told that we already have a suite of offices in Fort Lauderdale at your disposal, with a staff awaiting your direction."

Steve replies, "You know, Mr. President, I didn't vote for you. I still don't understand why you want me."

The President replies bluntly, "I know…but you are still the right man for the job."

Steve turns as the door to the Oval Office opens and Colonel Johnson walks in. After the President introduces the two men, he concludes the meeting.

As the Colonel ushers Steve out of the President's office, Steve wonders how President Baruch knows for whom he voted in the last election.

While they continue walking down the hallways and out of the White House, the Colonel informs Steve that he will be escorting him to the Pentagon so he can get started on his assignment. During the ride through Washington in the Colonel's chauffeured limousine, they discuss sports, the pending World Series, and general bullshit. At breaks in the conversation, Steve still wonders how the President knows how he voted.

The two men spend the better part of the day and early into the night at the Pentagon reviewing procedures, personnel, and the latest intelligence information about Interplex LTD, the company that is now managing Port Everglades. Steve will be responsible for heading up a staff of ex-military personnel and will be in charge of the southeast region of the United States. Since it is still illegal to deploy U.S. military troops within the borders of the United States, the President established this non-military security force to make it all "legal."

Steve finally arrives at his hotel room about 11:00 p.m.

that evening. His flight to Fort Lauderdale is at 10:30 the next morning, so he decides to go right to bed without watching any of the offerings on late night TV. Before he nods off to sleep, he feels a sudden urge to pray a Rosary, but he shrugs it off. He falls asleep dreaming of the Amalfi Coast, sans his wife.

# CHAPTER SEVEN

Steve arrives at the airport early the next morning, but he does not need to go through the normal pre-flight security before boarding his flight. Being a member of Homeland Security has its perks.

Upon entering the airplane, he chats with the flight crew, all of whom he knows from previous flights, and eventually buckles himself in his seat for takeoff. As the plane begins its flight back to Fort Lauderdale, Steve reviews the personnel records Colonel Johnson gave him at the Pentagon. He needs to familiarize himself with his new coworkers, and he also needs to devise a plan for getting Angie and Geo to agree to come on board.

The flight attendant brings him his coffee. It will get cold.

Diane sips her coffee at about 30,000 thousand feet, somewhere above the Midwestern United States. Her assistant, Tammy, and Phil, her agent, left California for Florida the night before and are waiting for her at Ventura Country Club. Diane is busy reading the final script and is becoming familiar with her character and her lines. Shooting will start in four weeks and she hopes she will be ready. The more she reads the script, the more involved she gets.

Eventually, her coffee gets cold.

When Steve's flight arrives in Fort Lauderdale, he says goodbye to the flight crew and heads for his car in the parking garage, hoping that no one has dinged his new Corvette. The 'Vette is the car he always dreamed of, and now that he has it, he feels like a teenager whenever he drives it.

As he steps off the curb and into the crosswalk for the parking garage, a large white limousine nearly runs him over. He shakes his head and proceeds to where his car is parked. No dings. His car still looks good.

After paying the garage attendant, Steve drives through the maze around the airport and follows the signs to I-595 West. When he enters the highway, he notices that the same white limousine that nearly ran him over at the airport is stopped on the side of the road with the hood up, and the driver is standing nearby on a cell phone. Always willing to be helpful, he pulls off the road quickly to see if he can lend a hand. As he approaches the driver, he realizes that he knows him from his job as air marshal at the airport.

Steve calls out, "Hey, Rick! You nearly ran me over at the crosswalk! What's up?"

"Sorry, man. I was in a hurry. It's the tranny; the car just died. I'm calling for another car, but it's going to be awhile."

"Who are you drivin' that's so important?"

"It's Diane Summers. She's heading to Ventura Country Club. She's supposed to be in town for a movie shoot. Nice way to be introduced to South Florida hospitality, stuck on I-595."

With a smile on his face, Steve replies, "Maybe I can help."

He walks to the limo and taps on the window. Diane

pushes the button to roll it down, and Steve introduces himself.

"Miss Summers, my name is Steve Ciccone." He flashes his Homeland Security ID. "It's going to be awhile before a new car can come out here to get you. If you like, I can drive you to your hotel and Rick can bring your luggage later." He points toward his Corvette.

Diane glances at the Corvette and then takes a look at Steve's Homeland Security ID badge before replying, "Well, I didn't know that government jobs paid so well. But if it's no trouble, I accept your offer."

Diane would not normally take an offer from a stranger, but she is immediately attracted to Steve and is impressed by his Homeland Security connection. She has been divorced for seven years and has not dated or been involved in the social scene for a while. In fact, she's surprised when she realizes that she's feeling a bit giddy, like a teenager going on a first date.

Steve tells Rick that Diane has agreed to allow him to drive her to her hotel, and he asks Rick to deliver her luggage as soon as he can. Then, he escorts Diane to his car, and they take off.

As the Corvette makes its way down the highway, Diane glances at Steve and says, "Steve, I want to thank you for the ride. I really didn't want to sit on the side of the road waiting for a new limo."

With the smile still on his face, Steve replies, "It's my pleasure. I've admired your work for years. Besides, no one is going to believe me when I tell them who I drove around today. I must say, you're better looking in person than on the screen."

"Thank you, but you know, I just came off a long flight

from California. Would you like to join me for lunch? It's the least I can do to thank you for helping me."

Surprised by the invitation, Steve nonetheless agrees immediately, and punches the 'Vette to go faster. As the Corvette screams down I-595, they are pinned back in their seats, each of them anticipating an interesting lunch break.

After about twenty minutes, Steve pulls up to the country club and valet parks his car. As he helps Diane out of 'Vette, she asks him to wait for her in the lounge so she can check in and freshen up. When they enter the lobby, Diane walks to the reception desk and Steve heads for the lounge, where he orders a beer and calls Angie.

"Hey Ang, it's Chic."

Angie replies, "Welcome home. How's the Prez?"

The smile reappears on Steve's face as he replies, "Get together with Geo. I'll fill you both in later tonight at your place. But besides that, guess who I'm having lunch with today? It's Diane Summers!"

Shocked, Angie replies, "The actress? No fuckin' way!"

Steve describes his initial meeting with Diane as he drinks his beer. He thinks, *This is going to be a very interesting lunch.*

Tammy greets a very frantic Diane at the door to her hotel suite.

"Tammy, I need to borrow a change of clothes! I have a lunch date in a few minutes with a knight in shining armor!"

Confused, Tammy replies, "A knight? In armor? What's wrong with your clothes? What's going on, Diane?"

Diane grabs Tammy and drags her into the bedroom, saying, "I'll tell you while you help me look good!"

Steve is on his second beer when Diane walks into the lounge. He stands and thinks, *Wow, she's hot!* Together, they walk to the hotel's restaurant.

After being seated at a small table near the windows,

Diane glances at the menu, then stares into Steve's eyes and says, "Steve, I'd like to hear a little bit about you. I don't like breaking bread with strangers." She smiles.

"Well, there's not much to say. I'm retired from the New York City Police Department and I'm currently working for Homeland Security. I just came back from Washington this morning. Not to brag, but I met with President Baruch, and now I'm on a special assignment here in Florida."

"Wow, you met Baruch!" Diane was very impressed. "My knight in shining armor is a dignitary, too!"

She notices the white ring of skin on the finger of his left hand where his wedding ring was, and asks, "So, Sir Knight, are you married?"

Steve sighs. "I was, for thirty-five years. My wife died last year, and this is the first time I'm having lunch with a beautiful woman when it's not her. You know, she always asked me if I would love her for the rest of her life and I always answered, no, I'll love you for the rest of *my* life. How ironic!"

Steve shrugs off a tear, but Diane cannot. They order lunch and continue their conversation, which soon turns toward Diane's acting career. She tells Steve that she will be in town for a couple of months, shooting a film.

"Steve, you must come and visit the set once we start shooting. I'd like to introduce you to my friends and fellow cast members." Diane hopes Steve will stop by so they can get to know each other better.

Steve replies, "That sounds like fun. Sure thing!"

Diane gives Steve her phone number at the hotel and asks for his number so she can let him know when he can visit the movie set. When the waiter comes by with the check, Diane insists on paying for lunch, reminding Steve that it's her treat for his kindness earlier in the day.

After the bill is paid, Steve boldly says, "Diane, since you bought lunch, please let me buy you dinner."

Trying to withhold her excitement, Diane replies, "Okay, it's a date. But I'll be busy tomorrow, so how about Saturday?"

Surprised by her acceptance, Steve answers, "Great! I'll give you a call to discuss the details about Saturday."

After leaving the restaurant, they head toward the lobby, where Steve says goodbye to Diane and leaves the hotel. Steve cannot wait to brag to Angie and Geo about who he was on a first date with, and Diane cannot wait to get upstairs to tell Tammy what happened at lunch.


Later that night, Steve meets with Frank and George at Duke's Saloon. When the three of them get together, they always call each other by the nicknames of Chic, Angie and Geo, respectively.

Angie starts right in. "First, you meet with the President, then you have lunch with a famous actress, and now you're in my saloon. Come on, spill the beans!"

"Okay, okay! First things first; The President is starting a paramilitary group in the U.S. to help the locals cope with terrorist activities. Apparently, Port Everglades is now being run by a company from Dubai, so he wants me to head up a group in South Florida. I told him that you two guys would join me, and I said I wouldn't do it without you."

Angie says, "If you want me, I'm in, but only for our country, not for Baruch."

Geo replies, "The economy hasn't turned around yet, so I'll give Baruch the benefit of the doubt. Besides, you want this, so it works for me." Changing the subject, he continues, "But the real story is, how did you meet Diane Summers, and how did you end up having lunch with her, you dog!"

Chic relates the entire two days' experience, from Baruch to Summers, and ends by telling them that he exchanged phone numbers with Diane and that they're going to dinner on Saturday. The three of them toast Chic's new lady, then his new job, then their new jobs, then their old jobs, then anything else they can think of. Luckily, Chic and the guys don't have to report to work until Monday, because they all sleep at the bar that night.

The next day, Diane has a meeting with the film's director and her fellow cast members. The movie will start shooting in three weeks, but all Diane can think about is her lunch with Steve and how much she wants him to call.

Chic wakes up late in the morning with a headache that would kill a horse. Angie and Geo look like they were rode hard and put away wet. Each of them takes time to kiss the porcelain receptacle, because none of them are as young as they think they are.

Chic eventually makes his way home. He showers and then stretches out on the bed to try to get a little more sleep. Before falling asleep, he once again feels the need to pray a Rosary. This time he does, vowing to call Diane after he wakes up. He nods off, dreaming of the Amalfi Coast, again without his wife.

Mahmoud and his bodyguard have been waiting for a while at the designated park bench in Gorky Park. They arrived in separate cars, because Mahmoud has special plans for his bodyguard later that day. Mahmoud is carrying five hundred thousand euros in an attaché case that he's cradling in his lap. It's late and he's getting tired of waiting for Sergei to drop off the package, but they will wait a little longer. He knows that he must be patient when dealing with an addict.

Sergei finally enters the park. He is anxious and knows he is running late. He had a problem getting the uranium out of the facility, because the vessel containing it is larger and heavier than he thought it would be. He is barely able to carry the case to the bench. Heroin has left this addict rather thin and gaunt and the case is unyielding; it is quite heavy for him. He smuggled it out of the nuclear material reclamation facility in a garbage container, then retrieved it later from a dumpster after paying the janitor off in vodka and Cuban cigars.

The uranium is stored inside a cylindrical, stainless steel vessel that was inserted into a lead-lined transfer case. The stainless steel cylinder renders the uranium safe for transport, but it does not provide a complete shield against all of the radioactivity, thus the extra precaution of the lead-lined case. A good bit of lead is needed to hide the uranium from scanning devices at docks and airports, and also to prevent potential health problems in anyone who comes near it.

Sergei and Mahmoud shake hands briefly. No talking, no delaying. Mahmoud gives Sergei the attaché case filled with money, and his bodyguard takes the lead-lined case from Sergei. Sergei leaves quickly with his prize while Mahmoud makes a phone call.

"*Salaam Aleichem.* The package was delivered. The payment was made."

He hangs up, turns to the bodyguard and says, "This is a good day for Allah. Make sure our Russian addict makes it home and has a good night's sleep."

Mahmoud climbs into his Mercedes while his bodyguard puts the case containing the uranium into the trunk of the car. He drives off quickly and heads for a private airport to catch his prearranged flight to Dubai. The bodyguard leaves in the second car to tuck in Sergei.

The next morning, Sergei does not report for work at the spent nuclear reclamation facility. His supervisor calls his apartment, but there is no answer. This is unusual, and a security team is dispatched to check on him. After knocking several times at the door to his apartment and receiving no answer, they break the door down and find Sergei lying dead on his bed from an apparent drug overdose. The needle is still in his arm. They search the apartment and find a small stack of euros under the bed. In his haste to clean up the apartment, the bodyguard left some of Sergei's payoff money behind.

At the same time, back at the nuclear processing facility, an audit of inventory reveals that twenty-five grams of spent uranium 235 is missing.

Panic sets in.

Steve finally wakes up early that afternoon and calls Diane. He's feeling much better after his night with the boys and makes arrangements to pick Diane up the next day at 7:00 in the evening. He wonders where he should take her for dinner and decides to try one of the many restaurants on trendy Las Olas Boulevard. He doesn't normally frequent that part of town, but he wants to impress Diane with a good meal. He doesn't know that Diane doesn't care where they go for dinner; she is just happy that he called.

Steve eventually remembers that the next day is Sunday, the thirteenth day of the month, a special day. When his wife was alive, they would visit a visionary in Hollywood, Florida every thirteenth day of the month, whenever it didn't conflict with his work schedule. After his wife died, Steve became more casual in his Catholic devotions, but today he decides that the next day he will attend Mass and then visit the visionary.

The visionary in Hollywood has been receiving visions and messages from the Virgin Mary since 1994; every thirteenth day of the month, hundreds of people gather at her house to pray the Rosary and to hear the message that the Virgin Mary gives her. Then, through the visionary, the Virgin Mary blesses all the people.

Tomorrow will be the first time Steve will go there without his wife, and suddenly, he once again feels a strange urge to pray the Rosary.

His thoughts are interrupted by his ringing telephone. Steve picks the phone up and answers, "It's your quarter."

"Steve? This is Ken."

Ken is Ken Peters, son of Ronnie Peters, "The King" of NASCAR. When Steve was a teenager, his uncle was an engineer and crewmember for Ronnie Peters Racing. At the time, Steve was a promising NASCAR driver, but he decided to join the Army instead of continuing on the driving circuit. Ken Peters is now retired from the racing circuit and spends most of his time with Ronnie Peters Stock Car Adventure, a program that gives regular folks a chance to drive a stock car on local racetracks across the U.S. Each time the Peters' visit Florida, they call on Steve.

Steve shouts, "Ken! How the hell are ya? And how's your dad?"

"We're all doin' fine, but how are you holding up? We're still praying for you. Are you okay?"

"Yeah, I'm fine, thanks. You guys aren't back here at Homestead, are you?"

Ken answers, "We sure are. You comin' down tomorrow afternoon?"

"Wouldn't miss it!"

"Good! We'll talk then."

Steve hangs up and calls both of his sons. He invites them to the racetrack the next day with their families. Then, he calls Diane for the second time that day.

"Hi, Diane, this is Steve again. I know we're scheduled for dinner tonight, but what are you doing tomorrow afternoon?"

Diane had planned to hang out at the pool, but since the weather forecaster was predicting unusually chilly weather, she was wondering how she would spend the day. Now that Steve called, she is ready for whatever he has in mind.

Steve tells Diane that he has a surprise for her and asks to pick her up at 1:30. When she agrees, he advises her to dress in shorts, even though it will be chilly. With tomorrow shaping up to be a busy day, Steve begins to get ready for his dinner tonight with Diane.

At 7:00 p.m. sharp, Steve arrives at Diane's hotel suite. As they drive toward Las Olas Boulevard for dinner, he still cannot believe that he is about to have dinner with such a beautiful and famous woman.

Las Olas Boulevard is located in downtown Fort Lauderdale. The street is lined with special shops, art galleries, boutiques, restaurants, and sidewalk cafes. People hang out in the area, walk around, and show off.

Steve would rather be at Duke's Saloon having a burger, but he wants to make a good impression on Diane, so he chooses a trendy sidewalk café for their dinner. As they sit at their table enjoying a glass of wine, people walk by, stare, and point. Occasionally, Diane gets asked for an autograph, and she obliges. There are no paparazzi following her here, only a few camera flashes now and then.

Diane says apologetically, "Steve, I'm sorry you have to put up with this. Do you want to leave?"

Steve shakes his head. "This is no bother, and your company is worth it. But now, it's your turn to tell me about yourself."

During their meal, Diane tells him everything, from her arrival in Hollywood to her failed marriages. She has no children, just three Academy Awards, a People's Choice Award and a plaque on the sidewalk Walk of Fame.

After dinner, they take a stroll down the street. They stop for ice cream and window shop, but when the outdoor temperature starts to slide downward, they walk quickly to Steve's car and drive back to the hotel.

At the hotel, they have a nightcap in the hotel lounge. Later, when Steve walks Diane up to her suite, they kiss passionately in front of her door before saying goodnight. Steve tells Diane that he cannot wait to see her again tomorrow. When Diane finally enters her suite, she finds Tammy waiting to hear all about her date. The two women sit up for hours, talking about Steve and unexpected encounters.

Steve wakes up early the next day. After attending Mass, he calls each of his sons to ask them to meet him for breakfast with their families. They both decline, saying they will meet him later at the racetrack.

Steve is disappointed, because he wanted to tell them about Diane before they met her later that day at the racetrack. He decides to go jogging instead, then shower and head for the apparition site.

When Steve arrives at the apparition site, they are already praying the Rosary. He joins in with the prayers of the crowd while waiting for the message from the Virgin Mary. The visionary is a middle-aged Cuban woman and the message is given to the crowd in Spanish. Occasionally, the volunteers provide a simultaneous translation into English. Today they translate as the Virgin Mary gives Her message.

*"My dear little ones, I want you to always remember this day because it is very important for all of you, not only for My little ones, the children of My Heart, those whom My Loving Son gave to Me on the Cross when He said to John, one of His most beloved apostles, 'Here is your Mother, Woman, here is Your son.'*

*"My little ones, I don't want the prohibitions made by the servants of My Beloved Son, Jesus, in the Church to be made an echo. I want you to know that it is not easy for men to do what they do, to bring Jesus' flock together in a total conversion to the Infinite Love of Jesus; they follow the precepts of the Church. You—be sure that nothing distracts you, that nothing separates you from His great Love, and do not doubt that We are always at your side, helping My little ones to find the Path that He left.*

*"Now I want you to know that I have chosen this moment to speak during the Rosary because it is the Mystery of the Conception of My Beloved. How proud I felt and how glorified I am to see that God looked upon His little servant to give Birth to the Savior of the World. My little ones, that is how every mother who conceives and then gives birth to a being who did not ask to be brought into this world should feel, but do you know how many children are being murdered at this very moment when I am appearing here with you as a result of runaway youth, young people who are corrupt and out of control? Millions and millions of beings today have been cruelly murdered, and in whose name do they do it? In the name of their wickedness, in the name of their vices, and in their lack of love for all that God and His Loving Son have created.*

*"I want you, My little ones, to unite in a prayer of*

*love for all those children who have been killed and all those children who are outcasts of society, those who were conceived, even though they had not asked to be brought into this world.*

*"I want you to know that the Fury and the Pain of My Beloved Jesus is as great as His Love, and in the same way that He Rewards, He will also let His Arm fall to punish the wicked.*

*"Humble yourselves, My little ones, and ask for forgiveness, because all who ask shall receive. Love and convert. Do not wait, do not wait.*

*"Great misfortunes will take place in the world that will make you turn back and ask for Justice to be imposed with love.*

*"With the greatest infinite Love, I bless all of you and everything you bring with you. I want you to know that My Beloved Jesus will put His Hands on My little one [the visionary] for a general blessing, so that by uniting their hands together, you will receive all of His Love and all of His Blessings.*

*"I love you. I am your Loving Mother, the Virgin Mary. Amen."*

The apparition site is a very peaceful place. There are many images in the sky that day and many people give testimony of being healed. Steve waits to be blessed by the Holy Spirit through the hands of the visionary and the Virgin Mary. He collapses in the Spirit, as do many others.

While he is in the Spirit, he sees the Virgin Mary and his wife, smiling at him. When he comes out of the Spirit, he makes a donation of thanksgiving for the beautiful experience, picks up a copy of the messages from the previous month and turns to leave, feeling wholly refreshed.

On the way out of the apparition room, Steve notices Joe Ruffolo, one of the volunteers. He stops to say hello.

"Hi, Joe, it's been awhile. Where's your wife, Christine?"

They shake hands as Joe replies, "Christine is inside typing up the message. Where's your wife, Julie?"

Steve explains the circumstances of his wife's death, and eventually the conversation turns to their children.

Steve says, "You and Christine are always asking about my sons, but I have never asked about your children."

Joe replies, "Well, we have one daughter, Alicia. She's a Captain in the Marines and she's stationed down at Homestead Air Reserve Base. We just found out that she'll be leaving for Afghanistan soon. We often try to get her to come here, but it's hard to convince her. Please pray for her."

"No problem, Joe. She'll be in my prayers. Say hello to Christine for me."

While Steve walks back to his car, his mind turns to Diane. He needs to pick her up soon and he doesn't want to be late. He jumps in his 'Vette and heads out to the country club.

When Steve arrives at Diane's hotel, he goes directly up to her suite and knocks at the door. Tammy answers the door and coos, "So, you're Steve. Diane will be right out. Have a seat."

Diane does not keep him waiting long. When she walks out of the bedroom she is as dazzling as ever, even in shorts.

"So, where are we going today?" she asks, then greets him with a passionate kiss.

Steve is not prepared for such a greeting and quickly says, "It's a surprise, but we need to leave now. It's about an hour's ride away from here."

They say goodbye to Tammy and walk to Steve's car. He points the Corvette south and opens her up. They're running late, but he plans to make up the time.

As they cruise down the turnpike, Diane quietly wonders what they will be doing and where they are going. Steve breaks the silence.

"Well, Di. Oh, hey, can I call you Di? I feel like I've known you forever. I'm sure you'd like to know where we're going today. We're heading to Homestead-Miami Speedway, where you'll meet some old friends of mine and also my two sons and daughters-in-law."

Diane's interest is now piqued. "Di is fine, but Homestead-Miami Speedway?"

Steve exits the turnpike and turns toward the racetrack. "Steve, what are we going to do at the racetrack?"

Steve explains his connection to Ronnie Peters, to NASCAR, and to stock car racing. Then he explains what NASCAR is and what a stock car is, because Diane doesn't seem to know much about them.

Soon, the racetrack looms in front of them. Steve checks in with the guard at the gate, drives through the tunnel, and parks just outside pit row. Now, Diane has an idea of what she is in for.

Steve takes Diane's hand as they walk under the pit suites toward pit row, with the roar of the race car engines a constant backdrop. Steve notices his sons and daughters-in-law near the pit wall and walks Diane over to join them. When John and Mike turn toward their Dad, their jaws drop.

Steve beams, "Boys, I'd like you to meet a friend of mine, Diane Summers. Diane, these are my sons, John and Mike."

Diane extends her hand and says, "Nice to meet you both. You two are as handsome as your father."

John and Mike are speechless, so Steve nudges his sons.

"Are you guys going to introduce Diane to your wives?"

John wakes out of his coma first.

"Diane, this is my wife, Carla, and that's Mike's wife, Jeannie."

As the women exchange greetings and start talking among themselves, the boys pull their Dad aside.

"How did you pull this off, Dad?" Mike asks. "Diane Summers, holy shit!"

Steve shrugs, "She was stuck on the side of the road. I picked her up and drove her to her hotel. What's the big deal?"

Mike continues, "I'm glad you put yourself back in the hunt, Dad. It's been almost two years."

The men walk toward their women and take their hands, leading them toward pit road to meet with Ken Peters. Steve is still beaming as he introduces Ken to Diane.

"Hey, Ken! This is Diane."

"Hello, Diane! It's so nice to meet you, but is this your first experience with racing? You look a little nervous."

Diane is not sure why she is being asked about racing, but she replies, "It sure is, and I sure am."

"Don't worry, Steve will take care of you. Come with me, you need to suit up."

Diane raises her eyebrows in surprise, but allows Ken to walk her over to his crew, who helps her put on a fire retardant suit. When she's suited up, she walks back to Steve, who is also wearing a fire retardant suit.

Still uncertain of what's about to take place, Diane takes Steve's hand as they walk over to one of the Ronnie Peters Stock Car Adventure staged, and race-ready cars.

The Ronnie Peters Stock Car Adventure gives everyday persons an opportunity to drive stock cars on a racetrack so they can get the feel of being a professional stock car race driver. The Ronnie Peters cars are replicas of stock cars that are raced on the Cup circuit, with a few differences.

Normally, stock cars have only one seat up front for the

driver, but the car that Steve and Diane will be using today is specially set up with two seats in front so a passenger can ride along. The extra ride-along seat is for people who don't want to drive the cars themselves, but still want an adventure they will never forget. The other differences are that the bodies of these cars are fiberglass instead of sheet metal, and the engines are 650 horsepower instead of 850.

Before Steve and his family arrived at the track, Ken led one of the day's classes for a group of every day drivers who paid for the Ronnie Peters experience. With that class finished for the morning, the session that Diane and Steve attend is a private experience for Ken's friends.

After the safety lesson ends, Steve helps Diane climb into one of the available race cars through the passenger's side window. Then Steve climbs in on the driver's side, while one of the crew members straps Diane in.

Diane turns to Steve and says, "I've seen this racing on TV, but I never dreamed I would be doing this. How fast will we be going?"

Steve chuckles. He finishes buckling himself in and snaps the steering wheel in place, then turns to Diane and says, "With luck, about 170."

Steve flips the ignition switch and the monster roars to life. He takes the car screaming down pit road and enters the track in turn one. Diane is screaming, too. Steve pulls out onto the backstretch and heads toward the outside wall. Diane is yelling at him to slow down. The noise is deafening. They can't hear anything but the rush of air and 650 horsepower exploding out of the exhaust. Steve speeds up. They hit the next turn and the G forces push Diane up against the roll cage.

As they hit the front straightaway, Diane stops screaming, turns to Steve and smiles. Steve hits 170 and backs off as he approaches the first turn, and this sequence continues for ten laps around the track. After the tenth lap, Steve pulls off at pit road, comes to a stop, and shuts the beast off.

Diane exits the car with a huge smile and heads over to Steve to give him a big hug and kiss. NASCAR just got a new fan. The couple walks happily back to the staging area to remove their fire suits while Steve's sons prepare for their solo turns around the track. One at a time, each of them will drive race cars around the track for eight laps each, following pros that are driving their own cars.

While John and Mike are enjoying their drives, the women get to know one another, while Steve talks with the crew.

"I have to ask you guys, what do you think of Daniella Patterson, the heart throb of IRL racing, coming over to NASCAR? She's only won one open wheel race. How do you think she'll do in our circuit?"

Ken responds, "She's a talented driver, but it'll take a few years for her to be able to compete with the rest of the pack. The two cars are so different that it's going to be hard for her. With the Indy Racing League cars, she's used to a low center of gravity and an extreme amount of down force to keep the cars on the track. We drive giant 'bricks,' with little down force. It will be good for NASCAR, though, and I wish her a lot of luck. She's currently running a limited schedule in the Nationwide series and there are rumors that she may run in one of the last Cup races this year."

The women's giggling interrupts the men's conversation. Steve walks toward them and says, "You girls aren't talking about me, are you?" Everyone laughs at his question and the conversation continues while they wait for John and Mike to finish their laps. Ken beckons to Steve, who leaves the women to rejoin his friend.

"Steve, you looked good out there today. You should have been a driver!"

Steve smiles, "You're probably right."

Nodding toward Diane, Ken adds, "I don't know how you pulled it off, but you two look great together. Are you going to keep her around awhile?"

Steve replies, "I like her, but we just met. I don't know where we're going with this, but I hope it'll last—at least for a little while."

Steve is starting to fall hard for Diane. He knows it may not last, but he can dream.

Mike and John have finished their drives, and now Carla and Jeannie are riding along with the pros, each of them screaming their entire way around the track.

As the group watches the girls, Steve and Ken continue to catch up on old news, welcoming Steve's sons and Diane into their conversation.

When the girls' rides are over, Mike and John help them out of their suits while each of them brags to their wives that they hit about 140 mph on their solo drives. As the group chatters away, Steve invites Ken to lunch, but Ken takes a rain check.

"Gotta' get this show on the road."

Steve and his family thank Ken for a fabulous day, and then head over to a local restaurant for a late lunch.

After lunch, the group splits up and Steve drives Diane back to her hotel. He insists on walking Diane up to her suite, and when they arrive at her door, Diane invites him in. While she goes off to refresh herself, Steve makes himself comfortable on the couch. When Diane reenters the room, she joins him there.

"Steve, I want to thank you for today. It was the best time I've had in years. I also enjoyed meeting your family, they're great!"

Diane gives Steve a passionate kiss and asks if he wants

to spend the night. He agrees but then pauses and says, "Where's Tammy? Is she here?"

Laughing, Diane replies, "Tammy has her own room and she's not coming in here tonight." When Diane puts her arms around Steve's neck, he returns her passionate kiss.

# CHAPTER EIGHT

Early the next morning, Colonel Johnson is waiting in Steve's office at the Fort Lauderdale branch of the Federal Security Agency, commonly known as the FSA. This is the paramilitary group the President set up to help local authorities deal with terrorist threats and other national emergencies. Steve was scheduled to meet Colonel Johnson there at 9:00 a.m., but he's running late, because he's still at Saint Malachy Church. The Mass has just ended and only a few persons remain in the church, lighting candles and praying. Steve is sitting alone in the rear of the church when Father O'Donnell, the pastor, walks over and sits next to him.

"Steve, you look troubled."

"Hi, Father. Since Julie died, I've been conflicted between my job and my faith. I don't know how to reconcile the two, and lately, I've been feeling more mortal. I keep feeling as though I need to pray the Rosary, but I don't know why."

"Steve, as we get older, we tend to come closer to God. We naturally feel more vulnerable, and you also miss your wife. You don't need to be concerned, just remember that you're providing a service to our country. Look deep into your heart and you will find the answer. If you want, I'll stay with you awhile and we can pray together."

Steve glances at his watch. "I'd like to, but I can't stay, Father. I'm late for a meeting. Can I call you?"

"Any time, Steve."

After Father O'Donnell gives Steve a blessing, Steve thanks his pastor and quickly leaves the church.

When Steve finally arrives at his office at 9:15 a.m., he finds Angie and Geo waiting in the reception area, bullshitting with his secretary. As he rushes past the secretary's desk, she informs him, "The Colonel's inside, Steve."

Opening the door, he spies the Colonel standing near the window. "Good morning, Colonel. I'm sorry I'm late, I had a late night. Were you waiting long?" Not wanting to give the Colonel time to ask questions about why he is late, he quickly continues, "I'd like to introduce you to Frank and George, the other parts of the package we discussed."

The Colonel interrupts, "We'll get to know each other later. Let's sit down. I have some disturbing information that we need to work on right away." When everyone is settled, he continues, "The Russians have reported that there are twenty grams of uranium 235 missing from a nuclear waste reclamation facility located just outside of Moscow. Just yesterday, Interpol reported that Sergei Andropov, a scientist who works at the facility, was found dead of an apparent heroin overdose in his apartment. Five thousand euros were found with the body.

"Interpol has also informed us that they have been tracking Mahmoud Attan, an official at Interplex, a multi-national conglomerate based in Dubai that manages seaports across the globe. You may already know that Interplex now operates Port Everglades, here in Fort Lauderdale.

"As part of their investigation of Attan, Interpol has also intercepted an interesting cell phone conversation that

Attan had in Moscow with a man in Pakistan the night before Sergei was found. Information from that phone call ties into what CIA operatives inside al-Qaida have been reporting—that leaders of al-Qaida are trying to obtain radioactive material for a dirty bomb."

Geo exclaims, "If those assholes obtain that missing uranium and are able to blow it up, the blast area will be a dead zone for generations!"

Nodding his head, Colonel Johnson resumes, "That is why we need to set this FSA office up in Fort Lauderdale. We need to get up and operational as soon as possible. We believe that Attan, with his influence at Interplex, will help al-Qaida smuggle that radioactive material through the port and into the U.S. Gentlemen, it is your job to stop him, and fortunately, we may have caught a break. When Interpol conducted a sweep of Sergei's apartment, they found a higher than normal radioactive reading, which may make tracking this stuff easier, if we can locate the person who's been exposed to the radioactivity. But we still have a lot of work to do."

The Colonel hands out hard copies of the information he presented as the group dives into what they have just heard and brainstorms for the rest of the day.


Meanwhile, halfway around the world, Mahmoud Attan carefully stores his package in a safe place and then informs al-Qaida that the purchase of the uranium 235 has been made. He prepares to wait for instructions about when and how to transfer the goods to the next operative.

As soon as al-Qaida receives word that the uranium is in their possession, they begin to set their plans in motion. Within eight weeks, they intend to contaminate the Capitol and the immediate vicinity in D.C. for generations to come.

Their plan is to smuggle the uranium into Port Everglades and then transport it to Washington. They already have an operative in D.C. who is also waiting for instructions. The operative has been ordered to combine the uranium with an explosive and then ignite the dirty bomb in front of the Capitol.

The al-Qaida operative is Abdul Kalib, a solitary 'sleeper cell' placed in the U.S. for just such a mission. He was trained as a munitions expert in Syria and has been employed by the Yellow Cab Company in Washington, D.C. for the past year.

Unfortunately for al-Qaida, the Department of Homeland Security and the FBI have been monitoring Kalib for months.

After a long day, Steve is heading home with an attaché case full of homework. As he drives, his cell phone rings.

"This is Steve."

Steve's lawyer is on the other end of the line.

"Steve, this is Tom Lynch. I just received your settlement check. Can you stop by the office tonight to sign some papers and get your money?"

"On my way."

Steve changes direction, turning north from Broward Boulevard onto I-95, and hauls ass. He screams into the parking lot in front of his lawyer's building, rushes inside and up the stairs to the second floor office, not waiting for the elevator.

Tom is in the conference room when Steve arrives. He calls out for Steve to join him at the round conference room table while they sign the legal documents that release FPX and the Teamsters Union from any further litigation involving Julie's death. After all the papers have been signed, Tom hands Steve a check for twenty-five millions dollars.

Since this was an out of court settlement, Tom tells Steve that he cannot divulge where the money came from or how much money he has received.

"I already took out my legal fees from the settlement. This is all yours. Congratulations!"

Steve is speechless. He had asked Tom not to tell him how much the settlement would be. When he rereads the amount on the check, he exclaims, "Holy shit!"

Tom laughs and reminds Steve that he had previously set up a meeting for them at Steve's bank the next day to handle his new finances.

Steve guesses that he is going to be late for work again.


That night, Steve lies in bed, wide awake and restless; he cannot sleep. He keeps thinking about al-Qaida, his late wife, their planned retirement in Italy, his two boys, and Angie and Geo. His thoughts return to al-Qaida and then finally turn to Diane. It's late, but he calls her anyway. As her phone rings, he calms down.

"Hello, Diane? It's Steve." They talk happily for hours about nothing, and about everything.

# CHAPTER NINE

Hoping that the next few weeks will be rather uneventful while he settles into his new role for the President, Steve takes time out to set up trust funds for his two sons. He also hires a real estate agent in Positano, Italy, to search for a small villa for his retirement home. He still wants to retire in Italy, even though Julie won't be with him.

On the dating front, Steve and Diane are falling more and more for each other as their dating becomes more and more frequent. Late one Saturday morning, Steve picks Diane up in front of her hotel, exits the parking lot, and points his 'Vette westward, toward I-95.

"So, what are we doing today?" Diane asks.

"I thought we'd go 'old school.' We're headed to Executive Airport in Fort Lauderdale to visit a display of World War II aircraft that's open to the public this weekend."

They drive in comfortable silence on northbound I-95 and after a short time, exit at Commercial Boulevard West, toward the airport.

Steve parks in the area designated for the event and locks his 'Vette. He grabs Diane's hand as they walk toward the display area adjacent to the runway.

Steve smiles when he spots the aircraft. "Isn't she amazing? She's a completely restored B-17 Flying Fortress. They gave her that nickname because of her reliability and also because of the eight machine gun turrets positioned on her fuselage. The U.S. flew thousands of these over Germany, and thousands of them were shot down. This is the only one left in flying condition. She's seventy-five feet long and has a wingspan of one hundred and four feet. She has four Wright Cyclone engines rated at 1200 horsepower each, with a top speed of just under three hundred miles per hour. Her payload, the amount of bombs she carries, is seventeen thousand pounds."

"Wow, that seems like quite a lot!"

"Yeah, she was good for her time in history, but to compare her to a B-52 of today, well, a B-52 carries three hundred thousand pounds!"

Diane is suitably impressed as they walk around and under the B-17, and is also happy that no one in the crowd seems to recognize her.

"Steve, this is truly amazing. But now that we've looked over this plane, are you planning any other activities for today?"

Steve smiles and guides her over to the ticket table next to the B-17. "The group that maintains this aircraft, tours the country trying to raise money to support this plane and the other B-17's they're trying to restore. So today, we're going to help them. We're going for a ride!"

"On the *plane*?"

Giving Diane a sly smile, Steve purchases two tickets and then guides her toward the aircraft. They board the plane by climbing a ladder underneath the fuselage and are greeted by the pilot. Steve makes a beeline for the bombardier's seat in the nose of the aircraft, where he's surrounded by a giant glass canopy that affords him a perfect view of the entire area around the plane. Diane sits in the navigator's seat, behind the pilot.

After the couple is properly strapped in and the crowd

is moved to a safe distance, the B-17 pilot flips a switch, and one by one, each Cyclone engine awakens with a high-pitched whine from the starters, which then becomes a deafening roar as each engine ignites.

The B-17 slowly creeps out across the runway, and as her speed accelerates, she suddenly soars skyward toward the Everglades, as if she was making another bombing run over Berlin.

Although their philanthropic flight is only a short, twenty-minute ride around South Florida, it's the thrill of a lifetime for Steve and Diane.


While Steve is happy to be spending much of his time with Diane, he is still feeling conflicted about his faith, so he arranges a meeting with Father O'Donnell at Saint Malachy Church.

"Father, thank you for meeting with me again."

"That's why I'm here, Steve. What do you want to talk about?"

"Well, lately, I've been waking up at 3:00 in the morning with an urge to pray the Rosary. I don't think of myself as being very religious, so I want to know if you can tell me why this is happening. I've been to the Marian apparition site in Hollywood and I've been told that this is the Virgin Mary's way of telling us to pray."

After a few thoughtful minutes, Father O'Donnell replies, "I cannot officially comment on the apparition site, but I've been there, and you are correct. Our Lady wants us to pray for the world. I would like you to attend Mass more often, but you're a spiritual individual in your own way. As I've told you before, your spirituality should not affect your job and what you do for this country. You're protecting us from the evil in the world, and the Virgin Mary knows this.

That's why She's asking you to pray, to pray for the world. Don't worry. She's praying for you, and so am I."

"Father, every time I speak with you, I feel so much better."

Father O'Donnell smiles and suggests that they pray a Rosary together. Steve quickly agrees, and takes out his Rosary beads as they begin the prayers.

A three-week lull follows Steve's meeting with his pastor, during which Chic, Angie and Geo, and the personnel assigned to their bureau, study the intel they received from Interpol and the CIA. Things seem to be quiet for the moment, with no new information arriving. It seems like the old cliché—everything's quiet…too quiet.

Meanwhile, in the eastern Caribbean, a late-season tropical depression has formed. It quickly becomes a tropical storm and is given the name of Donald. Tropical Storm Donald's track is currently sending it toward the east coast of Florida. Steve is in the office, monitoring the progress of the storm. His agency was created to assist local authorities with security concerns that may arise from any source, so he must be ready for anything. Within forty-eight hours, Tropical Storm Donald becomes Hurricane Donald, but the storm looks like it will turn northward and away from the Florida coast. Steve places what he hopes to be his last call to Sam Jennings, the head of the hurricane tracking center in Miami.

"Sam, this is Steve from the FSA, looks like we lucked out again."

"You're right, Steve. Unless the storm does a complete turnaround, South Florida will only get rain squalls, beach erosion, rip tides and high waves."

"Well, Sam, the surfers will be happy. I sent all pertinent information to our Charlotte office, which will take over monitoring the storm as it heads north. Thanks for your help."

Hurricane Donald's track takes it near the coast of South Carolina. Donald with winds in excess of 110 miles per hour cause coastal flooding, and a widespread power outage, creating havoc in the Myrtle Beach area.

It seems that South Florida dodged another bullet, and Steve is relieved that he does not have to deal with this problem, as he has enough on his plate already. He stands the office down from this potential crisis, and returns his attention to al-Qaida.

The calm returns for two more weeks, then there's a hiccup. As Steve is reviewing information on Interplex's port operations, his receptionist knocks on the door.

"Mr. Cicone? Line one."

"Who is it?"

"It's Colonel Johnson."

Steve reaches for the phone. "Yes, Colonel?"

"Steve, I have a situation."

"Shit. That means I have a situation. What's going on?"

"I recently helped you set up your office down there in Florida. Now, I need you to help me set up an office in Dallas, Texas."

"Why Dallas?"

"NOAA is predicting a busy hurricane season for the Gulf of Mexico next year. We need to get an FSA office in that area in case there's a national emergency. The office in Dallas will be set up to monitor the Port of Galveston on the upper Texas coast and the oil refineries in the Gulf of Mexico from a safe distance, in case of a direct hit in the Gulf Coast area. It shouldn't take you more than a couple of days to brief Ed Rodriguez, the Dallas agency chief. Besides, there's a lull in our current project right now, so the timing is perfect. You can set things up, take the weekend off, and be back by Monday."

"No problem. I'm sure you already have my tickets and reservation set. I'm guessing I leave tomorrow?"

"You got it. Your tickets are at the Continental Airlines check in desk. Ed will meet you at the airport in Dallas. We updated him with your profile, so he knows what you look like, and he has your hotel info. Just brief him on what you've done so far. I'll fly down next week."

"Okay, Colonel. Take care."

Steve calls Angie and Geo to fill them in on his plans for the next few days. They wish him well and let him know that they will fill in for him at the office. Before Steve calls his sons about his schedule, he phones Diane to let her know that he will be out of town until after the weekend. Then, he heads home to pack for his trip.

The next morning, Steve takes his time getting to the airport and arrives with just a few minutes to spare. Because of his new FSA ID, he does not have to go through normal airport security, so he does not have to be at the airport hours before his flight. He walks quickly to the gate, waits about ten minutes, and boards his flight to Dallas.

If airplanes in this corridor were allowed to fly in a straight line, traveling from South Florida to Dallas would be a fairly short flight. But because Eglin Air Force Base uses the eastern Gulf of Mexico as a pilot training range, all airplanes flying to Texas must travel over the Florida peninsula, then west along the Gulf coast. This restriction increases flight times from Florida to Dallas to about two and a half hours.

Steve uses the down time during his flight to relax until his scheduled arrival in Dallas just before lunchtime. Ed meets him near the baggage carousel, and after Steve retrieves his luggage, they drive directly to the FSA office, where lunch has been brought in. Steve and Ed work through lunch, reviewing what Ed has accomplished so far.

"Ed, there are a couple of things you need to do right away. Number one is to surround yourself with professionals and get the local enforcement agencies on your side. After that, you need to recruit your staff and create an environment in which your team is working with you, not for you."

For the next two days, Steve and Ed review personnel records and intel reports on al-Qaida, while Steve fills Ed in on the looming situation in Fort Lauderdale.

On Sunday night, Steve calls Diane to set up a lunch date for the next day.

After his flight arrives in Fort Lauderdale late Monday morning, Steve drives directly to the FSA office to check in with Angie and Geo, and to fill them in on his meetings with Ed Rodriguez and the progress of the new Dallas office. He ends the briefing early, because he wants to visit Diane on the set of her movie before their lunch date.

The movie is being shot on location at the Museum of Art in downtown Fort Lauderdale. When Diane's scene ends, the crew breaks for lunch. When Diane sees Steve, she rushes over to give him a big kiss, and then introduces him to the rest of the cast and crew.

Amid the general conversation, Steve suddenly hears a familiar voice say, "So, this is Steve."

He turns, finding himself face-to-face with Clete Westbrook, the movie's director.

"Steve, it's nice to meet you! She talks about you all the time."

Steve excitedly shakes Clete's hand and replies, "Nice meeting *you*, Mr. Westbrook! I think you're great! I've been a fan since you starred in all of those spaghetti westerns."

Clete laughs. "Steve, you don't look that old. Listen, enjoy your lunch and bring her back on time. We restart shooting in an hour."

Because the movie is being filmed in downtown Fort Lauderdale, they don't have to drive far for lunch. They quickly arrive at Tony's Pizza on Andrews Avenue, where Steve orders a personal pizza and Diane orders a salad.

Steve takes Diane's hand and says, "Di, I'm planning a small trip to Italy to look at some property my broker found. Do you think you can come with me?" Steve had previously told Diane that he received a settlement from Julie's death, but he did not tell her the amount.

"Well, it really depends on the movie shoot, so I'll have to let you know when I'll be free. But I'd love to go with you!"

"Great! I really didn't want to go alone."

Steve is relieved, but his relief is short-lived. Even though he returned from his business trip just that morning, there's no rest for the weary, as his cell phone suddenly rings while they are eating lunch. Apologizing to Diane, he cuts the lunch short and drives her back to the set, then rushes back to his office.

As he runs into the building, the receptionist tells him that Angie and Geo are waiting for him in the conference room. Steve bursts into the room, and as he sits down at the conference table, he asks, "Okay, guys, what's up?"

Angie begins. "The package is about ready to be moved. The CIA intercepted a cell phone call between Mahmoud and Aziz Zarqawi Aziz. We believe Aziz is second in command to Usama Bin Laden. Mahmoud told Aziz that the package was ready to be transferred. Then Aziz told Mahmoud that one of his representatives would contact him about when, how and where to deliver the merchandise for shipment. CIA agents within al-Qaida have told us that it will be coming in by freighter."

Steve interrupts, "Do we know the name of the freighter?"

Looking down at his notes, Geo replies, "We have information that the freighter is called the *Crescent Star*. That ship has docked in the U.S. on many occasions, usually delivering brand name clothing manufactured in Bangladesh and Pakistan. It's currently inbound to the Port of Dubai and should arrive in six days. It's set to leave Dubai three weeks later for Port Everglades. We still don't know who the transporter is aboard the ship, or who his contact is in Florida, but the CIA and Interpol are working on that. The ship is scheduled to arrive in Fort Lauderdale in twenty days, so that means we have less than seven weeks to stop it. The one good thing is that the uranium should still be in its lead container inside a transfer case. The bomb will need to be assembled here."

There is dead silence for about five seconds, then Steve begins to give instructions to his friends, his fellow team leaders.

"We need to get someone inside the operations of the port as soon as possible. Geo, we need to put you into the Harbormaster's office. His office controls all ship movement into and out of the port, and that office also assigns the pilots who board each ship to guide them through the channel with their fleet of tugs. Berths for the container ships are located at the end of State Road 84, the main entrance into Port Everglades from Federal Highway. That entrance offers perfect access to the container berths for us and the local security force that will be supplied by BSO, the Broward Sheriff's Office. We'll need help from the FBI to get you into the Harbormaster's office, but we already have agents working at the port as longshoremen. They were placed there when Interplex took control of the operations."

Turning to Angie, Steve continues, "Ang, I need you to get Geo into the port ASAP. Then I need you to call BSO and fill them in on the situation. I'll contact Colonel Johnson to give him the skinny."

"Okay, guys. Let's get started."

The three friends leave the conference room and get to work.

Halfway around the world, Mahmoud is sitting in his office in Dubai when his secretary buzzes him.

"Mr. Attan, your 4:00 appointment is here. Shall I send him in?"

"Yes, please."

Mahmoud stands as a tall, dark man enters.

"Mr. Attan, Mr. Aziz says you are expecting me."

Mahmoud prepares to greet his visitor traditionally, with a kiss to both cheeks, but the man backs off.

"Let us get down to business. I do not have much time. The ship is the *Crescent Star*. It will be here in six days. Your company controls the Port of Dubai, so getting to it should be no problem. On the morning of the day after the ship docks, you are to bring the merchandise onto the ship and locate a crewmember by the name of Bashir. He is easily recognizable, for he has no right ear."

The dark stranger stands up, turns, and walks toward the door. Just as he is about to open it and leave, he looks back at Mahmoud and says, "Praised be Allah." Then, he leaves.

Mahmoud is relieved. Now, he can finally get rid of the uranium. He sits back down in his chair and turns to stare out his window, fifteen floors above the city of Dubai.

Steve finally gets off the phone with Colonel Johnson. Everything has been set into motion to deal with the *Crescent Star* when it arrives in Fort Lauderdale. All he can do now is wait and hope that more detailed information becomes available soon.

As he sits in his office, Steve realizes that for the next six weeks he will have little to do, unless something drastically changes. He decides that now would be a good time to take his trip to Italy to look at those villas, since the trip should only take a couple of days. He calls Colonel Johnson back to let him know that he will be taking a short trip out of the country before things get heated up.

Before leaving the office, he puts Angie and Geo in charge while he's out of the country, and heads home. He wants to call Diane before making his travel plans, and then he needs to get in touch with his real estate broker in Positano.

# CHAPTER TEN

"Hello, Diane, it's Steve. Sorry about having to leave our lunch so quickly this afternoon."

"That's okay. Is there anything I should be concerned about?"

"No, and if there was, I couldn't tell you about it anyway."

Diane is concerned, but doesn't let on. "Soooo, how did you like visiting my part of the world today?"

"I had a great time, but I always have a good time with you."

"Me, too, Steve. Me, too."

"Di, remember when we talked about going to Italy? Well, I know this is really short notice, but my window of opportunity is open now and I have to go this weekend. It will only be for two or three days, tops. Does that work for you?"

Diane exclaims, "Actually, that works out great! We break from shooting this weekend, because Clete has to go back to Hollywood. When do you want to leave?"

"Let me set up all the details. I'll make the reservations and call you back. Di, you really don't know what this means to me. Love you!"

Steve hangs up the phone, suddenly realizing that he has just said the "L" word.

Diane is taken aback. As she walks into her bedroom, she mumbles out loud to herself, "He said, 'love you', but he didn't give me a chance to tell him the same thing!" She was upset and elated at the same time.

Forty-eight hours later, after a whirlwind of packing and planning, Steve and Diane are at Miami International Airport, ready to board a new 787 headed for Naples, Italy. Steve's real estate broker, Stefania Rossi, made all their reservations and will pick them up at the airport in Naples. Feeling wealthy after receiving his settlement check, Steve requested a private, double sleeping compartment for their eight and a half hour flight across the Atlantic, and after dinner on the plane, the couple retires to their private room and becomes members of the Mile High Club.

When they arrive at Naples International Airport, Steve and Diane grab their luggage, make it through customs, and then notice a fairly attractive, middle-aged woman holding a sign with Steve's name on it. Steve approaches the woman and introduces himself and Diane. The woman is Stefania Rossi, Steve's real estate agent. They exchange greetings and kisses, and then Stefania escorts them to her car. As she drives them out of the airport, she reviews their itinerary.

"I have booked a suite for you at the Hotel Rufolo in Ravello. There are two villas in the area that I would like you to see and Ravello fulfills all that you are looking for. It is nestled high on a peninsula on the Amalfi Coast, just west of Salerno, approximately 80 kilometers from here. Ravello is north of the town of Amalfi, about 1.5 kilometers from the coast and is situated on a high ridge about 350 meters above the Mediterranean. From the town, the view of the sea and the coastline is breathtaking. Ravello has a population of about two thousand. I think you are going to love it there. I will drop you off at the hotel today and we can look at the villas tomorrow. That should give you enough time to rest after your long flight."

The drive to the hotel takes about an hour and a half and is a beautiful trip up into the mountains. Stefania drops the couple off at the Hotel Rufolo and tells them that she'll return to pick them up at 9:00 the next morning. Steve and Diane check in, have a light afternoon meal at a nearby restaurant, then return to their room. As Diane unpacks their clothes, Steve heads for the balcony. The view is spectacular, with small fishing boats speckling the water below the hotel. The sun is setting over the Mediterranean, and at this one thousand-foot elevation, he can see up and down the coast for miles.

Steve calls Diane to be by his side on the balcony. In the warm October night, he slowly turns toward her and says, "Di, we've known each other for almost two months now. I told you that I received a large settlement because of Julie's accident, but I didn't tell you the amount." Pausing to take a deep breath, he continues. "My net worth now is approximately twenty million dollars. I always wanted to retire on the Amalfi Coast, but I don't want to be here alone. I love you Diane, and I want you to be here with me. Will you marry me?"

Steve slips a four-carat diamond ring onto Diane's finger as Diane holds her breath. "I know you have a career, and…"

Diane quiets him mid-sentence with a kiss. "Steve, my career is near its end and this movie will be my last. I love you, too, and of course I'll marry you!"

They kiss again, hold each other close, and watch the sun dip into the sea. Diane doesn't know where to look first—at the sunset or at the ring on her finger. Emotionally and physically exhausted, they return to their room and go to sleep.

The next morning, the newly engaged couple waits in the hotel lobby for Stefania. When Stefania arrives, the first thing Diane does is show off her new engagement ring. Stefania is very happy for her clients. There are kisses for everyone and Stefania offers to buy them lunch as a celebration of their love.

The happy group exits the hotel and heads for the first villa on Stefania's list. It's located a short distance from the hotel, less than one kilometer outside the heart of Ravello, and just off the *Via Madonna dell'Ospedale*. The villa has four bedrooms and two and a half baths, a formal dining area, and a breakfast nook. It has a fully updated modern kitchen with central air, and there is a veranda outside with a covered arbor. A retaining wall overlooks the Mediterranean nine hundred feet below. Just off the veranda is a small lemon orchard with its own wall overlooking the Mediterranean Sea.

When Steve walks into the villa, his jaw drops in amazement. This is just what he was looking for! Steve turns to Stefania and declares, "Stefania, this is it! I don't want to look at any other houses. How much?"

"It's listed at 800,000 euros, about $1.1 million dollars."

Glancing at Diane, Steve asks, "What do you think?"

Diane gazes around her, and then smiles. "Are you *sure* you don't want to look at anything else?"

Taking her by the hand, Steve says, "This is exactly what I want, exactly what I've dreamed of, so there's no need to look at anything else. The house is perfect, the town is perfect, and you're a perfect fit here."

Steve turns to Stefania and announces his decision. "We'll take it."

"*Molto bene!*" smiles the real estate broker. "Congratulations once again! Let's walk around the house and grounds before I take you back to the hotel. After I drop you off, I'll go to my office, contact the sellers, and work on all the papers that are needed to start the purchasing process."

"Stefania, I've already made arrangements with my bank to wire transfer the funds I'll need. As soon as you have everything ready, it will be done."

The group tours the rest of the villa and then Stefania returns the happy couple to the hotel, where Steve and Diane have a snack and talk excitedly about their new home. Stefania will meet them again later for lunch.

The soon-to-be residents of Italy decide to take a walk around the center of town before regrouping with Stefania. They decide to enter the historic Villa Rufolo after crossing the *Via dei Rufolo*.

Steve remembers the villa from his research on the Amalfi area when he and Julie were planning their retirement in Italy. Steve stops on the entrance pathway after paying the villa's entrance fee, and briefly relays what he remembers to Diane.

"Before we go in, let me tell you what I know about this villa. The Rufolo's were once a powerful family in the area and the villa was their family home. The villa was also used by the Popes as a vacation home in the 1600's, but it's now basically just a shell of a house. However, the grounds are maintained as beautiful gardens that overlook the Mediterranean, and during the summer, many public concerts are held here."

The couple tours the house and then walks around the gardens, pausing to take a seat on a stone bench near a cypress tree. The view from this vantage point is incredible. They hold each other close and stare at the Mediterranean below while talking about their new life together.

When they finally leave the villa, Steve notices a panetteria across the street. The shop's name is on a sign above the door. Reading the sign, he says, "Di, there was a La

Stella's bakery in Little Italy that I used to hang out at when I worked for the NYPD. Let's go in."

As they approach the counter, Vincenzo, the owner, walks out of the rear of the shop. Steve takes one look at the owner and blurts out, "Vince?"

Vincenzo looks up and says, "Oh, my goodness, it's Steve Ciccone! What the hell are you doing here?" He rushes out from behind the counter and gives Steve a bear hug.

Steve and Vince Fiore had been friends while they both lived in New York, getting together with their wives for dinner on a regular basis. Vince and his wife, Stella, had opened a bakery in New York City after immigrating to the United States in 1980. After living in the U.S. for twenty-five years, they sold the business for a huge profit, moved back to Ravello, and continued their bakery business in Italy.

When Steve turns to introduce Diane as his fiancé, he notices a questioning look on Diane's face and explains, "Di, I used to go to Vince's place in New York all the time! He makes the best bread! I was really upset when he sold the place. Who would ever have thought that we'd end up in the same town in Italy?"

Puzzled at Steve's introduction of Diane, Vince asks, "What happened to Julie?"

Steve briefly explains the tragedy of Julie's death and the circumstances of meeting and courting Diane.

Sighing, Vince says, "I don't know if I should express condolences or congratulations. I'm so sorry to hear about Julie, but at the same time, I want to congratulate you and Diane. Still, that doesn't explain why you're here in Ravello. Are you on vacation?"

"Yes and no. I received a cash settlement from Julie's death, and guess what? I'm buying a villa right outside town! We're moving in as soon as the paperwork is done!"

Vince happily welcomes them to Ravello. "Wait 'till I

tell Stella you're here!" As he claps Steve on the back, he gives Diane another look. "Hey, are you Diane Summers, the actress?"

Blushing, Diane nods her head.

"Steve, you've really come uptown! Stella is not going to believe me when I tell her about all this!"

"Vince, we're having lunch with my real estate broker this afternoon to sign the initial paperwork to buy the villa. Why don't you and Stella come to our hotel suite about 7:30 tonight? We can catch up and share a bottle of wine together. We're staying in Suite 210 at the Hotel Rufolo."

Vince smiles. "Sounds great! See you then. Stella is going to *flip out!*"

Before Steve and Diane leave the panetteria, Vince walks behind the counter, grabs a paper bag and places a couple of sfogliatelle into it. He gives the bag to Steve.

"Here, enjoy. But you better start to learn Italian if you don't want to be taken for a tourist!"

Steve thanks Vince for the sweets and bids him goodbye. Then Steve and Diane walk back to the hotel, marveling at their good fortune at already having friends in their adopted country.

Later that afternoon, when Stefania meets them for lunch, she tells them that the sellers have accepted their offer to purchase the villa. During their meal, Steve signs the initial paperwork. Even with the time difference, Steve was able to contact his bank and have the money transferred for the down payment. Now, Stefania can work on getting the sale finalized. If all goes well, the villa should be Steve's in about eight weeks.

Stefania toasts the couple's success and their engagement with a bottle of Prosecco, and after some small talk, their lunch ends. Stefania decides to go back to her office, because she has much to do. She needs to contact the sellers and the bank, and notify the local government about the pending sale. But before they leave the restaurant, Stefania offers to manage the property for Steve and Diane until they move in. By hiring someone to represent him, Steve will not have to appear at the final closing.

After lunch, the happy but tired couple retires to their hotel suite. They must prepare for Vince and Stella's visit tonight and pack for their return flight home tomorrow. After putting some things in their suitcases, Steve orders a bottle of wine from room service and they both lie down for a quick nap.

A knock at the door wakes Steve from his afternoon nap. When he looks at the clock on the nightstand, he calls to Diane, "Di, its 7:30! It must be Vince and Stella."

Steve rises from bed, walks out of the bedroom and opens the hotel room door. When Stella sees him, she greets him with an enthusiastic hug and kiss.

"Congratulations, Steve! I can't believe you're here. It's so great to see you again!"

When Diane walks out of the bedroom, Stella rushes over to greet her as well. "Hello, and congratulations to you too! Let me see your ring!"

Diane returns the greeting and then ushers the group to the balcony, where they sit around a small table.

Vince begins the conversation. "Steve, I still can't believe you ended up here in Ravello, and with Diane Summers on your arm to boot!" Turning to Diane, he says, "Diane, I've seen all your movies. I especially liked you in the remake of Bus Stop. I think you did a better job than Marilyn Monroe!"

"Well, thank you, Vince. You've linked me with very good company."

Steve fills his friends in on his children and what has taken place in his life since he saw them last—Julie's death, meeting President Baruch, and meeting and falling in love with Diane Summers. Then it's Vince and Stella's turn to update Steve on their lives, and Diane's turn to get to know her new friends. The group talks for hours and goes through three bottles of wine and assorted snacks from room service.

Eventually, Vince looks at his watch. "Oh, no! It's just past midnight! I have to go to work in four hours!"

The friends quickly exchange phone numbers say their goodbyes. Steve tells Vince, "I'll give you my address in Italy as soon as I know it."

After the Fiore's leave, the future Mr. and Mrs. Ciccone rush off to bed. They have a long day tomorrow, and a long flight home. They fall asleep in each other's arms as the moon glistens off the surface of the Mediterranean, like sparkling diamonds floating on the water.


Because of a layover in Paris, the lovers do not make it back to Florida until the following evening. Steve drops Diane off at her hotel, kisses her goodnight, and goes home for some much-deserved sleep.

Late the next morning, Steve makes a few phone calls. He wants to talk to each of his sons to tell them about his engagement and his purchase of the villa in Ravello. He receives unexpected news with his first phone call to John.

"Hi, John, it's Dad."

"Dad! How was your trip to Italy?"

"Great! I have good news!"

"That's great, Dad. I have news, too. But you go first."

"Okay, John." Steve takes a deep breath. "I bought my retirement villa in Ravello, and I asked Diane to marry me!"

"Holy shit, Dad! Did she say yes?"

"She sure did!"

There's a pause on the line, and then, "Wow! My step-mom is going to be Diane Summers! When's the wedding?"

Steve laughs, "Wow is right! Give us a break, we just got back! But it will probably happen within the next year. Okay, now it's your turn. What's your news?"

Another pause. "How do you think Diane will like being a grandma?"

Steve shouts, "Holy shit is right! That's great news, John! How's Carla? Is everything all right?"

"Carla's fine Dad, everything is fine. You know, that trust fund you set up for us came just in time! Funny, Mom is still helpin' me out."

Steve is silent for a moment as he remembers Julie and their life together. "John, give Mike a call, okay? I want to take you all to brunch. But don't tell him anything about my engagement."

"No problem, Dad. I'll leave that up to you."

Steve hangs up with John and makes his next call to Diane to invite her to brunch with his family. His final calls are to Angie and Geo. He wants to give them the good news, too, and to get an update on any new information at the FSA office.

Steve is still beaming after all his phone calls, and he cannot wait to see Diane's face when she finds out that soon, she's going to be called "Grandma!" But before leaving for the family's brunch, he takes care of one last task by contacting a real estate broker in Fort Lauderdale. He wants to sell his house and then buy a condo near the beach so he and Diane will have a place to stay in Florida when they visit from Italy. Their ideal plan is to spend winters in the states and the rest of the year in Ravello.

While Steve is celebrating with his family in Fort Lauderdale, it is late at night at the Port of Dubai. Mahmoud Attan climbs out of his limousine as soon as the driver parks at the berth alongside the *Crescent Star*. As President of Interplex, his executive identification badge gives him full access to the port with no questions asked. Holding the large transfer case that contains the uranium, he approaches the container ship's gangplank. The captain of the ship is expecting Attan's arrival and meets him on deck as he climbs aboard.

"I have luggage for a man called Bashir."

Eyeing his visitor, the captain replies, "Please remain here. I will get him for you."

Attan watches as the captain enters the bowels of the freighter. He turns to the dock and signals his chauffer to start the limousine's engine. When the captain returns, a deckhand is following behind him. Mahmoud makes sure the man has no right ear and then hands him the case.

"Take care of this, and may Allah be with you."

When the transfer is complete, Mahmoud quickly leaves the freighter, making his way down the gangplank and into the waiting limousine. Bashir watches him leave and then returns to his bunk, case in hand.

# CHAPTER ELEVEN

Monday comes too soon for Steve, as he sits in his office going over intelligence reports. Predictably, his phone soon rings and Colonel Johnson is on the line.

"Steve, Mahmoud has transferred the goods onto the *Crescent Star* in Dubai. It's crunch time. That ship will be in Fort Lauderdale in four weeks."

"We already started the ball rolling. Geo reported to the pilot of the port this morning, and as you know, we already have men in place as longshoremen. I've briefed Sergeant Williams from BSO and will meet with him again tomorrow morning to finalize our plan. He's in charge of security at Port Everglades."

"Good, Steve. I'll let the President know what's happening and I'll keep you informed about the location of the ship. We'll be tracking it by satellite and a Seawolf Class attack sub will be waiting for it off the Florida coast. It will track the ship as it nears our coastline and will follow it to Fort Lauderdale. If we need to, we'll blow the ship out of the water, but that will be a last resort. The ship is owned by the King of Saudi Arabia, and blowing it up is an incident we want to avoid."

"Right, Colonel. Got ya covered."

Steve hangs up. Now, the hard work begins. He calls Geo to give him the latest information from Colonel Johnson and asks Angie to come into the office. Steve wants Angie to accompany him to the port to scope the area out. They need to have as much real world information as possible for their planning meeting with Sergeant Williams the next the morning.

While he waits for Angie to arrive, Steve contacts the local Coast Guard Commander at Port Everglades to briefly fill him in on the situation and invite him to tomorrow's meeting with the BSO Sergeant. As he wraps up the phone call, Angie walks in.

"Okay, Chic. What's up?" When Steve and his friends are alone together, they resort to their informal nicknames.

"Ang, the uranium has been transported to the freighter in Dubai. It's scheduled to be here in about four weeks. I just got off the phone with Commander Thomas Elliot of the Coast Guard unit at Port Everglades. Tomorrow, we're having a meeting with Sergeant Williams of the BSO unit in charge of port security, along with the Commander Elliot. I'll want you at that meeting, but I also need you to come with me now to scope out the port."

Bashir puts his precious cargo in the travel trunk located next to his bunk. The intel the CIA has is incomplete, as Bashir is not working alone. There are four other agents working with him aboard ship, and all of them are equipped with automatic weapons that they smuggled aboard.

The operation planned for Fort Lauderdale will not run as smoothly as everyone hopes.

On Tuesday morning at 9:00 a.m., Steve calls his meeting to order. In attendance with him are Frank "Angie" Angelo, BSO (Broward Sheriff's Office)  Sergeant Brook Williams, and Coast Guard Commander Thomas Elliot. George "Geo" Jackson is already working at the Harbormaster's office, so he will not attend.

Steve starts the meeting.

"Gentlemen, all of you have been briefed about a possible terrorist breach at Port Everglades. Now let me fill in the details. A scientist at a nuclear waste reclamation facility outside of Moscow recently sold some spent uranium 235 to al-Qaida, which intends to use it in a dirty bomb that they hope to explode outside of the Capitol building in Washington, D.C. Due to the extreme radioactivity of this material, any explosion containing uranium 235 would render the immediate area around the blast site uninhabitable for generations. In four weeks, a freighter named the *Crescent Star* will be docking at Port Everglades. One of its crewmen is in possession of this uranium, and he goes by the name of Bashir. I have information on this man that I will be sharing with you all later. We currently have agents working as longshoremen at Berth 4, near the Convention Center off Eisenhower Boulevard. George Jackson is currently working with the pilot of the port to make sure the *Crescent Star* freighter docks at Pier 4, Slip 2, Berth 4 when it arrives in Fort Lauderdale."

Addressing the sergeant, Steve continues, "Sergeant Williams, you will be responsible for shutting off the port's entrances at State Road 84, Eisenhower Boulevard, S.E. 17th Street, and here on Eller Drive."

Steve points to a map of Port Everglades.

"We'll also need your SWAT team staged at the end of SR 84 where it intersects with Eisenhower Boulevard. We'll compliment your team with our men."

Addressing each man in turn, he says, "Frank, a portable radiation detector is being sent to us from the FBI. I'm told it's like a Geiger counter on steroids. A Hazardous Materials

Safety team (HAZMAT) is also coming in from Homeland Security in case we need them. Commander Elliot, your assignment is to secure the port on the water side by blocking off the berth after the ship docks, and also blocking off the inlet and the Intracoastal Waterway. Colonel Johnson will be our liaison between the White House, the Pentagon, the CIA and the FBI. He has contacted Homestead Air Reserve Base and they will provide us with two Apache attack helicopters for air cover during the operation. Frank, before the freighter docks, you will be deployed with the SWAT team and George will be with the pilot of the port. As you know, the pilot takes control of large vessels entering the channel to Port Everglades to guide them safely to their berths. I will position myself at the top of the parking garage near the Convention Center. It's a four-story structure, the tallest structure at the port. It will offer me a clear view of the freighter in case a sniper is needed. The information we have is that there is only one crewmember involved in the transportation of the uranium. He's a member of the Taliban and his name is Khalil Bashir. He's very recognizable, because he has only one ear."

Steve passes out a photograph of Bashir, along with a photograph of the container the uranium is expected to be transported in.

"Gentlemen, each of you has been given a written brief of all the information we have available, as well as an overview of the details of this meeting. We will meet again in two weeks, and then on a daily basis during the final week before we implement this mission."

Frank remains behind after Steve adjourns the meeting. He looks straight into Steve's eyes and says, "Well, we're knee deep in the hoopla now! Does Diane have any idea what you're getting yourself into?"

Steve shakes his head. "No, but I guess I better give her

some idea of what's goin' on. Come on, Ang. Let's take an early lunch."


The previous two days had been fairly hectic for Diane. She told Tammy and Phil that she is engaged to be married and that she will be retiring from show business, which means that they will be basically out of work after the wedding.

Diane asked Tammy, her personal assistant, to continue working for her until the wedding, promising that she would help her find her another job and pay her a salary until she could find new work. Tammy was very happy for Diane and agreed to remain with her for as long as she's needed. Phil, her agent, has other clients, so even though he's disappointed, he'll be okay.

Diane also told the movie's cast and crew about her new plans and they responded by holding an impromptu engagement party for her on the set this morning.

After the party was over, the studio presented the cast and crew with some unexpected news. They informed everyone that they decided to shoot the balance of the movie on a sound stage back in Hollywood, and requested that they prepare to leave Florida within forty-eight hours.

Diane is not overly upset about having to return to California unexpectedly, because aside from being away from Steve, the studio's change in location fits perfectly into her plans. She would have had to leave Steve for a while anyway, since she needs to put her California house up for sale and start her wedding preparations. The couple has not set a firm date yet, but they would like to be married by next spring. Diane needs to decide on a theme for the reception, buy a dress, choose the flowers, contact the bridesmaids, and take care of all the other details involved in planning a wedding.

Steve calls Diane when he arrives home from work

and invites her to his house that evening for a home cooked meal. Diane is happy to share an evening with her fiancé, and tells Steve that she'll ask her limo driver to drop her off at sevenish. Steve defers to Diane's timetable, because it will give him more time to prepare dinner.

After a quick shower, he begins to cook. He decided to make a simple pasta dish with spinach, almonds, onions, artichoke hearts and diced tomatoes. This dish is one of his specialties and is very easy, very quick, and very good. Another reason that Steve likes this particular dish is that it goes well with a bottle of Lambrusco, his favorite wine.

The doorbell rings as the pasta goes into the boiling water. When Steve opens the door, he is greeted by a big kiss from Diane. "I missed you! We haven't seen each other in almost two days!"

"Missed you too, but I've been so busy it seems like we were just in Italy this morning!"

Diane follows Steve into the kitchen and watches as he prepares dinner. "Steve, it smells so good! I didn't realize you could cook. Well, in the kitchen, that is."

Steve chuckles. "Dinner's done." He gives Diane a peck on the cheek as carries the food from the kitchen to the table.

As they start to eat, Steve hesitates before beginning to speak. "Di, I need to tell you what I'm currently involved in."

Diane interrupts him. "Well, I have some news for you, too, but you go first."

There is a pause, then Steve begins. "You know that I'm currently in charge of the Fort Lauderdale bureau of the FSA, the Federal Security Agency. The President is setting up bureaus across the U.S. to interface with local authorities in case of national emergencies, natural or manmade, or in case there are any major security breaches to our homeland. Well, we recently learned about a terrorist plot involving Port Everglades and I'm currently working on the problem with other federal agencies. The situation should be resolved in about four weeks, but until then, I'm going to be quite busy and quite scarce. I can't tell you anything else, because as the cliché goes, if I tell you, I'll have to kill you. I hope you understand. I promise that after this is all over, I'll fill you in about what actually happened."

Diane is taken aback. "Are you in danger? Will you be okay? Will *we* be okay? Steve, please don't do anything stupid, especially not *now*!"

Steve takes her hand and gently squeezes it. "Everything will be okay. The local police are involved, and so are Homeland Security and the FBI. We'll be fine, I'll be fine. Besides, I'm too old to do something stupid, and I want a long and happy life with you."

Steve leans across the table and caresses Diane's cheek. "Now, what do have to tell *me*?"

Diane takes a large gulp of wine. "Well, I found out today that they're moving the movie shoot back to the studio in Hollywood. I have to leave Thursday morning to return to California to finish the movie. It's a good thing, though, because I'll be able to start our wedding plans there. I need to sell my home and prepare for my new life with you. I was hoping that you could come out and help, but I understand that you'll be busy."

"I'll be happy to come out and help however I can, but not for at least four weeks. I could come out for a while after things are wrapped up here. Is that okay with you? Besides, I want to take a peek at your life out there in Hollywood."

Diane smiles, "That will work out fine. But you know, I'll be back in South Florida around the nineteenth of November. I just hope you won't be jealous about what I'll be doing until then!"

Steve jokingly replies, "Jealous! I hope he's smaller and older than me so I can kick his ass!"

Diane laughs as she clears off the table. "Actually, there will be a lot of guys, and I'm pretty sure they're way younger than you."

"Okay, you've piqued my interest. What's up?"

"Because we filmed most of the movie here in South Florida, the studio thought it would be good for me to promote the movie in Florida. By the way, it's scheduled to be released this summer. So…I'm going to be the Grand Marshal for the last NASCAR race at Homestead-Miami Speedway! Isn't that ironic? I was hoping you could be with me on that day."

Steve is happy and upset at the same time. "You know I can't wait to be with you at any time, but that little job I have to take care of? If everything goes as planned, it'll happen on the same day as the race."

"Oh, no!" Diane's smiles fades after hearing Steve's explanation, but then it brightens again as a thought comes to her mind. "But you know you don't have to wait to be with me. I'm here now."

With the dinner dishes forgotten and the limo sent away, Diane prepares to stay the night.


At 5:00 a.m. on Thursday morning, Steve drops Diane off at the airport for her flight to California, before heading to the office. The goodbye is tearful, and they promise to talk to each other every night.

Once he's at the office, he and Angie spend the day going over the daily intelligence reports on the *Crescent Star*, along with all the rest of the hoopla. They run various scenarios over and over, trying to prepare for the worst, while poring over satellite photos of the *Crescent Star*, Port Everglades, and the Port of Dubai. This will become their daily routine, repeated every day until the freighter docks at Fort Lauderdale.

# CHAPTER TWELVE

Friday, 5:30 p.m., Duke's Saloon:

Steve walks into the saloon and waves at Angie behind the bar. He sits on the nearest stool and waits for his Jack on the Rocks.

"Geo should be here any minute. It's about time we got together." Angie pours himself a beer; "Any new information on our one-eared asshole?"

"No, SSDD; except that the radiation detector arrived today. It's pretty neat. It's about the size of a portable computer."

At that moment, Geo walks in, walks over to his main squeeze, who is serving drinks at one of the tables, and gives her a pat on the ass. He turns toward the bar and sits down next to Steve, where a beer is already waiting for him.

Steve looks at him and smiles, "How's the new job?"

"Great, if you like workin' for a living; I can't wait until all of this is over so I can be retired again. Oh, did I ever get a chance to thank you for this bullshit?"

Steve puts his arm around Geo as Angie laughs. "Come on, ya love every minute of it. How is the pilot taking all of this?"

"Good, Chic. I filled him in on the operation, where we want the freighter to dock, and all the other bullshit. I'll be on the bridge with him when we do this."

Ang chimes in, "Hey, we're going to be armed, aren't we? I'm not going in naked, am I?"

Chic begins to laugh mid-drink and nearly expels Jack Daniels out of his nose. "Shit! I just pictured you naked. That image is now burned into my brain! Look, I got Glock 18's for the both of you. By the way, they're fully automatic and come with 30-round clips."

Ang is a little shocked. "Automatic hand guns, SWAT, Coast Guard, Apache's. Are we preparing for WWIII?"

"Look, I'd rather be prepared for the worst than take things lightly and get fucked. Ever since the CIA screwed up the intel on Iraq, I don't trust them to get it all right." Changing the subject, Steve asks, "Hey, Ang, how about another round, and some wings?"

The three friends spend the better part of the night eating wings, drinking, and telling war stories. Eventually, Steve looks at his watch. It's almost midnight. "Oh, shit! I gotta' call Diane."

Ang and Geo let him have it, "Great! Pussy-whipped already and not even married yet!"

Steve gives them half a peace sign as he leaves the bar. "I'll call you tomorrow."

As he climbs into his car, he sets his 'Vette on autopilot and heads home to call Diane.

The next morning is Saturday, and Steve wakes up late, feeling like shit. He makes himself a pot of coffee and calls his sons to invite them over for dinner. As he is reading the morning paper, the phone rings. It's his local real estate agent.

"Steve, I have a condo for you to look at. It's right on the beach at the end of Oakland Park Boulevard, eighth floor, ocean view. I'll come by to pick you up at 11:30, okay?"

Steve agrees, hangs up and finishes his coffee. Then he goes off to do the three S's: shit, shower and shave.

The real estate agent arrives right on time and drives Steve down to the ocean. The condo they have come to see is part of a large, fifteen-story, multi-building complex with pools, spas and a private beach. The unit they are looking at today has three-bedrooms and a large wraparound balcony with an ocean view.

When Steve sees something he likes, he goes for it, and he likes this condo, so he makes an offer. He doesn't worry about selling his house, because he knows that Geo has always liked his place and that he is currently looking for a house to settle in with his waitress girlfriend, so he decides to sell it to Geo on the cheap. Everything is falling into place.

After the agent drives him home, he decides to take a nap before beginning to prepare for the family dinner that evening.

It may be the first week of November, but when the family arrives, Steve is outside on the patio grilling steaks. Mike calls out, "Need help, Dad?"

"No, Mike. Just bring out some beers."

The wives set the table as Steve and his sons bullshit while he cooks. When the steaks are done, he brings them into the dining room and everyone sits down to eat.

After Steve says grace, he announces, "I need to fill you all in on some news. Diane had to go back to Hollywood to finish filming her movie, and while she's there, she's going to start planning the wedding. We don't have a date yet, but it will be sometime this spring."

As the family begins to chatter about wedding details, Steve interrupts them to continue his announcement. "In the other good news, I bought a villa in Italy! You guys know it was always my dream to retire on the Amalfi Coast. Now, I won't be doing it alone. Oh, and I also put a contract on a condo in Fort Lauderdale! I don't need this house anymore, so Diane and I will be using the condo when we come into town. We plan to spend winters here with you and our grandchildren!"

The family is stunned by all of Steve's news, but at the mention of grandchildren, John and Carla smile, while Steve grins at Mike and Jeannie and says, "You guys are next!"

Mike and Jeannie grin sheepishly while Mike retorts, "That villa better have extra bedrooms so we all have a place to sleep when we visit!"

As the family laughs and clinks their drink glasses together in a toast, Steve clears his throat before delivering more news. "Guys, I'm also involved with a security problem at the port, so I'm going to be out of communication for a few weeks."

Concerned, John says, "I know you Pop, don't do anything stupid."

"Why does everyone think I'm going to do something stupid? Look, I'm too old for something stupid. Besides, I'm the one in charge, so I won't be in harm's way. I'll fill you guys in on everything after it's all over."


While Steve's family is enjoying their time together, the *Crescent Star* is pulling out of her berth in Dubai and heading for the Suez Canal on her way to Fort Lauderdale. The attack sub *SSN Bridgehampton* is unofficially tracking the *Crescent Star* as it leaves Dubai and heads into the Persian Gulf. The sub will have to break off surveillance when the *Star* enters the Suez Canal, though, because officially, the United States doesn't have attack subs in that part of the world. The *SSN*

*Nemo* will pick up the *Crescent Star's* track in the Mediterranean and then follow her the rest of the way to Fort Lauderdale.

Sunday is a very quiet day for Steve. He has nothing planned, so he heads down to Duke's Saloon and watches football all afternoon.

On the other hand, Sunday is a very busy day for Diane in California. She is spending the day with Tammy, shopping for wedding gowns, bridesmaid gowns, flowers and photographers. Diane also books their reception at the Beverly Hills Hotel for the first weekend in August, and needs to tell Steve that she went ahead and chose a date for their wedding.

It's a busy day for Bashir, too, but a deckhand aboard a freighter is busy every day. Bashir cannot wait to get to America to fight the infidels. He is prepared to die for Allah if he needs to, and his four partners on board are equally as dedicated. Along with the automatic weapons they smuggled aboard the ship, they also have a small charge of plastic explosives. If circumstances dictate, they won't hesitate to blow up the container of uranium, no matter where they are.

The next day is Monday, and Steve sits in his office reviewing reports of the *Crescent Star* passing through the Suez Canal. He picks up the phone to call Geo at the port and asks him to arrange a quiet lunch meeting with the pilot who has been assigned to guide the *Star* to its prearranged berth. Steve cautions Geo to make the meeting as private as possible.

At the appointed time, Geo picks up three sub sandwiches at Quiznos and meets Steve and the pilot of the port under the western span of the 17th Street Causeway Bridge near downtown Fort Lauderdale. They sit together on a bench overlooking the Intracoastal Waterway while Geo introduces the pilot to Steve.

"Steve, this is Herman Schmidt, our contact in the Pilot's Office at Port Everglades."

Steve does not waste time. "Herman, we picked this spot to have our meeting so we won't bring attention upon yourself and your office. I know that George has already filled you about our situation. Since we don't know how involved Interplex may be in this plot, we had to keep our meeting quiet. We're going to need the *Crescent Star* to dock at Pier 4, Slip 2, Berth 4. After the ship arrives at its berth, we've arranged for a blockade of the port by land, sea and air. Are you on board with all this?"

Herman replies firmly, "I wasn't happy when Port Everglades was taken over by Interplex. You have my complete cooperation."

"Good. The *Crescent Star* is a handy-sized freighter, five hundred twenty-five feet long. It has five cargo holds. George will be on the bridge with you when you guide her in. We already have men in place at the dock and we'll keep you in radio communication with them. If you do as we say, there won't be any problems. George will keep us abreast of any changes that day. Any questions?"

"Yes. How many terrorists are involved aboard the *Star*?"

"As far as we know, just one, a deckhand named Khalil Bashir. But we'll be prepared for more, just in case."

They eat their sandwiches in silence and when Steve finishes eating, he returns to his office. Geo and Herman remain on the bench talking quietly while watching the pleasure ships cruising up and down the Intracoastal Waterway.

The rest of the week goes by fairly smoothly, without any incidents. Steve reviews daily reports on the *Crescent Star*, which is now approaching the Straits of Gibraltar and is about to enter the Atlantic Ocean. The *SSN Nemo* is very vigilant, following close behind the ship while remaining undetectable.

During the week, Steve makes several calls to Homeland Security, which has recently positioned their HAZMAT team at the port. He wants to keep everyone in the loop.

On Friday afternoon, before leaving the office for the weekend, he hands Monday's briefing report to his secretary and asks her to make several copies. On his drive home, he mentally reviews his weekend, hoping that he has nothing to do. Suddenly, his cell phone rings. Glancing at the incoming call display, he sees that it's Colonel Johnson.

"Yes, Colonel. What's up?"

"Steve, I've made arrangements for you to meet Sergeant Williams and some of our Special Forces personnel at Markham Park's gun range to get you familiar with the weapons you'll have at your disposal for the operation. Are you free tomorrow morning at 8:00?"

"Sure am, Colonel. I'll be there at 8."

"Good. Just give the person at the front desk your name and he'll direct you to the enforcement officer's range. I'll be coming into town on Sunday night, so I'll see you at the meeting on Monday. Good shooting, Steve."

Steve hangs up. Now he hopes that at least his Sunday will be quiet.

As he is eating dinner that evening, his cell phone rings again. This time, it's his real estate agent.

"Hi, Steve, this is Tom. I have good news! You're now the proud owner of a condo on the beach!"

"Wow, that's great! When do you think we'll close?"

"Probably not until after Thanksgiving, but it should be before Christmas. Does that work for you?"

"Works fine for me, Tom. Just call me with the date."

"Will do Steve, and congratulations."

Thinking to himself that the timing is perfect, he decides to give Diane the news when he calls her this evening. He sits back down to finish his dinner, then clears off the table and turns on the TV to watch Fox News.

Later that evening, the phone rings again. This time, it's Diane.

"Hi, Steve! I thought I'd call *you* for a change. Miss me?"

"Hi, Di! Miss you a lot! How's our wedding coming along?"

Sighing deeply, Diane says, "Well, I had to book our reception, so I chose the first weekend in August. Are you okay with that? I'm sorry I didn't ask you first, but it was the first opening they had available. I hope you're not angry!"

"Angry? You couldn't possibly make me angry. August is great! Get your gown yet?"

"Sure did. Wait 'till you see it! And I'm so glad August is okay. I love you!"

"Me, too! But I also have some news for you. I placed an offer on a condo on the beach and it was accepted! We'll probably go to closing next month. Di, I can't wait for you to see it. And I can't wait to see *you!*"

Mushy babble continues for an hour. If only Angie and Geo knew!

Saturday morning, 8:00 a.m.:

When Steve arrives at the gun range, BSO Sergeant Brook Williams is waiting inside, near the front desk. They greet each other and ask to be escorted to the professional range, where they meet more members of the team.

"Steve Ciccone, my name is James Nelson. We're here from the Department of Homeland Security."

James Nelson is ex-Navy Seal and ex-CIA. He was recruited into Homeland Security and is now scheduled to head the FSA office in New York. James proceeds to introduce Steve to the rest of the fifteen-man team, and then Steve introduces the team members to Sergeant Brook Williams.

After the introductions, James takes charge. "Steve, we're here to familiarize you with the weapons we'll have available for this mission. The boarding party will be equipped with P90's. They carry a thirty-five round horizontal clip. If you remember the TV series Stargate SG-1, the P90 is the weapon that was used by the SG teams. Now Steve, we know how proficient you are as a sniper, so for you, we have a Barrett 107 .50 caliber semi-automatic, with a Leupold scope."

"Hoorah! I know that fine weapon has an effective range of 7,000 yards, but that it's most accurate at 2,500 yards. And I also know its projectile travels 2,700 feet per second and that a halfway decent rifleman can shoot ten rounds in less than ten seconds. So, when do we start making some noise?"

They make noise for about forty-five minutes. During a break in the shooting, Steve invites James to the meeting at the FSA on Monday morning, and thanks him for the training session. Then he and Sergeant Williams leave the gun range to grab some breakfast. The rest of the men remain at the range and continue to make noise for the better part of the morning.

Sitting in a booth at a nearby restaurant, Steve and Sergeant Williams spend the time getting to know each other.

"So, Brook, how long have you been with BSO?" Steve has already read Brook's bio, but he wants to see what the Sergeant has to say about himself.

"Well, Steve, I've been with BSO for three years, but

before that I was a grunt in Mosul, going door to door, looking for the Taliban. But you must have read my bio, so you know all that." He takes a drink of his coffee and looks at Steve.

Steve smirks. "Just like to know who I'm going to party with."

At that, they raise their coffee cups and tap them together, then wink at each other and dig into their breakfasts. When they leave the restaurant, they high five each other as they walk to their cars. After Steve climbs into his 'Vette and Brook climbs into his cruiser, each of them hauls ass out of the parking lot.

Driving home, Steve muses, *All of our plans seem to be coming together. Now, if Khalil will just cooperate, everything will be just fine.*

Sunday morning after church, Steve speaks with his pastor again. His talks with Father O'Donnell are helping him to embrace his faith and resolve his issues with morality and justice.

While he's still in the church parking lot, he places a call to his son, John.

"Hey, John! Got anything planned for today?"

"Not really, Dad. Mike and Jeannie are coming over for a barbeque and then we're watching football."

"Mind if I join you? I'll bring the beer."

"No problem, Dad. See you about noon?"

"Great! See ya then."

Steve hops in his 'Vette and heads home to change out of his Sunday clothes. He has just enough time to call Diane and get the beer.

# CHAPTER THIRTEEN

At 8:58 a.m. on Monday morning, Steve is getting out of his 'Vette in the FSA office parking lot when a brand new Camaro Z28 roars up and pulls into the parking space right next to his. A young, attractive, female Marine gets out of the car and heads into the building. Steve follows her in.

As they wait for the elevator, Steve asks, "Excuse me. Are you going to the FSA office?"

"Yes, Sir."

"Well, my name is Steve Ciccone and I'm in charge of this bureau. Are you here for a meeting this morning?"

"Yes, Sir. My name is Captain Alicia Ruffolo. I'm an Apache pilot assigned to the Panther Squadron based at Homestead Air Reserve Base. I'm your air cover, Sir."

The elevator door opens, and as they enter it, their conversation continues.

"I thought there were supposed to be two Apache's. What happened?"

"My squadron was reassigned to Afghanistan. I was chosen to stay behind, and I'm temporarily assigned to the FSA. As soon as this mission is complete, I'll be joining the rest of my squad. But don't worry. With a full armament of Hellfire missiles and a front mounted, sight activated, 30 mm chain gun that shoots 625 rounds per minute, one Apache will do just fine, Sir."

"Wow! I guess so. But from now on, please call me Chic. By the way, Ruffolo sounds familiar to me. Do you know Christine and Joe Ruffolo?"

"Why, yes, I do. They're my parents. How do you know them?"

When the elevator reaches their floor, the doors open into the FSA bureau office.

"I know them from the apparition site in Hollywood. I met them there."

"Wow, small world! They've been volunteering there for years. It's been awhile since I've been there, though. I guess I should go down there again."

"You know, I just returned from a trip to Italy and I stayed at a Hotel Rufolo."

"Yeah, my Dad talks about going there all the time, but I don't think we're related to those Rufolo's."

Steve's secretary informs him that everyone is already present in the conference room, so when Steve enters, he commences the meeting as Captain Ruffolo takes a seat.

"Good morning, everyone. Each of you should have the latest briefing information in front of you. But before we review the details, I'd like to go around the table so each of you can introduce yourselves to the group."

Steve reviews the reports while the introductions take place. The brief interlude allows him to collect his thoughts.

"Now that we know each other, I'll begin, and I'll try to be as brief as possible. For James Nelson, our ex-Navy Seal and ex-CIA team member, and Captain Alicia Ruffolo, the two new additions to the team, I'll first give a quick overview.

"Almost eight weeks ago, a Russian scientist stole some spent uranium 235 and sold it to al-Qaida. Al-Qaida plans to use the uranium to construct a dirty bomb that will be detonated in front of the Capitol in Washington, D.C. Our job is to stop them at all costs. The radioactive material is coming into this country on a freighter named the *Crescent Star*, which is due to dock here in Fort Lauderdale in about two weeks. James and Sergeant Williams are in charge of the SWAT team that will board the ship and capture our terrorist friend, Khalil Bashir. Please refer to your information packet for his bio and a photo. Captain Ruffolo will provide air cover for the mission. Frank Angelo will be with the boarding party that will monitor radiation levels and he will also be in charge of bringing in the Federal Emergency Management Agency's recovery team (FEMA) to properly transport the uranium after we secure it. George Jackson is currently working with the pilot of the port at Port Everglades and will be on the bridge of the *Crescent Star* as they guide her to dock at Berth 4."

Steve points to a satellite photo of Port Everglades.

"I'll be stationed atop the parking garage and will be sniper backup. The *Crescent Star* is currently entering the Atlantic Ocean. It's being followed and tracked by attack sub *SSN Nemo*. They'll keep us updated on her position.

"Oh, a couple more things; Coast Guard Commander Thomas Elliot will be our sea cover and will blockade the port while this operation is in progress, and the local police, under the command of Sergeant Brook Williams, will also blockade the port on land. Any questions?"

Thomas raises his hand. "Steve, will we be using deadly force, or are we going for capture?"

"If our intel is correct, Khalil is the only bad guy on board the *Crescent Star*. We'll try for capture, but you can dish out what you receive."

After more discussion, Steve adjourns the meeting until the following Monday, when daily meetings will occur until the ship docks.

About ten miles off the northern coast of Africa, at a depth of two hundred feet, the *SSN Nemo* stealthily monitors the *Crescent Star,* which is on a direct course for the United States. With fifteen years of experience as a submariner, Commander Andrew Paine scans the sonar screen and looks over the infrared readouts of the *Crescent Star's* location. He directs his crew over the con to bring the *Nemo* up. He's a bit of old school and wants to take a look through the periscope. As the *Nemo* eases up to periscope depth, the Commander looks through the scope. The moon is shining off the aft bow and sparkling off the ocean's surface.

"Transmit her coordinates, and someone get me a coffee."

The week goes by uneventfully, with daily talks between Steve, Colonel Johnson, and the FBI to discuss the continuously-updated intelligence reports. But Friday does not come soon enough for Steve. Even with all the stress of the impending mission, he knows that he has to start packing up his house for his move to the condo.

On Friday night, Mike and Jeannie meet John and Carla at a steak restaurant at the large casino resort complex in Hollywood. Steve has often wondered if it was just a coincidence that the Virgin Mary's apparition site is located in the same city as a large casino complex.

As the families wait for their orders, Mike asks, "So, what do you all think of Dad's new life?"

"Look, I think it's great," John says. "Dad looks happy, and Diane looks great!" He immediately gets an elbow to the ribs from Carla.

"John, she's going to be your stepmother and our child's grandma!"

Mike agrees with John. "John, you're right. Dad looks great and Diane fits in perfectly with the family. And with her career, he doesn't have to worry that she's after his money!"

Jeannie adds, "Carla and I had a great talk with her at the track. She seems very down to earth."

Carla agrees. "She'll make a good grandmother."


A couple of towns away, Steve is talking with Angie and Geo at Duke's.

"Hey, guys. We set the wedding for the first week of August. I want you both in the wedding party, and Ang, I'd like you to be my best man."

Ang agrees immediately and the group toasts Steve's new life. But they quickly decide not to continue toasting, because they realize they aren't as young as they used to be.

Even though Steve is happy to be with his friends, he leaves early because he has a couple of calls to make. When he arrives home, he kicks off his shoes and calls his son, John.

"Hello, John. It's Dad."

"Hey, Dad. What's up?"

"Diane and I set a date for our wedding. It's going to be the first weekend in August. I want you and Mike to be in the wedding party."

"Perfect timing, Dad. Mike and Jeannie are with us now. That saves you a phone call."

"You're not talking about me, are you?"

Smiling, John says, "No, not now. We were, about an hour ago, though! Let me put Mike on."

"Hey, Mike! We set our wedding date and I'd like you to be in the wedding party. It'll be the first weekend in August.

The wedding will be in California and I hope all of you can come out there." With a chuckle, he adds, "I'd pay for your tickets, but you guys have enough money now!"

"Yeah, that's great! We'll all be there! How's your condo shopping coming along?"

"You know me! I already have a contract on one. If all goes well, I'll be moving in next month. Geo's going to buy my house, so I'm all set. How are you and Jeannie doing? Any news I need to know about?"

"We're still practicing, Dad. We don't want to do anything artificial with special drugs, because we don't want three or four kids at once. We're pretty optimistic, though. We hope to have good news shortly. How's Diane?"

"She's good. We talk every night. Oh, by the way, she's coming back into town for the race at Homestead, because she's the Grand Marshal for the last race of the season! Can you believe that? Ken has a suite for us on pit row. I know you guys were planning to be there anyway, but unfortunately, I'll be busy at Port Everglades that day. I don't know if I'll be able to make it there or not."

"That sucks, Dad. We're all praying that everything goes well."

"Pray for the country, too. Listen, I gotta' go. I love you all. Kiss Jeannie and Carla for me, and if you want to, kiss John, too."

Mike laughs. "We love you, too, Dad."

Mike hangs up and plants a huge kiss on John's lips, while John smacks him on the back of the head.

As soon as Steve hangs up with Mike, his phone rings. It's Diane.

"Hi, Steve. Love you!"

"Hi, Di! I was just about to call you. Is anything wrong?"

"No, I have some good news. When we moved the movie shoot back to Hollywood, we were able to finish it earlier! Now it's due to be released around the beginning of March. They want me to do additional promotion of the movie to generate interest, so I'll be coming down earlier than we planned to do some local shows and events. I'll be in South Florida on Monday!"

"Hey, that's great! Do you need to be picked up at the airport?"

"No, I have a limo. But you know what happened last time!"

They both laugh and continue talking for what seems like hours. They are like two young kids, both are in love and standing together in a doorway, having to say goodbye for the night, but not really wanting to. They are two people in love, 4,000 miles apart, yet as close as Siamese twins.

Sunday goes by like a blur for Steve as he packs some stuff and throws other stuff away. When he comes across some old photos stuffed away in a box in the attic, he stops in his tracks. The photos were taken on his twenty-fifth wedding anniversary, when he spent a long weekend in Bermuda with Julie. They were young then, but Julie always looked twenty years younger than Steve. Everywhere they went, people stared at Steve, thinking he robbed the cradle.

He smiles as he remembers the worst of those incidents. It was in Bermuda. They were eating breakfast in their hotel's restaurant, when the waiter asked how he and his daughter were doing. Julie laughed out loud, and she never let him forget it.

He carefully places the photos back in the box and marks them for his son, Mike. He does not want to lose the memories, but he does not want Diane to feel insecure in their new relationship, either. When he finishes clearing out the attic, he cleans himself up and goes to bed.

Monday morning's meeting at the FSA office goes off without a hitch. The *Crescent Star* is in the middle of the Atlantic and is on schedule to arrive in Fort Lauderdale early Sunday morning. Everything is in place. FEMA has arrived in town, BSO is all set, the bomb squad has been briefed, and the Coast Guard has brought in an additional patrol boat to assist in closing off the port. All the players are prepped and anxious to get this over with.

When the meeting ends, Steve walks over to his desk and calls Homeland Security to fill them in on the latest intel and to give them the final details of the planned assault.


Four thousand miles away, Diane is boarding a plane for Miami. She cannot wait to see Steve again. Diane has a lot to talk to Steve about, with all the preparations she has made for the wedding and reception. She has photos of flowers, cakes, bridesmaid dresses, tuxedos and other wedding stuff. Because she has no children of her own, she is excited about getting input from Carla and Jeannie. Diane's previous marriages were based more on infatuation and convenience, but she knows this one will be different. This time, she's in love, and she wants this one to last.


Steve leaves the office early and goes home to shower and get ready to meet Diane and his family for dinner. He is anxious to finish this project so he can tender his resignation and prepare for retirement and his new life in Italy.

Steve drives over to John's house, where he meets Mike and Jeannie. They all pile into John's SUV and head to the local hotel and resort where Diane is staying on her current trip into town.

Steve calls Diane from the car. "Hi, Di. We're just pulling into the parking lot."

"Okay, wait for me in the lobby. I'll be right down."

They valet park the car and everyone walks into the hotel lobby, where they sit down to wait for Diane amid plush sofas and comfortable chairs. Jeannie touches Steve on the arm.

"Dad, you seem a little nervous. Are you okay?"

Steve squeezes her hand. "I'm fine, hon. I just hope you all take Diane into your hearts like I did. And between the bad guys, my wedding, my retirement, and a grandchild on the way, I have a lot on my plate right now."

Diane walks out of the elevator as the Ciccone family is hugging each other. When she sees what's going on, she runs toward them and joins in with the hugging.

After some small talk, the family walks over to the hotel restaurant. Steve orders a bottle of champagne as soon as they are seated. After the waiter pops the cork and serves everyone except Carla, who is having club soda, Steve proposes a toast.

"To John and Carla! Congratulations on your pregnancy, and many more!"

Everyone toasts the couple. Then, John stands and directs his attention to Steve and Diane. "To Dad and Diane! Congratulations on your engagement, and on your future life together. We love you, Dad!" Turning to Diane, he continues, "Diane, we welcome you into our family. You can't replace our mother, but you'll make a great grandma. We love you, too…Granny!"

Diane does not know whether to laugh or cry, because she is overwhelmed with joy. She stands up and walks around the table, giving kisses all around. Steve stands, giving John a hug, and high fiving Mike. Eventually, the group settles down and eats dinner.

After dinner, the family goes up to Diane's suite. Diane, Carla, and Jeannie sit down at a small table and begin talking about wedding stuff, so Steve directs his two sons to the balcony, where he whips out three Cuban cigars. The men enjoy the evening with a good smoke and some man bullshit.

"Wait 'till you see my new condo, boys. It has an ocean view with a wraparound balcony, a private pool, a beach, a gym, and a spa! And when you two come to Italy, it'll be my treat!"

They answer in unison, "Italy! We're *there*!"

But John adds, "Dad, it's going to have to be after the baby is born. By the time you're married and settled in, it'll be right around the birth date. In fact, if Carla is early, we may even miss the wedding. Her due date is August 17 and the wedding is August 2."

Not wanting to spoil the evening with a possible complication in the wedding plans, the conversation turns to football and hockey, and then eventually, to the bad guys.

"You all set for the mission this week, Dad? We're gonna' miss you at the race on Sunday."

"Mike, everything is set. I've surrounded myself with the best people I could find, so I'll be fine. I'll miss the race, but Diane will be there. She's the Grand Marshal, and I'm sorry I'll miss that. I'll record the race on my DVD player at home, but take a lot of photos for me, okay?"

"Sure will, Dad."

When their cigars are finished, they head back inside the suite. Diane has ordered dessert and coffee from room service, so everyone sits down and continues to talk about the wedding and to review Diane's photos. Steve likes the flowers and the decorations and the girls like the gowns. The night goes very well. It feels as though they have been a family for years.

When Steve and his family are ready to leave, Diane walks

them down to the lobby. Steve tells his sons and daughters-in-law to go ahead to the car, while he stays behind to say goodbye to Diane.

"Di, the night went great! I'll call you when I can. This week is going to be very busy for me. We all love you."

"Steve, I love all of you, too. But promise me that you'll be extra careful this week. We all need you."

They share a kiss in a corner of the lobby and then Steve reluctantly leaves the hotel.

He is fairly quiet on the ride home. His children are all for Diane and the wedding, and Steve is calm and happy.

The remainder of the week is busy for Steve. There are daily meetings at the FSA office, mock run throughs staged at private training grounds at Homestead Air Reserve Base, and daily updates on al-Qaida and the *Crescent Star*. Steve is pumped, but he is ready for all of this to end. He calls Diane every night and their talks calm him and take his mind off the serious tasks at hand.


Saturday morning.

Steve arrives at the office early. The latest intel puts the *Crescent Star* about two hundred miles off the coast of Florida. At a cruising speed of ten to twelve knots, she'll be ready to berth between eight and 10:00 on Sunday morning.

The shit will hit the fan about 5:00 in the morning, so tonight will be an all-nighter. Steve brought a change of clothes with him because he plans to crash on the sofa in his office. He doesn't want to leave the building this close to the start of the operation. Everything must go right; he can't afford to fail.

He calls Ang and Geo and asks them to meet him at the office. They bring pizza and beer and plan to stay there with him throughout the night.

During the night, Geo calls Herman at the port to update him with the latest information. Herman tells Geo to meet him in his office at 6:00 a.m. so they can prepare for the *Crescent Star's* berthing.

Everyone else is also on board, no pun intended. They will stage at the port's entrance at 7:00 a.m. BSO has closed the parking garage near Pier 4 so Captain Ruffolo can set her Apache helicopter there before dawn in an effort to keep the operation as inconspicuous as possible. Steve will join her there later in the day.

Chic, Angie and Geo try to get to sleep early that night on cramped chairs and an uncomfortable sofa. Each of them has slept in foxholes at some time in their careers, so these conditions are like being at a luxury hotel.

Diane is wide awake in her hotel room; she cannot sleep. She is worried about Steve and wonders what he'll be doing tomorrow. Attempting to clear her mind, she rises from bed to take a couple of nighttime analgesics. She knows that she'll have a long day tomorrow, but realizes that Steve's day will be much harder. She goes back to bed, says a prayer, and dreams of Steve and their wedding day.

# CHAPTER FOURTEEN

**Sunday, November 20, 5:00 a.m.**

When Steve wakes up, he walks over to wake up Angie, and then Geo. They change their clothes in silence and get ready for the day. It's been a long time coming.

Geo puts on his undergarment holster and straps in his Glock 18, also pocketing three 30 round clips. He inserts an earpiece in his ear so he can communicate with the rest of the team, then high fives Steve and Angie and leaves the office. He needs to get over to the pilot house at the port to wait for the *Crescent Star*.

Meanwhile, Steve calls Colonel Johnson at the Pentagon to get the freighter's latest coordinates.

"She's near the Bahamas, about two and a half hours from Fort Lauderdale. In about an hour, the captain should be contacting the port pilot for final procedures."

"Thanks, Colonel. We're all ready."

During today's operation, Geo will shadow the pilot of the port and will also remain in constant contact with Commander Elliot of the Coast Guard. In the hour before the *Star* arrives, the Commander will deploy two of the Coast Guard's patrol boats to make sure the port is secure. The port's parking garage, which was sealed off the week before, is swarming with HAZMAT team members and BSO bomb squad technicians. In order to keep the public away from the garage, construction signs were placed around the property, and passengers for the cruise ships that dock at the port are being instructed to use nearby Fort Lauderdale-Hollywood International Airport for parking. Shuttle buses have been arranged to transport them between the airport and the port.

At 6:00 a.m., Steve and Angie leave the FSA office. But before they reach the car, Angie runs back into the building to pick up the radiation detector he left in Steve's office. When he returns to the parking lot, Steve is in the car, waiting to drive them over to the port to meet with Sergeant Williams and his crew, and James Nelson and his assault team, at the port's entrance off SR 84.

At the command post that has been set up at the port's entrance, Steve and Angie greet James and Sergeant Williams, and then each of them begins to review the port's status reports and the latest intel received from several federal agencies.

All of them are using their earpieces to monitor communications between the various team members, when they pick up the sound of a helicopter approaching. In their earpieces, they hear, "Steve Cicone, Steve Cicone. This is Panther 3. I've just landed on the top level of the parking garage."

Steve replies, "10-4, Panther 3. Is that you, Alicia?"

"Yes, Sir. Where are you?"

"I'm meeting with the ground troops. I'll join you in about twenty minutes. How do you like your coffee?"

"Black, Sir. No sugar."

"Black it is, but cut out the 'Sir' shit. Call me Chic."

"10-4…Chic."

Wishing everyone Godspeed, Steve leaves the command post and heads for the parking garage as Angie puts on his bulletproof vest and begins to review last minute instructions with James and the Coast Guard team, and Sergeant Williams orders his patrol boats to seal off the port on the north and south sides.

At 7:15 a.m., Captain Emil of the *Crescent Star* contacts the Harbormaster's office to request a pilot. This is the call the team was waiting for. Herman immediately gets on the line and tells the captain that a tug will be sent to meet the *Crescent Star*, and that he and his assistant will board the ship to guide her in. The *Star* is now visible from land, about one mile off the coast.

Geo contacts Steve, who is now in the parking garage.

"Steve, she's here! Look east. We're getting ready to go out and board her."

As everyone listens in over their communications equipment, Steve takes control of the mission.

"Okay, men, the ball is in our court. The ship should be berthed in about an hour. You guys ready at the berth?"

"Ready."

"Sergeant Williams?"

"All set, Steve."

"Angie and James?"

"Ready to kick Bashir's ass!" assures James, as Angie chimes in, "All set, Chic. See ya later."

"10-4 guys. Colonel Johnson, time to deploy."

"We're on it, Steve. Good hunting, guys."

Steve loads his Barrett .50 caliber rifle, stands at his post on the top floor of the parking garage, and stares at the *Crescent Star*. He watches as the patrol boats move into position as the tug carrying Geo and Herman heads out of the inlet.

Steve turns to Captain Ruffolo, who is alongside him in the parking garage.

"It's party time! As soon as she reaches the end of the inlet, it's your time to shine."

Alicia gives him the thumbs up signal, and then they return their attention to watching the tug and the *Star* converge offshore.

At a little after eight in the morning, Diane is in the shower, starting the preparations for her busy day as Grand Marshal at the race at Homestead-Miami Speedway. A limo will pick her up in about an hour, even though the race doesn't start until 3:00 p.m. She needs to be at the track early in order to attend the various pre-race ceremonies that are scheduled for the day.

As busy as her day will be, her mind is not on the race, but on Steve, and she prays that everyone will be safe during today's operation.

Before driving down to the racetrack, John, Carla, Mike, and Jeannie attend early Mass together and light some candles for their Dad and the members of his team. After Mass, they go out for breakfast, and then they head down to the track to beat the traffic. Mike calls Diane from the car to let her know that they will meet her at the Peters' racing pit.

Aboard the *Crescent Star*, Khalil Bashir stows his gear and prepares for docking. He grabs the small piece of paper that contains the name and number of Malcolm Mohammed, his Fort Lauderdale contact, and places it safely in the clothes that he will wear onshore.

Malcolm Mohammed is a Florida-born terrorist, whose given name is Malcolm Jones. Malcolm is a recent convert to Islam, and now attends a local mosque. His role in the scheme is to transport the uranium to Washington and then hand it off to Abdul Kalib, the al-Qaida operative.

Halfway around the world, Mahmoud Attan sits in his Dubai office alone. He is waiting for Khalil Bashir to call him after the *Crescent Star* docks in Fort Lauderdale. He stares out over the skyline of Dubai, overly confident of his success over the infidels.

After Herman and Geo board the *Crescent Star*, they head directly for the bridge, where Herman immediately takes the helm. He positions the ship behind his tugboat and guides the *Star* into the inlet off the port, as Geo stands by.

Watching from the top level of the parking garage, Captain Ruffolo spots her cue. She quickly climbs into the Apache and lifts off.

Everything is about to go down. James Nelson, Sergeant Williams and their team members arrive at Berth 4 and intermingle with the men that Homeland Security had previously placed there as longshoremen.

When the Harbormaster's tugboat finally peels away from the *Star*, it gives a blast of its horn. This is the signal that everyone was waiting for.

At the port, the James Nelson's Homeland Security force secures the dock area; no one in, no one out. On the freighter, Geo flashes his Federal Security Agency ID and places the ship's captain under arrest. Captain Emil, who was not part of the terrorist conspiracy, remains quiet, although he is clearly shocked while Geo handcuffs him to the helm's chair and briefs him on what is about to occur.

As Geo watches, Herman slowly brings the *Crescent Star* to dock, while the *Star's* deckhands work with the dockworkers to batten down and tie off the freighter. When the gangplank is raised into position, the assault team springs into action. James assigns his team to guard the entrances to below decks, three forward, two at each cargo hold, and the rest aft.

News of these unexpected events spreads quickly throughout the ship, and when it reaches Khalil and his four terrorist accomplices, they react immediately. Khalil turns away from the corridor he was headed for and makes a beeline for the uranium that he stowed near his bunk, while the remaining terrorists grab their weapons and take up positions around the ship to oppose their attackers.

When the assault team arrives below decks, they are immediately met with automatic weapons fire and Steve reacts to the news with anger.

"What the hell? The CIA fucked up again! What's your status?"

Angie, who had hung back, responds, "We got resistance! I guess Khalil is *not* alone! Looks like three or four are armed with uzi's. The other teams are responding, and I'm splitting off from them. We need to find Khalil."

Back at the garage, Steve shakes his head.

"Alicia, stay close. This is getting ugly."

The marine pilot banks her Apache aft of the freighter and hovers there, waiting.

It is now close quarters in the hold of the ship, and James does not like it.

"All right, men! Let's clean this mess up!"

A fierce firefight ensues, which quickly ends the lives of two of the terrorists. However, in the resulting confusion, Khalil manages to make it to his bunk. He removes the canister of uranium from its lead travel case, grabs the plastic explosive and a detonating device, and heads toward the top deck. Angie's radiation detector immediately reacts.

"Steve, its Ang. I got radiation! He must have removed the canister from the case!"

On the top level of the parking garage, Steve sights the ship's deck through the Leupold scope.

"I'm covering the deck."

The two remaining terrorists manage to keep one of the assault teams at bay while they try to make their way to the aft deck of the freighter.

Khalil is able to avoid the firefight by climbing topside through cargo hold five. When Khalil arrives on deck, Steve spots the terrorist through his rifle scope and adjusts his focus to target him as he kneels down to press the plastic explosive onto the radioactive canister.

Wasting no time, Steve pulls the trigger, and the Barrett 170 roars to life. At 2,700 feet per second, the round enters Khalil's left temple and blows the right side of his head off. The canister containing the uranium falls harmlessly to the deck.

At the same moment, the remaining terrorists arrive at the ship's stern. When they emerge on deck and turn around, they stare directly at Captain Ruffolo in her Apache. The fanatics instinctively raise their weapons to fire at the behemoth hovering in front of them, but Captain Ruffolo is much quicker than they are. She sights through her 30 mm chain gun and unloads a ten second burst directly at them. One hundred and four rounds rain down on the deck at a rate of six hundred and twenty-five rounds per minute. Nothing is left of the radicals but teeth, hair, and eyeballs.

The sudden silence after Captain Ruffolo's burst of gunfire is deafening.

After a few seconds of quiet, Steve calls out, "Status report!"

James reports first. "All's quiet here. We'll continue to secure the ship."

Angie's next. "Need the bomb squad and HAZMAT team on deck. I think we got the canister."

Geo checks in. "Damn, you guys make a lot of noise! Steve, classic shot!"

Captain Ruffolo reports in. "Nice work, guys! Good guys, five, bad guys, nothing. Hope they don't make me pay for the damage to the freighter!"

After hearing from all team leaders, Steve makes a few observations of his own.

"Sergeant Williams, everything seems secure, but keep the port locked down until we're sure. Nice job, Commander Elliot! Continue to monitor all access to the channel and keep it blocked until we close out this operation. Hey, Alicia! Good shooting! See you back at the garage."

It takes several hours for the security teams to safely recover the package of uranium, round up all the crew members, and conduct a sweep of the ship. James Nelson calls Steve's cell phone to relay some information that was found during the search of the ship.

"Steve, we found a phone number and a man's name among Khalil's clothes in his bunk. It must be his local contact."

James gives the information to Steve and Steve forwards it immediately to the FBI. Within twenty-five minutes of receiving the contact's phone number, the FBI arrests Malcolm Mohammed at his home near Fort Lauderdale International Airport. Soon after his arrest, Malcolm comes clean with crucial information, enabling the FBI to break into Abdul Kalib's apartment in Washington, D.C. and rudely awaken him with an M-16 in his face. During a search of Kalib's apartment, they find the explosives that he was planning to combine with the uranium to create the dirty bomb.

After contacting the FBI, Steve calls Colonel Johnson

to give him the details his team obtained about the terrorist's plot, and then the Colonel passes that information on to Interpol. When the international authorities receive the information, they quickly assemble a team in Dubai and order them to race to Mahmoud Attan's corporate headquarters, on a tip that he is still at work. When they barge into his office, they find Mahmoud sitting at his desk, but before they can reach him, he throws his chair through the large window behind him, and jumps out. He lands violently on the front steps of Interplex's office building, fifteen floors below.

Hours later, a Predator drone armed with Hellfire missiles circles a Taliban encampment in the hills of Badakhshan province on the border between Afghanistan and Pakistan. When the drone acquires its target, it fires. Aziz Zarqawi Aziz, second in command of the Taliban, is sent to hell, along with several of his officers.

Today turns out to be a great day for the good guys!


Back in Fort Lauderdale, Steve orders his team leaders to attend a debriefing in the Homeland Security command trailer in the parking garage. The debriefing confirms that the uranium has been secured, the sea lanes have been reopened, and that as soon as Captain Ruffolo's Apache helicopter takes off for Homestead, the operations of Port Everglades can return to normal.

When the meeting adjourns, Steve looks around for Captain Ruffolo and catches sight of her as she is walking toward her chopper. He calls out, "Hey, Captain! I need a favor!"


The Apache helicopter lifts off from Port Everglades and heads south, but instead of flying directly to the Air Reserve

Base at Homestead, Captain Ruffolo will make a quick stop along the way.

Steve is strapped into the rear seat of the Apache. It's 2:15 p.m. and the race at Homestead-Miami Speedway is scheduled to begin at 3:00. Steve is hoping that he can arrive in time. He always wanted to make a grand entrance. As the chopper flies south, Homeland Security contacts Homestead-Miami Speedway through the local police department and alerts them about the incoming Apache helicopter.

As the helicopter flies over south Miami, Steve's cell phone rings.

"It's Steve. Start talking."

"Steve, this is President Baruch. The United States owes you a huge debt of gratitude! It's a shame that no one can know about it, though."

"Thank you, Mr. President. It is an honor, but you really have an entire team to thank."

"I know, Steve, but I wanted to make you my first call. I intend to call each of the members of your team personally. Please also accept my congratulations on your engagement to Diane Summers. Give her a kiss for me. Oh, and congratulations also to your son, John, and his lovely wife, on their pregnancy."

The President ends his call and leaves Steve puzzled once again. He wonders, *How did the President find out about his recent engagement, and how did he know about his son's news about the pregnancy?*


It's been a long day for Diane, but now it's race time. Diane is standing on pit row and the race cars are lined up and ready to go. As Grand Marshal, she is about to start the race with four famous words.

At the appointed time, Diane announces, "DRIVERS… START… YOUR… ENGINES!"

At the sound of the starting command, forty-three cars roar to life. Then suddenly, at the end of the front straightaway, an Apache helicopter lands, and all of the cars come to a screeching halt.

Steve taps the top of Captain Ruffolo's helmet, thanks her, and wishes her luck in Afghanistan. He knows that whoever faces her will be in trouble. He jumps out of the chopper and runs toward pit row.

Diane cannot believe her eyes! She leaves pit row to run toward Steve and when they reach each other, they embrace in a fervent hug and kiss as the crowd cheers them on.

When Alicia lifts her chopper off the ground, she banks it over pit road. As she passes overhead, she smiles and waves down to Steve, then quickly departs the track area.

From their suite above pit row, John, Mike, Carla, and Jeannie shake their heads while they watch the unbelievable scene unfold below them. They know what their father is capable of, but they are still having a hard time believing what they are seeing.

After the track is cleared, the field of cars begins to take their pre-race laps as they wait for the green flag start. Eventually, Diane and Steve join the family in the pit suite that Ken Peters arranged for them.

John grabs Steve's shoulder as he walks through the doorway.

"Dad! You need to fill us in on what happened today before it gets too loud to talk! How did it go?"

"It's a long story, and I won't be able to finish it before the race starts. Let's just say the good guys won this one. We stopped the terrorists in their tracks! I'll fill you in on the details later, because it's about to get very loud!"

As forty-three race cars squeal out of the far turn, the

drivers head down the front straightaway with pedals to the floor, screaming past the green starting flag in front of the pit suite.

The vibration of forty-three, 850 horsepower engines at full throttle rattles the chests of everyone present and makes verbal communication virtually impossible. Everyone puts in their earplugs and settles down to enjoy the race. The race is a long one, which makes for a long day for Steve.

During the post-race fireworks, Steve gathers his family together to give them the details of his day.

"Today, we stopped al-Qaida's attempt to blow up a dirty bomb outside the Capitol in Washington, D.C. The terrorists tried to smuggle radioactive material through Port Everglades, but with the help of local officials and the FBI, my team neutralized the threat and recovered the dangerous materials. The Marines also assisted by assigning one of their crack helicopter pilots to our mission, and she graciously helped me make a grand entrance at the track. So, I guess you can say we made history today in more ways than one."

At the conclusion of Steve's commentary, his family crowds around him in admiration and thanksgiving for a successful and safe outcome of the day's events, while Diane throws in a wet kiss. The group eventually makes its way to John's SUV to start their long ride home.

History was actually made twice today, as Daniella Patterson was the first woman to ever win a NASCAR cup, and al-Qaida's plan to target the U.S. Capitol was decimated!

# EPILOGUE

**September 3, just before dawn.**

Steve is standing in his backyard, staring at the Mediterranean as the sun rises over his shoulder and glistens off the surface of the water. He stares at the sea and thinks about the events of the previous few months that eventually led him here.

He smiles as he remembers how he quickly he resigned from the FSA when they finally closed the book on the mission at Port Everglades, and he is still happy that Colonel Johnson tapped George to take over his position.

Events in his life moved quickly after the mission ended. After he finished moving into his condo on the beach, he left for California to be with Diane, and for a few months after that, things went by in a blur. He remembers attending meetings with florists and photographers, and also a flamboyant wedding planner.

Just before the wedding, Steve moved into Diane's Beverly Hills mansion, even though a buyer for the house had been found rather quickly. They lived in the house together until the date of the closing, and then they moved into a room at the Beverly Hills Hotel, where they remained until their wedding day.

Oh, what a wedding it was! The theme of the reception was red roses, and Diane looked so beautiful! The wedding party was small, with Tammy acting as maid of honor, and Carla and Jeannie as bridesmaids. Angie was Steve's best man, and Mike and John were groomsmen, while George was an usher. Carla looked rather odd in her bridesmaid gown since she was nine months pregnant and looked as though she was smuggling a watermelon under her gown, but she had a wonderful glow about her that day.

The marriage ceremony took place in a garden on the grounds of the Beverly Hills Hotel, while the reception was indoors, behind two very large French doors that overlooked the garden. Steve and Diane enjoyed being the center of attention that day and they made and effort to spend time with each of their guests.

The day after the wedding, the happy couple left for a two-week tour of northern Italy, before arriving at their new home in Ravello.

After spending a few minutes watching the fishing boats on the Mediterranean Sea, Steve decides to walk into town to get something for breakfast. It won't take him long, as their house is located only half a kilometer outside of the city.

As he heads down the *Via Madonna dell'Ospedale*, he glances up the hill and notices that his neighbor, Giacamo, is tending his sheep with a shotgun strapped to his shoulder and a wineskin under his arm. It occurs to him that he is witnessing a scene that has not changed in over one hundred years.

Steve has settled in very nicely into his new life in Italy, but as much as he loves his adopted country, he cannot wait to get back to the states because he has still not met his new granddaughter. John says that she looks like Julie, and Steve is itching to see her and to act like a grandpa. Mike and Jeannie's twins are due in a couple of months, so Diane recommended that they fly home in time for their birth, which would enable everyone to be together for the holidays.

As Steve continues walking into town, he muses on Diane's career, as Hollywood is once again looming on the horizon. Diane ended her career in style after her movie was released, and was promptly nominated for an Academy Award for supporting actress. That means that Steve and Diane will have to attend the Awards show next year, which is something Steve is not looking forward to.

As he enters the center of town, he stops at several small stores to buy some mortadella, a melon, and a small wedge of sharp provolone cheese. The cheese smells like dirty feet, but he loves it. Before he returns home, he stops at Vince's panetteria. When he walks into the store, he sees Vince behind the counter.

"*Buon giorno, Vincenzo! Come va il pane di oggi?* How's the bread today?"

Vince laughs. "Your Italian is getting better. Not good, mind you, but better. Don't forget that you and Diane are coming over later for dinner. We want to get together with you before you leave for your trip to America."

Steve buys some fresh bread, but he doesn't notice the sfogliatelle that Vince put in the bag with it. He waves goodbye to Vince as he leaves the store.

On his way home, he takes a different path out of town, walking along the *Via dei Rufolo*, and eventually turning down the road to his house. Winter is coming and there's a definite chill in the air, but the air is clean and crisp, laden with the scent of lemons.

Steve enters the house quietly and sets up breakfast on the outside veranda. When he spies the free pastries in the bag, he laughs. A few minutes later, Diane steps out onto the veranda and puts her arms around Steve.

"Good morning, Mr. Ciccone."

"Good morning, Mrs. Ciccone."

The sound of Steve's cell phone ringing interrupts their first kiss of the day.

It's Colonel Johnson.

Book Two
Trihedral of Chaos
Trilogy

# The Falcon's Canticle

by Frank A. Ruffolo

# CHAPTER ONE

Steve and Diane finish their cappuccinos and sfogliatelle, say goodbye to Vince and Stella, and leave La Stella's panetteria. They pass the Hotel Rufolo and head back home down the *Via Madonna dell'Ospedale*. It is a beautiful spring day in the small mountain town of Ravello, Italy. The bougainvillea is in bloom and the smell of jasmine fills the air. The couple turns down a gravel road, and as they approach their villa, they notice a small red Fiat parked at their front door, next to their blue Fiat. As they pull into their driveway, a tall gentleman walks around the side of the house and waves at Steve. Steve sends a cold, sniper's gaze toward the tall man.

"*Buon giorno,* Steve."

"Colonel Johnson. Tell me you're on vacation."

Ignoring Steve's comment, the Colonel turns to Diane. "Mrs. Ciccone, I haven't seen you since the wedding. How are you?"

The Colonel reaches out his hand in greeting toward Diane, but before taking the Colonel's hand, she glances at Steve, who still has the Colonel in his crosshairs.

Colonel Johnson is chief of the FSA, the Federal Security Agency, and is Steve's former boss. The FSA was established by President Baruch as a liaison between the federal government and local law enforcement agencies in times of emergency; since it is illegal to deploy U.S. military troops within the borders of the U.S., the President set up this agency as a non-military security force in order to make it "legal."

However, Steve recently retired from the FSA, and he is not happy to see the Colonel.

"Chic, it would be rude not to invite our guest in." Diane opens the front door. "Would you like to come in, Colonel?"

"Only if your husband doesn't shoot me." The Colonel steps inside the villa as Steve continues his stare.

"I'll make some coffee. Why don't you boys sit out back and enjoy the Mediterranean."

Steve and the Colonel walk out to the back veranda as Diane fusses in the kitchen. They sit and face the Mediterranean Sea below.

"Okay, Colonel. Why are you here? I retired, remember?"

"I'm on a fact-finding mission. I need to know if you're available as a consultant. No management involvement, no massive commitment. I just need to know if you'd be available and would help if needed."

"Needed for what?"

Diane arrives on the veranda with two black coffees. "Chic, I'll leave you two alone now; I'll be inside. There's too much testosterone out here."

Steve takes a sip of his espresso and gently puts it down.

"Like I said, Colonel, needed for what? And how the hell did you find me?"

"Oh, you know, public records, bank statements. It was easy to find you once I arrived in Ravello, it's a small town. I'm staying at the Hotel Rufolo and I just took a stroll, asked some questions. Vince at La Stella's told me quite a story." After a pause, the Colonel continues. "Look, we opened another FSA office in Baltimore. Yours in Fort Lauderdale was the first and we'd like to have your experience and knowledge available, if needed."

Steve glances at his coffee, then stares at the Mediterranean, at the coastline, and at the olive trees growing near the veranda. He looks back inside the villa at Diane, who is reading a book, then eyes the Colonel with that cold, sniper's squint, as if he was measuring his target in the crosshairs and compensating for wind and distance.

The Colonel seems a little uneasy. Steve keeps him on target.

"My initial reaction is not just not no, but hell no. Look around, Colonel. Would you want to be here or in Baltimore? Shit, if God wanted to give Maryland an enema, that's where he'd stick the tube. I'll have to think strongly about this. Listen, you're on the government nickel here. Your hotel has a fine restaurant, how about you invite me and Diane to supper tonight, your treat. I'll give you my answer then. By the way, how's Geo doing since he took over the office in Fort Lauderdale?"

The Colonel takes a deep breath, easing his tension.

"Oh, he's doing fine. No concerns after the operation, except we did shoot up that freighter a little. The Prince was a little upset that his insurance wouldn't pay any claims."

"Yeah, but our oil dollars paid for that tanker. Eight o'clock tonight?"

"Eight's fine."

The Colonel waves goodbye to Diane as Steve escorts him through the house, toward the front door. After closing the door, Steve walks over to Diane.

"We're going to dinner tonight, Di. Put on something sexy, okay?"

# CHAPTER TWO

In the mountains of northeastern Afghanistan, al-Qaida continues to train recruits and suicide bombers to attack the West. A few years ago, Mossad, Israel's secret service, placed agent Moshe Saban deep undercover inside the terrorist organization. Because of his Persian roots, he was able to blend in well.

Moshe's father was stationed in Iran as a diplomat during the reign of the last Shah. When the Shah was overthrown by a populist revolution in 1979, Moshe's father and his Iranian secretary fled to Israel, where they married and had their only son, Moshe. Moshe's own wife and son now live in Tel Aviv, Israel.

Hidden behind a wall at the al-Qaida training site, Moshe observes the terrorist organization's current class of suicide bombers. As he watches their activities, he knows that NATO forces are busy tracking him through the signal originating from his cell phone. He also knows that they have dispatched a Predator drone to attack the site with rockets.

Back in Fort Dix, New Jersey, Air Force personnel are guiding the drone over the al-Qaida training site. After they receive confirmation of the target, the drone is directed to make its final attack run.

Moshe slips out of the camp and jumps on his horse as the rockets hit their target. The training camp is destroyed.

As Moshe rides out of Afghanistan and toward the Pakistan border, he does not realize that one of the suicide bomber trainees was able to escape from the camp before the rockets hit. Images from the Predator drone were relayed to Fort Dix after the attack, but they do not show any survivors. No one monitoring the camp knows that one of al-Qaida's trainees is determined to complete the mission he was being trained for. That recruit is working alone now, and is headed toward Pakistan, according to his orders. The recruit's ultimate mission is to explode a bomb on a crowded street in Tel Aviv, Israel.

# CHAPTER THREE

Even though Steve and Diane are only a short walk away from Hotel Rufolo, with Diane all dolled up in five-inch heels and a black cocktail dress that stops above the knee, they decide to take the Fiat instead.

As they walk into the hotel's restaurant, all heads turn to stare at one of Hollywood's most beautiful actresses. Steve puts his arm around Diane and whispers into her ear, "You know, I don't understand it, but every time we walk into a room together, everyone stares at me!"

Diane smiles and gives him a peck on the cheek. Steve catches sight of the Colonel and steers Diane toward the table where he is already seated. The Colonel stands to greet them.

"Mrs. Ciccone, you look stunning tonight."

Cutting in, Steve says, "Oh, I thought they were looking at me." He gives a wink to Diane as he pulls her chair out and seats himself at the table.

The Colonel pours three glasses of wine and proposes a toast.

"Health and happiness to both of you." Glasses clink together as the waiter arrives to take their orders.

"So, Steve, what have you decided? Can we expect your help if it's called upon?"

"Diane and I discussed it this afternoon, and you're

very lucky. My son, Michael and his family just moved to Maryland. He's a senior software engineer at a lab run by the federal government in Columbia. They have a five thousand square foot home with a separate apartment above a two car garage, so Di and I could stay with them if I have to go to Baltimore. We'd be able to use that time to visit with our grandkids. But I'll accept an assignment only if I'm a consultant. No responsibilities, no field work, and if I don't like it, I'm history. Got it?"

"Got it." Steve raises his glass, as does the Colonel, and they clink them together in agreement.

"Mrs. Ciccone, I must congratulate you on the Oscar nomination for your last film. I know you've announced your retirement, but are you planning to attend the Awards ceremony?"

"We sure are, Colonel, and thank you."

The Colonel raises his glass in another toast. "Best of luck to Diane Summers! You should have won a long time ago."


In separate hotels in Islamabad, Pakistan, two men have unrelated missions that will unite them together in chaos.

Moshe Saban's newest mission from Mossad is to infiltrate one of the international terror organizations sponsored by the Revolutionary Guard from Iran.

After preparing a new ID and creating new Iranian paperwork, Moshe sets out for a flight from Islamabad, Pakistan, to Tehran, the capital of Iran. His mission's code name is Falcon Canticle and his initial orders are to meet a CIA agent at the Tehran airport, where he will receive further details.

Meanwhile, Ahmed Vakal, the eighteen-year old suicide bomber from Syria who survived the Predator drone attack in Afghanistan, is also preparing for a flight, but his flight will end in Cairo. From there, terrorist sympathizers will transport him through Egypt to a location on the Egyptian-Israeli border, where he will travel through a smuggler's tunnel to gain entrance to the Gaza Strip. Once inside the hotly-contested Palestinian territory, he will receive his vest of explosives, various maps, and his ID, and then pass through another tunnel directly into Israel.

Ahmed is a Syrian Jew who was placed into an orphanage after his parents died in a car crash. He bounced from one abusive family to another and eventually converted to Islam. His abusive past and his knowledge of Hebrew make him the perfect foil.

Ahmed was recruited by Moshe Saban, as he played his part as a fellow terrorist. Ahmed's orders were to kill as many people as he could on a public street in Tel Aviv. Moshe believes that Ahmed was killed in the drone attack in Afghanistan, but as Moshe waits on line to check in at the airport, Ahmed has just taken off for Cairo. Within seventy-two hours, Ahmed hopes to meet his virgins in paradise.

Lisa Thomas is cooking breakfast in the large house at the top of Lewis Mountain Circle in Charlottesville, Virginia. She works as the live-in nanny, personal assistant and cook for the wife of Virginia's Senator, William Lewis. Lisa is thirty-eight years old, single, and has worked for the Senator's wife for the past six years.

Lisa's actual name is Risa Rashjani. She was born in the United Arab Emirates and was recruited by al-Qaida fifteen years ago to be trained in explosives and groomed to infiltrate the West. Risa is currently posing as a Southern Baptist, but she is actually a closet Muslim who is waiting for her orders. She is a sleeper agent of terror, the type of terrorist the FBI is most afraid of, a terrorist who has assimilated into Western society. She is working under the radar, where she cannot be easily spotted or tracked.

Rishad Amanni is another sleeper cell. He is from Saudi Arabia and is now living near Fort Lauderdale, Florida, posing as a medical student at Nova Southeastern University. Once a week, he goes to the Broward County Library in nearby city of Plantation to use their computers to check for online coded messages that are meant for him. He uses the library's computers because internet access from public computers is not normally traced.

Today, Rishad is reading through the personals column on the website of Al Jazeera, the Arab-language news network, where individuals can post requests and answers much like they used to do in the personals posted in local newspapers. Most of the messages are just meaningless communications, but intermingled within the normal nonsense are coded messages directed toward terrorist operatives across the globe. Rishad retrieves his coded message and writes it down: *When the eagle flies, the falcons sing. It has left the nest for plundering. She'll take two eggs and fly away; we'll sing again another day.*

Clutching the canticle, Rishad returns to his dorm room to decipher it in private. Fortunately, Rishad does not know that he was not the only one to see this message. The CIA is also monitoring Al Jazeera, and has labeled his message as a matter of interest.

# CHAPTER FOUR

Diane starts packing for their trip to Hollywood, California to attend the Academy Awards ceremony, commonly known as the Oscars. On their way to California, they will stop in Florida to visit John, Carla and their new granddaughter, Jenna at their home in Fort Lauderdale. The Fort Lauderdale stop will also give Steve a chance to visit his best friends, Frank and George, who continue to make their homes in the Sunshine State. After Steve retired to Italy, Geo took over the FSA office in Fort Lauderdale, while Frank continues to run the bar he owns in Pembroke Pines.

When the three friends get together, they refer to each other by their nicknames, which have stuck with them throughout the many years they've known each other. Frank is dubbed Angie and George is named Geo. Along with Steve, whom they've designated as Chic, the three friends make up the triumvirate they call the Three Musketeers.

When Steve and Diane arrive in Florida, they will stay at the condo they own on the beach in Fort Lauderdale. An airport shuttle bus will take them there, since Steve's son, John, has been minding his Corvette while they were living in Italy. Steve knows that it will be hard for John to give up the 'Vette when he arrives back in the States, but he's looking forward to driving it again.

The CIA office in Washington, D.C. has assigned a team of code experts to work on deciphering the message that was intercepted from Al Jazeera's website. The message has been forwarded to Colonel Johnson at the Pentagon because of its potential ties to national security. After reviewing the CIA's preliminary report, the Colonel decides to take a preventative measure by moving up the opening of the Baltimore FSA unit in the group of offices the government leased on the top floor of the World Trade Center Institute at Baltimore's Inner Harbor.

The Colonel tries to contact Steve at his home in Italy but the call goes unanswered, as the Ciccones are currently in a plane somewhere over the Atlantic. After hanging up the phone, he remembers that the couple is on their way to the Oscars, so he decides to contact Steve in another day or two, and then turns his attention to reviewing the resumes of several promising candidates for chief of the new FSA office.


Rishad Amanni deciphers the message that was sent to him through the Al Jazeera website. His orders are to book a flight from Fort Lauderdale to Washington, D.C., where he will need to communicate with Iran's Office of Foreign Affairs in order to obtain the name of his al-Qaida contact person. Because Iran has no official embassy in the United States, Rishad is directed to contact the Iranian office through Pakistan's Washington embassy. While seeming to be a hindrance, the necessity of using this roundabout route of communicating with Iran is actually an advantage for the terrorist organization because it avoids having calls or emails traced directly to al-Qaida.

As Rishad begins preparing for his trip to Washington,

he is unaware that he is about to embark down a highway to hell. There will be no virgins waiting for him in paradise.

In Tehran, Iran's capital city, Moshe Saban is preparing for bed in his room at the Lelah Hotel. He has a meeting the next day with Javeed Tavaazo at the Foreign Affairs Ministry, the agency that is generally believed to be the operating unit for Iran's organization of international terror, while the Iranians deny being involved in government-sponsored terrorism.

Before settling down for sleep, Moshe turns on the TV news and hears a report from Al Jazeera that there was a suicide bomb attack that day on a crowded street in downtown Tel Aviv. In the report, the bomber was identified as Amad Vakal.

Moshe sits on his bed, visibly shaken. In a daze, he mumbles, "I recruited that kid. I thought he died in the attack. I killed all those people."

His grief is interrupted by the ringing of his personal cell phone. He picks it up and glances at the caller ID display screen, but it does not show an identifying phone number. He answers the call on the second ring.

"Moshe, this is General Sandberg. I have some bad news. We picked up a coded message through Al Jazeera. We think there is going to be an attack on Washington, D.C. or at some other location in the United States. You need to get some concrete information when you meet with Tavaazo."

General Sandberg refrains from telling Moshe that his wife and child were killed in the Tel Aviv attack. He cannot afford to compromise Moshe's mission at tomorrow's meeting.

Moshe ends his call with the General, but continues to listen to the news from Al Jazeera while lying in bed. At the end of the broadcast, the reporter announces that ten people died in the attack in Tel Aviv earlier that day, and then he begins to read the names of the victims, which were obtained by the news agency after bribing a police official. Among the names listed are Moshe's wife and son.

At first, Moshe does not believe that what he is hearing is true, but when realization finally hits, he screams through choking tears, "I killed my family! I killed everyone! Those bastards, those *bastards*! They don't give a shit about anyone! Play by the rules, gather information, and you can watch them grow. No, NO! Now, I do it my way. They killed my family, now it's their turn. *An eye for an eye!*"

In anticipation of his father's arrival back in town, John drives Steve's Corvette to his Dad's condo on Fort Lauderdale Beach, with Carla and Jenna following behind in his minivan. As they head east on Oakland Park Boulevard, the three white towers that encompass the development containing Steve's new condo slowly come into view, each of them rising above the surrounding buildings like the wizard's castle in the Emerald City.

At the same time, George is heading for Duke's Saloon after a long day at the Fort Lauderdale FSA office. Steve had called a few days ago to let him know that he'll be in town for a couple of days before heading to the Oscars with Diane, and he asked Geo to meet him at Angie's saloon. Steve has not seen Geo and Angie since his wedding.

As soon as Rishad arrives in Washington, he eagerly makes his way to the Pakistani Embassy. After passing through the lobby's metal detector, he walks up to the receptionist and introduces himself, explaining that he is writing a paper for a political science class about the foreign policy of Pakistan's neighboring country of Iran, and that he needs to contact Javeed Tavaazo, an official in Tehran who is helping him with his project. He produces a letter of introduction from Mr. Taavazo that explains his request. The receptionist reads the letter and then places a call to her supervisor. After a ten minute wait, two large men in black suits and sunglasses exit the lobby elevator and walk to the front desk. One of the men takes Rishad's introduction letter and reads it, while the other makes a quick search of Rishad's backpack and pats him down for concealed weapons. When they are convinced that Rishad is not a threat, they instruct him to follow them into the elevator.

At the third floor, they exit the elevator and escort Rishad to a small office containing a desk and a computer, and then close the door, leaving him alone in the room. After a few minutes, which seem like hours to Rishad, a short, balding man enters the room.

"Mr. Amanni, we were able to contact Mr. Taavazo in Tehran. It is nighttime there, but he is still at his office. You can text him on that computer and ask him anything you want. When you are finished, just pick up the telephone and dial extension 132. I will return to escort you back to the lobby."

Rishad types out his name, along with the coded message, and waits for instructions. He types, <*This is Rishad Amanni. The falcon sings when the eagle flies. How must we hurt the infidels?*>

Almost immediately, his response arrives. <*Target their symbols of freedom. When the eagle gave birth, which were its first two eaglets? The Declaration of Independence and the Constitution.*>

<*What do I do?*>

<*You will contact Risa Rishjani. Her western code name is Lisa Thomas. You will receive a package and an envelope from the*

*receptionist in the lobby. Deliver the envelope to Risa. She will know what to do.* > The transmission ends.

Rishad logs off the computer and picks up the telephone. He dials extension 132 and sits back to wait for his escort out of the embassy. He does not know that all traffic in and out of the embassy is monitored by the FBI.

Rishad is now on their radar.

# CHAPTER FIVE

Steve is whistling as he drives his 'Vette down Pine Island Road toward Duke's Saloon in Pembroke Pines. After dropping their luggage off at the condo, he drove Diane to John's house, and is now on his way to catch up with Angie and Geo for a few hours, before returning to John's for dinner. He heads onto I-595 West, then turns south on I-75 and punches up the 'Vette to three digits on the speedometer. In less than ten minutes, he pulls into the strip mall and parks in front of Duke's.

As he opens the door, the bar erupts and everyone calls out, "CHIC!" He walks up to the bar, where Geo is sitting on a bar stool and laughing. Angie is behind the bar with his head down, laughing so hard he cannot breathe.

"Nice! It feels like I walked into an old TV sitcom."

Geo rises from his bar stool and gives Chic a big hug. At the same time, Chic reaches across the bar and high fives Angie.

"Well, guys...miss me?"

Angie gives Chic a cold one, and they clink their glasses together. Chic sits at the bar next to Geo, and then it starts.

"So, Chic. You gonna' be packin' at the Oscars?"

Angie adds, "Maybe he didn't understand you. You should ask him in Italian, *capeesh?*"

Before Chic can answer, he turns at the sound of the

front door opening and squints with a cold sniper's stare at a tall man who is entering the saloon.

"Oh, shit!"

Geo turns to check out the new arrival. "Sheeeeit!... Afternoon, Colonel!"

Colonel Johnson walks up to the bar and sits down next to Chic and Geo.

"Hey, Frank! I'll have a Sam Adams."

"We didn't invite you to this reunion," snaps Angie, slamming the Colonel's beer on the bar and causing a beer volcano to erupt out of the top of the bottle.

Chic glares at the Colonel. "Man, you're like a bad cold. There better be a good reason for you to be here. I'm tired you popping up in my personal life."

The Colonel takes a sip of his beer. "The CIA intercepted a coded message from Al Jazeera's website. They believe there will be an attack in Washington, D.C. sometime soon. But this time, they believe it's going to come from agents already here in the States. Steve, our new office in Baltimore will be open in about ten days. After you enjoy your excursion to Hollywood, we're going to need you back in Baltimore. George, I'll send all the information we have to your office, including the coded message. The more people we get involved, the quicker we'll be able to figure this out." The Colonel finishes his beer and leaves.

Angie cleans up the bar. "Chic, I thought you retired. You're like the Godfather. They keep dragging you back in."

"I am retired. This is consulting work. The only good thing is that this will give Diane and me an excuse to visit my son, Mike, while we're in Maryland. Now, how about some of your hot wings, and another round of beers?"


Moshe waits in a sitting room outside Javeed's office in

Tehran. He has introduced himself to the secretary as Darab Qalat, an al-Qaida recruit from the University of Tehran.

When Moshe meets with Javeed, he will claim that he was trained in Pakistan and Afghanistan, and that he was sent back to Iran to advise them about the latest terrorist techniques, and in turn, to be briefed on al-Qaida's current projects.

In reality, Moshe was informed by Mossad about the coded message the CIA intercepted, and he was ordered to meet with Javeed to try to gather vital information that could be passed on to Israel and the United States.

"Mr. Qalat, you can go in now."

As Moshe walks into the office, Javeed rises from his chair.

"Darab! Come in, sit. Welcome home." He calls his secretary on the intercom. "Bring us some coffee. Darab, your paperwork speaks for you. What can we do to assist you?"

"We know the great falcon, Iran, has targeted the U.S. and will be striking soon. I need background information on all persons you have in place and by what methods this mission will be carried out."

Javeed walks over to a file cabinet, pulls out three folders, and hands them to Darab.

"All the information you seek is there. We have targeted America's symbols of freedom—their Constitution and their Declaration of Independence. We will destroy them."

Moshe reviews the folders. "It looks like I have a lot of reading to do. I will do that later, at my hotel."

Javeed's secretary enters the room, carrying two small cups of coffee. Moshe takes one and drinks it down.

"Javeed, why don't we go to lunch to get better acquainted, since we will be working together quite closely? There is an excellent restaurant at the Lelah Hotel, where I am staying. That would be convenient for me, since I do not have a car."

"A very good idea. Let me inform my secretary of our plans, and then we will go."

Moshe follows Javeed to his car, a late model C class Mercedes. He makes a mental note of the color and license number. He intends to obtain as much personal information from Javeed as he can. He has much to do and not enough time to do it.



Rishad retrieves a package and an envelope from the receptionist in the lobby of the Pakistani Embassy and leaves the building. On the corner, there is a small park with a few benches. He sits down on one of the benches to read his instructions.

The package contains several hundred dollars in a small envelope, along with a map to Charlottesville, Virginia. That is where he will meet Risa Rashjani, the personal assistant to Senator William Lewis. Also inside the package is another envelope containing a detailed log of Risa's daily routine, as well as her photo. A third envelope includes a short memo instructing him to rent a car, drive to Charlottesville, and deliver the separate, sealed envelope to Risa.

After inspecting the contents of his package, Rishad hails a cab and instructs the driver to take him to Dulles International Airport, where he intends to rent the car.



It's now late in the afternoon. Steve says goodbye to his two best friends and points his Corvette north, back to Plantation. He does not want to be late for dinner. He and Diane plan to spend a couple of days with John, Carla and Jenna, before heading to Hollywood for the Academy Award ceremony.

# CHAPTER SIX

Moshe is at Tehran International Airport early the next morning. After his lunch with Javeed the day before, he returned to his room at the hotel and booked a flight to Miami, with a stopover in Madrid, Spain. He needs to get to Florida to find Rishad Ammani, the recipient of the coded message.

After a light breakfast, Javeed leaves his apartment to drive to work. As he starts his C class Mercedes, the last thing he hears is the key turning in the ignition lock. The ensuing explosion blows out most of the windows in the surrounding buildings and turns Javeed Taavazo into a large charcoal briquette.

In his rented Ford Focus, Rishad stands vigil at the base of Lewis Mountain Circle, waiting for Risa Rashjani to drive by. As described in his package, Risa's morning routine sends her into downtown Charlottesville, where she drops off Senator Lewis' children at a private school before stopping at a Starbucks for coffee.

Having memorized Risa's photo, Rishad knows when Risa passes by in the Senator's Cadillac CTS. He quickly maneuvers his car behind hers, and fifteen minutes later, they arrive at the local Starbucks. Rishad follows Risa into the store and gets in line behind her. He taps her on the shoulder and quietly asks, "Have you heard the falcon singing?"

Risa quickly turns around, looks at Rishad and says, "John! My gosh! What has it been? Two years?" She gives Rishad a hug and a kiss. "Let me buy you a cup of coffee." The pair moves to a corner table with their vendi frappachinos.

"So, ah, Lisa, what have you been up to?"

"Working for Senator Lewis. And you?"

"I went back to college. Listen, you left some of your personal letters and photographs at my apartment. I was visiting D.C. and decided to bring them by." He hands her the sealed envelope that he received at the Pakistani Embassy.

They sit and talk nonsense for ten minutes, then go off in different directions. Risa heads back to the Senator's house, while Rishad drives to Dulles International Airport to return the rental car and to catch a return flight to Fort Lauderdale. As far as he is concerned, his mission is complete.

Mossad's General Sandberg has sent out an official notice to the CIA and the FBI that they have lost contact with one of their agents in Iran, and that he is rumored to be in Spain. Included in the notice was a complete dossier on Moshe Saban, along with information on the death of his wife and son.

Moshe intends to lay low for a couple of days in Madrid. After arriving at the airport, he takes a cab to the Madrid Chamartin train station, where he pulls a key from his pocket. He walks to lock box number 127 and retrieves a carry-on bag that he had planted there a while ago in case he needed to find a safe place or had to get away quickly. Inside the bag is a few thousand dollars in U.S. dollars and Euro notes, some fake ID's, a change of clothes, and a 9mm Beretta with a silencer.

Moshe exits the train station with the bag and takes another cab to the Madrid Airport Hilton, where he books a small room to wait for his flight to Miami, Florida. While in his hotel room, he prepares a fake U.S. Passport and a Homeland Security ID card, which will allow him to enter the United States without scrutiny at customs, and will give him permission to carry a handgun.

According to his new ID, Moshe Saban is now Scott Sax, Homeland Security Officer, and a U.S. citizen residing in Annapolis, Maryland, at a Mossad safe house on Clay Street.

Under his new persona as Scott Sax, Moshe contacts Continental Airlines and reserves a seat on a flight that leaves Madrid in forty-eight hours, informing the airline that he will be flying to Miami on Homeland Security business. After the reservation is made, he takes a shower and then goes down the elevator to a tapas bar off the hotel lobby.

On their last night in Florida, Steve and Diane are hosting a small gathering at their condo on the beach. Steve, Angie and Geo are hanging out by the gas grill near the outdoor pool with John, Steve's son. Diane and Geo's girlfriend, Trisha, are lounging by the pool, waiting for their burgers, while John's wife Carla and their daughter, Jenna, are splashing in the pool.

In the morning, Steve and Diane will fly to California to attend the Oscars. After that, there will be no rest for the weary, as they will leave California the very next morning and head to Baltimore.

Risa, known in the West as Lisa Thomas, has returned to the Senator's house after her meeting at Starbucks and is now in her room, behind a locked door. She opens up the envelope that Rishad gave her and studies her mission. Her orders are to destroy the Declaration of Independence and the Constitution of the United States by blowing up the National Archives building, where the two documents are on display. To do so, she knows that she will need at least 1,000 pounds of ammonium nitrate fertilizer mixed with diesel fuel oil. Having been trained in explosives by al-Qaida, Risa only needs a reliable source where she can obtain the ingredients for her deadly cocktail.

Also in Risa's envelope is information on her contact, Rick Collins. A few years ago, Rick's family lost their farm to the federal government due to unpaid taxes. At the time, the bank would not remortgage their loan, and a large, corporate farming conglomerate eventually took control of the family business. In despair, Rick's parents committed double suicide over the loss of the farm, which had been in their family for one hundred years.

Ever since his parents' suicides, Rick has blamed the United States government for their deaths and for the loss of his family's livelihood. In his grief, he contacted al-Qaida through a lead on Al Jazeera's website and vowed to help them hurt the United States.

Al-Qaida is now ready to make use of Rick and to tap into his sense of revenge. He currently works part time at a local farm supply distributor, and is also employed as a farm hand at his family's former farm just outside of Charlottesville. For Rick, obtaining ammonium nitrate will be no problem at all.

Risa has been instructed to contact Rick and to develop a plan to deliver a homemade bomb into Washington D.C.

# CHAPTER SEVEN

It is early in the afternoon in Madrid, and Moshe Saban has just boarded a Continental flight to Miami as Scott Sax. He is very anxious to speak with Rishad Amanni, and intends to meet him within the next twenty-four hours. The plane slowly pulls away from the terminal gate while Moshe reads Sky Mall magazine.

When he boarded the plane, the flight crew was informed that he was Scott Sax, an officer of the Department of Homeland Security, and they pointed him out to the air marshal who was assigned to the flight.

As the plane takes off, two Mossad agents and an officer from Interpol arrive at the front desk of the Madrid Airport Hilton. They flash a photo of Moshe Saban to the front desk clerk and ask if he has seen him.

"Why, yes. He was a guest of ours for two days and checked out just this morning."

"Did he mention where he was going?"

"No, not at all. He was very quiet, very reserved. He said he was finishing his business trip before going home. Is there anything wrong?"

The officer from Interpol responds. "He is involved in some international trade, which we need to talk to him about. We need to search his room, please."

"No problem. It was room 231."

The desk clerk calls for the hotel's security manager, who escorts the agents to Moshe's room. The security manager opens the door with his passkey. As the agents enter the room, the Interpol officer asks the security manager to wait outside. They close the door and proceed to turn the room upside down, but find nothing of interest. When they exit the room, they ask the security manager if the hotel provides internet services to their guests. The security manager escorts them to a business office off the lobby that has been set up for the use of their hotel guests with computers, printers and phones. The agents contact local authorities for permission to search the computers and phone logs.

Steve and Diane rise early this morning, excited about their trip to California. They have an 8:00 a.m. flight to Los Angeles and they will be traveling in style, as the movie studio has booked them first class tickets. The studio has also arranged for them to be met at the airport by a chauffeured limousine, which will take them to the Beverly Hills Hotel. There, a suite has been reserved for them in Diane's name.

Diane has been away from the Hollywood scene for many months, and is not aware that she is the favorite for the Best Actress award. Steve, who is very supportive of Diane, will put on the good husband act, because he really does not give a shit about Hollywood and all that hoopla.

In Washington, D.C., Colonel Johnson waits in the lobby of FBI headquarters at 935 Pennsylvania Avenue. Field Agent Carol Lawson enters the lobby from the elevator and approaches the Colonel.

"Colonel Johnson, I'm Agent Carol Lawson. I'm here to escort you to a short briefing about a message that was intercepted by the CIA and brought to our attention. Would you follow me, please?"

The Colonel, who had risen from the chair he was sitting in, follows Agent Lawson into the elevator.

"So what is so important that you needed me here first thing on a Saturday morning?"

"All will be forthcoming in due time, Colonel."

When they reach the ninth floor, Agent Lawson and Colonel Johnson exit the elevator and enter a conference room at the end of a long hallway. Field Agent Lawson introduces him to the rest of the attendees, who are already seated.

"Gentlemen, this is Colonel Johnson of the FSA. Colonel, may I present General Sandberg from Mossad, Henri Gilbert from Interpol, and our own Troy Jacobs, an FBI encryption officer. Let's get this meeting started."

As Agent Lawson and the Colonel seat themselves, Troy hands the Colonel a file and starts the meeting.

"As you know, gentlemen and Carol, we have been monitoring the postings of personal messages on Al Jazeera's website for a while now. Though the postings themselves are not illegal, we have felt that terrorist agents across the globe could be retrieving their operating instructions from those personal messages. About a week ago, we flagged this message."

As Troy presses a button on a remote control device located on the table, the lights dim, a projection screen lowers from the ceiling at the far end of the room, and an overhead projector displays a message on the screen: *When the eagle flies, the falcons sing. It has left the nest for plundering. She'll take two eggs and fly away. We'll sing again another day.*

"We have determined that the falcon stands for the Republic of Iran, which as we all know, is a supporter of terrorism through Hamas and al-Qaida. Obviously, the eagle is the United States. The two offspring of the mother eagle that would be still around today are the Declaration of Independence and the U.S. Constitution. These documents are on display in the National Archives, just down the block from here."

The Colonel chimes in. "Are you implying that they're going to try to steal those documents?"

"Unlike what you may see in the movies, trying to steal those documents would be impossible. However, they could try to destroy them. A well-placed explosive device just outside of that building could do it, if it was timed to go off while the documents were on public display. When they are dropped down into their vaults, a nuclear device could not harm them. We feel that a sleeper cell in the United States has been given the assignment of destroying these two important documents. We continuously monitor all web access to Al Jazeera and have noted that for the past six months, there has been weekly access to that website from a public library in Plantation, Florida. We contacted that library and installed cameras near their computer terminals to monitor their usage. One individual has used the same computer over and over again."

Troy clicks a different button on the remote control to display a photo on the screen.

"Rishad Ammani, a medical student from Saudia Arabia, is enrolled at Nova University in Davie, Florida. As is routine, we have been monitoring his computer activity and cell phone usage. We found nothing of concern, except that we noted that he accessed Al Jazeera's personal columns on a weekly basis, which, as I mentioned before, is not necessarily a threat. However, we recently caught these photos of Rishad entering and exiting the Pakistani Embassy in Washington."

Troy displays the images on the screen. "These photos were taken about one hour apart from each other. As you can see, he enters the embassy carrying only a backpack, but he exits with a small package and an envelope. As we all know, Iran does not have an active embassy here in the States. However, they do have a satellite office operating out of the Pakistani Embassy. The day after Rishad's visit to the embassy, security cameras at Dulles Airport picked him up heading back to Florida. Further investigations revealed that he purchased all of his airline tickets with cash and that he rented a car here in Washington with cash. We feel that this activity is suspicious and that it could link Rishad to Iran's terror network. We have alerted the President, the D.C. police, and the executives at the National Archives. We recommended to the President that the Declaration of Independence and the Constitution be temporarily stored in their secure vaults and not raised into their upper chambers for display. The President has refused our recommendation, stating that we will not be held hostage to terror. Because we are not able to protect these treasured documents in the most secure way possible, if a strike is perceived to be imminent, the code word "Falcon" will be given to the Archives. Upon receipt of that code word, security guards will evacuate the building and properly store the documents. We are currently monitoring Rishad's movements and will be picking him up for questioning within twenty-four hours. General Sandberg will now brief you on another matter. General?"

The General rises, and with a touch of the remote control device, displays Moshe Saban's photo on the screen.

"Good morning. This is Moshe Saban, an agent with Mossad. Until a few days ago, he was working for us under deep cover, and was recently in Afghanistan and Iran, trying to infiltrate the Taliban's terror network. While working in Afghanistan, he directed a drone attack against one of the Taliban's training facilities. At the time, we believed that all present at the training camp were eliminated in the attack, but we were mistaken. Amad Vakal, one of Moshe's recruits, escaped the attack, and later blew himself up in the middle of downtown Tel Aviv, killing ten people. Two of those murdered were Moshe's wife and son. Moshe was scheduled to meet with Javeed Tavaazo, an official of the Iranian Foreign Affairs Ministry, which we believe is orchestrating the attack in D.C. Unexpectedly, Al Jazzera got ahold of the names of the victims of the Tel Aviv bombing and broadcasted them on their newscast. We lost contact with Moshe after that broadcast. We surmise that he heard the broadcast and learned about the death of his wife and son. The morning after the broadcast, Javeed Tavaazo was blown up outside of his town home by a car bomb. At that point, we lost contact with Moshe. We searched for him and traced him to Spain, but lost track of him again. We are reviewing security camera images from the Madrid airport of everyone who boarded flights to Miami. We believe Moshe is now in the United States, that he probably got a lead on a terrorist cell here, and that he will try to eliminate that cell. The best case scenario is that he does. The worst case scenario is that he will eliminate all the leads we have developed to locate terrorists and that you will have an incident here in Washington. Mossad is cooperating with the FBI and we have given them a dossier on Agent Saban."

Turning to Colonel Johnson, General Sandberg continues. "Colonel Johnson, we have put together a package that you can take to your FSA office in Baltimore. You were successful in stopping the recent terrorist incident in Fort Lauderdale. We hope that you can be just as successful now."

# CHAPTER EIGHT

Diane is looking out the window of a penthouse suite in the Beverly Hills Hotel. The Academy Awards ceremony is tomorrow evening and she still has not seen the gown that will be loaned to her for that evening. A knock at the door prompts her to call out, "Who is it?"

"Special delivery from Christian Dior."

Diane recognizes the voice and runs to open the door.

"Tammy!" She gives her former assistant a big hug.

"Be careful, Ms. Summers! You don't want to wrinkle the gown."

"Oh, to hell with the gown! How are you? Come in, come in!"

Tammy is holding Diane's gown draped over one arm, and has a shopping bag on the other arm. As she walks into the suite, she drapes the gown over a loveseat near the front door and drops the bag on the floor.

"I gave the designer your measurements, so I hope you haven't gained weight. The gown is floor length, off the shoulder, and it's an original. It's silver metallic silk and has a matching clutch bag. I also have shoes and a diamond necklace on loan from Tiffany. When you win the Oscar, you need to be in style!"

"But Tammy, I'm speechless! This is such a shock!"

"Look, Diane. You've been a great boss and I would

never leave you alone at this important time. You've been away from all the hoopla, but you're the odds on favorite to win. Of course I'll be here for you. Now, go try on the gown!"

With tears in her eyes, Diane grabs the gown and the shopping bag and steps into the bedroom.

While Diane is trying on her gown, Steve is renting a tux at the men's shop off the hotel lobby. As he talks with the clerk, his cell phone rings. Excusing himself, he answers, "Hello?"

"Steve, Colonel Johnson here. We have some breaking news and I'll need you in Baltimore first thing Monday morning. Plane tickets have been arranged and a car will pick you up at Baltimore/Washington International Airport. Don't tell Diane, but I have sources that tell me she's probably going to win an Oscar. She'll be busy for a couple of days with interviews and such, so I reserved a flight for her on Wednesday that will bring her up here to be with you. Check at the front desk. The tickets are there for the both of you. I'm not going to elaborate on the phone, but things will start to happen quickly. See you Monday."


Moshe Saban easily passes through customs at Miami International Airport using his credentials as Scott Sax, and with multiple ID's in his possession, renting a car is also easy.

At the airport's rental car area, he rented a pickup truck from Budget for about a week, telling the agent behind the counter that he is in town visiting his sister, a university student who needs his help to move off campus. Driving out of the airport, he follows the map he received when requesting directions to Nova University in Davie.

Moshe is looking forward to his encounter with Rishad Amanni, but it has been a long flight. He is tired, and had been prepared to wait until the next morning to put his plans into motion, but impulsively he decides not to wait. He decides to go ahead and do what needs to be done now. Besides, his lack of sleep will just make him more edgy, which he believes will not be a bad thing.

In less than an hour, he pulls off I-595 onto University Drive and heads south to the university campus. Passing several strip malls, he locates one that contains a firearms dealer, where he stops to purchase ammunition, a holster, and a set of handcuffs. In the same strip mall is an auto parts store, where he buys duct tape and jumper cables.

After placing his purchases in the pickup, he continues on his journey to meet Rishad. When he finally pulls onto the university campus, he notices that a campus police car is parked near the entrance. He pulls up next to the cruiser and gets out.

"Excuse me, officer. My name is Scott Sax and I'm with Homeland Security." He hands the guard his badge and ID.

"Why, yes, Scott. What can I do for you?"

"I have to go to Dorm Building 4 to speak to an exchange student. Can you take me there to avoid any complications?"

"Sure thing. Is anything wrong?"

"No, just some background follow-up on a student visa."

Moshe returns to his truck and follows the campus guard to Building 4, where they pull into the parking area and park their vehicles.

"Scott, follow me. I'll take you to the dorm manager. She'll be able to help you."

The pair walks inside the main lobby of the residence building and Moshe follows the security guard to the office on the right.

"Doris, Doris?"

Doris Kominsky walks into her office from the bathroom down the hall.

"Hi, Joe. Can I help you?"

"Doris, this is Officer Scott Sax from Homeland Security. He needs to speak to one of the students in the dorm."

"Well, Officer Scott. What can I do for you?"

"I need to speak to Rishad Ammani, an exchange student from Saudia Arabia. I believe he is in room 117."

"Yes, it's just down the hall. He's not in any trouble, is he?"

Moshe thinks to himself, *Boy, they really don't know how much trouble he is in*, but aloud, he says, "No, not at all, I just need to talk to him about his student visa."

"Joe, you can walk Officer Scott down the hall. Rishad should be in his room."

"Thanks, Doris, and if I don't see you again, have a nice day."

Moshe follows Joe down the hall until they stop at room 117. The guard knocks on the door.

"Who is it?"

"Campus security."

Rishad opens the door. "Yes? Is there anything wrong?"

"No, but we need to come in for a few minutes."

The men enter the small room and Moshe speaks first.

"Rishad, I am Officer Scott Sax with Homeland Security. I need to talk to you about your student visa."

Rishad is shaken, but tries to remain calm. He asks, "What seems to be wrong with my visa?"

"Nothing to worry about. You need to fill out some paperwork at the Fort Lauderdale office. Your file is missing some information about your parents. I'm here to take you to the office and drive you back. It shouldn't take more than an hour or two."

"I do not know why I need to do this. I am studying for a major exam."

"Look, I'm sorry for the inconvenience, but you have to come with me today to complete your file. If not, you'll be subject to deportation in violation of your visa."

"Okay, okay. Let's go and get this over with."

Moshe follows Rishad and Joe Rent-a-Cop out of the dorm building. Outside of the entrance, he fakes a phone call so Joe can leave ahead of them in his cruiser. When Joe is out of sight, Moshe directs Rishad to the rental pickup truck. As they approach the vehicle, Moshe steps behind Rishad and reaches around him to open the passenger door. When Rishad begins to climb in, Moshe whips his berretta out of its holster, and with a large thump, lands it on the back of Rishad's head. Before Rishad can slump to the ground, Moshe hoists him up by the waistband and throws him into the front seat. He quickly closes the passenger door and runs around to the back of the truck where he picks up a roll of duct tape, before darting to the driver's door and entering the pickup. Moshe uses the duct tape to cover Rishad's mouth and bind his hands and feet. Then, he quickly starts the pickup and heads off campus. In less than a minute, he sees the entrance to I-595 and heads west, toward the Everglades.

Moshe is looking for a desolate location so he will not be bothered while he enacts his plan. What better place to find some isolation than the Everglades? Continuing west, he winds up on I-75, locally known as Alligator Alley. He continues driving for about half an hour, and then notices a dirt road off to the right of the highway that seems to follow alongside a canal that stretches out into the Everglades. He slows down and pulls off the highway, heading away from civilization.

Meanwhile, just off I-64 near Waynesboro, Virginia, Risa Rashjani walks into a tractor supply store, and asks the female sales associate for Rick Collins.

"He's out back. I'll get him for you."

The young sales associate leaves the sales area, and a few minutes later, returns with Rick.

"Can I help you?"

Risa takes Rick by the arm as they slowly walk down the store's aisles.

"I need some help with fertilizer. You see, the falcons are singing."

Rick stops short and stares into Risa's eyes with some anxiety. After a short time, he regains his composure.

"Well, you came to the right place. What can I get for you?"

"Ammonium nitrate, 1,000 pounds or so." She whispers close to his ear. "Need diesel, too. Can you provide?"

"Look, we can't talk here, too many people, too many ears. Your shopping list is no problem. Pickup and delivery will be, though. Are you familiar with the Berkshire Apartments in Charlottesville?"

"Yes, it's near Starbucks."

"Good. Meet me there at 7:00 tonight, Building 200, Apartment 203."

"It's a date."

Risa gives Rick a quick kiss on the cheek, so anyone looking would think they were close friends, then she turns and leaves the store.

Risa has already formulated her plans and knows how she intends to deliver the bomb to the National Archives. She intends to use Senator Lewis' fifty-foot motor coach, which is well known in the D.C. area. The only problem she can foresee will be loading that much fertilizer into the motor coach.

Moshe drives the pickup to an area off the main dirt road, where there is quick access to a narrow canal and a clump of pine trees. Rishad is still out cold. Moshe positions the pickup for easy turn around and shuts her down. He climbs out and surveys the area, making sure he will not be seen. It is eerily quiet, no wind, and no sounds of life. He spies an alligator floating in the canal and notices what appears to be a large snake easing itself into the water.

With a sigh, Moshe turns to the pickup, opens the passenger door, and drags Rishad out onto the ground. After unbinding Rishad's feet and removing the duct tape from his mouth, he yanks off his shorts and boxers, leaving him naked from the waist down. He then rips open Rishad's shirt and drags him over to the tallest pine tree. Positioning Rishad spread-legged against the tree, he tapes his arms over a low branch and cuffs his wrists together. Rishad looks like a slaughtered cow that is hanging in a deep freezer.

After surveying his handiwork, Moshe climbs back into the truck and eases it close to Rishad. He pops open the hood and climbs back out, leaving the motor running. Grabbing the jumper cables from the truck bed, along with Rishad's boxers, he walks over to the canal and soaks them in the water. When he returns to Rishad, he slaps him in the face and torso with the boxers until he is soaking wet.

The water awakens Rishad with a jolt, and when he realizes the situation he's in, he tries to escape, but quickly finds that he can't move.

"Who are you? What is this? HELP, HELP MEEEEEE!"

Moshe pulls out his Beretta and places the muzzle against Rishad's forehead.

"No more yelling. No one can hear you anyway. Welcome to the Everglades."

"You are not Homeland Security! Who are you? WHAT DO YOU WANT?"

Moshe slaps Rishad in the face. "I said, no yelling. What I want is answers, and no, I am not Homeland Security. I am Mossad."

Rishad gazes wide-eyed at Moshe. "I know nothing. I am a student."

Moshe walks to the pickup and brings out a file folder from behind the front seat. He opens it up in front of Rishad.

"Do you know Javeed Tavaazo?"

Looking down, Rishad answers, "No."

"Well, he knows you. In fact, he gave me this file on you, and you know, the very next day, he mysteriously died in a car bombing. How about Risa Rashjani. Know her?"

"I know nothing."

Moshe breathes in with a deep, audible sigh. He walks over to the pickup, opens the hood, and grabs the jumper cables from the ground. He attaches one end of the cables to the battery terminals, red to red, black to black. Then he slowly walks back to Rishad, tapping the free ends of the cable together to cause large sparks and crackling sounds.

"Now, we can do this easy, or we can do this hard. It's your choice. Again, Javeed Tavaazo and Risa Rashjani?"

Rishad makes no move to speak.

With a shake of his head, Moshe grabs the red cable in his left hand, and carefully keeping the ends of the cables apart, allows the black cable to hang downwards. With his right hand, he quickly grabs Rishad's penis and testicles and pulls them forward, firmly clamping the red cable behind Rishad's testicles, at the base of his penis. Rishad moans loudly.

"Uh, uh. No yelling. Well, maybe in a while. Now, I'm going to tell you what I will do. If you don't answer my questions, I'll clamp the black cable to your right nipple. Then, you can yell all you want. Now, Javeed and Risa. Hmm?"

Rishad looks at the cables and stares at Moshe. "You are bluffing. You will not do this."

Moshe stares at Rishad and waits a few more seconds for a response. When none is forthcoming, he clamps the black cable to Rishad's nipple. Writhing in pain and shaking with convulsions, Rishad screams, while his bladder and bowels release their contents. Moshe removes the black cable and waits.

Crying in agony, Rishad whimpers, "Okay...okay. Javeed sent me a package to bring to Risa. She is going to try to destroy the Declaration of Independence and the Constitution. I delivered the package to her in Charlottesville, Virginia. She works for Senator Lewis, and that is all I know."

"Well, was that so hard? Do you know a Rick Collins in Charlottesville?"

"No, no. I just delivered a package. I don't know what was in it."

There is a long pause as Moshe stares at Rishad. Then, he lays the files on the ground next to Rishad's clothing, goes to the truck and unclamps the battery cables. He throws them onto the ground and closes the hood.

Rishad cries out. "What are you going to do with me?"

Moshe heads back toward Rishad and tapes his mouth closed with the duct tape.

"I was going to kill you, but that would be a waste of bullets. So, I'm just going to leave you here. Pray to Allah that someone finds you before the alligators and the snakes do."

Moshe climbs into the truck and drives toward the dirt road, leaving the tape and the jumper cables behind.

As Moshe drives back up the dirt road to Alligator Alley, Rishad frantically tries to free himself, knowing that the heat and exposure will do him in quickly.

Moshe has decided to drive directly to Charlottesville, stopping to rest on the way when he gets too tired to drive any further. It will take him sixteen to seventeen hours to reach Charlottesville, but with the long flight from Spain earlier in the day, he knows that he will need to stop for a long-deserved sleep.

Rick and Risa will have to wait another day.


As Rick Collins steps out of the shower, the front doorbell rings. He glances at his watch, noting that it's 6:43 in the evening, and thinks to himself, *I guess Risa is early.* He yells out, "I'll be right there!" as he pulls on a pair of gym shorts and a sleeveless t-shirt before answering the door.

"Come on in. You're a little early."

"I can't stay long. I dropped the Senator's children off at a birthday party earlier this afternoon and I have to pick them up by 7:30."

Rick closes the door behind Risa. He leads her into the dining area, where they sit at the table.

"I'm guessing you're going to blow something up. I can help. I have access to ammonium nitrate and diesel fuel. ANFO bombs, commonly known as ammonium nitrate and diesel fuel, are quite impressive. I can get you 1,500 pounds of nitrate and all the fuel you'll need. The nitrate will come from the supply store I work at and also from TriStar Foods. The fuel is available at the farm and is stored there to power the farm equipment. I can get fifty-five gallon drums from the store and the farm. You'll need five of them. How do you plan to deliver the package?"

"Senator Lewis and his family are leaving town tomorrow for a few days. He owns a custom built, fifty-foot motor coach. The back drops down and opens up as a deck, with French doors that lead into a large living area. He uses the coach for campaigning and he has also brought sick children from Bethesda Naval Hospital into D.C. on day trips to the Capital Building. So in D.C., this vehicle will not be an unusual sight. We can load the drums into the coach through the French doors. It will take time, but we can fill the drums with the nitrate and fuel oil once they are in the coach. I already have the detonation caps and the electronics that are needed to detonate the mixture. I have been waiting for this mission for years."

"Good. It will take me a day or so to fill your shopping list. Meet me at the store at 11:00 p.m. tomorrow night. You will need to leave the coach there. I know a few men who hate this government as much as I do. We'll start loading the coach at the store, and then drive it to the farm. There is an old, abandoned barn in the woods with a dirt road leading up to it. I used to play there as a kid when my family owned the farm. TriStar now owns it, with help from the federal government. I'll bring the coach there and we'll finish loading her up on Monday. It's my day off, so I won't be missed. Come to the store at 11:00 p.m. Monday night and I'll bring the coach to you there."

"No, that will not work for me. I will bring you the coach tomorrow, but I will stay with it until it is full. I can sleep inside. I am not letting the coach out of my sight."

"No problem, then. We're all set. See you tomorrow. By the way, what is your target?"

"The National Archives building."

After Risa leaves, Rick begins making the phone calls that will gather his work crew together.

Moshe has now driven as far as he can and pulls into South of the Border, a rest stop and tourist attraction along I-95 in South Carolina. He books a motel room for the night and crashes until morning.

# CHAPTER NINE

Diane wakes up early at the hotel in California. Tammy will be coming over soon with a hair stylist and makeup artist, compliments of the movie studio. Diane lets Steve sleep in and orders room service. She cannot wait to see his expression as he gets his face made up and hair styled. Diane really wants this event to go well, because this will be her last involvement with show business.

A few hours later in Fort Lauderdale, FBI Field Agent Jerry Myers and a small SWAT unit are entering the campus of Nova University. They are headed for Dorm Building 4, Room 117. Their plan is to surprise Rishad Ammani. They quietly enter the lobby and quickly make their way down the hallway to Rishad's room. With a large handheld door ram, a SWAT team member pounds the door open as they yell in unison, "FBI!" The noise brings students out into the hallway, as well as a very startled Doris Kiminsky, who runs out of her office and down the hall to find dejected FBI agents in Room 117.

"You guys are a day late, and which one of you is going to pay to have this door fixed?"

Agent Meyers responds, "What do you mean we're a day late? Do you know where Rishad is?"

"Don't you? Someone from Homeland Security took

him down to the Fort Lauderdale office yesterday, and he hasn't been back since."

"Fort Lauderdale office? There is no Fort Lauderdale office. Look, men. Search this room and take his computer." He turns toward Doris. "And you are?"

"I'm the dorm manager, Doris Kominsky."

"Well, Ms. Kominsky, I'm Agent Jerry Myers from the FBI. Let's go somewhere we can talk. I need to find out about your run-in with Homeland Security."

At the same time these events are occurring in Davie, a lone Seminole Indian, guiding his airboat down a canal deep in the Everglades for some morning hunting, spots a man through the overgrowth, and it seems that he's duct-taped to a pine tree. He pulls his airboat against the canal bank and climbs up to find a naked Rishad alive, but unconscious. He dials 911 on his cell phone, and through the phone's imbedded GPS chip, authorities are able to pinpoint his location and send help.

Jerry Myers follows Doris into her office and closes the door behind them.

"Okay, Doris. Tell me what happened."

"Well, Mr. Myers, there isn't much to tell. Officer Scott Sax, or that's what his identification said, walked in with Joe Simmons, one of our campus police officers. He said he needed to speak to one of our students, Rishad Ammani, about his student visa. I told him that Rishad's room was right down the hall. He and Joe went there, and a couple of minutes later, they left with Rishad. That was the last time I saw Rishad and Scott, or whoever he was."

"Okay, Doris, thank you. I'm going to have a sketch

artist from my office come here to get a description of the person who is calling himself Scott Sax. He should be here within an hour. Now, if you'll excuse me, I'll return to my team."

Jerry leaves Doris' office and heads down the hall to Rishad's room. As he walks down the hallway, he dials his office and arranges for an artist to be sent to visit Doris. The FBI agents take Rishad's laptop, along with other items of interest, and leave the dorm.

On the way back to his office, Jerry receives a call telling him that Rishad Ammani was found unconscious in the Everglades, with some files that may describe a security threat. Jerry detours to the emergency room of Broward General Hospital to meet the ambulance that is transporting Rishad to the hospital with a Florida Highway Patrol escort. On the way to the emergency room, he calls the FSA office in Fort Lauderdale and asks George Jackson to meet him at the hospital.

By the time George reaches the hospital, the FBI, the Florida Highway Patrol and the unconscious Rishad have already arrived. He parks his Explorer near the emergency room doors and walks up to Agent Jerry Myers and an FHP officer, who are standing outside the ER entrance.

"So, tell me Jerry, what's the skinny on this one?"

Jerry introduces George to FHP Officer Alvarez and then begins to fill him in.

"We've been tracking the activity of exchange student Rishad Ammani, because he's been accessing a Middle Eastern website that has ties to al-Qaida and the Iranian terror network. We caught him on a surveillance camera that's focused on the Pakistani Embassy in Washington D.C., which happens to contain a satellite office of the Iranian Embassy. We noticed that Rishad left the embassy with a package that he did not have when we caught him again later that day on a security camera at Dulles Airport, where he caught a flight back to Fort Lauderdale. We sent a detail to pick him up at his dorm room this morning, however, he wasn't there when we arrived. Doris Kominsky, the dorm manager for his building, told us that we were a day late, because he had left the day before with an officer who identified himself as Scott Sax from the Homeland Security Office in Fort Lauderdale. Well, as you know, there is no Homeland Security office in Fort Lauderdale, because they're based in Miami. We checked with Miami, and they don't have a Scott Sax listed as working for Homeland Security. About an hour ago, a Seminole Indian hunting off his airboat found an unconscious man he identified as Rishad Amanni after looking through some papers he found at the scene. Rishad was handcuffed and duct-taped to a tree next to a canal in the Everglades. The Seminole called 911, and EMT's, along with FHP Officer Alvarez, responded to the call. Officer Alvarez found this file on the ground under Rishad when they lifted him up to put him on the stretcher. It's from the Iranian Foreign Ministry Office and it contains dossiers on Rishad and someone named Risa Rashjani. Risa's profile also names a Rick Collins. Apparently, these individuals are sleeper terrorist agents based here in the United States.

"When they examined Rishad, the EMT's noticed burn marks near his testicles and on his right nipple. They also found a set of jumper cables at the scene. It looks like Rishad was interrogated and then left for dead."

George takes the file from Agent Myers and skims through it. He turns toward Officer Alvarez.

"You realize that what was said here stays here. This is a National Security issue. We thank you for your help, but I must ask you to leave us now so we can discuss this further."

"No problem, George. Take care, guys." Officer Alavarez

climbs into his cruiser and drives off. George watches him leave and then turns to Agent Myers.

"Wasn't someone from the Iranian Foreign Ministry just blown up? Javeed Tavaazo?"

"Tavaazo was killed in a car bomb."

At that moment, a doctor walks out to the parking lot.

"Agent Myers, your patient is semi-conscious. You can go in and see him, but not for long. He's suffering from exposure and dehydration. He should recover, but he won't be able to be discharged for a day or so."

"Thank you, Doctor, we'll be right in. I've arranged for an officer from the Broward Sheriff's Office to be assigned to guard his room. He should be here within ten minutes. We'll see Mr. Amanni now."

George and Agent Myers follow the doctor as he walks through the waiting area and enters the ER, pointing down the corridor to Rishad's room.

When they find Rishad, he is hooked up to an IV and is drifting in and out of consciousness. Agent Myers bends down and speaks close to Rishad's face.

"Rishad, can you hear me? Rishad?"

Rishad shakes his head and mumbles over and over again, "Mossad, Mossad, Mossad."

George pulls Jerry aside.

"Mossad? Wasn't there a bulletin recently that said Mossad lost contact with one of their agents who was under cover in Iran?"

"Yeah, Moshe Saban. Guess he's not missing anymore."

# CHAPTER TEN

Moshe awakens at 10:30 in the morning, just one half hour before checkout time from his motel room at the South of the Border rest stop in South Carolina. He uses his android phone to search for motels in Charlottesville, Virginia, and chooses a Red Roof Inn on Main Street. He then Googles Rick Collins and finds an old article about the Collins family, the farm they lost, and the suicides that resulted from it.

After checking out from the motel, Moshe grabs a quick breakfast before getting back on the road to Virginia.

He has an appointment with Rick and Risa that he vows to keep.


While Moshe is eating breakfast in South Carolina, Risa is waking up in Senator Lewis' motor coach in Charlottesville. Before dawn on Sunday morning, she drove the coach to the abandoned barn in the woods behind Rick's family's former farm, following closely behind his beat up Ford 150 pickup.

While the Lewis' are away on vacation, Risa has free reign to commit havoc. Stacked in the living room of the coach are fifteen, one-hundred pound bags of ammonium nitrate, and three empty, fifty-five gallon steel drums. At the abandoned barn are two more drums that are filled with diesel fuel, one of which is topped by a hand pump. With the help of Rick's friends, they'll divide the nitrate and the fuel oil among all five drums within the next forty-eight hours. Risa expects to drive the motor coach back to the Senator's house on Monday night, under the cover of darkness.

With most of her plans already set into motion, there is still one more thing that Risa needs to do. She has to configure a triggering device and set it to arm her deadly cargo. Her plan is to attack Washington, D.C. late Wednesday morning.

After climbing out of bed, Risa lays her prayer rug at the foot of the bed and says her morning prayers. She is preparing herself for her one-way trip to Washington on Wednesday. If all goes well, she believes that she will soon be with Allah in paradise.

Steve has not yet told Diane that he has to leave early Monday morning, the day after the Oscars. Diane's hairdresser has just left their hotel room, so before the makeup artist comes to prepare both of them, Steve decides to tell Diane about the Colonel's orders. He walks into the bedroom, where Diane sits in front of the vanity mirror trying on earrings.

"Di, I need to speak with you." Diane can tell by the tone of Steve's voice that something is wrong.

"Chic, you don't have cold feet about the Oscars, do you?"

"No, well...no. Look, when I was waiting for my tux yesterday, I received a call from Colonel Johnson. I have to go to Baltimore first thing tomorrow morning. That means right after the Oscars, no parties, no interviews, right back to the hotel. My flight leaves at 5:00 in the morning. There are also tickets for you to fly to Baltimore on Wednesday. "

"Well, that's okay, because I wasn't planning on partying

all night. I was just going to make an appearance at the Paramount party, which is right here at the hotel."

"Di, you are going to be the life of the parties, and of Hollywood!"

"Oh, you're so sweet." She gives Steve a kiss.

"No, well, yeah, well." He grabs Diane's shoulders and sets her down on the chair in front of the vanity.

"Diane, you have to be a very good actress tonight."

"What are you leading up to, Chic?"

"Colonel Johnson told me that you're going to win the Academy Award for best actress. That's why your tickets are for Wednesday. You'll have parties, interviews, and TV, and all the Hollywood bullshit to deal with. And I'm sorry I won't be here with you for all that. But something is going down in D.C., and that's where I'll be."

Diane is speechless. She stares at Steve, and then a smile slowly comes over her face.

"You're kidding me, right?"

"No. The Colonel has access to guarded information. You are the winner."

At that moment, there is a knock at the door. It is the makeup artist, and Diane has started to cry for joy.

The makeup artist is going to have to earn his salary today.


Before leaving Broward General Hospital, George asks Jerry Myers to return to the hospital Monday morning to try to interview Rishad again.

As he pulls out of the hospital parking lot, he remembers that Angie is organizing an Oscar Awards party at the saloon on Monday evening. Steve's friends cannot wait to see him and Diane walk the red carpet, and his family in Florida and Maryland are also hoping to catch a glimpse of the couple on

TV. All of them are praying that Diane will win the coveted award.

It is now early evening, and Moshe checks in at the Red Roof Inn in Charlottesville. He asks the desk clerk if there is a small diner nearby where he can get a quick dinner. He wants to eat at a local place where the town folks go, not at a chain restaurant, so he can furtively listen for information about Rick Collins or his family's tragedy. The desk clerk recommends The Blue Moon Diner on Main Street. He says that Joe, the owner, has been there for over twenty years and that he knows everything and everyone in town.

Moshe goes into his room, takes a shower, and heads to the diner.

Working late at the FBI office, Jerry Myers looks up to see the sketch artist he sent to meet with Doris at Nova University approaching him. The artist is holding a drawing of the man who identified himself as Officer Scott Sax. Jerry grabs the drawing and compares it to the photo of Moshe Saban that was circulated in the dossier issued by Mossad. With a low whistle, he can't believe his luck. It seems too good to be true. It looks like an exact match.

# CHAPTER ELEVEN

Steve and Diane are heading to the Kodak Theater in their chauffeured limousine, courtesy of Paramount Pictures. Steve is dreading the walk down the red carpet in front of the thousands of people lining the streets and in the bleacher seats outside the theater. Steve gives Diane's hand a gentle squeeze of reassurance. Diane looks over at Steve and gives him a wink.

"I'd give you a big wet kiss, but it would ruin my makeup. I don't know how I'm not going to say anything about knowing that I won."

"I don't know how I'm going to tolerate wearing this tux all night. But you'll be fine. Give 'em hell."

The limo stops in front of the waiting crowd. The driver gets out and opens the door for Diane and Steve to exit among cheers and flashing camera lights. Hand in hand, the couple proceeds down the red carpet.

"Diane, Diane Summers!" Diane is called over by the Entertainment Network's live TV reporter, Tina Jefferies.

"Diane, you look fabulous tonight! Who are you wearing?"

"Thank you, Tina, you look good yourself." Steve melts into the background. "It's Christian Dior."

"So, tell me, Diane. What do you think of your chances tonight?"

Diane glances quickly at Steve, who has a boyish smirk on his face. "Why don't we ask my husband, Steve. Steve, what do you think?"

Diane reaches out and takes Steve's hand to pull him toward the microphone and cameras.

Watching live coverage of the Academy Awards event are Steve's family at their homes in Maryland and Florida, along with his friends, who are gathered together at Duke's Saloon. At Diane's antics, they call out with the same mindset, "Diane dragged Steve onto the TV!"

The red carpet reporter continues her questioning. "So tell me, Steve, do you think Diane will win tonight?"

Steve glances at Diane and then looks straight into the camera. "I definitely think she'll win, but I'm sort of biased. If the Academy didn't vote for her, they made a big mistake."

"Well, we thank you for stopping by and saying hello. Good luck, Diane."

"Thank you. Good night, Tina."

Diane and Steve walk off camera to flashing photographers' lights and cheering fans.

As Diane and Steve enter the Kodak Theater in Hollywood, Moshe Saban is entering the Blue Moon Diner in Charlottesville, Virginia. He approaches the counter seating area and sits at one of the stools. A waitress walks over and hands him a menu.

"Evenin', Hon. Want somethin' 'ta drink?"

"Water's fine." He notices her name tag. "Tell me, Sarah, does Joe make a good burger?"

"Our half pounder with grilled onions is the best in Virginia. But how do you know Joe? You're not a regular here. In fact, I never saw ya before."

"Name's Scott Sax. I'm a reporter for USA Today. The

desk clerk at the Red Roof Inn said Joe's the man who knows everything about everything. I'm doing a story about the Collins family and how the government ruined their lives."

"Yeah, that just wasn't right. The government took that land right from under them. We think it was a payoff to TriStar."

"Wow. Well, give me that famous burger and a coke, and ask Joe if he'll talk with me."

"No problem, Hon." The waitress writes up the order and enters the rear cooking area to get Joe.

Within fifteen minutes, a tall, skinny man emerges from the kitchen looking a little like Abe Lincoln without a beard. He walks down the serving aisle in front of the counter and drops a beautiful burger in front of Moshe.

"Name's Joe. What do ya need 'ta know?"

"I'm Scott Sax, an investigative reporter for USA Today. I want to do a story on the Collins family and the tragedy that ended their lives. What can you tell me about Rick and his late parents?"

"It was a damn shame. Mary and Tom Collins ran that farm all of their lives. Tom's grandfather and his young bride came here in the early 1900's from England. They bought a block of land just outside Charlottesville and kept it in their family until one year ago. They farmed mostly tobacco, and in the later years, switched to corn and soybeans. Two years ago, Tom got sick. Now, bein' an old tobacco farmer, Tom was a heavy smoker, but he smoked his own, not the store bought stuff. What happened was he caught the flu and it turned into pneumonia. He was only in the hospital ten days when they discovered he needed a double bypass. Farmers don't have the greatest health insurance, so they mortgaged the farm 'ta pay his bills. Rick and his mother tried 'ta keep the farm going while Tom was on the mend, but he was outa commission for close to six months, then a drought hit and their crops couldn't support 'em, so they fell behind in their mortgage payments and didn't pay their taxes. They went to the bank and the IRS to try to negotiate a payout, but no one wanted anything 'ta do with 'em. Then TriStar Foods suddenly came in. The feds seized the farm and within days, TriStar was the new owner and Mary, Rick and Tom were out on the street. Funny, just before all that happened, our new Senator, Gordon Lewis, who lives right here in Charlottesville, was elected. He ran as an Independent 'ta distance himself from the Washington assholes. Then, after he was elected, he switched 'ta the Democratic Party, pissin' off everyone who voted for him. The funny thing is that Senator Lewis was a tax attorney before he got into politics, and his largest campaign contributor was—you guessed it—TriStar Foods. "

Scott feigns writing all this down in between chowing down on his burger.

"That's incredible, Joe. This will make a great story. So, tell me, what happened to Rick?"

"Rick was never the same after his parents passed. The mayor and the city councilors rose up a stink about the whole deal and gave TriStar a hard time. TriStar eventually bought a place for Rick 'ta live in and gave him a job on his old farm, but it's just a figurehead position. They pay him as a consultant and he goes in a couple of times a week. He also works part time at the tractor supply store on 64. Rick has been hangin' out with a small paramilitary group called The First Virginia Militia. They all hate the government, and when Baruch became President, they really started to recruit. The local authorities have been monitorin' their activities, but there's nothin' but war games in the mountains. However, they started 'ta collect large supplies of munitions. I hear the FBI is also gettin' interested."

"Joe, you've been a great help, and this burger is

outstanding. Thanks for the info. I'm going to try the tractor supply store tomorrow to see if I can meet Rick."

The men shake hands and Moshe leaves cash on the counter, then heads back to the motel for a good night's sleep. Tomorrow, he'll deal with Rick.


"Jeannie, are the boys asleep? They're about to announce the winner for Best Actress!"

"I'll be right in, Mike."

Mike calls his brother John in Florida.

"John, its Mike, I wanted to be connected with ya at the announcement."

"Hey, Mike. Carla and I are up. We tried to keep Jenna awake, but she fell asleep on the couch."

"Jeannie will be right in. She just put the twins to bed."

Even though they are almost 900 miles apart, the couples watch live coverage of the Academy Awards ceremony together, while at Duke's Saloon in Plantation, the entire bar waits in anticipation.

"...And the envelope please. The winner is...Diane Summers, for her role in *Las Olas!*"

Screams and yells erupt from Maryland to Florida, and the applause is deafening in the Kodak Theater. At her seat, Diane's face registers amazement as her name is read. When she turns to Steve to give him a kiss, she whispers, "How'd I do? Did I look surprised?"

Steve smiles, "Your best performance ever!"

Diane quickly rises and scampers up to the stage to accept her award. While Steve is giving Diane a standing ovation, his heart fills with admiration and love for his wife. He thinks to himself, *This will probably be a long night, but what the hell. I'll sleep on the plane.*

# CHAPTER TWELVE

It's early morning when Agent Jerry Myers arrives at Broward General Medical Center, but Rishad is awake and he needs to be questioned. The agent nods at the BSO officer standing guard outside the room and goes in.

"Good morning, Rishad. My name is Jerry Myers and I'm a field officer with the FBI. We need to talk."

Rishad looks up. "How do I know you are who you say you are?"

"Well, I have a digital recorder here to capture what you say, and I don't have jumper cables. So, let's get to it. Who is Risa Rashjani?"

In a subconscious attempt to protect himself, Rishad folds both hands over his groin, but says nothing.

Jerry Myers moves closer to the bed, places his hands over Rishad's hands, and stares into his eyes.

"A little sore this morning? Lucky you're not dead. Look, I don't have all day to visit with you. Who is Risa Rashjani?"

At this second question, Jerry applies downward pressure on Rishad's hands and Rishad starts to grimace.

"Okay, okay! What do I get for cooperating with you?"

"Probably deportation, but no jail time. On the other hand, if you don't cooperate with me and this Risa person turns ugly, you could be facing the death penalty as an accessory. So, again, who is Risa?"

As if considering his options, Rishad looks away from the agent and then replies, "All I know is that I deciphered a message that told me to contact the Iranian government. I did what I was told and was given a package to deliver to Risa in Charlottesville, Virginia. We met at a Starbucks. I gave her the package and then I left."

"And what is she supposed to do?"

"I don't know anything about that, except that her assignment has something to do with someone or something in Washington."

Jerry lifts his hands from Rishad's and leaves the room. He tells the BSO officer to handcuff Rishad to the bed and to call for federal marshals. He locates Rishad's doctor and asks him if Rishad can be moved to a more secure area. The doctor says it would be uncomfortable for Rishad, but possible. Jerry arranges for Rishad to be moved and then places a call to agent Carol Lawson at FBI headquarters in Washington.

Following Joe's directions, Moshe has no trouble finding the tractor supply store where Rick Collins works. After walking into the store, he quickly locates a clerk and asks for the manager. Soon, an overweight, middle aged man walks out of an office and approaches Moshe.

"I'm the manager here. Can I help you?"

"Yes. I'm Agent Scott Sax with Homeland Security." He flashes his phony ID. "Where can we go to talk in private?"

Flustered, the fat man answers, "Well, I guess we can go to my office. Follow me."

Moshe follows the manager to a small room off the sales floor and waits while the manager closes the door behind them. Turning to Moshe, the manager asks, "Now, what is this all about?"

"Do you have an employee working here by the name of Rick Collins?"

"Rick? Why, yes. What's wrong?"

"Look, you keep asking me questions. That's not how this is going to work. I need to see his employee file."

"Don't you need a warrant for that kind of information?"

"Warrant, WARRANT? Are you really going to make me get a warrant? One phone call and I get a warrant! Then, I'll call out a complete team and shut this place down, oh, maybe for a week. Now, get me the file."

The manager walks over to a file cabinet, pulls out Rick's employment information, and hands it to Moshe. All Moshe wants is Rick's address.

"Is this information current and up to date?"

"Yes, Sir."

"I'll need to take this file with me. Is Rick working today?"

"No, he has the day off."

"Okay, listen to me carefully. Don't tell anyone about this meeting or try to contact Rick. It's a matter of national security. I'll contact you again within twenty-four hours."

Moshe leaves the store with Rick's file and returns to the motel. He intends to pay a visit to Rick very soon.


Luckily, the Paramount Awards after party was held at the Beverly Hills Hotel where Diane and Steve have a room, so they didn't have to travel far when the party wound down at 3:00 in the morning. Steve's flight leaves at 5:15, so he quickly showers, changes clothes, and gives Diane a hug and kiss before leaving for the airport.

"Honey, you were great tonight, and I'm sorry I can't be with you at your time of glory. But, I'll see you at the airport in Baltimore on Wednesday."

"Steve, I'm the one who's sorry that I can't go with you today. And you really did great, putting up with all this bullshit. I love you, Steve. I can't wait 'till Wednesday."

They kiss again and Steve grabs his bags and reluctantly leaves the hotel for Los Angeles International Airport.

Diane's plate is full for the next two days with media interviews that will keep her very busy. She walks into the bedroom and sits on the bed, gazing at the Oscar she just won.

In Virginia, members of the First Virginia Militia have responded to Rick's request for help and they are now busy helping him pour the nitrate and fuel oil into the 55 gallon drums that are standing in the living room of Senator Lewis' motor coach. The going is slow and cautious. They do not want to cause any sparks that may start a fire and cause premature detonation of their crude bomb.

Risa is on site, overseeing the operation in her role as a trained munitions expert for al-Qaida. She estimates that they should be finished by late afternoon. Her plan is to drive the motor coach away from the farm after sunset, under the cover of a moonless night.

Early that morning, Moshe leaves the Red Roof Inn with the small passport-sized photo of Risa Rashjani that he took from Javeed Tavaazo's file. Before heading for Rick's apartment at the nearby Berkshire Apartments complex, he programs the GPS app on his Android phone with Rick's address, then stops at a Cracker Barrel for breakfast and at a hardware store to get another roll of duct tape. If Rick is not at the apartment, Moshe will pick the lock and wait inside until he returns.

Steve is fast asleep as his flight soars over the Rockies, headed for BWI Airport in Baltimore, Maryland. He manages to get a couple of hours of much needed sleep after the whirlwind events of the previous night. He needs his sleep, because any further rest during the next seventy-two hours will come at a premium as Risa's plan unfolds and possibly changes the political course of the United States.

Diane, however, is not able to get any extra rest. She is scheduled to appear on one of the morning news shows via live feed from a media room that has been set up in the hotel. She will be on national TV at 5:30 a.m. California time and needs to put on her best camera face, even though she is dead tired.

# CHAPTER THIRTEEN

As Steve picks up his luggage at BWI, he is approached by Carol Lawson from the FBI.

Extending her hand in greeting, she says, "Steve, I'm Agent Carol Lawson, FBI Washington."

"I thought Colonel Johnson was meeting me."

"I'm taking you to his new office in Baltimore. We'll update you there. A lot of stuff came down recently, and more will happen quickly."

When they exit the terminal, Carol guides Steve to a black SUV that she parked earlier in the airport's short-term parking garage. In relative silence, the FBI agent drives Steve toward Baltimore's Inner Harbor.


In California, Diane has returned to her suite and is finally getting some well-deserved sleep. Her next interview is not until late afternoon, and then she will appear with Jay Leno on *The Tonight Show*.


The black SUV arrives at the World Trade Center Institute at Inner Harbor, Baltimore. Carol and Steve exit the SUV and head into the building's lobby, taking the elevator to the top floor. When they open the door to the FSA office, they are immediately directed to a conference room, where Colonel Johnson has arranged a meeting to introduce Steve to Sam DeVito, chief of the FSA office in Baltimore and a twenty-year veteran of the FBI. Waiting inside the room are Colonel Johnson, Sam DeVito and General Sandberg.

After everyone seats themselves, short introductions are made around the table, and then Colonel Johnson starts the meeting.

"Okay, let's get started. I called this meeting because we believe there is an imminent threat against the United Sates from a terror cell within our borders, the type of threat that is the most difficult to stop."

From a projector linked to his laptop, Colonel Johnson sends information to a screen at the far end of the conference room.

"General Sandberg, your renegade Mossad agent, Moshe Saban, has shown up here in the states, and is probably in Charlottesville, Virginia, as we speak. We know that he interrogated Rishad Ammani, an exchange student from Saudi Arabia, and left him for dead in the Everglades with files that he probably took from Javeed Tavaazo, the Iranian foreign ministry officer who was blown up in his own car. We believe that the bomb incident was also arranged by your missing agent."

The Colonel displays photos of Moshe and Rishad on the screen.

"A Seminole Indian cruising by on his airboat saw Rishad duct-taped to a tree off a canal in the Everglades, and called 911. We interrogated Rishad and now have him in protective custody. He told us that there's an agent from al-Qaida in the Charlottesville area by the name of Risa Rashjani, and in the files from Iran, the name Rick Collins is mentioned. We've been monitoring Rishad's actions for a while, and we know that he gave a package to Risa last week. After that meeting with Risa, we have reason to believe that their targets are the Declaration of Independence and the Constitution of the United States."

He continues, "Gentlemen, the problem is, that although we reviewed city records in Charlottesville and interviewed local residents, we cannot find a Risa Rashjani living in the area. It's obvious that she's using an alias, but we just don't know what it is. Until we can find more information on her, we must turn our attention to Rick Collins.

"We discovered that Rick's family recently lost their family farm because of unpaid taxes. The farm was bought by TriStar Foods, which has since hired Rick on as a consultant. Rick also works part time at a tractor supply store. Locals believe the sale of the family's farm may have been arranged through a payoff to Virginia Senator William Lewis. He's a tax attorney who lives in Charlottesville, and he received a very large campaign contribution from TriStar Foods. Although we have not established a link between TriStar and the Senator at this time, the situation looks suspicious."

The Colonel indicates Rick's photo on the screen. "Getting back to Rick, he's been linked to a paramilitary group called The First Virginia Militia. Carol Lawson can fill you in on what we know about that group, since the FBI has been monitoring its activities over the past year. Carol?"

Carol stands and takes the Colonel's place at the head of the table.

"The First Virginia Militia started out as a bunch of men disillusioned with the federal government, and that is why we think Rick was drawn to join them. However, since President Baruch took office, a more radical, racist tone has taken over the group, and they are now being linked to a local chapter of the KKK.

"We believe that our only link to Risa is through Rick Collins and/or Moshe Saban. We sent a photo of Moshe to the local authorities in Charlottesville and instructed them to be on the lookout for him, and we're sending a team into Charlottesville early in the morning to monitor Rick's activities. We also put the National Archives on alert for a possible attack. They moved the two original documents to their bomb proof vaults and have put two replicas on display, so the public is not aware of any changes."

Steve interrupts. "Look, if we think an attack is imminent, we need to have plans in place to block off the entrances to downtown Washington. The two bridges over the Potomac that could be accessed from Charlottesville are the Theodore Roosevelt Memorial Bridge and the Arlington Memorial Bridge. My guess is that they'll use the first one, since it leads directly to Route 50 and the National Archives. Risa could possibly take the long route to 95, but I assume she's going to try to destroy our treasures, and if she's transporting explosives, she'll probably take the shortest route. Now, for the amount of explosives that would be needed for this job, a car or SUV will not be big enough, so I think we should be looking for a box truck. Oklahoma City comes to mind. If Rick has access to a farm and works for a tractor supply outlet, he has access to ammonium nitrate and diesel fuel. Again, Oklahoma City. Sam, you need to contact the Washington police and the President, because we're going to need the National Guard to cover those bridges."

Carol continues. "I agree. We need to put our plans into place immediately, and we need to make them available to everyone involved. I'll get surveillance started on Rick Collins as soon as possible. I don't think we have a lot of time here, so we need to get to work. If there is nothing else, gentlemen, we need to adjourn this meeting."

After the meeting, Steve, Sam and the Colonel get together, and Steve starts the conversation.

"Listen, Sam. You and the Colonel need to share this

information with the FBI, the Washington police and the White House. If we don't get a handle on this Risa chick, aside from stopping every large truck or bus coming across the bridges into Washington, there is no way to prevent this attack. If Risa uses 1,500 to 2,000 pounds of ANFO, made from ammonium nitrate and fuel oil, it will level a city block. Even if she doesn't get close to the National Archives, the collateral damage will be intense wherever it goes off."

Sam replies, "I agree, Steve. Colonel, you need to get the White House on the phone. We need to start this right now."

Stifling a yawn, Steve says, "Gentleman, since I'm only a consultant, I think I've contributed enough today. I need to get a car with a GPS so I can get to my son's house and crash 'till morning. I haven't slept since Saturday night, and I'm not as young as I think I am."

The Colonel pats Steve on the shoulder. "No problem, Steve. I'll have Sam's receptionist reserve a vehicle for you after she connects me with the President."

When Colonel Johnson leaves the room, Steve turns to Sam.

"So how'd you get volunteered for this gig?"

"The Colonel brought me down to the White House and we met with the President. The President asked for my help, and I couldn't say no."

"You too, huh? They got me the same way."

"Listen, how about we take an early lunch, then, I'll drive you to get your car."

"Lead the way. You're the boss."

Sam leads Steve out of the office and down to the Inner Harbor to get some crab cakes, while the Colonel speaks with the President to fill him in on the current situation.


Moshe Saban arrives at the Berkshire Apartments and

knocks on Rick's door, but there is no answer. With the lock picking kit that all good spies carry, he makes quick work of the locked door and lets himself in. He enters the apartment, relocking the door behind him, and puts a roll of duct tape on an end table in the living room.

He quickly surveys the rest of the apartment and locates a computer on a small desk in the bedroom. He powers it up and waits for the home screen to appear. He examines the desktop screen, and nothing appears unusual. Next, he checks the Outlook files and finds emails to various militias and neo-Nazi groups across the United States. After reading a few of them, he shuts the computer down and goes into the kitchen, where he opens the fridge.

Mumbling to himself, he says, "Hell, might as well get something to eat while I wait for ol' Rick to get on home."

Moshe finds a frying pan and makes himself some scrambled eggs, then pours himself a glass of Arizona Iced Tea. He takes his plate of eggs and his glass of iced tea into the living room to watch TV while he eats. Moshe has no set time schedule and figures that Rick will be home eventually.

The rented Ford Fusion pulls off Route 108/Clarksville Pike, and enters Beaverbrook Road. Within a couple of blocks, Steve pulls into the first brick house on the left that has an in-law suite over the garage. He cannot wait to see his son, daughter-in-law and new twin grandsons, but he is also in desperate need of some sleep. He lifts his luggage out of the trunk, beeps the Fusion shut, then walks slowly up to the front door and rings the doorbell. Inside the house, Jeannie runs to get the door, because she does not want the ringing doorbell to awaken the twins from their nap.

"Dad! Wow, you were supposed to call. Come on in!" Jeannie gives her father-in-law a hug.

"Di will be flying in on Wednesday. She's a little busy right now."

Jeannie closes the door behind them.

"Wow, ya think? She looked great! I can't wait to congratulate her."

"Hey, what about me?" Steve says with a smile.

Mike walks in from the kitchen. "You looked great, Dad!" Smiling, father and son exchange a man-hug.

"So, where are my grandsons?"

"They're taking a nap. Let me take your luggage and get you a beer while Jeannie gives you the nickel tour of the house."

"House? You can put my villa and my condo inside this thing and still have room."

Jeannie takes Steve through the five bedroom, three and one half bath Colonial, and then shows him the separate in-law suite with a bath and kitchenette. Mike catches up to them in the apartment over the garage and hands Steve his beer.

"Here, Dad. So, what do you think?"

"Wow! Beer's cold!"

"Dad!"

"Guys, this place is great! Congratulations to you both! Now, if you would excuse an old man, I haven't slept since Saturday night. I need a nap, too. Besides, Di's going to be on Jay Leno tonight and I want to be awake to see her."

After Mike and Jeannie leave the in-law suite, Steve drinks his beer, then crashes on the bed and is asleep in an instant.


Rick and his crew have been working all day to store the ANFO bombs in the motor coach, and it is now late afternoon. They decide to remain with Risa until nightfall and then leave under the cloak of darkness, so they won't be noticed. After Risa wires the detonation circuits, everything will be complete. She will do that back at the Senator's house on Tuesday, before heading to D.C. on Wednesday morning.


While watching the local news on Rick's TV, Moshe decides to give General Sandberg a call. He uses Rick's home phone because he doesn't want the General to know who is calling. He dials the General's international cell phone number, not realizing that the General is actually nearby, in Washington, D.C.

In his hotel room, General Sandberg picks up his ringing cell phone and stares at the number on the display screen. Puzzled, he answers the call.

"Shalom."

"General, it's Moshe."

"Moshe! Where are you? What is happening? What are you doing?"

"My job, my way. I'll be in touch again, but an attack on D.C. is coming. I believe it will be within days, if not hours."

"I think they know that. Rishad was very talkative."

"Again, doing my job, my way. But I didn't plan on him being found. Bye, General."

The General sighs deeply and quickly places calls to the Israeli Embassy and to Carol Lawson at the FBI.

# CHAPTER FOURTEEN

Determined to be a good grandpa, Steve volunteers to help his daughter-in-law get his grandsons off to bed. After they're settled in for the night, he heads toward the family room with Jeannie to watch Diane on *The Tonight Show With Jay Leno,* to see how she's holding up. Mike is already on the sofa, waiting for them.

"Good grief, Mike. Do you feed your kids nothing but Mexican food? I told Jeannie to call a hazmat team out to dispose of the diapers. I don't remember it being so gross, but your Mom always did most of the diaper duty back then."

"So does Jeannie. I help out when I'm home, but she's a saint. I'm going to the kitchen. You two want anything?"

In unison, they call out, "Gimme a Dew!"

"Dad? Mountain Dew?"

"I have a feeling I'm going to be busy in the next couple of days. Dew's fine."


At 10:30 that evening, Risa drives the motor coach out of the old barn, following Rick's pickup truck as he leads her off the farm toward the Senator's house on the hill. When they reach a junction in the road, Rick turns the opposite way and heads home alone, knowing that Risa will continue on up the hill.

When Risa arrives at the house, she plans to take a well-deserved shower and get a good night's sleep so her mind will be clear in the morning for the task of wiring the explosives. She wants to be sharp to avoid any mistakes that would result in the Senator's house blowing up or in wiring the explosives incorrectly so they would not blow up at all.

Moshe is preparing for an evening of fun. He screws the silencer onto his Beretta and shuts the lights in the apartment but leaves the TV on, positioning himself on the living room sectional so that he faces the front door. Within a few minutes, he hears footsteps in the hallway that stop at the apartment door. After a short pause, he hears a key being inserted into the lock.

On the other side of the door, Rick stops before turning the key in the lock, thinking to himself, *I didn't leave the TV on, did I?* Shrugging that thought aside, he continues turning the key that unlocks the dead bolt, and slowly opens the front door.

"Rick, Rick, Rick. Come on in. Been waitin' for ya."

Rick stares down the barrel of the 9mm Beretta.

"Who the hell are you?"

"Now, now, Rick. That just might be the last question you ask me tonight. Close the door, you're letting out all the AC."

Rick slowly closes the door and turns toward Moshe.

"Let me see your hands, Rick. That's a good boy. Now take that roll of duct tape off the end table and sit down on that chair near the dining room table." After Rick is seated, Moshe continues. "Very good. Now tape your legs around the front legs of the chair."

It takes a few minutes for Rick to complete the task.

"What are you going to do?"

Moshe rises and walks over to Rick. "Right now, I'm going to bind your arms behind you through the back of the chair."

Moshe uses the duct tape to bind Rick tightly to the chair. Before Rick has a chance to speak again, Moshe tapes his mouth shut.

"Hope you don't have sinus problems, or you could suffocate. Now, Rick, I have all the time in the world, so let's get started. Who is Risa Rashjani?"

All he hears is mumbling. "Oops, I forgot the tape."

Moshe rips the tape off Rick's mouth, which causes Rick to let out a robust yell. At the sound, Moshe places the silencer against Rick's temple and cups his hand over Rick's mouth.

"No yelling, or the tape goes back on. Now, who is Risa?"

"I don't know any Risa."

"Well, a lot of important people say you do. And one of them is dead."

"Who the hell are you?"

Moshe punches Rick in the face, breaking his nose. Blood gushes from Rick's nose and runs down his face, onto his t-shirt.

"I'm the guy who wants to know who Risa is. We can get this over with real quick or we can do this all night. Again, Rick. Who is Risa?"

Rick looks up at Moshe and exclaims, "Go fuck yourself!"

"Now, Rick, no need to get vulgar."

Moshe walks over to a floor lamp in the living room, unplugs it and brings it into the kitchen. He rummages through the drawers and finds a large carving knife that he uses to cut the cord off the lamp at its base. Then, he walks over to Rick, grabs the back of his chair and drags him over to the outlet where the lamp had been plugged in a few minutes ago.

"Rick, you really need to take that bloody t-shirt off."

Moshe cuts through the sides of Rick's t-shirt and pulls it over Rick's head, then goes into the kitchen and runs the t-shirt under the water. He returns to where Rick is sitting and wipes away the blood from Rick's bare chest that is still dripping from Rick's nose. Then, he wipes Rick's face with the same t-shirt.

"There. Feel better?"

With the carving knife, Moshe strips the coating from one end of the power cord to expose two inches of copper wire. He then grabs the cord and pulls it apart like a turkey wishbone, so that he now has two separated power cords, each about one foot long. Moshe then plugs the other end of the power cord into the outlet and walks back to Rick. Holding the two exposed ends out in front of him, Moshe touches them together slightly, which causes a large spark. Rick starts to sweat profusely.

"Now, Rick, let's start this again. As soon as I get what I need, I leave. Okay? Are you paying attention, Rick? Who is Risa Rashjani?"

When Moshe receives no answer, he picks up the roll of duct tape from the floor and tapes Rick's mouth shut. Then, he takes one end of the power cord and touches Rick's chest with it. Rick starts to shake his head, no, but Moshe touches the other end of the power cord to Rick's chest, and then 117 volts of electricity course through Rick's body, causing him to go into convulsions. Moshe know that he has to be careful, because if the cord remains connected to Rick too long, his heart will stop.

After two seconds, Moshe pulls the cord away and Rick slumps in his chair. He's unconscious, but alive. Moshe waits patiently for Rick to come to.

Back in Maryland, Steve, Mike and Jeannie are watching a rerun on TV, waiting for Diane to be announced on stage at the Academy Awards ceremony.

"...so, without waiting another moment, the Best Actress winner is, Diane Summers!"

Diane walks through the curtain from backstage to a thundering round of applause. The entire Ciccone family is filled with pride and Steve is the proudest peacock of all.

"Doesn't she look great!"

Mike puts his arm around his father. "You did good, Dad, you did real good."


It takes about an hour, but Rick is slowly coming to. Moshe slaps Rick's face with his bloody, water soaked t-shirt to speed things along.

"Feeling better, are we? You know, Rick, we can do this all night."

In the parking lot outside Rick's apartment, a white van parks in a guest spot. The van contains a surveillance unit from the FBI. Carol Lawson sits in the front seat with another agent.

"Look. His pickup is parked across the lot. He must be home. I'll put a bug under the fender so we can track him."

Carol slips out of the van and nonchalantly approaches the pickup. When she reaches the truck, she quickly attaches the bug and returns to the van.

Back in the apartment, Moshe pulls the duct tape from Rick's mouth. Now Rick has two second degree burns on his chest, along with a broken nose. He is exhausted and somewhat disoriented. He whispers, "Who are you? What do you want?"

"Wow, you're not too bright, are you, Rick? I'm the man

who wants to know who Risa Rashjani is, and why she knows you."

"She's a friend."

"Oh, Rick. A redneck like you has a raghead for a friend? Talk to me, Rick. It's going to be a long night."

"I don't know anything."

Moshe puts fresh duct tape over Rick's mouth and shocks him a second time. Once again, Rick goes into convulsions, but this time, his bladder and his bowels evacuate. Rick is now unconscious and Moshe shakes his head. He did not think it was going to be this hard to break Rick, but Moshe is very patient. He goes to the fridge and grabs a beer, confident that Rick will eventually talk.

Moshe and Rick go round and round until dawn. Then, Moshe makes himself some eggs for breakfast. He sits near Rick while he eats.

"You're needin' a shower, Rick. You're beginning to reek." Rick has dried blood around his nose and mouth and six burn marks on his torso. Moshe finishes his eggs and pulls a chair up in front of Rick.

"Rick, you impress me. Better men than you have talked way before this. But I got nothin' else to do, so let's start again."

"Look, I told you, she's just a friend!" Moshe shocks him again and Rick passes out.

"This is getting old, Rick, and boy, you stink."

Moshe grabs the back of Rick's chair and drags him into the bathroom. He puts Rick and his chair into the shower and turns on the cold water. It takes about thirty minutes for Rick to come to.

When he's conscious again, Moshe lays Rick's chair down in the shower, with Rick still strapped to it. The back of the chair is lying on the shower floor, with Rick's lap facing upward. Moshe walks into Rick's bedroom, grabs a pillow off the bed, and takes the pillowcase off. He brings the pillowcase with him into the bathroom and slips it over Rick's head. Then, he grabs the hand held shower massage and turns the water on full blast, setting it to a hard massaging stream. He then reaches under the pillowcase and removes the tape from Rick's mouth while angling the pulsing water through the pillowcase, into Rick's mouth, and up Rick's nose.

"You know, Rick. Waterboarding always works."

Gasping for air, Rick tries to get some words out, but the only words that come through his gulps and gags are, "Okay! Okay! Stop! Stop!"

Moshe turns off the water. "Ready to talk, Rick? I can do this all day."

"No, no, I'll talk. I'll tell you everything I know, just don't do that again!"

Moshe lifts the chair up to a sitting position and removes the pillowcase from Rick's head.

Rick begins talking. "Risa is a terrorist. She works under another name for Senator Lewis. She's going to blow up the National Archives building."

"How is she going to do that?"

"I got her some ammonium nitrate and diesel fuel. She has 1,500 pounds of it. She's going to deliver the payload using Senator Lewis' motor coach."

"Fifteen hundred pounds. That'll blow up a city block. When is this going to happen?"

"She's a munitions expert, and she still has to wire the detonator. It'll probably happen either today or tomorrow."

"The Senator, where does he live?"

"On Lewis Mountain Circle, in a big house at the top of the hill."

Moshe glances at his watch. "Let's hope she hasn't left yet."

With no hesitation, Moshe puts a 9mm round in Rick's left temple. Oblivious to the collapsed body, Moshe searches through Rick's pockets and takes his keys. He stands up, brushes himself off, and leaves the apartment, locking the door behind him.

It's now about 8:00 in the morning and Rick's neighbors are leaving for work. Moshe appears to be just another commuter on his morning routine as he walk in front of the white van in the parking lot and enters Rick's pickup.

Carol has seen Moshe's photo in Rick Collins' file, so when Moshe passes in front of the van, she stares at him.

"I know that face."

Carol opens the complete file on codename Falcon and exclaims, "Damn it! The guy in the white pickup truck that left about five minutes ago was Moshe Saban, the missing Mossad agent! We need to go in and check on Rick!"

Carol and her assisting agent, Joe Hamilton, rush to Rick's apartment. When there is no response at the door, they break in with guns drawn. As they enter the apartment, they carefully survey the interior, noticing the power cord on the floor that had been cut and spliced open. Joe is the first one to reach the bathroom.

"Carol! In here!"

Carol walks into the bathroom and recoils when she glimpses the gruesome sight of a tortured and dead Rick Collins.

"Damn it to hell!" Carol calls the local police, then her office, and then Colonel Johnson.

"Colonel, it's Carol Lawson. Our missing Mossad agent paid a visit to Rick Collins. Rick's dead. Whatever Rick knew, Moshe now knows. My team is investigating all the local hotels, so we should find out where Moshe is staying. He was here today and I ID'd him, but I didn't put the face with the name until after he left the scene. He's driving a white pickup; I think it's a Dodge. I called the locals to help cordon off the apartment and I gave them the info on the pickup. I'll stay here until our forensic team arrives."

"Damn! I'll put my team on alert."


FSA Chief Sam DeVito's team is listening to a briefing by Colonel Johnson in the ready room when Steve walks into the room.

"Sorry I'm late. I'm not used to your morning traffic patterns."

"Sit down, Steve. Let me bring you up to speed. As I was saying, Moshe Saban, the renegade Mossad agent, is in Charlottesville, Virginia. We believe he's hunting down Risa Rashjani, a terror cell operative who has been ordered to target the National Archives for one of al-Qaida's terror schemes. Unfortunately, we believe that when Moshe killed Rick Collins, he eliminated our only lead to Risa. We hope that Moshe contacts his ex-boss, General Sandberg, again soon. We sent his photo to the local police in Charlottesville, and they have issued an APB out on the white Dodge pickup truck that we think he's driving.

"In the last conversation that General Sandberg had with Moshe, he told the General that he believes an attack in the U.S. is coming within days or hours. Therefore, beginning this morning, all trucks and large RV's will be stopped and inspected before crossing over the Potomac at the Theodore Roosevelt Memorial Bridge and the Arlington Memorial Bridge. A National Guard unit has been moved to Fort McNair to help with the investigation."

Steve interrupts. "Colonel, we need to set up a crew on a high overlook position to oversee both bridges. I recommend the roof of the Lincoln Memorial."

"Good idea, Steve. Sam, we'll need to get permission

from the Department of the Interior before we can put people on top of the Lincoln Memorial. Steve, you'll be in charge of setting up this part of the operation."

Colonel Johnson continues. "People, we still have no handle or ID on Risa Rashjani. Obviously, she must be using an alias and has integrated herself into the local community of Charlottesville. The way I see it is that we have only two chances at preventing this attack. If Moshe finds Risa first, we have to hope that he'll stop her, or if we find him, we have to stop her together."

Risa has finished her morning prayers and is gathering up the wiring supplies and various electronic and detonation components before she heads over to the motor coach. She needs to wire all of the drums in a parallel circuit, so they will all detonate at the same time. She intends to use the motor coach itself as the power source by first connecting the bomb's wiring to the coach's cigarette lighter, and then attaching those wires to a mercury switch that she will fasten to a head band. With the head band on her head, the bomb's circuit will be completed when she bows her head down and touches her chin to her chest. At that angle, the mercury switch will activate the blasting caps that she has placed into each drum of explosives. Risa knows that if she is killed before she can set off the bomb, the inferno will still be ignited when her head slumps downward, even though she may already be dead. She also knows that depending on where she is when the bomb goes off, the original target may not be affected, but the collateral damage wherever the explosion takes place will be devastating. Either way, she knows that her terrorist mission will be accomplished.

Risa expects that it will take approximately two hours to wire all the explosives. She wants to retire early this evening so she can get enough sleep before leaving for Washington at 5:00 in the morning. The trip to D.C. will take about three hours, which will place her and her cargo in downtown Washington at about 8:00 in the morning, the middle of rush hour.

Moshe has had no sleep this evening, but he is still pushing himself onward, heading steadily toward Lewis Mountain Circle, a lonely, winding, two lane road leading to Senator Lewis' mountaintop retreat in Charlottesville. Halfway up the mountain, he is stopped by what appears to be a fortress. A high, cast iron gate and walls of brick topped by broken glass block any further passage. Moshe turns his pickup around and heads back down the road, pulling over to the side to wait. He has pulled stakeout duty before, and time is on his side. From what Rick told him, he doubts that Risa has left the farm yet. He guesses that nothing will happen until morning. Moshe opens the driver's side window so he can hear any passing motor vehicles and decides to take a well-deserved nap.

Before going out on morning patrol, Desk Sergeant Troy Davis briefs Charlottesville's finest.

"Okay, troops, one last thing. On your way out, pick up a photo of Moshe Saban. He's a renegade Israeli agent and we believe he's driving a white Dodge pickup. He's armed and dangerous. There is apparently some sort of terrorist threat that may have its roots right here in Charlottesville. Be on the alert for any box trucks or large vehicles that you don't recognize as being familiar to the area. The FBI sent several teams to search local hotels for information on Moshe and to gather information on any unusual activity. Be safe out there."

# CHAPTER FIFTEEN

It is almost noon and Risa has just finished wiring up the ANFO drums in the motor coach. She goes back into the house to pack up her personal belongings, then places them into the large motor coach. This trip will be one way and she does not want to leave any evidence behind. She returns to the house again to recite her afternoon prayers in the privacy of her room and prepares to retire early, because she wants to leave at five in the morning.

Halfway down the mountain road, where Moshe has parked just off the pavement to wait for Risa to drive by, he gets out of the vehicle to stretch his legs and empty his bladder. He walks down an embankment about fifteen feet below where he is parked, but before he can get down to business, he hears a car driving up and he quickly hugs the ground, lifting his head just enough to take a peek. The car is a police cruiser belonging to the Charlottesville police department. It seems that an officer is making a routine visit to Senator Lewis' house.

When the officer spots the white Dodge pickup on the side of the road, he notes that it matches the description of the vehicle in the APB he was briefed on at the beginning of his shift, so he stops to check it out. Moshe watches silently from below the embankment, but he knows that he cannot allow anything to stop him now. When he realizes that the officer is wearing a bulletproof vest under his uniform, he acts quickly. Quietly climbing back up the embankment, he grips the 9mm, thankful that he had previously attached the silencer, and waits for the perfect shot. When the officer turns toward the embankment, Moshe gets off two quick shots to his chest. The concussion from the impact of the bullets immediately knocks the police officer to the ground, taking the wind out of him and incapacitating him for about ten minutes. Moshe runs up to the road and drags the officer around to the back of the pickup, out of sight of anyone who may drive by.

Before the officer regains consciousness, Moshe takes the cop's stun gun from its holster and gives him a jolt of electricity, providing him enough time to swap clothes with the officer. The Charlottesville police officer is larger than Moshe, so the cop's uniform fits loosely and Moshe needs to pull the belt on his pants up to the last hole. After placing his own clothes on the officer, he drags him into the driver's seat of the Dodge pickup and handcuffs him to the steering wheel, using the cop's own handcuffs. Then he turns the truck's steering wheel to the right and puts the transmission in neutral. After closing the pickup's door, he walks over to the police cruiser, which is parked just behind the white Dodge, and climbs in. The keys are in the ignition, so Moshe starts the cruiser up, puts it in gear, and drives forward, gently tapping the Dodge to force it down the embankment, rendering it invisible from the road.

Confident that the pickup can't be seen from the road, Moshe drives the police cruiser about 200 yards forward and pulls it off the road at a billboard near a fork in the road. The right fork leads into a wilderness area and the left fork heads into town and eventually to the interstate, the most probable route that Risa will take. He drives the cruiser behind the billboard, gets out, and checks the trunk to see if there is anything in there that he can use to help him stop the motor coach. He is pleasantly surprised when he spies a Benelli M2 tactical shotgun. He takes it out of the trunk and places it in the front of the cruiser, in a harness that has been set up over the center hump.

Moshe gets comfortable in the cruiser, preparing to continue his wait for Risa to drive by. His position behind the billboard is perfect. He has a clear view of the road, but is far enough inside the tree line where he cannot be seen, but can quickly reenter the road. Moshe knows that the Charlottesville police officer will be missed at the end of his shift, but he has seen police cruisers in driveways around town, so he hopes that there won't be an immediate search for the missing officer.

Suddenly, the police cruiser's radio comes alive.

"Car 123, go to Tactical 3. Reilly, Tact 3."

Moshe has to think fast. He switches to the Tact 3 frequency on the radio and starts to cough. With a rough and raspy voice, he mumbles, "Reilly, Tact 3."

"Danny! What the hell happened to you?"

Moshe fakes a couple of coughs. "I woke up with a scratchy throat. Been downhill ever since. Feel like shit." He coughs again.

"Shit. I wanted to meet you for a late lunch, but you should go home. I'll call it in and cover your area."

"10-4. I'm headed home. Thanks."

Moshe smiles. This development will keep him in the clear. Now he can sit back and wait as long as necessary.


Back in Baltimore, Steve requests a sniper from the FBI unit to complete his team. He wants two snipers to position themselves on the roof of the Lincoln Memorial, while he covers the Arlington Memorial Bridge. He assigns Javier

Melendez, the FBI sniper, to cover the Theodore Roosevelt Bridge. He requested that a National Guard unit be placed on call at a local armory to shut down both bridges over the Potomac and to pull traffic control duty, if needed. The FBI has also placed a team on standby under the direction of Sam DeVito at FSA headquarters in Baltimore, waiting for their deployment to the field.

After everyone is in place, Steve decides to take a quick break and calls Diane on her cell phone.

"Hi, Di. How's my girl?"

"Chic! I can't wait to see you. I'm tired of all this Hollywood B.S."

"Miss you, too. Wait 'till you see the twins! You won't believe Mike and Jeannie's house, either."

"I can't wait to be with you all. Don't forget to pick me up at the airport tomorrow. I'm taking the red eye flight. I arrive at 9:00 a.m."

"Di, I'm a little tied up here. I may not be able to meet you, so Mike will pick you up. I'll try to be there, if I can. If not, I'll catch up with you at Mike's house later."

"Is there anything I should be concerned about?"

"No, just routine duty. Besides, you know what they say. I can't tell you without killing you."

"Well, don't do anything stupid. You're retired, remember? I want you around awhile."

"Wow, déjà vu. No problem, Di, I'm just a consultant. Gotta' go now, still love ya."

"Love you, too, Steve. See you tomorrow."


FBI agent Carol Lawson gathers her team together to review what information they've gathered so far.

"So, gentlemen what do we know?"

"Moshe was staying at the Red Roof Inn. He checked

out yesterday. We went into the room, but it had already been cleaned, so we found nothing. We learned that he went to the Blue Moon Diner and that he spoke with the owner. We spoke to him, and he told us about Rick's farm and the militia he joined. We raided their headquarters and took several members into custody for questioning. We have no further information."

"Okay. Let's concentrate our efforts on interrogating the captured militia members. The Charlottesville police are currently looking for Moshe. I'll connect with them in the morning. Let's get some rest now, and start again at seven."

# CHAPTER SIXTEEN

At 4:30 in the morning, Risa finishes her morning prayers and prepares for her drive to Washington. As a parting gift to Senator Lewis, she blows out the pilot light in the fireplace located in the family room near the kitchen, and then opens the jet, allowing gas to flow out. She walks over to the kitchen stove and does the same thing, allowing gas to flow out into the kitchen. Then she places a saucepan in the middle of the kitchen floor and fills it one quarter of the way with the powdered chlorine that is used for maintenance of the Senator's pool. She then pours about one half cup of brake fluid over the chlorine and quickly exits out the back door. In about four minutes, the chlorine/brake fluid mixture will ignite, destroying the house on the hill. Risa climbs into the Senator's motor coach and backs the vehicle out of the driveway, down Lewis Mountain Circle.

Moshe is still in the police cruiser at the bottom of the hill. He's been there since yesterday morning and is now half asleep. When he opens the window to help clear his head with the cool morning air, he hears the approaching motor coach as it winds its way down the mountain. As he watches the headlight beams through the trees, he is jolted by a loud explosion from the top of the hill. The chlorine has worked its magic on Senator Lewis' house.

After watching Risa drive by, Moshe starts up the

cruiser. With blue lights flashing and siren blaring, he pulls out onto the road and heads after the motor coach. In the background, he hears sirens blaring from fire and emergency vehicles that are heading to the Senator's house.

Moshe pulls up alongside the motor coach and signals for Risa to pull over, and Risa complies. Moshe parks behind the coach and walks his way up to the front. Risa opens the driver's window and looks down.

"Good Morning, Officer. Is there anything wrong?"

"Can I see your license and registration, please?"

Risa pulls the information out of her wallet and hands it to Moshe.

"Well, Lisa. Where are we going so early in the morning?"

"I have to pick up some children from the oncology ward at the Naval Hospital in Washington, and then take them to the zoo for an outing that is sponsored by Senator Lewis."

Moshe looks at his watch. It's almost 5:00 a.m. He looks up at the terrorist and hands back her ID.

"You have a safe drive. You headed to I-95 or I-29?"

"Going by way of 29. I-95 is too far out of the way."

"Well, take care. It's a long ride."

As Risa drives off, Moshe heads back to the cruiser and immediately calls General Sandberg. The phone rings twice, and then the General answers.

"General, it's Moshe. It's going down this morning. Risa Rashjani is posing as Lisa Thomas, an employee of Senator Lewis. She is driving his black motor coach into Washington via Route 29. I couldn't try to stop her, as the coach has bulletproof glass. I'm posing as a police officer and noticed the glass when I pulled her over. I also noticed that she's wearing a headband, which is wired. I believe she has a mercury switch in the band. If her head drops, it will probably set off explosives. Let the FBI know. They can't let her into Washington, because the collateral damage from any explosion will be great. I'm going to let the Charlottesville police know what's going on. Oh, by the way, I think she blew up the Senator's house."

Moshe shuts off his cell phone and gets on the police radio in the cruiser.

"I have an all points alert. My name is Moshe Saban from Mossad, and I have commandeered Officer Reilly's cruiser. You will find him halfway up Lewis Mountain Circle, handcuffed inside a Dodge pickup truck off the side of the road and down an embankment. Risa Rashjani, whom you may know as Lisa Thomas, is driving Senator Lewis' motor coach to Washington, D.C. The coach is loaded with 1,500 pounds of ammonium nitrate fuel oil bombs. She plans to blow up your National Archives. I will follow her in your cruiser. Do not try to stop her. She has a kill switch, and she can blow up that bus at any time. Fifteen hundred pounds of ANFO will level a city block. If she thinks anything is wrong, she will self-destruct. I will keep you posted on her position, so keep everyone off the roads. Oh, she blew up the Senator's house."

There is a moment of silence, and then the dispatcher comes on the air.

"We located Officer Reilly. The firemen spotted the pickup on their way to the Senator's house. We'll keep the roads clear. Keep us posted on Tactical 3."

"Will do. Good luck."

Steve is awakened at 5:30 a.m. by a call from Sam DeVito.

"This better be good."

"Operation Falcon is on. Our terrorist is headed to Washington. Be ready in ten minutes. I dispatched a helicopter to pick you up. It'll be on your son's front lawn."

"Shit." Steve ends the call and rushes to get ready. He

dresses quickly, no shave, and leaves the apartment over the garage just as the helicopter lands. Steve climbs in and looks back at his son's house as the lights come on in Mike's bedroom, as well as in all the bedrooms in the neighborhood. Sam is in the helicopter.

"We're headed to the Lincoln Memorial, where we set up our field headquarters. Your sniper teams were airlifted on site a few minutes ago, and the National Guard has been dispatched to help the Washington police. Moshe contacted the Charlottesville police and they put out an APB to all the neighboring towns between them and us. Moshe is following the motor coach in a Charlottesville police car."

"Did he try to stop her?"

"Apparently that was his goal, but she's driving Senator Lewis' motor coach, which is fitted with bulletproof glass. The coach is loaded with 1,500 pounds of ANFO bombs and she wired herself to them. If anything happens to her, the coach will ignite."

"Does she work for the Senator?"

"Yeah, her alias is Lisa Thomas. She's the nanny and is also his personal assistant. Oh, by the way, she blew up his house."

"Damn, Sam. Fifteen hundred pounds of ANFO will blow up a city block. We can't let that bitch cross the Potomac, and we can't spook her, or she'll blow up the Virginia countryside and kill hundreds."

"You're right, Steve. We need to stop her on one of the bridges. That way, if she detonates, the only collateral damage will be to the bridge."

"It will have to be in the middle of the river and on the Theodore Roosevelt Memorial Bridge. It's longer, and there will be less of a chance of someone getting hurt. We have to make sure she chooses the right bridge. I'll keep a sniper on the roof of the Lincoln Memorial, but I'll take up a position on the overpass on the east side of the Potomac, on Route 50. The Lincoln Memorial will be over two thousand meters away."

"Okay, Steve. We'll get it done. We only have about two hours to pull this off."

"Let's hope she's a slow driver."

As the helicopter ferrying Steve heads to the Lincoln Memorial, Carol Lawson catches up to Moshe on US 15 East in her van. She follows Moshe as Moshe follows the motor coach, each of them keeping Risa in their sights.

# CHAPTER SEVENTEEN

After their helicopter lands behind the Lincoln Memorial, Sam and Steve exit quickly and run toward the portable command center. The National Guard has cordoned off a section of D.C. east of the Washington Monument, west of the Potomac, north of the White House, and south of the Jefferson Memorial.

Sam and Steve enter the command center and join Colonel Johnson, General Sandberg from Mossad, and representatives from the D.C. police, the Arlington, Virginia, police, and Captain Juan Carlos of the National Guard. When Sam and Steve arrive, Colonel Johnson begins a briefing.

"Gentlemen, this is what we know. Risa Rashjani was working for Senator Lewis of Virginia, and is currently driving to D.C. in the Senator's motor coach, which is loaded with explosives. She is currently on Route 15 and is heading northeast to 29. She'll connect to 50, and will then probably come across the Theodore Roosevelt Bridge. We have to stop her on the bridge in order to avoid major collateral damage in the surrounding areas."

Sam DeVito adds, "I've directed the Arlington police to clear all the streets and highways that lead to the Theodore Roosevelt Bridge, as well as to the Arlington Memorial Bridge." He points to a large map on a table, as they all circle around it. He continues. "The National Guard, as well as the D.C. police, are covering the eastern area, within this section."

Captain Juan Carlos breaks in. "The National Guard has large trucks and armored vehicles. We can block the bridges on the east side as a last resort, if we can't stop the coach. She may blow the vehicle up, but we won't let her drive through to D.C. I also suggest that we get the Air Force involved and have them send an F-18. They can take out that bus in the middle of the bridge. Of course, they will also destroy the bridge."

Steve speaks up. "Gentlemen, Sam and I set up snipers on the east side of this area. One of them will be located on the roof of the Lincoln Memorial, and I chose to take up a position on Route 50, on the east side of the river. But I have just decided to alter that course of action. We need to try to disable the coach without blowing it up, in order to give Risa the opportunity to surrender. We cannot just take a kill shot. If Risa is wired to the explosives, a kill shot will have to disable the wiring and kill her at the same time. Trying to accomplish such a precise shot while compensating for deflection of the projectile as it passes through bulletproof glass will be almost impossible. We need snipers on the Memorial and also on Route 50 East and Route 50 West.

Pointing to the map, Steve says, "I'll take up a position on the roof of the Best Western Motel in Arlington. From there, I'll have a clear shot at the rear of the motor coach. A Barrett .50 caliber will penetrate an engine block, and the motor coach's engine is in the rear. By seizing up the motor, the coach will stop without detonating the explosives. It will then be up to our terrorist and the Air Force as to whether the explosion will actually be set off. But we need to be prepared in case the explosion does go off. The blast from that many explosives will create a concussion that will spread out for a half mile or so. We had better prepare the police and our teams. I suggest that we evacuate the Best Western, as most of their windows would probably blow out.

"Sam, I turn the floor over to you."

"Okay, look. This is all going down at or near 8:00 this morning. Captain, I need you to bring your armored vehicles in to block off Route 50. Colonel, I need to task you with getting an F-18 ready for air coverage. I will contact the Coast Guard and have them block off the river north and south of the bridge.

"But for all our plans to work, we need to make sure Risa chooses the right bridge to cross. Let's release a phony scenario to the media that shuts off southern access to the Arlington Memorial Bridge from Route 50; perhaps a major accident that forces Arlington police to close the access roads. Then, Risa will be forced to take the Theodore Roosevelt Bridge.

"Steve, the snipers are yours, one on the east side of 50, one on the roof of the Lincoln Memorial, and you on the roof of the Best Western. Captain, any chance you can get Steve some armor piercing rounds, just to make sure we stop that bus?"

"No problem, Sam. He gets whatever he needs."

"Good. Let's get to work. We have a lot to do and only a little over an hour to do it."

Diane has left Hollywood, and is on her way across the United States. Her flight is scheduled to arrive in Baltimore in less than two hours. When she flies first class, she is able to sleep more easily, so as she relaxes in her seat, she dreams of her house in Italy, with Steve at her side.

Moshe, Carol Lawson and Risa, are now approaching Catlett,

Virginia, and are heading toward Manassas. Moshe radios the unlikely trio's latest position to the command center, but when he glances down at the cruiser's gauges, he realizes that he's running out of gas and that he will need to break off soon from following Risa. He radios his situation to Carol Lawson, and she advises the command center that she will keep up the tail.

Moshe pulls off into a gas station as Carol drives by, flashing her headlights. But as soon as Moshe exits the car, he is swarmed by local police. They had been monitoring his radio frequency, waiting for a chance to apprehend him and place him under arrest for the assault of Officer Daniel Reilly and the murder of Rick Collins.

In the motor coach, Risa is unaware of the events swirling around her. She believes her mission will be fulfilled in a little over an hour. She laughs as she imagines the Lewis' reaction when they arrive home and see that their house is destroyed. As she drives, the lights of Manassas are coming closer, and so is her date with destiny.

# CHAPTER EIGHTEEN

Steve is busy setting up his Barrett .50 caliber rifle on the roof of the Best Western Hotel. The occupants of the hotel have been evacuated and moved to other local hotels, and the Arlington police are diverting as much traffic as possible from the southern approaches to Washington, D.C., trying not to draw too much attention to their actions.

Steve loads four armor piercing rounds into the rifle and takes sight at various vehicles that are crossing the Theodore Roosevelt Bridge, to help him hone in on his future target. Steve figures that two quick shots into the vehicle's engine block will seize the motor within seconds.

The snipers on the Lincoln Memorial and on the east end of the Theodore Roosevelt Bridge are also set up and ready, while the National Guard has pulled six Humvees and two Bradley troop transports onto to the overpass on the east side of the Potomac, ready to roll them into place to block any vehicles that attempt to enter the D.C. area. Colonel Johnson has arranged for an F-18 to be fueled and on standby at Andrews Air Force Base, ready to deploy, if needed. Arlington police are set, Washington police are set, and the Coast Guard is in place to stop boat traffic on the Potomac.

A few minutes earlier, Arlington police issued a fabricated report to the media of a major accident on Route

110. The report states that access to Arlington Memorial Bridge is currently blocked. The report was designed to require Risa to use the Theodore Roosevelt Bridge to cross the Potomac, the bridge they selected for their mission.

Steve looks at his watch. It's 7:35 a.m., and Risa should be arriving at his location within minutes. He settles himself down, and waits.

Carol Lawson reports that Risa is near Falls Church, Virginia, on Route 66, Custis Memorial Parkway, about eight miles away. Risa is currently unaware that anything is amiss, but in about ten minutes, all that will change.

Arlington police report in to the command center on Risa's location. They state that she is passing the bend on Route 66 and is heading south toward the Theodore Roosevelt Bridge. From his vantage point on the roof of the Best Western Inn, Steve listens to the police report on his head gear and looks north, spotting the motor coach as it approaches his location. Focusing on the task at hand, he doesn't notice that the early morning sun has just started to rise and that night is slowly changing into day. Steve watches his target as the motor coach moves south and turns onto the bridge. He notices a small car in front of the coach and hopes that the National Guard can work fast enough to close the bridge behind her, so no other cars will be around when he takes his shot.

As Risa makes the turn onto Route 66, the Annapolis police block any further traffic from entering the roadway. All surface streets are now blocked off, and so is boat traffic on the Potomac River. Steve takes aim as Risa starts crossing the bridge. He holds his breath and quickly gets off two shots that enter the rear of the coach and lodge deep inside the engine block. Risa feels the impacts when the motor coach jerks forward and the engine falters. Oil soon begins to spew out onto the road while the coach shudders and the engine seizes. The motor coach continues to creep forward slowly, until it comes to rest in the middle of the Theodore Roosevelt Bridge, over the western end of Theodore Roosevelt Island.

A quick call from Colonel Johnson causes the F-18 at Andrews Air Force Base to come alive and hit the skies. Steve lays low to watch as the drama plays out.

When the motor coach finally stops, Sam gets on a microphone attached to large speakers on the bridge, so he can speak to Risa.

"This is the FBI!" Sam knows that the FSA is a relatively unknown agency, so he draws on the formidable reputation of the Federal Bureau of Investigation, gambling that it will convince Risa to cooperate. "Risa Rashjani, we have disabled your motor coach, and we have blocked off the bridge. Your mission has been aborted. Please leave the coach and drop to the ground with your hands on your head. It's all over."

There is no response from Risa. The snipers on the Lincoln Memorial and at the east end of the Theodore Roosevelt Bridge have her targeted in their sights, and the National Guard has blocked off the bridge at the exit. Everyone sits and waits.

Risa realizes that her plan has been thwarted and that her intended target will not be hit. She slowly unplugs her headband from the cigarette lighter and disappears into the back of the coach. In anticipation of possible problems, she hooked up her Blackberry cell phone to the explosives as a backup detonator. Senator Lewis had given the phone to her to assist him in keeping appointments and to make it easier for her to be contacted by his office.

Risa removes the cell phone from a backpack and exits the coach. As she walks around the side of the vehicle, she raises her hands in triumph and shows off her cell phone.

Sam reacts immediately. "She's holding a phone! She'll set off the explosives! TAKE HER OUT NOW!"

The FBI sniper takes his shot, and his .308 round finds its mark dead center in Risa's forehead. Risa falls like a stone and drops the phone before she could place a call.

However, at that very moment, Senator Lewis' son, at Disneyworld with his mom, wants to call his nanny to tell her that he's about to have breakfast with Goofy. He uses his mom's cell phone to place a call to Lisa. When the Blackberry accepts the call, the coach suddenly erupts into a fireball, and vaporizes on the bridge.

On the roof of the Best Western Inn, Steve ducks quickly and waits for the concussion from the blast to blow over. Most of the windows on the floors below him blow out, and a forty-foot section of the Theodore Memorial Bridge shatters and falls onto the island beneath, and into the river. Car alarms in the neighboring areas erupt into an eerie song, and the explosion is heard over fifteen miles away, rattling windows in downtown D.C. and Arlington, Virginia. As Mike is getting dressed in Columbia, Maryland, he hears a low boom and looks out the bedroom window, but sees nothing.

From the bridge, a large mushroom shaped cloud rises skyward, as dust and debris fill the air, making the area appear much like lower Manhattan during the World Trade Center disaster. When the dust clears, the damage to the Theodore Roosevelt Bridge can be clearly seen, revealing a gaping hole in the middle of the span.

Sam takes immediate inventory, checking in with all of his men. There are no casualties or injuries.

Steve calls in to get a report.

"How's everyone down there?"

"We're all fine. How about you?"

"I'm aces. Can't say that for the bridge, though. That's gonna' fuck up traffic for a while."

Suddenly, the F-18 flies overhead, heading back to

Andrews Air Force Base after its mission is called off. Steve picks up his gear and makes his way down from the roof of the hotel to the lobby, where there is broken glass everywhere. He exits the hotel and calls Sam from his head gear.

"Sam, I'm gonna' need a ride."

"Stay at the hotel. I'll get Carol Lawson to pick you up, and we'll meet at the Lincoln Memorial."

Sam contacts Colonel Johnson. "Colonel, I'm tasking you to contact Senator Lewis on his trip to Europe and also the Senator's wife at Disney World, to give them the bad news about their house and their nanny/personal assistant."

The Colonel replies, "The White House is handling that through the Secret Service. Sam, Al Jazeera just ran a statement from al-Qaida. They're taking responsibility for this bombing."

"I guess this is all over the TV stations."

"Yeah, the hound dogs are on the loose."

Steve is standing in front of the Best Western Hotel, shouldering his 50 caliber rifle, when a white van pulls up and Carol Lawson beckons from the window.

"Steve! Hop in back. We'll go over to the Lincoln Memorial for debriefing."

Steve slides the side door open, climbs in the van, and slides the door shut.

"Man, that was some eruption! My ears are still ringing."

"Yeah, we did good. I don't think anyone was injured."

As Carol drives south to the Arlington Bridge, and over to the Lincoln Memorial, the local police are diverting traffic and preparing for a horrendous morning commute into D.C.

When they reach the mobile command center behind the Lincoln Memorial, local and national TV crews arrive with their remote satellite units. As they walk inside the command center, Steve mumbles, "Why couldn't they keep the TV guys away for a while?"

Inside the command center Sam DeVito, Captain Juan Carlos, and representatives from the Arlington and Washington police are already assembled. Steve glances at his watch. It's almost 9:00 a.m. and Diane will be landing at BWI within minutes.

Sam begins the debriefing.

"Okay! My thanks to Carol, from the FBI, for keeping us posted on all developments as our mission unfolded. General Sandberg and his team are currently headed to Virginia to pick up Moshe Saban, their rogue Mossad agent, from the Manassas jail. Colonel Johnson is on his way to the White House to brief the President, and from what I hear, the President himself has chosen to inform Senator Lewis and his family about today's events. Reports are still coming in, but so far, there have been no major injuries from the explosion. Some of our personnel have suffered cuts and ruptured eardrums, and they have been treated on scene. Except for the bridge, there was no major structural damage. Most of the windows on the east side of the Best Western Hotel were blown out, but the building itself is not damaged.

"Steve, good job stopping the bus! Carol, props to your sniper, the one who put Risa down. We located what we think is the cell phone she was holding, and it doesn't appear that a call was made from it. We are currently checking out the phone to try to get information about the explosion. Just to let you know, al-Qaida has already taken responsibility for this incident, and with the information we have about Iran, things are going to get interesting. The TV hounds are out, and I'll give them a statement soon. They'll also be asking about the morning commute, but that problem will be handled by the Arlington and D.C. authorities."

After Sam concludes his briefing, Steve pulls him aside. "Sam, I need a favor. My wife is landing at BWI, probably at this moment. Can I get a fast ride to Baltimore?"

Diane's red eye flight has already pulled into the terminal gate. When they landed, she tried calling Steve on his cell phone, but there was no answer. She deplanes and follows the crowd to the luggage carousel to retrieve her belongings. As she heads down the escalator to the baggage area, she sees Mike waiting for her. When she waves, he rushes over to meet her and gives her a big, welcoming hug.

"Welcome to Baltimore, and congratulations on your Oscar!"

"Oh, thank you, Michael! But where's your father?"

"Dad was whisked away this morning by helicopter, right from my front lawn. Al-Qaida attacked D.C. this morning. They blew up the Theodore Roosevelt Bridge, which crosses the Potomac from Arlington, Virginia. I heard the explosion from my house this morning, just before I left to pick you up. I haven't heard from Dad yet."

"Oh, no! I tried calling him after I landed, but there was no answer. Is everything okay?"

"I'm sure he's alright. He'll probably call you at any moment."

The helicopter that Steve arrived in earlier is still on the lawn behind the Lincoln Memorial. He re-boards it, and the chopper starts up. Within minutes, he is airborne and heading toward Baltimore. He takes out his cell phone to place a quick call.

Diane's phone rings as she and Mike are exiting the baggage area.

"Steve! Where are you? Are you okay?"

"Hi, Di. Welcome to Baltimore! I'm on my way to the airport, and I should be there in a few minutes. Listen, you'll be paged by Homeland Security. They'll give Mike a police escort to the tarmac, where my helicopter will land. I'll explain everything in about ten minutes. I love you."

When Diane hangs up, an announcement comes over the PA system at the airport. "Attention! Will Michael Ciccone please report to the police service center located on the lower level, near luggage carousel thirteen. Attention! Will Michael Ciccone please report to the police service center located on the lower level, near luggage carousel thirteen."

"Mike! Steve just said that you would be paged!"

Puzzled, Mike and Diane make their way to the Baltimore Police service center inside the terminal.

"I'm Mike Ciccone. You just paged me." An officer looks up from his desk.

"Can I see some ID, please?"

Mike takes out his wallet and shows his driver's license to the slightly overweight officer. The officer stares at it, and then looks back at Mike.

"Where are you parked?"

"Well, I'm here to pick up my stepmom. I'm on the third level, in hourly parking."

"Go to the parking garage and wait at the elevator on the third level. A police cruiser will pull up and escort you to where you need to go."

Bewildered, Mike and Diane glance at each other, but follow the officer's directions. They leave the terminal and walk to the hourly garage where Mike parked his car, taking the elevator to the third level. A few minutes after they arrive at the elevator, a police cruiser pulls up and the officer behind the wheel opens his window.

"Mike Ciccone?"

"Yes, Sir."

"Your car nearby?"

"Third car down that aisle." Mike points to his car.

"I'll wait here. Get your car, then follow me."

Still not knowing what's happening, Mike and Diane rush to his car and quickly load Diane's luggage into the trunk. Mike pulls carefully out of the parking slot and drives his car over to the police cruiser. When the officer sees Mike behind him, he drives toward the garage's exit, not stopping at the pay booth. After the cruiser leaves the airport area, its lights begin flashing and Mike concentrates on following the officer as he zigzags out onto Aviation Boulevard and around to Stony Road. The police car stops at an open grassy area, and the officer gets out and approaches Mike's car. Mike opens his driver's side window.

"Wait here. Steve will arrive shortly."

The officer returns to his car, and uses it to block off approaching traffic on the roadway. Within minutes, a Black Hawk helicopter swoops in and lands in the middle of the open area. Steve quickly exits the chopper, and as soon as he clears the rotors, the Black Hawk rises and heads back to Washington, D.C. Diane smiles at the sight of her husband and runs from the car to meet Steve halfway. When they reach each other, they embrace in a passionate kiss.

Taking a breath, Diane says, "Another flashy entrance, huh?"

"You know me! Now, let's restart my retirement, and go see your new grandkids!"

# EPILOGUE

Chaos is what a terrorist organization breeds, and they do not need to kill a large amount of people to achieve their goal. They only need to cause as much disruption and fear as possible, believing that "death by little cuts" will cause a slow hemorrhage of will and stamina for the enemies of Allah.

The United States must be successful one hundred percent of the time in stopping all acts of terror and violence, but terrorists need to be successful only once. They wait patiently in the shadows for the time to come when they can sing the praises of their accomplishments to Allah.

Although a bridge was destroyed in Washington, D.C., Al-Qaida is not satisfied with this triumph. They have ordered more sleeper cells into the United States, and they have renewed their ties with Iran to ensure its continued cooperation in their Jihad against the West.

May God bless us, and may He bless the United States of America. We need all the blessings we can get.

Book Three
# Trihedral of Chaos
Trilogy

# Yellowcake

by Frank A. Ruffolo

# PROLOGUE

**February 2008, Tuwaitha, Iraq**

The United States and Canada have reached a deal to remove a stockpile of concentrated uranium ore from Iraq. The uranium had been destined to be used in Saddam Hussein's nuclear program, and consists of 550 metric tons of yellowcake, the base ingredient for higher grade fuel enrichment. The material has been stored for years in fifty-five gallon steel drums, which are now corroded. The ore needs to be repackaged into shippable containers and airlifted from Bagdad to begin a two-ocean voyage to Montreal, where it will be processed into fuel for nuclear reactors.

The uranium ore is called yellowcake, because its color and consistency resembles that common dessert. Army Major Kevin Wilkens has been tasked with repackaging the material into approximately 3,500 secure barrels. The U.S. Army will supervise a select group of Iraqi nationals, who will perform the manual labor of filling and securing the barrels.

By itself, yellowcake is not highly radioactive, but safety precautions must still be taken to avoid inhaling any dust particles that may arise during the repackaging process. The stockpile is located in Tuwaitha, Iraq, and must be trucked to Bagdad International Airport, then airlifted to the island of Diego Garcia. That small British-held island in the Indian

Ocean is home to a U.S. military base, where the uranium will be transferred to an ocean freighter, then transported to Montreal.

Despite all precautions, al-Qaida operatives have successfully infiltrated the Iranian work crew that has been tasked with the repackaging process. As the operation gets underway, the old and corroded fifty-five gallon steel drums of yellowcake are being repackaged into Teflon-lined, stainless steel barrels, to avoid future corrosion.

The al-Qaida terrorist organization has devised a plan to intercept several of these barrels and to resell them to countries like North Korea and Iran, for use in their uranium enrichment programs, or to be used as a component in the manufacture of dirty bombs.

During the final days of cleanup and recovery of the corroded barrels, an official count of 3,505 barrels was issued by the work crew, but the actual count was 3,510 barrels, a difference of five barrels, weighing approximately 340 pounds each.

When the truck convoy carrying the last 300 barrels of yellowcake was halfway between Tuwaitha and Bagdad International Airport, it fell victim to several roadside I.E.D.'s, the improvised explosive devices favored by Iraqi insurgents. Two trucks in the convoy flipped over, scattering their cargo of stainless steel barrels of yellowcake across the desert road. Due to the chaos that ensued, insurgents were able to capture and steal two of the barrels.

This incident was not publicized, and since the total number of barrels loaded onto the cargo plane was more than was reported on the original paperwork, the United States government decided not to admit to a security breach surrounding their transfer of uranium ore out of Iraq.

Two barrels of yellowcake do not contain enough raw uranium for the refinement process involved in fuel enrichment, so al-Qaida destined them for use in the manufacture of dirty bombs targeted at the West. They were eventually able to smuggle the barrels out of Iraq through Syria, but due to continued wars in Iraq, Afghanistan, and Pakistan, and the death and capture of most of their top officials, the al-Qaida organization was put into temporary disarray. They put their plan for the manufacture of dirty bombs on hold, and in December of 2008, they buried the two barrels of yellowcake in the desert just outside the city of Al Annazah, Syria They remained undisturbed under the desert sands until November of 2011.

When al-Qaida was ready, the recovered barrels were relabeled as flour and transported to Syria's Port Baniyas on the Mediterranean coast, then shipped via freighter across the Atlantic Ocean and up the Saint Lawrence Seaway to Montreal, Canada. Ironically, the two stolen barrels of yellowcake were sent to the same place the original shipment had been sent to three years earlier.

Al-Qaida chose to ship the yellowcake to Montreal because of the city's lax security and its proximity to miles and miles of unguarded borders with the United States. The terrorist organization was able to easily smuggle the yellowcake across the U.S.-Canadian border, and it has been stored for some time in an old watermill west of Mooers Forks, New York, on the Great Chazy River. There, a sleeper terrorist cell has been lying patiently for their time to act, which is now.

# CHAPTER ONE

Just before sunrise, Steve Ciccone is standing on the balcony of his condo overlooking the Atlantic Ocean in downtown Fort Lauderdale. Steve and his wife, Diane, are back in Florida after spending some time at their villa on Italy's Amalfi Coast. They are in town to visit family for the holidays, after Steve recently retired from the FSA, the Federal Security Agency, for the second time. The FSA was established by President Baruch, and is the connection a liaison between federal government and local law enforcement agencies in times of emergency. The President set this agency up as a non-military security force, because it is illegal to deploy U.S. military troops within the borders of the U.S. This arrangement makes everything "legal."

Diane brings a cup of coffee out onto the balcony for Steve and settles into a deck chair to watch the sun paint the sky orange, yellow and red as it rises up out of the ocean. It's a warm morning for early December, about seventy-five degrees. A cold front is due to bring rain later in the day, and by the next morning, temperatures are forecast to be in the forties, downright chilly for southern Florida.

After finishing their coffee, the couple goes inside the condo to get ready to meet John, Carla and Jenna, Steve's son, daughter-in-law and granddaughter, for breakfast. They spent the Thanksgiving holiday with John's family in Fort

Lauderdale, and are planning to spend Christmas with Steve's other son, Mike and his family, at their home in Maryland.

Diane is Steve's second wife, the world famous Academy Award winning actress, Diane Summers, who retired from the Hollywood hoopla to live out the rest of her life with her true love in Southern Italy. With no family of her own, Diane was welcomed into the Ciccone clan and has become a beloved wife, stepmom, and grandma.

While Steve dresses in the bedroom, Diane calls out from the shower, "Steve, would you like to give me a hand washing my back?"

"You bet! But then, I guess we'll be late for breakfast."


Frank "Angie" Angelo, and George "Geo" Jackson, moved to Florida with Steve when each of them semi-retired from the NYPD. They still find time to hang out together and hope to remain best friends for life. When the three of them get together, they still call each other by their nicknames, referring to Steve as "Chic."

George took Steve's place as head of the FSA office in Fort Lauderdale after the incident with the *Crescent Star* at Port Everglades, and Frank owns a bar and grill in South Florida called Duke's Saloon, which is filled with memorabilia about the late, great actor, John Wayne.

Whenever Steve returns to Florida, the trio gets together as much as possible to catch up and reminisce about past adventures. This Saturday, Frank has planned a trip with Steve to Eglin Air Force Base in northeastern Florida, where the two of them can keep their sniper instincts and skills current. This outing to Eglin was part of their monthly routine, until Steve and Diane moved to Italy. The duo hasn't had their "man day" in over a year.

On Sunday, Frank has also prepared a gathering at his

saloon for Steve and Diane, and John and his family. George will be there with his girlfriend, and he has invited several employees of the FSA who worked with Steve on their last operation. It's been awhile since the group has been together, and Frank anticipates that the party should be a blast.

John picks up the phone to call his dad. The phone rings a few times before Steve answers.

"It's me. Start talkin'."

"Dad, what's up? Everything okay? You're almost an hour late."

"Yeah, well, we're just heading out the door. We should be there in twenty minutes or so. I guess I took too long in the shower."

Wincing, John says, "Spare me the details, Dad. I can just imagine!"

# CHAPTER TWO

Twin brothers Tom and James Moon grew up in the Plattsburgh, Albany, area of northern New York State, in a dysfunctional and abusive family headed by an alcoholic father. In a drunken rage, their father murdered his wife, then killed himself in front of the two teenage boys. Because they were both eighteen at the time, and of legal age, state and local authorities had no jurisdiction over their lives, and after the tragedy, they were both left to their own devices.

An insurance policy their mother had owned gave them enough money for a college education and rooms on campus at the State University at Albany. While taking a religious studies course at the university, the twins developed an interest in the Quran, and soon converted to the Muslim religion. On a pilgrimage to Saudi Arabia, they joined a Muslim extremist group that was linked to al-Qaida. Wanting to take advantage of the Americans in their midst, the group sent them to Yemen for terrorist training, and then directed them to return to the United States to establish themselves as a terrorist cell and to wait for future instructions from al-Qaida on how to assist them in retaliating for the killing of Usama Bin Laden.

The twins were eager to fulfill the role that al-Qaida assigned to them. They settled in Mooers Forks, New York, a few miles south of the Canadian border. Because Canada's security procedures aren't as stringent as those in the United States, terrorist groups find it much easier to enter the U.S. through the Canadian border, so the small town of Mooers Forks is perfect for al-Qaida's plans. In that area of New York, only the main highways contain protected border crossings, while the remainder of the border between the U.S. and Canada is unmonitored and unprotected. The town is also just a few miles from the Adirondack Northway, the main north-south route through New York State's Adirondack Mountains, and the northern part of the highway system that connects Montreal to New York City.

When Tom and James Moon arrived in Mooers Forks, they purchased an old grist mill and watermill on the Great Chazy River, then slowly renovated them. In the summer months, they offer inner tube rides on the river, with the watermill as the main attraction, and the grist mill housing an antique shop that keeps income coming in during the rest of the year.

Over a number of years, al-Qaida has sent several suicide bombers to the Moon brothers for deployment as terror cells across the United States. The latest recruits arrived with two barrels of yellowcake and instructions to start their Jihad against the West this winter. They need the Moon brothers' grist mill to grind the yellowcake into a fine powder for easier disbursement when they eventually explode it in their dirty bomb. These new suicide bombers were recruited from Yemen and Saudi Arabia, and have been working at the Moon brothers' grist mill, assisting inner tube rafters down the Great Chazy River.

Al-Qaida selected Grand Central Terminal in downtown Manhattan, commonly known as Grand Central Station, to be the recruits' first target in the use of the stolen yellowcake. If that attack is successful, the Moon brothers have been directed to use the yellowcake in further attacks across the United States and Canada.

Tom Moon is carefully preparing a piece of carry-on luggage for Josef Malik, the twenty-year-old recruit from Saudi Arabia. He lines the luggage with lead foil to mask any radiation that may leak from the yellowcake and set off the detectors that are deployed in all public places. He packs the luggage with several plastic containers that are filled with forty pounds of finely milled yellowcake. He adds one pound of plastic explosives, which the brothers acquired through black-market contacts and midnight purchases over the years, along with a detonation device that can be activated from outside the luggage by a trigger near the handle. The carry-on luggage is destined to become a dirty bomb, and is designed to disperse the radioactive yellowcake powder throughout a large area. Al-Qaida expects that the ensuing panic and cleanup will cost hundreds of thousands of dollars over a period of many, many months, carrying out their plan of "death by little cuts."

After the carry-on is packed and ready, Tom drives Josef to the nearby town of Plattsburgh, where the recruit will take a morning train to Schenectady, then transfer to Albany, the state's capitol. He will stay overnight in Albany at a small motel, then take the first morning train to Manhattan, his ultimate destination. If all goes well, Josef will be at Grand Central Station in New York City at the height of rush hour on Monday morning.

# CHAPTER THREE

Steve pulls his 'Vette into John's driveway in Plantation, a suburb of Fort Lauderdale. He crawls out of the car and walks around the vehicle to help Diane up and out.

"You know," Diane says, "as we get older, it's going to get harder and harder to climb out of this thing."

Steve puts his arm around Diane's waist, then lowers his hand and squeezes her ass. "But then, you don't feel like you're getting old."

When the doorbell rings, John looks out his living room window and sees the 'Vette in his driveway.

"It's Grandpa and Grandma! Jenna, go open the door."

Jenna opens the front door quickly, then runs outside to give Diane a hug around her legs. Steve picks Jenna up and gives her a hug and kiss as they walk into the house together.

"I smell bacon! Where's that lovely mom of yours?"

"Right here, Dad. Come and sit. We have some good news to tell you."

The group follows Carla into the kitchen, where everyone seats themselves around the large breakfast table. John brings a pot of coffee and joins them at the head of the table. After taking a deep breath, he says, "We wanted to say something on Thanksgiving Day, but we weren't quite sure. Carla went to the doctor yesterday, and we're pregnant!"

Amid shouts of joy, Steve stands up and hugs his son, while Diane gives Carla a kiss.

"Congratulations, guys! When's the date?"

"The doctor thinks it's June fourteenth."

"Do Mike and Jeannie know yet?"

"No, we thought we'd call them tonight, after Mike gets home from work."

Diane touches Steve's arm to get his attention. "Steve, since it's too early in the day to toast their good news, why don't we take them out for dinner tonight? We can call Mike and Jeannie before we go."

Turning to John and Carla, Steve inquires, "Okay with you guys?"

After receiving nods of agreement, he continues, "Good! Now, where's my pancakes?"


Claude Killeen, a French national al-Qaida recruited from a Muslim ghetto in Paris, has just arrived at Montreal's international airport. He walks outside the terminal and searches for a taxi stand where he can arrange for transportation across the U.S.-Canadian border to Mooers Forks.

Claude's appearance makes him the perfect terrorist. Rather than being a typical-looking terrorist with dark Middle Eastern features, he's a white male of French and Spanish descent, with light brown hair. His appearance makes it impossible to racially profile him and allows him to blend in easily among the masses, proving the perfect cover for a suicide bomber.


Josef Malik has checked into a "no-tell" motel in the city of Schenectady in upstate New York State. Since he is carrying no change of clothes in his luggage, he washes his underwear and socks while he takes a shower, hanging them on the shower rod to dry. He wraps a towel around his waist and steps out of the bathroom to recite his evening prayers before retiring for the night.

The train that Joseph plans to take to New York City will leave very early in the morning, arriving at Penn Station about 7:00 a.m. The early arrival in Manhattan will give Josef enough time to get from Penn Station to Grand Central Station, where he intends to cause as much havoc as possible to the city's commuters.

# CHAPTER FOUR

After driving all night, Chic and Angie finally arrive at Eglin Air Force Base's sniper range at eight in the morning. They are waived through the front gate with special permission from the FSA and Homeland Security.

While Angie walks 1000 meters down range to set up the first targets, Chic takes his Barrett .50 cal. sniper rifle out of the back of the SUV and sets it up for firing. On his way back to the shooting area, Angie checks wind speed and direction, and calls out to Chic, "Little or no wind at all! If it comes, it'll be at our backs. You think you can still do this, old man?"

"Yeah, we're getting kinda' old for this shit! My eyes are still good, though. It'll be no sweat, just like riding a bike. Once you know how, you never forget!"

"Yeah, but now you need one of those three wheelers, the ones with a basket in the front!"

Angie laughs at his own joke as Chic flashes him the Florida state bird. Still smiling at Chic, Angie drops to the ground to spot Chic's shots. Chic checks for wind, but notes that the air is now very still. He sights his target, loads a round into the chamber, then peers into the Leupold sight and squeezes the trigger. Like a dormant volcano roaring to life, the .50 cal. belches fire and sends her projectile toward the target down range.

Taking a look through his own scope, Angie turns to Chic and exclaims, "Damn! Dead center!"

Chic switches his rifle to semi-automatic mode and loads a clip of five rounds. Then he sights his target and gets off five quick explosions of belching fire.

After checking Chic's results, Angie removes his earplugs and pats Chic on the head.

"They're all grouped within eight inches of each other! I don't want you staring at me down the barrel of that thing! Hey, Chic, since we're such good friends, how about I take a couple of shots with that monster?"

Chic loads another clip and changes places with Angie. Deep down, they both know they probably won't be doing this for much longer. Angie takes a few shots with the .50 cal. and hits his target once or twice, which makes his day.

After a few more turns with the .50 cal., they walk down range to pick up their targets, then return to the shooting area to pack up.

As they're reloading their gear into the back of the SUV, they notice a Humvee coming toward them in the parking area. When the vehicle comes to a sliding stop near them, a young Corporal climbs out of the driver's side.

"Mr. Angelo and Mr. Ciccone?"

Glancing at the young soldier, Angie whispers to Chic, "Five bucks says he doesn't even shave."

Chic closes the back door of the SUV and turns to the Corporal.

"You found us. What can we do for you?"

"Mr. George Jackson of the FSA in Fort Lauderdale called us. He wants the both of you to follow me, please."

Angie turns to Chic. "If Geo's involved, we're in for it. But I guess we should follow this kid. He's so damn young, that I'm afraid if we say no, he might start to cry."

Chic turns around so the kid doesn't see him laugh, then Angie calls out, "No problem, Son. Lead the way."

Angie follows the Humvee out of the range area, and toward the tarmac of the base's main runway. When the Humvee pulls up in front of a large hanger, Angie pulls his SUV alongside it. The young Corporal tells them to wait as he runs inside the hanger. Within a couple of minutes, two Navy pilots emerge from the building and approach the SUV. From their uniforms, Chic and Angie immediately recognize them as members of the Navy's Blue Angel Squadron.

"Hello, Gentlemen. My name is Captain Joe Harmin, and this is Captain Kevin Walsh. As you may know, Eglin is home base to the Navy's Blue Angels. We're about to go up and practice. Would you like to join us?"

Angie and Chic gasp in unison. Then, Chic blurts out, "That son of a bitch! Captains, it would be our honor!"

Smiling broadly, the Captain replies, "Great! Follow us. But remember, if you throw up in our planes, you clean it up."

The pilots direct Angie to park his SUV nearby, then they usher the two friends into the hangar to be fitted with flight suits.

Their "man day" is turning out to be a day they will never forget.

# CHAPTER FIVE

Tom and James Moon open the Old Great Chazy River Mill early today. They recently decided to add a coffee shop to the grist mill, which they decorated with items and furniture from their antique shop, to increase their income over the winter months. Their justification for the addition to their business was their belief that the more income they could bring in, the easier it would be for them to complete their task of terrorizing the countryside.

As a result of an ad in the local newspaper, a small group of people has gathered outside the coffee shop to wait for the doors to open. The shop is quaint, with antiques on the wall, a small pot belly stove in the center the room, and living room-style furniture for the customers to relax in. Along with coffee, the shop offers pastries and gourmet cookies.

While Tom opens the door and greets the morning guests, James prepares to take their orders.

"Good morning, and thank you for coming in today! My, you guys are out early! My name is Tom, and my brother, James, will be happy to take your orders."

"Mornin' Tom. We came out early to beat the snow."

As the guests file in and sit down, James grabs his order pad and walks around to each seating area. The phone rings as Tom walks behind counter to check on their supplies, and he promptly answers it.

"Good morning, Old Great Chazy River Mill! How can I help you?"

On the other end of the line, Claude Killeen replies, "The Falcon is pleased to send me into your service. My name is Claude Killeen. I am at the bus depot in Plattsburgh, and I was told that you could pick me up."

"Well, good morning, Sir. Yes, we are open today, and yes, we can do that for you."

"Good. I am wearing a red beret. I will be sitting inside the building, facing the entrance."

"No problem. We'll see you in about an hour."

Tom hangs up the phone and gives James a quick nod. As soon as each of them can break away from their duties, they make their way to the rear mill room. When they are alone, Tom tells James about the phone call from the new recruit, and lets him know that he will be leaving the coffee shop in about thirty minutes to pick him up.

Before turning back to their customers, Tom asks Omar Saleem, one of their current recruits, to help James in the dining area while he drives to Plattsburgh.


On the tarmac at Eglin Air Force Base, a ground crewman straps Angie into the number three F-18 belonging to the Blue Angels, as Chic is strapped into the number four. Each of them is handed a sick bag as they are briefed on the emergency procedures.

"Okay, Mr. Ciccone. The life vest you're wearing will automatically inflate upon entering the water, in case we have a water-bound incident. If there is a catastrophic mechanical failure, Captain Harmin will inform you that you will be ejecting from the aircraft. That black and yellow striped handle near your left leg will ignite the ejection rockets under your seat. After Captain Harmin blows off the canopy, you need to tuck your chin into your chest and pull that handle toward you, then quickly cross your arms in front of your chest. Your seat will immediately eject and the parachute will automatically deploy. Don't worry, though. No catastrophic incident has ever occurred during these demonstration flights. Do you have any questions?" Before Chic can respond, the crewman continues. "Oh, just one more thing. If you think you're going to be sick, you need to remove your air mask and make good use of the bag provided. If you don't, you'll be breathing your own vomit, and let me tell you, cleaning out that mask is a chore you really don't want to undertake. Now, do you have any questions?"

"No, you covered it all."

"Good luck, Mr. Ciccone."

Chic looks over at the other F-18, sees Angie, and gives him a thumbs up. Angie returns the gesture as the canopies close and the F-18's roar to life. In unison, the ground crewmen for both jets step away from the F-18's and give the traditional salute to the pilots and passengers as the jets slowly taxi toward the runway.

At the end of the runway, the F-18's pause side by side to wait for permission to take off. Suddenly, and with precise timing, both pilots bring their war birds to life. With full throttles and afterburners blazing, the F-18's, with Harmin, Walsh, Chic, and Angie on board, are airborne within nine seconds.

Pulling their sticks toward them, the pilots shoot nearly straight up, leaving Chic's and Angie's stomachs on the tarmac. Thirty seconds later, they are at 23,000 feet. After one minute of flight time, Angie looks out over the Gulf of Mexico, and within another couple of seconds, stares at the horizon, barely making out the curvature of the earth before his jet makes a barrel roll and descends almost straight down. Within a few more seconds, the F-18 pulls hard to the right, and Angie blanks out from g-forces that approach 9 g's. At the same moment, Chic's ride pulls to the left, with the same results for Chic.

After their brief "sleep," Chic and Angie are informed by their pilots that each F-18 will be playing chicken with the other. At a closing rate of five hundred miles per hour, the pilots fly their planes directly toward each other, and at the last possible moment, flip their birds onto their wings and scream past the other F-18, not more than four feet apart.

After another barrel roll and then a slow bank downward, the F-18's head back to Eglin. Each flight lasted only a few minutes.

With similar conversations going on in both planes, Captain Harmin asks Chic, "So, Mr. Ciccone, how are you doing back there? You didn't throw up in my plane, did you?"

"My God! You guys get paid to do this?"

"Yeah, not bad, huh?"

The jets land together and taxi back to their hanger areas as the ground crewmen run out to help Chic and Angie deplane.


Over one thousand miles away, while Chic and Angie are giving each other high fives and man hugs, Claude Killeen enters Old Great Chazy River Mill in Mooers Forks, New York, and introduces himself to Tom's brother, James, and to Omar Saleem. After brief introductions, Tom escorts Claude into the rear mill room, while James continues to take breakfast orders, and Omar seat guests and buses tables.

"Claude, as a new recruit, you need to quickly familiarize yourself with how the bomb is created. The process is started in the mill, where we pulverize the uranium yellowcake for easier dispersal. The material is radioactive, but it's not dangerous unless it's ingested or inhaled. You must wear protective clothing during the production phase in order to prevent the uranium dust from accumulating in your lungs. The bomb has been designed to produce terror and chaos in the population, rather than actual physical damage. Remember, we're here to create havoc, we're here to create disorder, we're here to kill by little cuts.

"Now, I will give you your final mission. You are fortunate to have been chosen by al-Qaida to detonate a radioactive device in Miami, Florida, during the city's New Year's celebrations at midnight on New Year's Eve. May Allah go with you.

"Until your date with destiny, you will work here in the coffee shop as a waiter. Let me introduce you now to the rest of my team, and then you can get some breakfast. But first, join me in morning prayers."

After thanking the Blue Angels pilots and their crews for a fantastic experience, Chic and Angie climb back into their SUV and head south. Under normal driving conditions, the drive from Eglin Air Force Base to Duke's Saloon takes about ten hours, so they will need to lead foot it back to Angie's saloon to arrive in time for the party at 7:00 that evening. However, Chic decides to make use of some of the capabilities of the FSA's black SUV that he cajoled George into lending to him for this morning's target practice. As he pulls onto I-10 and heads toward the Florida Turnpike, he turns on the flashing blue lights, and grins at Angie. The SUV is no Corvette, but it will still haul ass.

"Pull your belts tight. Them NASCAR boys ain't got nothin' on me!"

With a low growl, the SUV hits triple digits.

"Jeez, Chic! You don't drive fast, you fly low!"

"Just like them Blue Angels, Angie, just like them Blue Angels!"

# CHAPTER SIX

John, Carla, Jenna, and Diane sit at a table together at Duke's Saloon, waiting for Frank and Steve to return from their "man day" at Eglin. The third member of their group, George Jackson, helps Frank at the bar on weekends, and has arranged this dinner party for his two buddies.

"Hope they left early enough, it's a ten hour ride. Those two have been up all night. They're not as young as they think they are."

"Well, George, yesterday we had an early bird dinner with John, Carla, and Jenna. Steve went to bed as soon as we got home, but I think he only got about three hour's sleep before Frank picked him up really early this morning. But he did take a nap before dinner yesterday afternoon. I hope Frank did the same."

At that, the door opens, and Frank and Steve walk in. They immediately look for George, and in unison, both call out, "You son of a bitch!"

They rush over to their friend and take turns giving him man hugs. When they turn to greet everyone at the table, John notices the blue caps on their heads.

"Hey, Dad! Why are you two wearing Blue Angel's caps?"

Frank leaves the group to head for the kitchen, while

Steve beams and replies, "Why don't you ask Geo? I have to see a man about a horse."

All eyes turn expectantly to Geo, as he takes an empty seat at the table.

"Okay, okay! Chic and Angie have been going up to Eglin Air Force Base for their man outings for years now, and I know that weekend together will probably become less and less frequent as we all get a little older, so I pulled some strings. I called my boss, Colonel Johnson, who is also chief of the FSA, and got them a ride with the Blue Angels. They're based at Eglin."

Everyone at the table is speechless as they turn to look at each other. Then Diane exclaims, "My God, that was perfect! Steve must have been in heaven!" Leaning over, she gives Geo a thank you kiss.

When Chic returns to the table, John quickly asks, "So, Dad, did you pass out?"

Chic shakes his head no and sits down. "I thought I was in pretty good shape, but those pilots are aces in my book. Yeah, 9 g's and blackout city. At least I didn't throw up. We took off, and in less than a minute, we were at over 50,000 feet. Geo, there are no words that can express what we experienced. You're the best!"

At 2:30 in the morning in Kandahar, Afghanistan, U.S. Marines and NATO forces are attacking a Taliban and al-Qaida convoy fifteen miles north of the city. After a brief fire fight, they take several prisoners, one of whom is a Taliban soldier named Aziz Zarqawi Aziz. Aziz became commander of al-Qaida after Usama Bin Laden was killed by Team 6 Navy SEALs in a covert operation directed by the CIA. When the troops recognize Aziz, they immediately separate him from the other prisoners and take him to a secure location.

There, he is bound and gagged, and a sack is placed over his head. After a quick discussion with headquarters, Aziz Zarqawi Aziz is rushed via Humvee to NATO headquarters in Kandahar.

Military leaders know that they cannot legally interrogate a prisoner with extreme measures in order to retrieve information that could be world changing, therefore, Aziz is quickly and quietly whisked to a covert interrogation facility on the island of Cyprus, far away from public scrutiny. There, various questioning techniques will be used to acquire any and all possible information.

Good for us, bad for Aziz.

John Ciccone stands at the table in Duke's Saloon and raises his glass.

"A toast to my Dad and his two partners in mayhem, who have been like uncles to Mike and me over the years. Angie, thanks for this dinner, you're the best! Geo, you and Angie have always been there for us and Dad. You're like brothers to him." Turning to Diane, he continues, "And let's not forget Diane. What can I say? We love ya!" Extending his glass to Steve, he concludes, "Enjoy your retirement, Dad, and try to stay retired this time! Let's face it, you're getting a little old for all that hoopla!"

Steve looks over at his wife, Diane, and gives her a wink. "You're only as old as how, or who, you feel!" Everyone laughs and raises their glasses to end the toast.

Over 1,800 miles away, Josef Malik says his nightly prayers at a flea bag hotel in Albany, New York, as he prepares for what he believes will be his morning meeting with Allah in paradise.

# CHAPTER SEVEN

Even though the party ended late the night before, Diane and Steve wake up early to take a walk on the beach before sunrise so they can get a view of the sun rising out of the Atlantic Ocean like a phoenix. The weather is typical for December, about sixty degrees, and not a cloud in the sky. It's still twilight as they stop along the shoreline and wait for the sky to present them with yellows, oranges and blues, as it creeps over the horizon.

After witnessing a spectacular sunrise, the couple walks off the beach and crosses over A1A. They are headed for an Italian bakery that is located just before the bridge over the Intracoastal Waterway.

After receiving their orders, they grab a small table on the outside deck to enjoy their cappuccinos and sfogliatelle, before walking back to their condo.

Geo steps out of the shower and dries himself off. He dresses quietly in order not to wake his sleeping girlfriend, then heads off to work. He likes to get an early start on weekday mornings, usually stopping at IHOP for breakfast before arriving at the office.

He notes that it's been relatively quiet in South Florida lately. Except for going through a hurricane, he hasn't had to deal with any major events since the *Crescent Star* incident at Port Everglades. He did play a minor role in ending the recent threat to the National Archives, but that merely involved passing along some information to the FSA office in Virginia.

He doesn't realize that his job is about to get very interesting.


Josef Malik is now on his way to New York City, with his carry-on luggage close by his side. His train is scheduled to arrive at Penn Station soon. With luck, he will be with Allah within the hour, and New York City will be in chaos for the first time since 9/11.


Geo has finished a short stack of blueberry pancakes and is reading the Sun Sentinel newspaper with his second cup of coffee. He glances at his watch; it's just before eight. He's not in any rush, as the office is just ten minutes away. He plans to leave after finishing the sports page.


The Moon brothers are serving their morning customers as usual, with one of the morning news shows playing on a wide screen TV. It's 8:00 a.m., and they are expecting to see their plan come to fruition at any moment. Tom turns up the volume on the TV to make sure all their customers will hear the report.


Josef Malik exits the train at Penn Station and heads up the escalator to the main floor. At the top of the escalator, he joins the thousands of people who are milling about on this typical Monday. Josef walks to the center of the main hall, stops to look around, then heads for the Third Street exit. At the curb he hails a taxicab, and tells the driver to take him to Grand Central Station.

Grand Central is located on 44th Street, about two miles east of Penn Station. Rush hour has just begun, so the short cab trip will take about thirty minutes.

When Josef finally exits the cab at Grand Central, he glances at his watch and notes the time; it's 8:00 a.m. He quickly enters the main terminal hall and pushes his way through the thousands of people who are scurrying about, focused on reaching their destinations. When he reaches the center of the floor, he looks up at the ceiling and yells, "ALLAHU AKBAR!"

A transit policeman turns just in time to see a large explosion, and a mustard-colored cloud rising from the center of the hall. Then he and hundreds of others are blown backwards by the yellowcake bomb's concussion.

The scene, reminiscent of the aftermath of the fall of the World Trade Center's Twin Towers, is marked by a dense cloud and then by dead silence, which quickly gives way to the sounds of blaring radiation detection alarms, and coughing, and moaning.

# CHAPTER EIGHT

Tom is busy serving his customers when the morning TV newscast is interrupted by a breaking news alert.

*"We have just received word that there has been an explosion in the main rotunda of Grand Central Station in downtown Manhattan. Initial reports indicate that the explosion may have been caused by a suicide bomber. We take you now to our reporter on the scene, Bill Jordan. What can you tell us, Bill?"*

*"We've been told that the police have cordoned off the area surrounding Grand Central Station, and that the FBI has sent in a field team. They're not letting anyone into Grand Central and they're stopping everyone from leaving. Victims of the explosion who have already exited the building are being escorted offsite and quarantined. Apparently, some sort of dirty bomb has been detonated here this morning. We're waiting for an official statement from authorities."*

*"Bill, how do we know that a dirty bomb was detonated?"*

*"At this point it is just speculation, but we have based it upon the actions of local emergency personnel, and from the arrival of a team from NAIRA, the Nuclear Accident or Incident Response and Assistance Operations program that was set up by the U.S. Army."*

*"Have there been any deaths due to the explosion?"*

*"No information has been released yet. We have been told that there will be an official statement for the press in about fifteen minutes."*

*"Okay. Thanks, Bill. We'll come back to you in time for the press conference.*

*"So, to bring everyone up-to-date, a bomb has apparently been detonated in Grand Central Station. As you can see from our helicopter over Manhattan, the Army is on the scene and is setting up what appear to be field hospitals and emergency treatment centers. There are also fleets of fire trucks and other emergency vehicles on site.*

*"We will stay on the air with this story and bring you updates as we receive them."*

As the broadcast continues, Tom turns toward his brother, James, gives him a quick wink, then launches into an act for the benefit of their customers.

"Oh, no! All those people! They finally did it, they bombed us!"

After enjoying their leisurely breakfast overlooking the Intracoastal Waterway, Diane waits while Steve finishes his coffee and signs the bill. As Steve sets his cup on the table, their reverie is interrupted by the ringing of Steve's cell phone. Steve glances at the phone's display screen and notices that the call is from his son, John.

"Mornin'! What's up?"

Steve shakes his head in disgust as he listens to John telling him about the explosion in New York City.

Across town, Geo has finished his breakfast and is also receiving a call on his cell phone. It's from his office at the FSA.

"Morning."

"Mr. Jackson, you need to come in ASAP. We're on high alert. There has been an incident at Grand Central Station in New York City."

"I'll be there in less than ten minutes. What's going on?"

"Colonel Johnson will update us within the hour. Apparently, a dirty bomb was detonated at Grand Central Station."

"Crap! The shit just hit the fan!"

Geo ends the call and hurriedly pays his breakfast bill.

In the back of his mind, Geo knew that this call had to come sooner or later. He knows that in order to defeat the terrorists, we have to be vigilant and on alert one hundred percent of the time, while the terrorists need to complete their mission only once in order to be successful.


Diane becomes worried when she sees Steve's reaction to the phone call. As soon as he hangs up, she asks, "Steve, what happened? Who was on the phone?"

"It was John. We need to get home quick."

"Is everything all right? Is it Carla?"

Steve takes Diane's hand and guides her quickly out of the restaurant. As they begin to walk briskly back to their condo, he answers Diane's question in a grim tone of voice.

"It's not Carla, they're alright. A suicide bomber detonated a dirty bomb at Grand Central Station."

Diane gasps and begins to cry as they walk across A1A. When they enter the lobby of their condo, Steve's phone rings again.

"This is Steve. Talk to me."

"Dad, it's Mike. Did you hear the news?"

"Yeah, those bastards said they would retaliate for killing Bin Laden."

"You're not going to get involved with this, are you, Dad?"

"I hope to hell not! Not again."

"Keep me posted, Dad. I'll see you in a few. You know, I have a bad feeling about this!"

"Yeah, me too, Son. Take care."

Steve pulls Diane close to him as they board the elevator to their floor.

"That was Mike checking in."

Wiping tears from her eyes, Diane asks worriedly, "What are we going to do now?"

Steve replies solemnly, "Kill the bastards."

# CHAPTER NINE

Geo enters the FSA headquarters in Fort Lauderdale and greets Sandra, his receptionist.

"Everyone in the situation room?"

"Yes, Sir, they are all waiting for you, and Colonel Johnson is already on the line for your meeting."

'Thanks, Sandy, and good morning." Geo rushes into the meeting room and greets his staff.

"Okay, gentlemen, this is what we're getting paid for." Directing his attention to Colonel Johnson through the speaker phone, he asks, "Colonel, what's the skinny?"

"The skinny, as you put it, is that at 8:08 this morning, a suicide bomber detonated a dirty bomb at Grand Central Station in New York City. Al Jazeera has reported that al-Qaida is taking credit for this attack. The explosion caused a wide area of contamination and the FBI is preparing a statement for the press that should be released in about fifteen minutes. Twenty-five persons are confirmed dead from the initial blast, and two hundred twenty-eight are injured. From what the FBI and our teams at ground zero can surmise, the bomb contained yellowcake, a fairly inert, but radioactive, uranium ore. Although the radioactive yellowcake is not in itself a health hazard, if it is inhaled or ingested in large quantities, the human body has no way of expelling it, and it can produce long-term health problems in persons who are not treated quickly. Everyone who was in the terminal at the moment of detonation was exposed and must be checked for radiation contamination. Grand Central Station will likely be shut down for months, because it will take that long for Hazmat crews to clean up the contamination. We do not expect that there will be any immediate side effects or illnesses associated with exposure to the yellowcake, except possibly in persons with existing respiratory problems, but the routine checking and examination of everyone in that station will cause chaos and fear, and that is exactly what the terrorists want."

Geo breaks into the conversation. "Colonel, what is the FSA assigned to do here in Florida?"

"I will be conducting similar meetings with every FSA office in the country. An extreme level of vigilance is now needed across the United States. Statements from al-Qaida have led us to believe that there will be more attacks, but we don't know when or where they will occur. This was a homegrown terror operation, sleeper cells, if you will.

"The one good piece of information I can share with you today is that we have just captured Aziz Zarqawi Aziz, who was Usama Bin Laden's replacement. He has been sent to a CIA base in Cyprus for extraordinary interrogation, so we hope to have more information on the terror organization's activities shortly. I will keep you posted on that situation.

"That's it for now, so I'll sign off. Good day, gentlemen."

Geo turns to his staff, "Well, people, the shit just hit the fan."


In Moers Forks, Tom and James Moon are cleaning up the dining area after the morning rush. They are still excited after witnessing the reports about Josef Malik's successful mission in New York City, but they have a larger job that is still pending.

"Tom, I'm going out back to talk to Claude."

James takes off his apron and walks over to the mill area where Claude is carefully pouring finely powdered yellowcake into small containers. Claude calls out, "Allah is pleased! We have avenged the murder of Usama!"

"Yes, but we're not done yet. We still have your mission to accomplish. Now, I will tell you how you will do that. When you detonate your bomb during the infidels' celebration in Miami on New Year's Eve, you will act as a street vendor selling Italian Ices, but your cart will be full of explosives and yellowcake, instead of flavored ices. Within ninety-six hours of New Year's Eve, you will drive to a room we have rented for you in Miami, and you will bring the vendor cart with you. Come with me now and I will show you your equipment."

Claude follows James into a storeroom, where the two of them inspect the vending cart.

James and Tom had originally assigned two targets to their first terror recruit. Grand Central Station in New York was the main target, and the international airport in Montreal, Canada, was the backup target. Because the New York mission was such a success, the airport in Montreal will now be the backup for the second mission, in Miami.

The TV has been on in the condo ever since Steve and Diane returned from breakfast. They've been watching the news coverage to get further information regarding the bombing in New York. The reporter for Fox News has been on the scene for hours, and is now being interrupted as the broadcast breaks away to cover the FBI news conference. Field Agent Robert Sansone approaches a dais near a field operation trailer in Rockefeller Center.

"At approximately 8:08 this morning, a suicide bomber detonated an explosive device at Grand Central Station. Initially, there were twenty-five fatalities, with an additional two hundred thirty persons wounded. These deaths and injuries are the direct result of the concussion produced by the explosion. The detonated device also contained a substantial amount of uranium ore in the form of yellowcake, which is radioactive. Yellowcake itself is not a hazardous substance, unless it is ingested or inhaled in large quantities. We have quarantined Grand Central Station and everyone who was inside it, and we have notified the local police and fire rescue teams to quarantine all persons who may have exited the building after the blast. We are also issuing an order for anyone who was inside the terminal during the explosion and who may have already left the area to seek immediate medical attention as a precautionary measure. While we do not feel that bystanders will be adversely affected by being exposed to the uranium, we strongly advise that they seek medical attention. Again, we do not believe that exposure to the yellowcake will be hazardous to your health, but we strongly advise you to seek medical attention.

"We estimate that there were three thousand people in the general vicinity of the bomb's detonation. All local hospitals have been placed on alert, and NAIRA, the Nuclear Accident or Incident Response and Assistance team, and FEMA, the Federal Emergency Management Agency, have set up field hospitals at Bryant Park. We estimate that Grand Central Station will be closed for the next sixty days so HAZMAT teams can decontaminate the building. All inbound trains and subways will be diverted to Penn Station and other locations in the tri-state area. The New York Transit Authority will operate shuttle buses to help commuters.

"At this time, we have not identified the suicide bomber,

*but al-Qaida has already taken credit for this attack as retaliation for the death of Usama Bin Laden.*

*"No questions will be taken after this briefing. The Mayor of New York City will hold a press conference at 12:00 noon and he will take questions at that time. Thank you."*

After the press conference ends, Steve turns the TV off, but the sudden silence is soon broken by a ringing telephone.

"Chic, it's Geo. The bastards did it to us again!"

"Yeah, and what are you guys doin' about it?"

"We're on high alert. I guess I'll be spending most of my time here at the office. I called Ang and told him not to expect my help at the saloon for a while."

"Well, you can't expect my help, either. I'm retired, remember? And Diane and I are going to Maryland for Christmas."

"I'll keep that in mind. I don't think anything will happen here. I'll keep you posted, though."

"Thanks. Godspeed, Geo."

Several weeks have passed since the New York explosion, and now Steve and Diane are planning to leave Florida to spend the Christmas holidays with Mike and his family in Maryland.

Tom Moon is also planning a trip. He is preparing to drive to the Islamic Center in Plattsburgh, New York, to meet with Imam Khalid al-Mohammed, who was born and raised as Benjamin Jackson in Albany, New York, but is now a member of al-Qaida. Al-Mohammed is helping the Moon brothers by replenishing their supply of explosives for Claude Killeen's New Year's Eve mission in Miami. Claude is anxiously awaiting that mission so he can spend New Year's with his virgins in paradise.

However, halfway around the world, enhanced interrogation techniques have begun to work on Aziz Zarqawi Aziz, and he is reluctantly spilling his guts to the CIA.

# CHAPTER TEN

Diane starts to pack for their visit to Maryland, so while she's busy, Steve relaxes on the balcony with a cold Peroni and stares thoughtfully at the Atlantic Ocean. When the phone rings, Diane picks it up while folding her winter coat into the suitcase.

"*Pronto*! Uh, hello?"

"Diane? This is Ken Peters. How are you?"

"Ken! It's been a while! I'm fine, how are you?"

"Good, all good. How's Steve? He isn't getting into this al-Qaida crap, is he?"

"I hope not, but you know Steve. So, to what do we owe this phone call? Are you in Florida?"

"Yep. I was hoping to catch you guys in town. We're back at Homestead, and I was wondering if you'd like to come down and put in a few laps."

"Wow! Let me get Steve." Diane carries the portable phone out to the balcony and taps Steve on the shoulder.

"Steve, honey. It's Ken Peters for you."

Steve nearly spills his beer as he grabs the handset. "Ken! How the hell are ya?"

"I'm fine, buddy. Feel like racin'?"

"Homestead? When? Soon?"

"Calm down, man. Look, it's Wednesday, and we just got in. How about Friday morning? You and Diane can come down, and if John and his family can make it, bring them, too. If not, I'll see the two of you. We'll race, then do lunch."

"That sounds great! See you Friday, and say hello to your dad for me."

"Will do, Steve. Take care."

Steve hands the phone back to Diane and exclaims with a smile, "We're goin' racin'!"

When Tom Moon enters the Islamic Center in Plattsburgh, he immediately seeks out the Imam.

"*Assalamu Alaikum,* Peace be upon you. I need assistance."

"*Wa alaikum assalaam,* And upon you be peace! You have been very successful, Tom! How may I assist you further?"

"I need more plastic explosives for my Miami excursion."

"Very well. I can have what you need within forty-eight hours. Come back Friday, after afternoon prayers. We'll have some dinner, and then I will give you what you need for Miami."

Tom leaves the Islamic Center and rents a motel room for a couple of nights. He needs to purchase several items for the coffee house while he's in town, but his true shopping list will be filled on Friday.

When the phone rings, Carla answers it. "Hello?"

"Hi, Carla. It's Dad."

"Hi, Dad, what's going on?"

"Ken Peters gave me a call, and he's back in Homestead with his crew. Are you guys available this Friday to do some laps?"

"Oh, geez. John's on duty 'till the weekend and I volunteer at Jenna's school on Fridays. Sorry, Dad, but we won't be able to make it. But you and Mom go, and have a good time. We'll see you for dinner on Saturday before you leave to see Mike, Jeannie and the kids."

"Okay, Hon. See you then. Bye!"

Steve calls out to Diane. "Di, John and Carla are busy on Friday, so we'll be on our own."

"Well, we're on our own right now. Want to do something about it?"

"Hmm, what do you have in mind?"

"Chic, I'm going into the bedroom. Wait five minutes and then come in. You'll find out."

Diane gives Steve a long, deep kiss and pushes her tongue deep into his mouth.

"That was just a tease. See you in five minutes."

Steve immediately sits down. Not because he wants to, but because he has to.

# CHAPTER ELEVEN

George Jackson has been at his FSA office in Fort Lauderdale, reviewing all the new intel coming in since the bombing at Grand Central Station. The final head count is thirty-five dead and two hundred sixty-five injured.

We won hands down at Port Everglades, and in Washington, D.C., we aborted their plans with collateral damage and no lives lost. But in New York, we lost. That was the worst attack in the U.S. homeland since 9/11, and because it was domestic terrorism, it may be almost impossible to trace.

Colonel Johnson is in his office in Washington, reviewing the information that was retrieved from the deep interrogations going on in Cyprus. After reading the report, he gives George Jackson a call in Fort Lauderdale.

"Mr. Jackson, Colonel Johnson on line one."

"Thanks, Sandy. Morning, Colonel."

"George we're starting to get information out of Aziz. He told investigators that the yellowcake was stolen from the large reserve that was discovered in Iraq and that was transferred to Canada in 2008. He also said the suicide bomber was named Josef Malik and that he was from Saudi Arabia. The only information we have on Malik at the moment is that he traveled to Canada on a student visa and entered that country through the international airport in Montreal.

With our northern border with Canada being so porous, with miles of unpatrolled areas, it's too easy to cross into the United States undetected, so based on more information received from Aziz, the FBI has begun to monitor an Islamic Center in Plattsburgh, New York. We believe the terror cell is located somewhere near that mosque. We sent an agent to that Islamic Center and he has successfully infiltrated the group that meets there. I'll update all the FSA offices by fax as information from him becomes available. If I contact you by phone again, it will be because we expect an incident in your district."

"Very good, Colonel. How is the investigation going in New York?"

"Well, the field hospitals have been dismantled. A total of three thousand, three hundred twenty-one persons have sought medical attention for radiation testing. Only a handful of them have been sent on for further treatment due to prior respiratory conditions. There have been no further deaths or injuries as a direct result of the attack and Hazmat teams are slowly decontaminating the building. We expect that procedure to take another sixty days or so to complete."

"How are Robert and his team doing?"

"Our office in New York is on lockdown. Their mattresses are out and they're working 24/7. We pulled personnel from the Boston office to assist in New York, and after the info came in about Plattsburgh, we sent personnel from Baltimore to that area. We're also opening a field office in Albany to keep closer tabs on the situation in Plattsburgh. I'll keep you informed. Take care for now."

"Thanks, Colonel. Godspeed."

George hangs up with the Colonel and asks Sandra to call his team together for a meeting so he can update them with the latest information. It will take a couple of hours to get them all in the office, so George schedules the meeting for late afternoon. He asks Sandra call out for pizza, then he goes to see a man about a horse.

It's now early Friday morning. Steve is nursing his second cup of coffee while waiting for Diane to get out of the shower. He cleans up the breakfast dishes and goes out to the balcony to finish the coffee. The condo has a nice view of the Atlantic Ocean, but it doesn't compare to the morning view from their balcony in Italy, with the Amalfi Coast, the Mediterranean Sea, and Mount Vesuvius in the distance.

Diane joins him on the balcony and comments, "Nice view, but it's not Italy."

"Yeah, Babe, not even close. We ready?"

"As they say, Gentlemen, start your engines!"

"Great! Let me hit the head, and then we'll be off."

Within minutes, they pull out onto Oakland Park Boulevard and head west. Under normal driving conditions, it would take almost an hour to reach Homestead, but since Steve still holds his Homeland Security identification, a "get out of a ticket free card," as soon as he reaches the Florida Turnpike, he opens the 'Vette up and hauls ass. In less than forty minutes, Steve and Diane pull into the tunnel at Homestead-Miami Speedway underneath the back straightaway, and head to the pit area. When Steve parks the 'Vette, Diane declares, "Last time we did this, you drove me around. Today, I want to drive!"

Steve smiles as they walk toward pit row to greet Ken.

For a fee, the Ken Peters NASCAR Racing Adventure enables customers to drive mockups of actual race cars on several racetracks around the country. The mockups are not as powerful as the actual race cars, with about 600 horsepower instead of 800, but they still give the average Joe the thrill of a lifetime. The Ken Peters Adventure ends their season each year at Homestead-Miami Speedway. After a taking short break, they start up again in February, when the NASCAR racing season starts.

Ken notices Diane and Steve approaching and walks out to greet them, giving Steve a man hug and Diane a kiss on the cheek.

"I'm so glad you guys could make it today! What's it going to be this time, Diane? Are you taking the ride-along or will you try driving yourself? Steve, I know *you're* driving!"

"I want to drive this time."

"Okay, then! You have some insurance paperwork to fill out and then you have to watch the training video. After that, we'll take you on a quick tour around the track in one of our vans. That's all because of the insurance bull. When you're done with the track tour, you'll get to drive your own car while following one of our professional drivers around the track. Just follow behind the professional and do whatever he does, he'll pace you at your own speed. But here's a bit of advice, Diane. If he screws up and hits the wall, do *not* follow him."

"Oh, that makes me feel better!"

Chuckling, Ken says, "Go ahead into the media room. They'll get you suited up and you'll complete all the preliminary bullshit. I'll stay here with Steve. We'll meet you at pit road when you're ready to ride."

Diane walks off with one of the professional drivers as Ken and Steve continue to talk.

"So tell me, how do you like living in Italy?"

"Ken, it's the best. The food is fantastic and the people are friendly. The bad thing is that the U.S. dollar takes a hit with the conversion rate, so it's rough on Americans. By the way, you think gas is bad here? It's nine dollars a gallon there! Listen, when you take your break this year, why don't you and your wife come over and stay with us awhile? We have plenty of room and we'll be going back there right after the first of the year."

"Wow, it's a date! We've never been to Italy. Besides, it'll be good to go somewhere I won't be recognized."

"Yeah, over there, it's soccer and Formula One. When you make your reservations, book a flight that goes into Naples. I'll pick you up at the airport. It's about an hour to an hour and a half ride to my villa. Depending on traffic, it could take a little longer, but the view on the way is outstanding, so you probably won't even notice the time."

"Thanks, Steve! I'll check with my boss and give you a call. How are your kids and grandkids?"

Steve pulls out his wallet and shows Ken the treasured photos of his family like a proud Grandpa should, as Diane walks by, all suited up and ready to take her tour of the track.

"Showing Ken photos of the grandkids?"

"They're beautiful, Diane, congratulations! I must say, you sure don't look like a grandmother!"

"Thank you, Ken. You're quite a gentleman. Now, let's get this track thing done so I can drive!"

Diane climbs into the van as Ken and Steve head to the media center so Steve can fill out his insurance paperwork and get suited up.


In New York, Tom Moon and Claude are working in the storeroom at the grist mill, preparing Claude's equipment.

"Claude, this is the false bottom of your vendor's cart. The top of the cart will be filled with the Italian Ices that you will be offering for sale. You will be going to Miami two weeks early so you can establish yourself as a street vendor in Bayfront Park, and you will stay at the Intercontinental Hotel. That is where they will hold the celebration on New Year's Eve. There will be thousands of people at the celebration, so it will be a glorious triumph for our cause! Let's go upstairs now. I will show you where the hotel is through a Google map on my computer."

"Is Bayfront Park near the hotel?"

"Yes, it's perfect! It's adjacent to the hotel, in the same complex. Come, I will show you. You will start working there on Monday, and you will leave here late Friday night. I have all your paperwork in place. Come, come."

They walk to Tom's office, where he Googles the Miami location and prints out a map with directions to Miami from Mooers Forks.

# CHAPTER TWELVE

Imam Khalid al-Mohammed and Farid Kalil, the Mosque's newest member, are unloading a van filled with explosives and detonation devices into a storeroom at the rear of the mosque.

"Sir, may I ask who this is for?"

"One of our family members needs to rid his farm of pests. He will be picking these items up after prayers. Come inside. We will have some tea."

Khalid does not know that Farid is an agent of the FBI.

Steve helps Diane climb into her race car, a mockup of the Number 48 car, last year's champion. One of Ken's pit crew members fastens the car's steering wheel to its post, and tightens Diane's seatbelts. Diane is strapped in so securely, she feels as if she's one with the car.

In the driver's seat, Diane is sitting directly behind the engine and on top of the exhaust, with only a thin sheet metal floor beneath her. Luckily, today's outside air temperature is only about sixty-five degrees, but on a hot day summer day, the temperature inside the cockpit of the race car could quickly reach in excess of one hundred twenty degrees.

The crewman begins a quick briefing by pointing to the instrument panel.

"When we're ready, I'll start the engine by flipping this switch. Right above that switch is a red warning light. If at any time during your laps that light should come on, you need to put the car in neutral, shut the engine by flipping this switch down, and pull off the track. The red lever on the floor next to the shifter is the fire extinguisher. If for any reason you see smoke or flames, pull that lever."

Looking at Diane, the crewman continues, "These instructions are only a precaution. We've been doing this for years and nothing has ever happened, but we need go through all this for insurance reasons."

After a pause, he asks, "Are you ready?"

When Diane gives him a thumb's up, the crewman flips the engine on with a roar, and after that, Diane cannot hear anything else but her heart beating in her chest. Luckily, the first car she learned to drive had a manual transmission, so she draws on that experience as she depresses the clutch and eases into first gear, slowly following her scout car off pit road and into the first turn.

Quickly, the two cars exit the turn and enter the back straightaway. Diane cannot believe the power she has under her control, and as she enters the second turn and explodes onto the front straightaway, she screams as she flies past pit road and a surprised Steve.

"Damn, Ken! She's flyin'!"

"Yeah! We got her logged in at 140! Not bad for a girl."

"Come on, Ken, that wasn't politically correct. True, but not correct!"

As they laugh, Diane continues around the track for ten more laps, before being directed back into pit row.

When Diane finally brakes to a stop in the pit, Steve and Ken walk out to greet her and to help her climb out of the car through the driver's window. After she's out of the car, she turns to Steve, gives him a big hug and shouts, "You were right! That was better than sex!"

Steve smiles while Ken laughs so hard he can hardly breathe.

"Okay, Di. Now I'll show you how it's really done, and tonight, we'll see if it was better than sex."

It's Steve's turn to climb into the Number 48 car. He doesn't need a scout car, so he'll be on his own as he drives around the track.

Firing the car up, he's out on the track in a flash, leaving behind a patch of rubber. While Ken helps Diane remove her racing gear near the pit wall, Steve is already roaring down the front straightaway. As Diane catches a quick glimpse of him passing by, she yells, "Wow! He's going *really* fast!"

Ken chuckles and says, "Diane, to put it in perspective, you were hitting speeds of 140 miles per hour, but Steve is probably going in excess of 175. If Steve had remained with NASCAR, he would have been one of the best stock car drivers ever. He has a natural ability to drive on the edge of chaos. Aside from our lifelong friendship, the main reason I invite Steve here every time we're in town is to see what a talented a driver he is and to imagine the career he could have had in stock car racing."

Steve roars by again as Diane, Ken and the rest of the crew, including Ken's professional drivers, enjoy the show.

# CHAPTER THIRTEEN

This morning, Claude is busy loading equipment into the trailer that he will be towing to Miami. The Moon brothers will be able to help him after they finish with the morning coffee crowd at the restaurant.

Claude is perfect for this mission, since he's a French national without Middle Eastern ties. With his heritage in the romance languages of Europe, he can speak fluent French, Italian, Spanish and English, which is perfect for selling Italian Ices in culturally-diverse South Florida, and is also a perfect cover for an Islamic terrorist.

When Claude reaches South Florida, he has been directed to make his first stop at a wholesale distributor in the city of Hialeah to pick up a supply of Italian Ices for his vendor cart, before checking in at his Miami hotel. After checking in, he has been told to bring his vendor cart to his ultimate location at Bayfront Park.

George Jackson is reading the morning fax update from Colonel Johnson. The FBI agent who infiltrated the mosque in Plattsburgh has reported that a shipment of explosives is on its way into the country, destined for a member of the city's Muslim community. As a result, two FBI agents from Albany have been assigned to monitor all activity at the mosque.

At the detention center on the island of Cyprus, Aziz Zarqawi Aziz is still being interrogated, but aside from revealing the name of the suicide bomber and his route into the United States from Canada, the only other information he yielded is that terror networks in the United States are currently targeting the country's railway infrastructure. But sadly, that plan has already come to fruition at Grand Central Station.

Steve pulls his ride into pit row after finishing his twentieth lap, and stops in front of applauding onlookers. After shutting Number 48 down, he unfastens his seatbelt, removes the steering wheel and his head gear, and extricates himself from the car by climbing out of the window. Diane runs over to give him a hug.

"Ya know, Di? You were right. This *is* better than sex!" Steve gives Diane a slap on the butt as they walk over to the pit wall.

"Hey, Ken! That was great! Where are we going for lunch?"

"That depends on how much you want to spend. Since I treated you to a day of fun, you can treat me to lunch!"

"Well, there aren't too many places around here. How about Ruby Tuesday's? You can pig out at the salad bar."

"Okay, sounds good. Why don't you two go ahead and I'll catch up in a few."

Steve removes his fire suit and walks hand in hand with Diane out to his car. Ever the gentleman, he opens Diane's door and helps her climb in on the passenger side before settling himself in on the driver's side.

As they pull away from the racetrack's infield and exit out of the tunnel that passes under the track, Diane declares, "So, you were, uh, *are*, quite a driver! Do you think you missed your calling?"

"Sometimes I wonder, what if? But you know I'm happy about how my life turned out. The war called me into the service and after Vietnam, I just kept that military mindset and went into law enforcement. If I didn't make that choice, I wouldn't have married two wonderful women and had two great sons and grandkids. I have no regrets, but I damn sure like to race! It's too bad NASCAR doesn't have a senior circuit. I'd be all over that like white on rice!"

"You looked good out there, and Ken says that one of the main reasons he invites you is just so he can see you drive."

"Well, let's hope I can still keep accepting. It *is* fun out there. Hey, you did good, too!"

Smiling, Diane replies, "It really isn't better than sex, but it's a damn close second."

After a few more minutes of driving, they pull into the restaurant parking lot and walk inside to get a table while they wait for Ken. Within fifteen minutes, Ken arrives and they start their lunch.

"Sorry about that, guys. I had to give some final instructions to my crew. We head back to North Carolina today for a well-deserved rest."

Diane orders a peach tea while the men order draft beers, and all of them order avocado turkey burgers, along with the salad bar. Within minutes of choosing their salad accompaniments, they are all sitting down again and enjoying their food.

"So tell me, Steve. When can Linda and I come to visit you two in Italy? We only have a small window of opportunity before my schedule starts up again."

"Let's see, Diane and I are spending the holidays with Mike and his family up in Maryland, then we return to Fort Lauderdale during the first week of January to close up the condo. After that, we head home. How about the week of January tenth? You have my email address. Send me your flight info and I'll pick you up in Naples. Remember, it's winter there, so pack accordingly."

"The tenth it is! Linda will be in shock."

The three of them clink their glasses together in a toast to friendship as their waiter arrives at the table with their burgers.

# CHAPTER FOURTEEN

After evening prayers, Imam Khalid al-Mohammed approaches Tom Moon and greets him as Mustaffa Amin, Tom's Muslim name, then the men proceed to the Imam's private quarters for a light dinner.

While the Imam is occupied with dinner, Farid Kalil, the undercover FBI agent, hangs around the storeroom area, trying to look busy. He wants to stay nearby to see if he can find out if Tom is the person the explosives are intended for. Within twenty minutes, Tom and the Imam emerge from the Imam's private quarters and approach the back storeroom.

"Farid, please come here. We need your assistance." Turning to Mustaffa, the Imam continues. "Drive your van around to the back. Farid will help you load up." Mustaffa bows and kisses the Imam on both cheeks, before walking off to get the van.

After Mustaffa parks the van near the building's back door, Farid discreetly takes his photo with his cell phone camera, and then helps him load the explosives. Farid hopes to pick up some information as he works alongside Mustaffa.

"So, you must be having a serious pest problem if you need such a large amount of explosives. Imam al-Mohammed tells me you are having a problem on your farm?"

"Yes, quite a large problem. There are many rats that I need to take care of."

"Many rats, huh? Are you near the river?"

"Yes, just outside of Moers Forks."

"Well, good luck, and may Allah be with you."

"Thank you, and with you."

After saying goodbye to the Imam, Tom, also known as Mustaffa, drives away from the Islamic Center. When he is out of sight, Farid uses his cell phone to send Tom's photo and the van's license plate number to the FBI field office.

At the same time, the two FBI field agents who were sent to monitor activity at the Plattsburgh mosque have just arrived at a local hotel.

But they are a day late and a dollar short.


Tom arrives back in Moers Forks late Friday night. Claude helps him transfer the explosives from the van into a trailer that Claude will tow behind a used pickup truck the brothers purchased for his trip to Miami. They also made arrangements for him to pick up a supply of Italian Ices in Hialeah when he arrives in South Florida. They estimate that if Claude travels one thousand miles a day and stops only once on the way down, he should reach Miami sometime Monday morning. That would allow him enough time to pick up the Ices, check in at his hotel, and be at his station in Bayfront Park by late Monday afternoon.

The next morning, Claude begins to put the bomb together, using one hundred pounds of the yellowcake. His training in Pakistan prepared him well for the proper way to wire explosive devices. The explosion will be glorious.


Colonel Johnson places a call to Benito "Ben" Ramirez, chief of the New York City FSA office, and finds him still at work. Ben was a twenty-five year veteran of the FBI before he was tapped to run this FSA facility.

"Ben, do you ever go home?"

"Not since the bombing, Colonel. Nowadays it's 24-7. I guess it's a good thing I'm divorced, so there's no one to go home to."

"Well, I guess that's as good a reason as any to spend so much time at work. Anyway, the reason I called is that it seems we caught a break up at the mosque in Plattsburgh. As you know, the FBI has been monitoring that mosque for a while with an undercover agent, and that agent has given us some good intel. We have been hearing rumors that the Imam there is linked to al-Qaida, and the agent just found out that a member of the mosque named Mustafa Amin recently picked up a cache of explosives and detonators. The van he was driving is registered to a Thomas Moon from Mooers Forks, New York, and the agent thinks that Mustafa Amin is Tom Moon's Muslim name. Based upon this information, the FBI sent two more agents to the area, and they arrived in Plattsburg a few hours ago. They will hook up with local authorities and travel to Mooers Forks to pay Mr. Moon a visit, as soon as we can get a judge to issue a search warrant. Since Mooers Forks is so close to Montreal, the international entry point that we traced the Grand Central Bomber to, this lead may be the one. I'll let you know what the FBI finds out."

"That sounds like good news, Colonel! Maybe I'll get to go home tonight after all. Thanks."

# CHAPTER FIFTEEN

George arrives at the office early Saturday morning to see if any new information arrived overnight about Tom Moon and the situation in Mooers Forks. After reading the latest fax from Colonel Johnson, he prepares to send an email to his team to update them with the details.

With his staff off for the weekend, it takes him some time to locate everyone's email addresses. First, he had to remember Sandra's password in order to gain access to her computer. Then, he had to log into her Outlook account to send a master email to all of her FSA contacts.

Little does he realize that this weekend will probably be the last one he has off for the rest of the year, thanks to al-Qaida.

Diane sits on the condo balcony and gazes at the Atlantic Ocean while drinking a cup of coffee. Steve is sleeping late this morning, so Diane is enjoying the morning solitude. After flipping through the morning newspaper, she grabs her Nook to continue reading a science fiction thriller about the End Times and how God will inform the world of His Son's Second Coming by sending the Archangel Gabriel to the earth with a message. She hopes she won't be distracted as she reads continues to read, because she cannot seem to be able to put the book down. That hope disappears when Steve walks out of the door and asks for a cup of coffee.

Ben Ramirez is also reviewing the latest fax from Colonel Johnson. The phone rings as he sits in the New York office of the FSA, on the eightieth floor of the Empire State Building.

"Ramirez? This is Sansone from the FBI."

"Mornin' Bob. What's going on?"

"Good news. If you read your fax this morning, you were updated on the break we got at the Islamic Center in Plattsburgh. This morning, we're raiding a grist mill in nearby Mooers Forks, because we believe the owners, Tom and James Moon, are linked to al-Qaida. Tom was the one who picked up a large amount of explosives at the mosque yesterday. Also, when Imam Khalid al-Mohammed's name came up during interrogations of Aziz Zarqawi Aziz in Cyprus, Aziz confirmed that the Imam is tied to al-Qaida. Based upon that confirmation, we're preparing a SWAT team that will raid the mosque later this morning. I'll send an update as soon as both of these missions are complete."

"That's great! I also have good news. Did you get your briefing on Grand Central? The HAZMAT teams are planning to re-open the lower levels. Commuters will be able to switch from track to track again, but they won't be able to ascend to the main level just yet. Even so, this will help to ease some of the travel and commuting issues. They still feel the rest of the building won't be open for at least another forty-five days, but they're making progress."

"Excellent. Listen, I have to go; there's a plane waiting for me. I need to get to Plattsburgh. Talk to you later, Bob."

The raid at the grist mill on the banks of the Great Chazy

River won't be easy. The team will consist of members of the FBI, the Department of Homeland Security, local police, and New York State Police. The team must not only secure the road that runs along the river, but also the river itself.

Because Mooers Forks is an unincorporated community in the eastern part of the town of Mooers, New York, police were pulled from Mooers and nearby Altona to join with personnel from the New York State Police station near the U.S.-Canadian border, and the Department of Homeland Security.

Two teams of two FBI agents each will man "go fast" inflatable Zodiacs to cut off any attempts at a water escape along the Great Chazy River, while sixteen men will break up into teams of eight men each to cover the front and back of the grist mill. New York State troopers have been assigned to block off the two nearby roads with their cruisers.

Later that morning, another raid is scheduled at the Islamic Center in Plattsburgh, which will be conducted by Plattsburgh SWAT police.

Everyone is set; the missions are a go.

In their shared apartment at the old grist mill, Tom and James are oblivious to the events that are about to surround them. As they arrive in the restaurant area of the mill, they begin to prepare for their day, unaware that the first customers to enter that morning will be the FBI.

As Tom mops the floor and James starts to brew the morning coffee, the front door is suddenly shoved open with a shout.

"This is the FBI! Everyone down on your knees!"

Tom and James freeze in place and are quickly overcome by the fast-moving agents. A potentially difficult situation is neutralized within seconds when they are forced to the floor and handcuffed. Tom and James are swiftly escorted out of the building as the eight-man teams survey the property and secure the building.

A few minutes later, two Middle Eastern employees of the mill are stopped at a road block on County Road 16 and taken to the local police station for questioning.

Lead FBI agent Janet Caffiero's intercom suddenly crackles as Sergeant Fred Upton calls her with a discovery.

"Agent Caffiero, this is Sergeant Upton. You need to come into the back of the mill area."

When Janet arrives in the back room, she immediately notices the barrels of yellowcake and its residue on the millstone.

"Sergeant, contact HAZMAT immediately and get them out here ASAP, and tell your team to keep searching. Who knows what else we'll find."

Janet walks through the café area and out of the building to speak to Tom and James.

"Before I read you your rights, would either of you like to explain what we found here?"

"Not without our lawyer!"

"Well, that's just great. The government and the system you obviously hate are the ones you're hiding behind. Praise be to Allah, right?"

Janet turns to one of the state troopers and directs him to read the brothers their Miranda rights and then take them into custody. Then she heads back into the mill area, where she finds Sergeant Upton examining the plastic explosives and detonation devices his team has discovered.

Janet calls the Albany FBI office to give them the details of the raid and to tell them to be extra careful when raiding the mosque in Plattsburgh. Within minutes, Ben Ramirez and Colonel Johnson are updated with information from the Mooers Forks raid. They will brief Agent Sansone upon his arrival in Plattsburgh, before he conducts the raid on the mosque.

# CHAPTER SIXTEEN

George Jackson is cruising down I-95, on his way to join Frank Angelo at Steve and Diane's condo for brunch. He knows that this will be the last time the three friends will be able to be together this year, because Steve and Diane are leaving late that night to spend Christmas in Maryland.

As George turns off I-95, his cell phone rings.

"George speaking!"

"Hey, George. This is Colonel Johnson. Taking the weekend off?"

"Yeah, I'm going to meet Angie, Chic and Diane for brunch."

"Well, you might want to know that we hit pay dirt with our raid this morning at the terror cell in upstate New York. It looks like it was home base for the Grand Central bomber. Sansone from New York City is about to lead another raid at the Islamic Center in Plattsburgh. We believe that mosque was the cell's connection to al-Qaida. Say hello to Steve and Diane for me. I'll keep you posted as more information comes in."

"Excellent! That's great news, Colonel! Talk to you soon."

FBI Field Agent Bob Sansone is meeting with the Plattsburgh

raiding team at the helipad at Plattsburgh International Airport. The team consists of members of the Bureau of Alcohol, Tobacco, Firearms and Explosives, commonly known as ATF, along with Homeland Security, local police, and New York State troopers.

The Islamic Center mosque is a three building complex situated on a small tract of land on Cumberland Bay. The area along the bay is largely undeveloped, except for the land occupied by the mosque, which erupts out of the ground like a pimple on the face of progress.

Cumberland Bay is connected to Lake Champlain, which crosses over the U.S.-Canadian border, therefore, the United States Coast Guard will patrol the bay behind the mosque during and after the raid, to stop any escapes by water. Local police have been directed to set up road blocks at Margaret Street to the north of the building, and Point View Terrace to the south.

At the airport, the ATF's SWAT team is preparing to board a waiting Black Hawk helicopter. At a pre-arranged signal, the SWAT team will rappel onto the roof of the Islamic Center complex and make their way down the side of the building, while New York State troopers and a second SWAT team from Homeland Security accompany Agent Sansone in a frontal assault. Through micro transmitters on each person's vest, all members of this operation will be in constant contact with each other, as well as with Agent Jonathan Baddour, also known as Farid Kalil, the mole who infiltrated the mosque, and who is currently inside of it.

George valet parks his car after passing the security guardhouse at Steve's building. When he enters the building's marble foyer, he makes his way to the elevator and punches the button for the third floor. After a short ride, he exits the elevator a few steps down the hall from the Ciccone's apartment. As he approaches their door, he notices that it is slightly ajar, so he gives a quick knock and walks in.

"Hello? Anybody home?"

"Out here on the balcony, Geo."

As George steps onto the balcony, Steve hands him a cold Peroni beer.

"You guys always leave the front door open?"

"Angie saw you pull up as he walked into the lobby, so we left the door open for you."

"Where is that old fart?"

"You know him, he's in the kitchen helping Diane with the food."

"Old fart, my ass! I'm the youngest one here, not including Diane. Give me a beer, will ya?"

When Frank walks onto the balcony, the three friends are together again, acting as if they were never apart. Over thirty years of stories bring these men together more like brothers than friends.

Diane gazes at Chic, Angie, and Geo from behind the sliding glass door, and smiles. She realizes that as life goes on, these three soul mates will get together less and less frequently, so she lets them talk awhile before announcing that dinner is ready. After a few minutes, she wipes a tear from her eye before walking out to join them.

"Hey, we need to add some estrogen to all this testosterone out here! Somebody hand me a beer!"

The conversation slams to a halt, and in disbelief, all three men shout, "*Beer?*"

# CHAPTER SEVENTEEN

Morning prayers at the Islamic Center mosque ended thirty minutes ago, and the mosque is emptying out quickly.

Outside the main mosque are two buildings. A storeroom is in one building and the Imam's living quarters are on the first floor of the other building, with meeting rooms and classrooms for Quran studies on the second floor.

Homeland Security is assigned to breach the front of the mosque, while ATF enters through the roof. Within minutes, everyone is in place and Agent Sansone gives the signal. "Okay, Gentlemen, LET'S ROLL!"

When Agent Sansone gives the go signal, the ATF team takes off in the Black Hawk helicopter, and three convoys of black SUV's head for the mosque, while the Coast Guard positions its patrol boat fifty yards offshore from the raid area.

Agent Jonathan Baddour, the FBI mole known as "Farid", hears the go signal in his earpiece and quickly walks into the kitchen area off the women's ablution room to be near the Imam. The prayer hall and the front foyer are almost deserted, except for a few volunteers who are cleaning up.

In a few minutes, the ATF team rappels down from the hovering Black Hawk, and with a handheld ram, they quickly breach a door on the roof. At the same time, Agent Sansone and the Homeland Security team enter the mosque's front lobby and quickly subdue everyone inside.

When Imam Khalid al-Mohammed becomes aware of the intrusion, he immediately pulls a small detonation device from his pocket, just as Agent Baddour rounds a corner and comes upon him in the mosque's kitchen. The agent quickly pulls out his weapon and commands, "I'M WITH THE FBI! DROP THAT DEVICE!"

The Imam stares quizzically at the agent, whom he thought was a believer in his cause, but in a matter of seconds, he makes a move to explode the device. Before the movement can be completed, Baddour fires a shot and the device flies out of the Imam's hand, along with two of his fingers. At that same moment, the Homeland Security team pours into the kitchen shouting, "DROP YOUR WEAPON AND GET DOWN ON THE FLOOR!"

Agent Baddour places his weapon on the floor and slowly pulls his badge out of his pocket, raising it high over his head, while the Imam writhes on the floor in pain and tries to stop the flow of blood from his missing digits.

Agent Sansone is the last one to enter the room, and when he sees Baddour, he yells, "He's FBI! He's one of us!"

At Sansone's command, the Homeland Security team stands down. Agent Baddour seizes that moment to grab a dishtowel from the counter and begin to wrap up the Imam's hand, applying pressure to the wounds.

"Get EMT's in here, and someone try to find his missing fingers!"

After a thorough search, the mosque is declared to be neutralized, with ten of its members taken into custody for questioning and the Imam rushed to CVPH Medical Center under armed guard, accompanied by his fingers.

Agent Baddour directs Sansone and the ATF team to the outside building that houses the storeroom. The team cordons off the area and calls in the bomb squad to secure the room. Meanwhile, Homeland Security conducts its own search of the mosque, the out buildings and al-Mohammed's living quarters, and confiscates the Imam's computer and all of his written materials.

Both of this morning's raids are judged to be a success. No one was killed in either raid, and there was no desecration or damage to the mosque. Everything is good.

Good guys two, bad guys nothing.


At Steve's condo, Diane is serving espresso to the boys. The brunch was a typical Italian buffet consisting of mortadella, sopressata, various cheeses, and fresh fruit. To finish the meal, Diane brings out cannoli and rum cakes while Steve passes around a bottle of Sambuca to flavor the coffee.

Happy to be surrounded by good friends, Steve takes a moment to stand and give a toast.

"To Diane. Great meal, babe! And to great company!"

George's cell phone rings while the others are toasting their hostess. George excuses himself from the table to answer the call.

"George speaking. Yes, Colonel… Great! All went well? …Huh? …They should have shot his balls off! …Good. I'll wait for your formal report. Thank you, Colonel."

When he hangs up from the call, George turns to Steve. "Colonel Johnson says hello."

"Damn. I wish that man would forget my name. So Geo, whose balls should be shot off?"

"This morning, the ATF, the FBI and Homeland Security raided a terror cell in Mooers Forks, and a mosque in Plattsburgh."

"Mooers Forks?"

"Yeah, it's a sleepy little town just outside of the sleepy, bigger town of Plattsburgh. It looks like the Grand Central bomber came from that cell in Mooers Forks and that the mosque was his connection to al-Qaida. They found a cache of explosives that the Imam was storing there. An agent shot off a couple of his fingers."

"Well, you're right! They should have shot his balls off!"

Diane had been listening quietly to the conversation, but decides to interrupt.

"Listen, guys. My waning estrogen is quickly being overpowered by all the testosterone out here. I'm going inside to do the dishes."

As Diane exits the room, Angie jumps up to join her.

"I'll help you, Diane. Let's leave Chic and Geo to all that hoopla. Besides, if I hear any more, they'll probably have to kill me. Unlike those two heroes, I'm getting too old for that shit."

# CHAPTER EIGHTEEN

John and Carla's house in Florida is brightly decorated for Christmas. They always put their decorations up the weekend after Thanksgiving, which is coming in handy this year, as they are celebrating an early Christmas before Steve and Diane head to Maryland.

While John and his father are watching the late NFL football game on ESPN Carla, Diane and Jenna are resetting the table for dessert. During a commercial break, John notices that it's now dark enough for the outside lights to come on, so he asks his Dad, "Before we sit down for dessert, do you want to see our Christmas lights?"

"Sure, Son. Besides, since we won't be here for Christmas, we have some gifts in the car for Jenna. I can bring them in now and she can open them before we eat."

Father and son walk out the front door into the chilly Florida night. Standing on the sidewalk, Steve looks back at the house and admires his son's handiwork. It's a simple holiday display with an animated flood light that focuses glimmering snowflakes onto the house, while a large star hovers over the roof and shines down upon a Nativity scene.

"Simple and to the point, Son. It's what Christmas is all about."

Steve walks over to his car and pulls out a couple of gifts for Jenna, then joins John to return to the warmth of the house. Sneaking the gifts under the tree before Jenna can catch him, he silently motions to John to call the others into the living room.

John calls out, "Carla, why don't we have dessert in the living room, near the tree?"

Surprised at her father's suggestion, Jenna rushes into the living room, since she knows that the only time they eat near the Christmas tree is when gifts are being opened. At the sight of the pretty, wrapped boxes with large bows, the child opens her eyes wide in delight.

As Jenna frantically rips open her gifts, Diane retrieves a couple of envelopes from her purse for John and Carla.

Handing three envelopes to Carla, Diane says, "We didn't want to forget you two, so Merry Christmas!"

"Diane, there are three envelopes here."

"Well, you have one on the way, right?"

While everyone is oohing and ahhing over Jenna's gifts, Diane goes into the kitchen and returns to the living room with coffee, hot chocolate, and Christmas cookies.

Jenna loves her new Barbie doll and Barbie house, and of course, the pink Barbie Corvette, and she gives her grandparents a big hug and kiss.

When Carla opens the Christmas envelope from Steve and Diane, she is overwhelmed and immediately shows the contents to John – airline tickets for their family to travel to Italy for the summer, and a beginning nest egg for their unborn child consisting of one thousand shares of common stock in a well-regarded company.

Kisses and hugs abound as the family enjoys dessert and each other's company.

Later that night, John drives Steve and Diane to the airport in his Dad's Corvette. Steve and Diane will be away for a while before they head back to Italy, so he doesn't want to leave the car unattended at their condo while they're gone.

He knows that John enjoys driving the 'Vette, so he asks him to take care of it until he returns to the States.

While the Ciccone's are flying at 30,000 feet on their way to Baltimore, Claude Killeen is pulling into a Days Inn off I-95 in Florence, South Carolina. He plans to sleep for a few hours before heading out on the road again. He estimates that he should arrive in Miami by Monday afternoon.

At this point, he is unaware of the recent developments in upstate New York.

After the Moon brothers were taken into custody, they were placed in Plattsburgh's city jail and then quickly transferred to Fort Drum Army Base to await further processing. Imam Khalid al-Mohammed will follow a similar path when is released by the surgeon who reattached his two fingers. There have been no leaks of these developments to the press, because the FBI and the CIA want to continue to interrogate the evildoers before they are tried in the court of public opinion.

When they were arrested, all three suspects immediately requested lawyers, believing that they will be able to hide behind the law and their constitutional rights.

According to the law, the federal government can only hold them incommunicado for forty-eight hours before being forced to yield to their attorney-client privileges. However, the attorney general of the United States is preparing to file a petition in Manhattan's Federal Court early Monday morning to classify these three individuals as enemy combatants. If the court sides with that petition, they will be incarcerated at a federal detention facility until a military tribunal can be scheduled.

Government lawyers believe that the reclassification of these suspects from civil criminals to enemy combatants is in the bag, because al-Qaida has already taken responsibility for the bombing at Grand Central Station, and because the federal judge who will be petitioned in the case is known to have a sympathetic ear.

# CHAPTER NINETEEN

**Monday, December 6**

Steve awoke early this morning, so instead of lying in bed, he decided to get himself a cup of coffee in his son's kitchen in Columbia, Maryland. His daughter-in-law, Jeannie, had just joined him at the breakfast bar when news broke over the morning TV program that Assistant Attorney General Sid Walters scheduled a press conference for 9:00 a.m. that day in front of the Federal Courthouse in downtown Manhattan.

"Boy, that's going to be an interesting news story."

"Dad, don't tell me you know what that's all about!"

"Okay, I won't."

Upon entering the kitchen, Diane overhears the tail end of their conversation and asks, "You won't what?"

"Well, morning Di. Why are you up so early? We didn't get in until almost 2:00."

"Don't change the subject. What won't you do?"

"Tell Jeannie about the news conference the Feds are having this morning."

"Hmm. Jeannie, let's wait to see what they say. Steve will fill us in if he can. Anyway, right now, I'm starved. Anyone want some eggs?"

Three heads turn toward the bedroom when they hear the twins wake up with howling tears and Mike calling to

Jeannie to help him get them dressed. As Jeannie leaves the kitchen, Steve winks at Diane and says, "Over easy, Hon."

After hearing the announcement about that morning's press conference on the car radio, Claude calls Tom Moon to check in, but there is no answer. He hangs up the phone and continues driving south.

Claude is committed to carrying out his assignment and is determined to allow nothing to prevent him from completing it. That is what a soldier of Allah is trained to do.

With one twin on Steve's knee and the other on Diane's knee, the Ciccone family watches the news conference conducted by Sid Walters.

*"Good morning. On the morning of Saturday, December 4, the FBI, along with the ATF, Homeland Security, the Coast Guard, and local and state authorities, raided two locations in upstate New York, near the Canadian border. The first raid was conducted in Mooers Forks, at a grist mill along the Great Chazy River. The owners of the mill, brothers Thomas and James Moon, were taken into custody there, along with two foreign nationals. We confiscated large quantities of explosives and yellowcake at that location, and we believe the yellowcake is the same powder that was used in the dirty bomb at Grand Central Station.*

*"This morning, Thomas and James Moon have been charged with an act of terrorism, thirty-five counts of murder, and two hundred and sixty-five counts of attempted murder. They have been classified as military combatants and will be held at Fort Drum in upstate New York.*

*"The second raid on December 4 took place at an*

*Islamic mosque and cultural center in Plattsburgh, New York. Imam Khalid al-Mohammed, who was injured in the raid, has been taken into custody, and a large cache of explosives was confiscated from this site. The Imam has been linked to al-Qaida, therefore, he has also been charged as a military combatant. As soon as he is released by his doctors, he will also be incarcerated at Fort Drum.*

*"An undercover agent was able to infiltrate the mosque in Plattsburgh and has provided evidence against the individuals currently in custody. We are also reviewing files and computer hard drives that were taken from both locations. We know that Tom and James Moon were members of the Plattsburgh mosque and that they received explosives from Imam al-Mohammed. It is our belief that the suspects in custody are responsible for the attack at Grand Central Station and on the people of the United States.*

*"Background information will be released on these individuals as soon it is declassified. Since this is an ongoing investigation, I cannot make any further comments or field any questions at this time. I would like to thank the local, state and federal law enforcement personnel who were involved in these raids, as well as the United States Coast Guard. The identity of these brave men and women will not be disclosed due to national security concerns. Thank you."*

At the conclusion of the press conference, there is dead silence in the Ciccone family room as all eyes turn toward Steve.

Steve rises from his chair, and holding his grandson, Frank, against his left shoulder, pats Frank's back and asks, "We won this battle, but will we win the war?"

Turning to his daughter-in-law, he asks, "Jeannie, what do you feed these kids? It smells like something died inside this diaper."

"I'll get it, Dad." Mike rises from the couch and takes Frank into the bedroom to get him cleaned up.

Relieved of his grandson, Steve's attention is caught by sudden movements at the window. "Look, it's snowing!"

George Jackson is in his office, reading the faxed update from Colonel Johnson. He is interrupted by Sandra, his receptionist.

"Mr. Jackson, Colonel Johnson is on line one."

"Morning, Colonel. Looks like we won one!"

"Don't get too excited, George. We may have another problem. Our initial review of the computers and files found during the raids has turned up another name, Claude Killeen, a French National. That same name came up during the interrogation of Aziz. Apparently, Killeen is an operative of al-Qaida and another member of this terror cell, but unfortunately, we don't know where he is.

"All FSA offices are now on high alert. Get out your mattresses; this is going to be a long and bumpy ride."

# CHAPTER TWENTY

It is now late Monday afternoon and Claude has just checked himself into the Intercontinental Hotel in Miami, Florida. He enters his assigned room, number 311, and quickly takes a shower.

During Claude's training with al-Qaida and his subsequent infiltration into the United States, he sported a long, unkempt brown beard and long brown hair, but while he was still in Mooers Forks, he shaved off his beard and dyed his hair blonde, cropping it close to his scalp. With the blue contact lenses that he is now wearing to cover his brown eyes, this blonde-haired, blue-eyed Frenchman will blend into South Florida quite nicely. With identification papers to match, he will be difficult to find.

Claude dresses quickly and leaves the hotel. He needs to get to the vendor in Hialeah so he can purchase Italian Ices and dry ice for his cart. With New Year's Eve a little over three weeks away, he should have plenty of time to establish himself as part of the landscape in Miami's Bayfront Park.


Interrogation officers from the CIA are scheduled to arrive at Fort Drum first thing Tuesday morning. The timing of their arrival is convenient, because Imam Khalid al-Mohammed has just been released for travel by his attending physician, and he will also arrive at Fort Drum Tuesday morning.

As expected, the legal system is having a field day with this case. After the news broke, the ACLU filed a petition to have Tom, James and Khalid reclassified as criminals instead of military combatants. Their argument is that the suspects are being denied their constitutional rights to a free trial as citizens of the United States, and that they are being denied their due process of law. Ultimately, the courts will decide how these individuals will be judged.

Steve and Diane had hoped to take Mike and his family out for dinner this evening, however, six inches of snow on the ground and still more falling have put a halt to those plans.

Steve stares out the window of the small apartment over the garage at Mike's house and turns to Diane.

"Well, I guess we're staying in tonight. I noticed a Chinese take-out place about a few blocks up the road, just before the turnoff into this development. I wonder if they're open."

"Do you know the name of the place?"

"I think it's Kim Sum's or Kim Luc's. Try calling Information."

Diane dials 411 and asks for the number to Kim Sum's in Columbia. Steve was right, and they are open.

"Steve, it's called Kim Sum's. They're open and they'll deliver, even in this snowy mess."

"Good. I'll go ask Mike and Jeannie what they want and then we can place the order."

Steve walks down the steps into the main house to tell his family about the revised plan for dinner while Diane writes down the restaurant's telephone number. Then, she follows Steve down to the family room.

George doesn't notice that it's still snowing. He's in his office, reviewing the latest information sent by the Colonel.

His stack of paperwork now includes a photo of Claude Killeen, which he will distribute to local authorities so they can be on the lookout for him. The only problem is that no one knows that the photo no longer resembles the terrorist they are seeking.

After reading through all the material he has received, George gathers his staff together for a late meeting. Late meetings and long hours are becoming the norm now, at least until this situation is resolved.

# CHAPTER TWENTY-ONE

**Friday, December 10**

The next morning, Agent Sansone has a quiet breakfast at the Herrings Inn near Fort Drum. He is lost in thought, reflecting on the dismal fact that after three days of interrogation, they have made no progress in extracting information from the Moon brothers or the Imam about a potential terrorist attack in the United States. They will resume questioning of the three suspects at Fort Drum this morning.

Meanwhile, in the cities of Mooers, and Mooers Forks, New York, many people are coming forward to talk about the Moon twins after seeing a hotline number advertised in the local newspaper and on the local TV station. Police officers and FBI field agents are following up on all leads and are visiting all businesses near the old watermill on the Great Chazy River.

This morning, they are following up on one particular lead from Ken Silvers, a used car sales manager at the Chevrolet dealer in Ellenburgh Depot, about ten miles from Mooers Forks. Officer Joe Daily from the Mooers police force is on his way there to take a statement from Silvers.

In Maryland, the new day brings a break in the weather,

with almost no trace remaining of the snow that had fallen the day before. With Mike having to work every day until Christmas week, Steve and Diane decide to take advantage of the better weather to get the rest of the family out of the house for a while.

Diane helps Jeannie get the twins dressed for a late morning treat. Rumor has it that an Italian ice cream parlor in Catonsville has the best gelato in the area. It is quite nice today – sunny, with the high forecasted to be in the low forties. Not bad for December in Maryland. When the twins are dressed, everyone climbs into Jeannie's minivan for the twenty minute ride to the ice cream shop.

Agent Robert Sansone is getting restless. He's been waiting in an interrogation room near the brig at Fort Drum for the arrival of an attorney from the American Civil Liberties Union. Finally, the door opens and a young attorney introduces himself.

"Agent Sansone, my name is Jeff Klein, with the ACLU. I have a court order for the release of Kahlid al-Mohammed from military custody. He will be transferred immediately to a civilian prison and tried as a United States citizen."

Although Agent Sansone expected this tactic, he is still upset at the news.

"Are you guys out of your minds? If you go through with this, we won't be able to get any valuable information out of Khalid, and on top of that, you'll be giving him a platform to spew his propaganda and venom to the entire world!"

"Khalid is a citizen of the United States, along with Tom and James Moon. The court has decided that the evidence against the Imam does not warrant his classification as a military combatant. It is most unfortunate that the Moon brothers will not be transferred out of here along with the Imam. You are denying them their constitutional rights."

"Yeah? And what about the rights of the victims at Grand Central Station?"

"Agent Sansone, Kahlid must be released. If you don't comply with this order, you will be held in contempt of court. Two state troopers are standing by to accompany Khalid to the Clinton Correctional Facility in Dannemora, New York."

"The only contemptible person in this room is you. Get the fuck out of my sight."

When Klein leaves the interrogation room, he instructs two guards to remove Khalid from his cell and to begin the process of transferring him into public custody.

After the transfer is complete, the guards return to the cell area, this time leading Tom Moon to the interrogation room for another day of questioning. Today, he will be questioned only by Agent Sansone; the CIA won't be involved. It's a good cop, bad cop thing. Robert Sansone will play the good guy today in the hope that a crucial piece of information will be revealed.

Tom is wearing a gray jumpsuit and looks like he has not shaved for days. His feet are shackled and his hands are cuffed behind him. Sansone asks the guards to release Tom's hands. The guards comply, but they shackle his feet to restraints in the floor before they allow him to sit down. Robert stares at Tom, but does not say a word, because he knows that the first one to talk is the one who loses. Fifteen minutes elapse before Tom speaks.

"Look, if you're just going to stare at me and not say anything, then let me go back to my cell."

"Well, good morning to you, Tom. You look a little unkempt. Would you like a shave?"

"Cut the crap, Sansone. You don't care if I shave or not."

"Okay. Where is Claude Killeen?"

"Never heard of him. Friend of yours?"

"Khalid al-Mohammed says you know him."

"You're striking out. Never heard of him, either."

"Come on, Tom. We have an eyewitness that identifies you as a member of the mosque in Plattsburgh, and he says that you personally received explosives from Khalid. Also, the yellowcake we found at your mill is an exact geological match with the uranium that was exploded at Grand Central Station."

"Allah is pleased, so I am pleased. Three days of this nonsense, and I am still not talking." Turning toward the door, he yells, "GUARDS, GUARDS! Get me outa' here!"

Tom sits back and laughs as the guards release his shackles from the floor, handcuff his hands together and take him back to solitary confinement. Within minutes, they return to the room with Tom's brother, James.


Officer Joe Daily pulls into the Chevy dealership in Ellenburgh Depot and makes his way into the used car department.

"Is Ken Silvers in?"

"He's in his office. I'll get him for you, Officer."

The salesman walks quickly into Ken's office to advise him that a uniformed police officer is waiting to see him. Ken steps out of his office and waves at the officer, motioning for him to join him. Officer Daily enters Ken's office and closes the door behind him.

"Mr. Silvers, I'm from the Mooers police task force that is investigating the Moon brothers. You called our hotline and said you had some information."

"Yes. When you released information about Tom Moon, I remembered that he was here about two weeks ago and that he bought a pickup truck. Paid cash, too."

# CHAPTER TWENTY-TWO

Robert Sansone stares across the table at James Moon. James says nothing and just looks at the floor. Employing the holdout strategy again, Robert waits for James to speak first, but this time, it does not work. James quietly stares at the floor as his left leg twitches up and down. Agent Sansone sits and waits. After thirty minutes, he asks, "Nervous, James?"

James stops twitching and takes a deep breath. He raises his head slowly and stares at Robert with a smile that is reminiscent of the photo of Jared Loughner, the man who was charged with the shooting of U.S. Representative Gabrielle Giffords in Arizona. Then, he quickly becomes sullen again, lowering his head and staring at the floor, while his leg resumes its twitching.

After another twenty minutes of silence, Sansone becomes frustrated and calls the guards in to take James away. As they escort him out of the interrogation room, James turns to look at Robert and says, "It was nice talking with you today. See you again soon?"

Agent Sansone is puzzled. Did he make progress, or was he conned? As he sits in the room alone, his cell phone rings.

The caller informs him that the two foreign nationals who were nabbed near the grist mill have been turned over to ICE, the U.S. Immigration and Customs Enforcement agency, and are being deported. He is also told about the tip that James recently bought a pickup truck that was not found at the mill. Sansone decides to drive to Ellenburgh Depot to personally interview Ken Silvers, the person who turned in the tip.

He'll talk to the Moon brothers again on Monday.

As Steve stands before the display case at Café Di Roma, he looks over the various flavors of gelato.

"Hey, Di! Looks like back home in Italy. Wonder how it tastes."

The clerk picks up on Steve's interest and asks, "Sir, would you like a sample?"

"Sure! How about some of the pistachio?"

The sales clerk grabs a tiny sample spoon and scoops a dollop of pistachio gelato into a small cup, handing it to Steve. Smiling, Steve takes the prize and places it on his tongue.

"Di, it's pretty good! Almost as good as back home. I'm impressed."

Steve is pleasantly surprised to find gelato in Catonsville, Maryland, that is almost equal in quality to what he can find near his home in Italy.

Since it's almost lunch time, the family decides to grab a table and order lunch before they indulge in some of the delicious gelato for dessert.

Robert Sansone has arrived at the used car dealership and is now sitting in Ken Silvers' office.

"So, Mr. Silvers, Officer Daily reported that you sold a late model white Ford F250 pickup truck to Tom and James Moon."

"Yes, it was a 2007 F250, with a trailer hitch. They said they were buying a boat and that they needed to tow it to the river."

"They paid cash for the truck? Isn't that a little unusual?"

"No, not at all. This is farm and wine country, and a lot of our sales are for cash. The only unusual thing is that the sale was completed so quickly. They came in and wanted a pickup truck with a hitch, so I showed them the F250. When they asked for a price, I told them the amount and they took it, without even asking to test drive it. I practically had to force them to try it out before I took their money."

"Did they seem nervous or edgy, or was there anything else out of the ordinary?"

"No, they were quite calm. It was just a very quick and decisive sale."

"They didn't even ask for the CARFAX report?"

"Excuse me, Agent Sansone, can you repeat that? I didn't hear you."

"Oh, nothing, just mumbling to myself. Mr. Silvers, here's my card. If there's anything else you remember, please call me."

Agent Sansone is puzzled. He knows the investigation at the grist mill didn't reveal a pickup truck or a boat or anything else that could be towed, so after he leaves the car dealership, he drives over to the Mooers police station to see what the FBI field operations team has retrieved from Tom's computer.

# CHAPTER TWENTY-THREE

Agents of the CSIS, the Canadian Security Intelligence Service, working in partnership with the Department of Homeland Security and the FBI, are reviewing recent security video tapes of passengers inbound to Montreal Trudeau International Airport. After reports indicated that two of the terror suspects entered Canada through that facility, they are trying to establish exactly when Claude Killeen and the late Josef Malik arrived in the country.

The CSIS agents' endless days of reviewing hours and hours of tapes are finally producing results. A man resembling Claude Killeen is seen on video tape exiting the main terminal and hailing a taxi. The agents make a note of the taxi's number and then contact the taxi company to request access to their pick up records.

In Mooers, New York, Robert Sansone enters the FBI operation center. He approaches three agents who are reviewing the evidence they collected at the watermill and the mosque.

"Gentlemen, what do we have so far?"

"Not much, Bob. It looks like most of their business transactions were conducted in cash. We froze their checking and savings accounts, which have a combined balance of a little over forty-seven thousand dollars. We also found six thousand dollars in cash in a safe in the corner of the storeroom where we found the twenty-five pounds of plastic explosives."

"How about the computer? Any valuable info there?"

"Apparently, the hard drive had just been defragged and reformatted. That doesn't remove all the old data, however, so we sent it to our lab in Manhattan to retrieve the hidden information. We should have a report within a week or so. We did find references to Claude Killeen in emails that were sent to Khalid al-Mohammed that basically stated that Killeen had arrived successfully and was eager to go to work. We also found emails referring to a trailer and a cart, but have no idea what that means."

"Well, guys, I just came from a Chevy dealer about ten miles from here. He sold the Moon's a pickup truck with a hitch because they said they wanted to tow a boat. It looks like what they wanted to tow was a trailer. Now, since we found no truck, no trailer, no cart, and no Claude, I think we can assume they are all together somewhere else. Check with local and state police and see if they have any intersection cameras between here and Plattsburgh. Maybe we can find that pickup and trailer on tape. Also, put out an APB to local law enforcement and the FSA on a white 2007 F250 and trailer. Someone may have seen something, somewhere."

The squeal of an incoming fax stops George Jackson from leaving the office, even though he's been there for fifteen hours straight, and is the only one there this evening. He picks up the paper, reads the update, and curses out loud.

"Well, shit! Be on the lookout for a white Ford pickup truck and a trailer! With all the lawn care companies down here, there has to be hundreds of 'em! The FBI is right on the ball, as usual."

George throws the fax away and goes home.


Grandpa Steve and Grandma Diane are keeping the twins occupied while Jeannie prepares dinner. The family is eagerly awaiting Mike's return home from work so they can enjoy the stuffed shells and wedding soup that Jeannie is busy cooking in the kitchen.

The soup is sure to hit the spot, because the temperature has dropped after the sunny weather earlier in the day, and it is expected to plunge into the low twenties overnight.

When Jeannie hears Mike pull his Legacy GT into the driveway and inside the open garage, she calls out, "Frankie and Donny, Daddy's home!"

# CHAPTER TWENTY-FOUR

**Monday, December 13**

Robert Sansone is heading back to Fort Drum for another round of interrogations. With him is Agent Karen Harris, a criminal profiler from the main FBI headquarters in D.C. Sansone wants her to observe James Moon, since his actions during the last interrogation were unusual, to say the least. Robert believes that if any information is to come out of the Moon brothers, it will be from James. As he drives, his cell phone rings. The call is from the headquarters of the police department in Champlain, New York.

"This is Sansone."

"Mornin'. This is Lieutenant Jason Campbell of the Champlain, New York police. We got a hit on that pickup truck you're looking for. Late Friday night, December third, a white Ford F250 pulling a white trailer was recorded on the intersection camera at Route 11 and I-87. It turned right and headed south on the Interstate."

"Were you able to see who was driving?"

"Not clearly. The driver was wearing a baseball cap, had long dark hair, and was wearing weird sunglasses."

"Damn! He didn't want to be identified on surveillance cameras. Can you bring that tape over to our field office in Mooers? They'll send it to our lab in Manhattan to try to get a closer look at the driver. Hey, thank your guys for this info!"

"Okay, will do."

"Karen, that was the Champlain, New York police. They got a hit on the pickup. From the description we have so far of Claude Killeen, it looks like he was probably driving. We're hoping to get more details from the taxi company at the airport in Montreal."

"Yeah, and hopefully, I'll be able to get a read on James Moon."

Robert calls the FBI office in Manhattan to tell them that the white pickup and trailer are heading south on I-87. Surveillance cameras at every intersection and toll booth south of Plattsburgh will now be reviewed for images of the truck. But finding the pickup may be almost impossible, since they have no idea where it is heading.

The next day, Steve and Diane decide to do some sightseeing while they're in Maryland, so they rent a car and head into D.C. Their first stop is the Basilica of the National Shrine of the Immaculate Conception, often referred to as America's Catholic Church, since it is the largest Catholic Church in North America and one of the ten largest churches in the world. The Basilica is four hundred fifty-nine feet long and contains over sixty separate chapels dedicated to the various apparitions and titles of the Virgin Mary, to whom this minor basilica is dedicated as the patroness of the United States.

As Steve and Diane marvel at the statues, artwork, and mosaics, Steve realizes that they are visiting the shrine on the thirteenth day of the month, the day when the Virgin Mary gives a monthly message to the world through a visionary near their home in South Florida. When he quietly reminds

Diane of the date, they spend a few moments kneeling in prayer in one of the shrine's many pews.

After touring the rest of the shrine, they decide to make their next stop the Smithsonian Air and Space Museum near Dulles International Airport.

On their way to the museum, the weather in D.C. turns nasty. The December sky becomes gray, with the temperature hovering between thirty-five and thirty-eight degrees, and wind and occasional sleet adding to the agony. When Steve spots a Starbucks, he parks near the store so they can get some hot coffee.

Steve brings two Venti Café Mochas to the sofa, where they sit side by side inside the store, away from the cold.

"Wow, Steve. That basilica reminds me of the grand, old churches in Italy. Too bad the kids and grandkids aren't with us."

"Well, we have a camera full of photos for them to see, and anyway, they can visit the shrine themselves. They do live nearby, you know. Besides, the weather today is ugly and the twins would be miserable."

"Come on, Steve. They're used to this weather, not like us,…" She cuts herself short.

"I know, Di, we're old farts. We live in Italy in the spring and summer and spend the fall and winter in Florida. We're not used to this weather. What are we going to do when we can't travel anymore?"

"I'll bring your espresso out to the veranda and we'll wrap each other in blankets and keep each other warm as we enjoy the Mediterranean."

Diane scoots over and snuggles closer to Steve as they drink their coffees and try to get warm.


FBI Agents Robert Sansone and Karen Harris wait for Tom

Moon in the interrogation room at Fort Drum. After he is escorted in and shackled down, his defiant silence begins anew. Robert breaks the silence after only a few minutes.

"Mr. Moon, we have some information to share with you today. Unfortunately for you, we know that you recently bought a pickup truck and that you got your explosives from the mosque in Plattsburgh. Also unfortunately for you, we're currently tracking that pickup truck south on I-87."

Robert's phone rings suddenly and he answers.

"This is Sansone."

"Agent Sansone, this is Special Agent Fred Wallace with the Canadian Security Intelligence Service. The taxi company in Montreal reports that Claude Killeen was driven to the Greyhound Bus Terminal, where security cameras show him boarding a bus for Plattsburgh, New York. He was wearing a baseball cap and sunglasses and had long, dark hair with a dark moustache, and a short, cropped beard. We contacted your Homeland Security Department and asked them to get the local police in Plattsburgh to review security tapes at the Plattsburgh bus terminal. They just confirmed that Tom Moon picked up Claude from the bus."

"Perfect! Thank you very much, and please thank your team for all their help."

Robert disconnects from the call and turns to Tom.

"That was the Canadian Secret Service. We have Claude Killeen on video tape taking a bus to Plattsburgh, and we have you and Claude on tape in Plattsburgh leaving the bus terminal together. Do you still deny knowing him, Mr. Moon?"

Tom is silent, but beads of sweat now appear across his forehead and start to drip down his face.

"Getting warm, are we, Mr. Moon? Have I hit a nerve? Is there a crack in your armor?"

"I have nothing to say to either of you." Tom sits back in his chair, stares at the ceiling, and begins to laugh.

Robert calls the guards. They lead Tom out of the room and replace him with James.

James takes his place in the hot seat and is shackled to the floor restraint by the two guards, who then leave the room. Agent Sansone quickly begins his interrogation.

"James, more information has come to us since we last talked. We know you guys bought a pickup truck, and we traced Claude Killeen from Montreal to Plattsburgh, where Claude and your brother, Tom, were recorded on security cameras together. Your Imam is also throwing both of you under the bus for the bombing, because he doesn't want to be executed like the two of you. So, what do you have to say now, Mr. Moon?"

"Imam al-Mohammed would not abandon us. You are lying."

"Come on James. Why would I lie? Look, Aziz Zarqawi Aziz, your boss, linked Khalid al-Mohammed to al-Qaida. The Imam gave you explosives, and the yellowcake we found at your mill matches the yellowcake at Grand Central Station. You guys are toast. We're screening your computer for hidden info and we know that Claude drove the pickup truck and trailer out of Champlain. So, tell me James, where did he go, and what is he towing?

"Listen, if you guys are so smart, figure it out yourselves before it's too late. I will not cooperate, so you better get on the stick. GUARDS, GET ME OUTA' HERE NOW!"

James gives both agents that wild stare and smiles as he is unshackled and led from the room.

When they are alone, Agent Sansone glances at Karen and asks, "Well, what do you think about the Moon twins?"

"I don't think either of them will let anything slip out under normal interrogation techniques; they have been too well indoctrinated. They have both been trained very well, but the weak one is James. Tom is tough. He broke out in a nervous sweat, but then caught himself. I don't believe that Tom will break, but that James is your best bet."

"You don't think he will break under normal questioning?"

"No, not at all. The CIA was here before you and they got nowhere. Look, to be blunt, waterboarding works, period. But try to prove that to the Attorney General and President Baruch. By the way, that wild stare that James gives, I think it's an act. He doesn't show any other symptoms of having a mental or behavioral disorder, except that he's a radical Muslim terrorist."

As Robert and Karen leave Fort Drum, Agent Sansone calls the FBI's main office in Manhattan to speak to the director.

"Director Hollberg, this is Sansone. I'm coming down there tomorrow. I need a meeting with Sid Walters."

"Okay, Sansone. And the reason for this meeting is?"

"Waterboarding, Sir, waterboarding."

# CHAPTER TWENTY-FIVE

**Tuesday, December 14**

On the twenty-third floor of 26 Federal Plaza in New York City, Assistant Attorney General Sid Walters walks into FBI Director Vince Hollberg's office, where Robert Sansone is already waiting.

"Good morning, Gentlemen."

"Good morning, Sid. This is Agent Robert Sansone. He's working the Moon case."

"Good morning, Mr. Walters."

"Just call me Sid. Now, what is this all about?"

"As you may be aware, CIA interrogation experts and I have been interrogating the Moon brothers. Yesterday, Agent Karen Harris, one of our leading profilers, was with me while I talked with the Moon brothers again. In case you don't know, we located Claude Killeen, a missing terror cell member, on an intersection camera leaving Champlain, New York and heading somewhere south. During my last interrogation session, James Moon basically said that we need to find Claude Killeen before it's 'too late.' Karen Harris' opinion of these two men is that we will not get any further information from them with standard interrogation techniques. She feels these two gentlemen were too well trained and coached to give up any information. We fear that Killeen is setting things up for another attack, but the only people who know the where and when are the Moon brothers. It is Karen's opinion, and also my own, that we need to use extreme interrogation techniques to get this information out of the Moon brothers as soon as possible. That's why I asked for this meeting. We need the Attorney General's approval to go forward, and ultimately the President's approval. If we don't get it, we fear that we may have another Grand Central-type incident sometime soon. I'm convinced that Claude Killeen has yellowcake and explosives with him, wherever he's going. So, the ball is now in your court."

"Damn, you're serious about doing this?"

"As serious as a heart attack, and it needs to be done now. So, why are we still sitting here?"

Sid Walters turns to the FBI Director.

"Vince, do you support this plan?"

"Sid, I need to go through the chain of command. If you're uncomfortable, I'll call the President myself and throw you and the Attorney General under the bus. Those people have killed citizens of the United States, and they will do it again. If it comes out that this administration could have stopped another attack and didn't, who do you think the President is going to blame? Your boss, or me?"

Sid stands up, walks over to the window and looks out at the Hudson River. After a moment, he declares, "Shit, I better get to work, then. Vince, I'll call you as soon as I know something."

The men shake hands and then Sid leaves the office. After the door closes, Agent Sansone turns to the FBI Director.

"Sir, he better get it done, or we're in deep kimchee."

Sid Walters needs a face to face meeting with his boss in order to get this request approved, so he instructs Director Hollberg's assistant to commandeer the Justice Department's

New York helicopter on his behalf so he can get to D. C. as quickly as possible.

Before leaving the building, Sansone makes his way to the FBI's forensic lab to check on the technician's progress in retrieving hidden data from the Moon brother's hard drive, but he's disappointed to learn that there has been no progress. The technicians tell him that they won't have any information until the end of the week.

It's now late afternoon, and Steve and Diane are still out sightseeing. Steve wants to take Diane to Baltimore's Inner Harbor before heading back to Mike's house for dinner. He asks Diane to call Jeannie to let her know that they'll be a little late returning home, but when Jeannie answers the call she tells Diane not to worry; she was just planning to warm up the leftover wedding soup and make a salad for dinner. After hanging up the phone, Diane suggests to Steve that they surprise Jeannie by bringing some crab cakes home to supplement dinner.

When they arrive at the Inner Harbor, Steve parks the rental car at a public garage, and then they walk down East Pratt Street, adjacent to the harbor. The wind has all but died down and the sun is about to set. During their leisurely walk around the harbor, they remember the crab cakes and decide to stop at the Watertable restaurant to order them as take out. While waiting to place their order, Steve glances out the window and notices that the Trade Center, the location of the Maryland FSA office, is just across the street. When he turns to point the building out to Diane, he bumps into Sam DeVito, head of the Baltimore FSA office.

"Gee, they'll let anybody in this place!"

"Steve! How the hell are ya? Retired yet?"

"Was always retired, remember? Sam, I'd like you to

meet my wife, Diane. Diane, this is Sam DeVito. He manages the FSA office here in Baltimore."

"Hi, Sam. I guess you two guys worked together before."

"Diane Summers! I've been a fan of yours for years. You look more beautiful in person than on the screen. What are you guys doing in Baltimore this time of year?"

"Thank you for the compliment, Mr. DeVito. Steve and I are here visiting his son and family for Christmas."

Interrupting Diane, Steve says, "Sam, I guess you've been pretty busy since the bombing in New York."

"Yeah, we're on high alert. I'm down here getting some food for my staff. We've been working long hours."

Smiling, Steve says, "That's exactly why I retired."

The clerk notifies Sam that his order is ready, so he walks up to the cashier to pick it up. After paying, he says goodbye to Steve and Diane and leaves the Ciccone's waiting to place their own order. Within forty minutes, the couple is back in Columbia enjoying good food and good company.


When Sid Walters' helicopter arrives in D.C., he rushes to the Justice Department for his hastily arranged meeting with Attorney General Gloria Simpson.

Meanwhile, Robert Sansone heads home to his loft apartment in New York's Greenwich Village. He knows that there's no point in going back to Fort Drum until he receives a response to his waterboarding request, so he intends to make use of this time to catch up on personal stuff, all the while hoping that Sid Walters is successful in his mission.

# CHAPTER TWENTY-SIX

**Wednesday, December 15**

Standing in the West Wing of the White House, in the hallway outside of the Oval Office, are Colonel Johnson of the FSA, U.S. Attorney General Gloria Simpson, and Assistant U.S. Attorney General Sidney Walters. They are anxiously waiting to meet with President Baruch to discuss the possibility of using enhanced interrogation techniques upon the Moon brothers. It will ultimately be the President's decision whether or not to approve the use of those techniques, and as he is a lame duck President, having been voted out of office in November, his decision will have consequences for future administrations.

The people of the United States voted against the President in the last election because they believe he is an anti-capitalist and that he is too weak on terrorism and too far left on social issues. With the economy currently experiencing a double dip recession, unemployment at ten percent, a fourteen trillion dollar debt, and a government managed healthcare system that no one wanted, President Baruch was proclaimed a one-term president by a wide majority of voters.

"Gloria, how confident are you that you can convince Baruch to approve our request?"

"Colonel, for the sake of the United States, I hope I'm very convincing."

After several more minutes of tense delay, a Secret Service Agent quietly opens the door to the Oval Office and ushers them inside. The President guides his visitors to the Oval Office's lounge area, where they sit together informally.

"Sorry about the delay. We have the new administration's transition team here and it's getting a little hectic. Gloria, you, ah, requested this meeting late last night, so I'm assuming, since you, ah, brought these distinguished gentlemen with you, that this is not just a social call. What's going on with the Moon brothers?"

"Well, Mr. President, the CIA and the FBI have been interrogating Tom and James Moon for several days, but no information has been forthcoming. However, we have learned through other sources, that there is another member of the Moon's terrorist cell. His name is Claude Killeen and he's a French National who has recently gone missing in the United States. We have evidence that the Moon brothers recently purchased a white Ford pickup truck with a trailer attached, and we have video confirmation that a person matching Claude description is driving a similar vehicle heading south on I-87 near Champlain, New York. We have no information on where that vehicle is going or what Claude intends to do, except that we believe there will probably be another attack in the United States. James Moon has issued a veiled threat stating that time is running out, and that if we don't locate Claude Killeen soon it will be too late. Mr. President, I am here this morning at the recommendation of the CIA and the FBI. They believe that without enhanced interrogation techniques, we will not be able to get the information we need to find Claude Killeen quickly and to protect the citizens of the United States."

"Gloria, you want me to give you the authorization to

torture those suspects? That is the one thing I wanted to eliminate during my presidency!"

"Mr. President, you know that enhanced interrogation supplied you with the information to find and eliminate Usama Bin Laden. So, no matter how you want to spin it, it does work."

"Yes, but that information was obtained by the prior administration."

Colonel Johnson stands up.

"Mr. President, President Bush was the last president who had to deal with a surprise attack on this country, and that was over ten years ago. Now, *you* are dealing with a surprise attack on this country. Do you want to be known as the president who could have saved the country from a second attack, but didn't? As of now, you are still the leader of this country. Mr. Baruch, I will be very blunt and to the point. Right now, your legacy as president is probably the worst in this country's history. If Claude Killeen is successful in what he intends to do, your name in the history books won't be worth a damn."

"Well, Colonel, why don't you, ah, tell me how you really feel? Gloria, what is your official position regarding this request?"

"Mr. President, the courts have ruled that Imam Khalid al-Mohammed must stand trial in the civilian court system. He is pleading guilty to aiding and abetting, has lawyered up, and is now plea bargaining. The only potential sources of information that we can now tap are Tom and James Moon. The FBI is currently trying to extract information off Tom's computer, but in my opinion, even if they are successful in retrieving worthwhile leads from that hard drive, you will still need to approve this request so we can obtain specific details."

Sid Walters interrupts the conversation.

"Mr. President, I believe that you need to make your decision now. We should not wait twenty minutes, let alone several days."

"Very well, points taken. Gloria, transfer the Moon brothers to the Guantanamo Bay detention camp and classify them as security risks. At the same time, tell the FBI that they, ah, need to provide me with more information about a possible terrorist attack on this country." Glancing at each person in turn, the President continues, "I approve the use of enhanced interrogation techniques at Guantanamo, whether the FBI obtains any new information or not, but, ah, don't let them know that last part just yet. I want them to work hard to extract as much information as possible from all sources in the time that it takes them to get the Moon brothers to Cuba. If they aren't able to gain any credible information during that time, they may go ahead with enhanced interrogation once the suspects arrive at Guantanamo. That's it. Time's up, people. I have another meeting to attend."

President Baruch rises and walks briskly out the door, leaving the trio staring at each other in amazement. Gloria breaks the silence.

"Okay, Gentlemen, let's go. We have work to do."

As they walk down the halls of the White House, Gloria reaches for her cell phone and dials the United States Marshals Service to make arrangements for transfer of the Moon brothers, while Sid calls FBI Director Vince Hollberg.

As their calls conclude, two White House staff members pass their group in the hallway while discussing the ESPN press conference that is currently under way with the President speculating on which teams will play in the Super Bowl.

When the group overhears those comments, they realize that President Baruch rushed off from their meeting to attend that press conference, and each of them silently thanks the American public for voting him out of office.

Fortunately for the Moon brothers, it's too close to Christmas to begin the process of moving them to Guantanamo, so the transfer will be delayed until after the holiday. It will take about one week to get the brothers and the proper CIA personnel to the military's Caribbean detainment and interrogation facility, so the date for their arrival in Cuba has been set as Sunday, December 26.

That deadline allows the government only five days to find and stop Claude Killeen before the enhanced interrogation techniques begin.

# CHAPTER TWENTY-SEVEN

**Friday, December 17**

FBI Agent Robert Sansone is in his office, drinking a Blue Spoon Company mocha latte while going over the morning reports and the latest intel from the raids in Plattsburgh and the ongoing interrogation of Aziz Zarqawi Aziz in Cyprus. When his phone rings, the voice on the other end is Director Vince Hollberg, who wants to see him immediately.

Latte in hand, Robert heads toward the Director's office. He knocks on the door and enters.

"Yes, Director?"

"Mornin' Bob. Close the door and sit down."

"Yes, Sir."

"The CIA and the U.S. Marshals are moving Tom and James Moon to Guantanamo. The President has approved enhanced interrogation, as long as we can get credible leads from that hard drive we're trying to decipher. The folks in the lab should know if there is anything worthwhile sometime today. My sources at the CIA are telling me that Tom and James won't be at Guantanamo until the day after Christmas, due to the normal slowdown around the Christmas holiday. That means that things are at a standstill until probably Sunday or Monday. I hope Claude keeps quiet until then."

"Director, this morning I reviewed the report on the

information we retrieved from Khalid's hard drive. When our analysts combined that information with the information we recently received from Aziz in Cyprus, they believe that al-Qaida wants to target something big around the beginning of the year. New Year's Eve celebrations, the Presidential Inauguration, and the Super Bowl were all mentioned."

"Well, let's hope our boys can pull even more info off that hard drive. The Super Bowl is in San Diego, so I'll call our office there and then give Colonel Johnson at the FSA a heads up. I'll also alert our main office in D.C. You get down to the lab and pressure them. We can't cancel any of those events, so we need some intel that pinpoints a definite location. Let me know when you have something. We need a city."

"I'm on it, Sir."


Mike is taking a half day off from work today and will be on vacation all of next week, until New Year's Day. The day is a warm one for December in Maryland, with the high forecasted to be in the fifties. The weather service expects the warm temperature to be short lived though, as their data indicates that a cold front will be passing through the area the following week, bringing with it a white Christmas.

Mike intends to spend the afternoon today picking out a Christmas tree and he hopes that his dad will go to the tree lot with him. He wants to choose the family tree with his Dad, just like he did when he was a child, only this time, he will be the one paying for it.

Mike gives Jeannie a quick call as he leaves the office.

"Hi, Hon. Just leaving work now. I should be home in ten minutes. Need anything?"

"Yeah, we're going to order a couple of pizzas to eat while we decorate the tree. Stop and get some beer."

"Okay, will do. Love ya."

Mike stops at the local supermarket to purchase a couple of six packs of Peroni beer and then walks down the frozen food aisle, trying to decide whether to bring home some gelato for desert, as well.

Following Director Hollberg's instructions, Robert Sansone is in the FBI forensic lab, waiting for any information that can be retrieved from Tom Moon's hard drive. He does not have to wait long, as computer geek Bob Harrington soon calls out, "Agent Sansone, we have something!"

Sansone jumps up and rushes over to Bob's work area.

"What do you have?"

"I was able to come up with a history of the websites that were recently hit. There are hotel websites in Philadelphia, Atlanta and Miami, as well as municipal websites in all of those locations. There are also two websites that sell ice cream vending carts and a website that sells beauty supplies."

"Good work! Get me a printout of each site so I can assign agents to investigate them, and get Director Hollberg on the phone."

"Agent Sansone, we're not done here. I should have more information shortly."

"Good. Keep me updated, but now, get me Director Hollberg."

Steve helps Mike carry the seven-foot balsam fir tree into Mike's living room.

"Wow, Hon! That's a tall tree! What did it cost?"

"You don't want to know."

Jeannie sits on the floor as she helps Mike and Steve guide the trunk of the tree into the tree stand.

While Mike and Steve hold the tree upright, Jeannie walks a few feet away and eyeballs it to make sure it's perpendicular to the floor before Mike tightens the support screws that clamp the tree into the stand.

When it's securely in place, Mike cuts the netting from the tree and then stands back to watch as the branches quickly unfold into their natural beauty. After he positions the tree into just the right place in the corner of the room, Jeannie pours some water into the tree stand.

"Mike, I ordered the pizzas. They should be delivered in about ten minutes."

Looking around the room, he asks, "Where are the boys, and where did Dad go? He was just here!"

"He's helping Diane put the boys to bed. Too bad they're not a little older so they can enjoy the tree trimming with us."

"Well, if we had gotten busier six months earlier, they might have been old enough." Mike and Jeannie exchange a hug and kiss just as Steve and Diane walk back into the room.

"Hey, hey, *hey*! Are you two working on another set of twins?"

Before they can reply, the doorbell rings. Jeannie grabs her credit card and walks to the front door to get the pizzas, while Steve goes into the kitchen to get a six-pack of Peroni.


As soon as Agent Sansone passes on the information the FBI lab technician retrieved from Tom Moon's computer, FBI teams in Philadelphia, Atlanta and Miami begin checking for hotel reservations that may have been made for Claude Killeen by Tom or James Moon.

Since the next day is Saturday, they will have to wait until Monday to contact city clerks in each of those cities to see if any vending permits have been issued to the Moon brothers. They will also contact vending cart and beauty supply companies to see what purchases they may have made.

FBI Director Hollberg has just concluded his call to the Director of Homeland Security. He put them, the FSA, and his own bureau in San Diego on high alert in case the Super Bowl is the terrorists' target. FSA offices in Philadelphia, Atlanta, and Fort Lauderdale have also been advised that a terrorist attack may be planned in their general areas for New Year's Eve, and in D.C., the Secret Service and the local police have been advised to increase their surveillance for the upcoming Presidential Inauguration, even though they are always on high alert for such a momentous event.

Although Miami is the Florida city that Tom Moon was investigating on his computer, the Fort Lauderdale FSA office is being called into duty because the agency has no office in Miami. As chief of the Fort Lauderdale office, this crisis could be the first one that George Jackson has to face after taking the office over from his buddy, Steve, when he retired and moved to Italy.

# CHAPTER TWENTY-EIGHT

**Monday, December 20**

On Southeast Sevier Avenue in Knoxville, Tennessee, two FBI agents are pulling up in front of Ice Cream Carts, Etc., to start their investigation into why the company's name appeared on Tom Moon's computer. As the agents pass through the front door of the business, they are met by a sales clerk.

"Can I help you, Gentlemen?"

As the agents present their ID badges, the lead agent responds, "Good morning. My name is Agent Fred Jackson, and this is Agent Christine Dinardi. Is the owner or manager available?"

"Why, yes. Ah…I'll get him."

In a few seconds, a rather portly older man makes his way to the front of the store.

"I'm Domenic Sorrento, I own this place. What do ya need?"

"Is there a place we can talk in private, Mr. Sorrento?"

"Sure, sure. Follow me to my office."

Sorrento leads them into a back office, and then he closes the door behind them.

"Mr. Sorrento, I'm Agent Fred Jackson with the FBI, and this is Agent Christine Dinardi. We are part of the ongoing investigation of the Grand Central Station bombing in New York City."

"Okay, but what does that have to do with me?"

"Several of the suspects we have in custody have visited your website. We're wondering if you've sold any ice cream carts to a Tom or James Moon from Mooers Forks, New York, or if you've sold any carts in the Champlain, Plattsburgh, or Schenectady areas of upstate New York within the last few months."

"Well, the names Tom or James Moon don't sound familiar, but I have sold carts in New York. Let me check my sales records. I have them cross-filed by region, just to see how my website is working out. I'll just access my computer here. Hold on a second."

Domenic accesses his sales files, and within seconds, responds, "Well, I haven't sold any ice cream carts in upstate New York, but I did sell an Italian Ice cart about one month ago to an Islamic mosque in Plattsburgh. It was shipped to the attention of Khalid al-Mohammed."

"Can you print out that order for me, Mr. Sorrento, and do you know how it was paid?"

"Sure, it's printing right now. I believe it was paid by money order. Let me see… Yes, it was a money order. Is there anything else?"

"Yes. Do you know how it was ordered?"

"Yeah, it was done by phone, and the money order followed in the mail. Nothing unusual, except that I never thought I would be selling an Italian Ice cart to a mosque."

"Did you question their purchase, Mr. Sorrento?"

"Yes, in fact I did, and they said they were having a fund raising event and were going to sell Ices, among other things."

"Mr. Sorrento, thank you for your cooperation. Since this is an ongoing investigation, be advised that you cannot tell anyone about our visit today or about the information you have given us. It's a matter of national security."

"Sure, sure. No problem, agents. Here's the information I printed for you."

The agents thank the owner once again and then leave the premises.

Other members of the FBI team are investigating the municipal and beauty supply company websites that were found on the Moons' computer, but so far, they have not collected any new information. A separate team of agents is reviewing all reservations made within the past thirty days at the three hotels listed on the computer. They are looking through over two thousand reservations for any ties to the Moons or to Khalid al-Mohammed.

# CHAPTER TWENTY-NINE

**Wednesday, December 22**

Director Hollberg looks up as Agent Sansone enters his office for their morning meeting on the Claude Killeen investigation. He waits patiently for Sansone to settle himself before beginning.

"Tell me something good, Bob."

Rifling through his notes, Sansone replies, "Well, what I can do is tell you where we are in the investigation, Director. We confirmed that Khalid al-Mohammed purchased an Italian Ice vending cart that was delivered to his mosque in Plattsburgh, but that cart was not there when we raided the place. Also, Claude Killeen has not registered under his own name at any of the hotels we found on Tom's hard drive, and no one who has checked in recently fits the description we have of Mr. Killeen, so we're assuming that he's using an alias and that he has altered his appearance. We haven't found any reservations that were made by Tom or James Moon, either, so we're digging deeper. Agents are reviewing all reservations at those hotels for the entire month of December to see if any of them include a white Ford pickup truck or if any seem out of the ordinary. As of yesterday, we received one hit from the Glenn Hotel in downtown Atlanta. Apparently, a man checked into that hotel with a Ford pickup that fits our description, but when we checked him out, we found that he's at the hotel on business and is scheduled to leave before Christmas.

Sansone pauses while the Director jots down some notes. Then he continues.

"Because of the internet searches about vending permits that we found on Tom's computer, we have advised local police in Philadelphia, Atlanta and Miami to be on the lookout for any new or suspicious street vendors peddling Italian Ices, and to strengthen their plans for surveillance at their respective New Year's Eve celebrations.

"When we looked through the suspects' cell phone records, we found that Tom Moon made many calls to mosques in various cities from Plattsburgh to Albany. We're checking out those leads, but the Imams we've questioned so far haven't been very cooperative. I'm afraid it's going to be hell trying to get search warrants to investigate all those mosques."

Sansone pauses a second time while the Director makes some notes:

"Director, our forensics team has been working nonstop on the computers we confiscated from Tom Moon and the Imam, but they haven't been able to extract any further useful information. Adding to that problem is the major blizzard that has hit the Plattsburgh area, blanketing it with thirty inches of snow. We'll have to wait until the roads clear before we can send another team up to Mooers Forks with a sketch of Claude Killeen to see if anyone recognizes him."

"Sansone, you know that under the Patriot Act, Homeland Security doesn't need a formal search warrant if they consider a situation to be a national security risk, so I'll get them right on those mosques. Get me a list of the ones that were contacted by Tom Moon; maybe something will shake out there. If not, we better hope the CIA at our base in

Cuba extracts useable information from the Moon brothers. Did you get any information from the city clerks in Philly, Atlanta, or Miami?"

"Nothing so far. Due to staff layoffs the upcoming holidays, each city said they won't have any information on new street vending permits until next week. The only thing they did say is that there's no record of Claude Killeen being issued a permit in the last three months."

Along with the FBI, George Jackson and his staff in Fort Lauderdale are reviewing reservations from hotels in the South Florida area, because the Hotel InterContinental's website in downtown Miami was bookmarked on Tom's computer. The hotel is the location of the city's New Year's Eve celebrations, where the "Big Orange" ball rises, instead of falls, during the night's festivities.

The hotel is the perfect location for an evil deed, but so far, there is no indication that Claude Killeen is there. For the past few days, he's been working hard as a vendor of Italian Ices in Bayfront Park. His counterfeit ID identifies him as six-foot tall Guido Rivera, and his ID photo shows a man with blonde hair and blue eyes, a far cry from the real Claude Killeen. The blonde hair dye, shoe lifts and blue contact lenses are a great cover-up, and for every day that he works at Bayfront Park, Claude is becoming less and less suspicious on the local scene.

The municipal parking lot adjacent to Bayfront Park is where Claude has been parking his truck and trailer. At the end of each day, he has been pushing his cart back to the trailer and then driving the truck and trailer to a local storage warehouse, where he is storing the loaded trailer overnight.

He has been driving to Hialeah and paying in cash whenever he has needed to replenish his stock of Italian

Ices, or the dry ice that is needed to keep his product cold, so none of his transactions are traceable. And since he parks his vehicles away from the hotel, there is no record of a truck or trailer attached to his reservation.

A Miami-Dade police officer approaches Claude as he stands at his cart and serves the occasional Italian Ice.

"Can I see your ID and permit, please?"

With a strong European accent, Claude responds, "Yes, certainly, Officer."

Claude shows the officer his New York State driver's license and his temporary street vendor's permit from Miami.

"Mr. Rivera, you have a Miami vendor permit and a New York State driver's license. Can you explain this?"

"*Si*, yes. I am staying at the Intercontinental Hotel until my wife comes down to meet me. She will be here right after New Year's. As soon as she comes into town, we will find an apartment and I will transfer my license to Florida with my permanent address."

"You better make sure you register down here soon. It's illegal to drive here more than thirty days without a Florida driver's license."

The officer hands the identification cards back to "Guido", and then orders a Cherry Ice. Claude gives him the ice, but refuses to take any money for it. The officer thanks him and leaves.

When the officer is out of sight, Claude takes a deep breath and wipes the sweat from his brow.

# CHAPTER THIRTY

**Friday, Christmas Eve**

From their solitary confinement cells at Eglin Air Force Base, Tom and James Moon quietly await their flight to Guantanamo Bay, Cuba on the day after Christmas. CIA interrogation experts will already be on the island, having left McLean, Virginia on Christmas morning in order to be set up and ready for the tough interrogations that are sure to follow the brothers' arrival.

All other members of the teams investigating the Moon brothers will have a couple of days off to enjoy the holiday. Robert Sansone is planning to celebrate the birth of Jesus Christ at his parent's home in Massapequa, New York, but he will be praying that the CIA will be able to acquire detailed information during their continued interrogations in Cyprus, and the upcoming interrogations in Cuba. He knows that if something doesn't break quickly, another terror incident that is presumably scheduled for the New Year will be impossible to stop.

Steve is looking out the window of the mother-in-law apartment over his son's garage while Diane takes a shower. The local weather report calls for light snow this evening.

Even though it's Christmas Eve, he decides to give George Jackson a call to see how he's doing with the investigation in Florida.

"Hey, Geo. How's it hangin'?"

"A little low, Chic, a little low."

"Man, you sound beat. What's up?"

"We got credible evidence that there could be an incident this New Year's Eve in Miami. We've been working 24/7 trying to get details, but no luck yet. Those two assholes we got in upstate New York are on their way to Cuba."

"Guantanamo?"

"Yeah. The CIA is gonna' waterboard the bastards. Look, if anything points to Miami, I'm gonna' need your help. This will be the first crisis I'll be handling since we shot up that ship in Port Everglades. I need your guidance and support, buddy."

"Well, I'm up here in Maryland for Christmas, but we're going back to Florida for New Year's Eve. Angie always throws a good party at his saloon. I guess I could leave here earlier if you need me, as long as the FSA pays my way."

"Well, let's hope nothing comes of all this. Listen, wish your family a Merry Christmas for me, okay?"

"You too, man, and wish me luck when I tell Diane about all this."

"Tell me about what?"

Steve turns and gazes at Diane as she stands in the doorway, dripping wet and wrapped in a towel.

"Well, what did you hear, Di?"

"I heard, 'I guess I could leave early if you need me.' That wasn't Colonel Johnson, was it?"

"No, that was Geo. Something may be going down in Miami, and if it does, he wants my help. I guess I owe him for that Port Everglades thing, and no, I'm not going to do anything stupid."

Diane shakes her head and walks to Steve's side to give him a kiss.

"You can't get this out of your blood, can you? That's one of the reasons I love you so much."

Steve smiles as Diane drops her towel.

Hazmat crews have been working for days, painstakingly cleaning up the yellowcake contamination in Mooers Forks and Manhattan. The old watermill on the Great Chazy River should be clean within forty-eight hours, and while the lower level of Grand Central Station is already clean, the main floor is still closed to the public. The city expects to reopen it in another two weeks, which would be about two weeks ahead of schedule.

One positive result of the Grand Central bombing is that security measures at airports and border crossings between Canada and the United States have been increased dramatically. However, with the miles and miles of uncontrolled borders between the two countries, illegal immigrants continue to cross at will, along with foreign and home grown terrorists.

# CHAPTER THIRTY-ONE

Checking the vicinity to be sure he is alone at his rented U Store storage bay, Claude slowly and delicately begins to wire the explosive yellowcake device into the false bottom that James Moon installed into the Italian Ice vending cart. Claude is preparing the dirty bomb ahead of time, so that it will be ready to detonate at the stroke of midnight on New Year's Eve.

After he finishes wiring the main device, he wires a backup detonation device and sets it to go off automatically a few minutes after twelve, in the event that he is unable to detonate the main device at midnight.

When everything is in place, he steps back and admires his handiwork, knowing that all he needs to do to complete his mission is to press a small button that is located inside the cold chamber of the vending cart. He tries to envision the explosion, which in his mind's eye, will be glorious. Thousands of people are expected to be in front of Miami's Intercontinental Hotel to celebrate the rising of the "Big Orange" ball at midnight on New Year's Eve, and he smiles at the thought of sending so many infidels to hell.


At the end of another long work day, George Jackson stops at Duke's Saloon to have a Christmas drink with his buddy,

Angie. When he walks into the bar, the patrons turn toward the door and shout in unison, "GEO!"

Grinning broadly, Geo proclaims, "Wow, what a greeting! I feel like I'm on TV! Angie, get me a bourbon, *and* a beer!"

Geo makes himself comfortable at the bar while Angie hands him a Daniel's and a Bud.

"Man, I haven't seen you in a while, Geo. What's the skinny?"

Downing his Jack in one gulp, Geo picks up the beer and says, "You know what they say, if I tell ya I gotta' kill ya."

"Bullshit, Geo, bullshit."

"Yeah, you're right. Actually, there may be some shit going down in Miami by New Year's Eve. If it happens, I got Steve coming in to give me support. Are you in?"

"Not just no, but hell no. I know *I'm* getting too old for this stuff, not like the two of you. Steve has retired, how many times? He has a family and a trophy wife, and he's still getting involved with this shit. And you, you're older than he is. Shit, you're older than me! You got a fine woman, a fine pension, and as long as I'm breathin', you got a place to work to keep yourself busy. Retire, Geo. Settle down and act your age."

"You know, you may be right, maybe I will. I just gotta get through New Year's." Holding up his beer, he says, "Merry Christmas, Angie."

"Merry Christmas, Geo, and Godspeed. If anything goes down, be sure to get the bastards."


Snowflakes are beginning to fall as Steve and Diane follow Mike and Jeannie and the twins out of Saint Paul's Church in Ellicott City after Christmas Eve Mass. The church was established in 1838, and is one of the oldest in the Baltimore area.

As they wait for Jeannie to get the twins strapped into their car seats, Diane shivers and asks her husband, "When's the last time you had a white Christmas, Hon?"

"Hmm, I guess it was thirty years ago in New York, when I was a cop."

The falling snow mesmerizes the couple, until Mike interrupts the moment.

"Hey, you two love birds get into the car, will you? You can make snow angels later, if you want. I'm hungry."

"Oh, hell, Mike! You were born hungry!"

After a twenty-minute ride back to the house, Jeannie makes BLT sandwiches while Mike and Diane feed the twins. Steve uses the time before their late night snack to go to the garage apartment to pack a suitcase for himself, in case he needs to leave for Florida the next morning. He has not said anything to his son and daughter-in-law yet, and he hopes he won't have to.

When he walks back into the main house, everyone is sitting around the Christmas tree. He walks over to the front window and watches as the falling snow is reflected through the light from the streetlight across the road. Opening the front door, he walks out onto the small porch and gazes at the quiet and peaceful scene. He doesn't hear a sound—until he's hit in the back of the head by a snowball thrown by his son, who had sneaked out the back door to surprise his father on the porch. The two men scramble over the snow-covered lawn trying to gather enough snow to make more ammunition, while Jeannie records their struggles with her cell phone.

Smiling broadly, Diane wraps her arm around Jeannie and whispers, "Merry Christmas," as the twins hold onto their mother's legs and laugh at their father and grandfather rolling around in the snow.

# CHAPTER THIRTY-TWO

**Christmas Day**

It's Christmas Day, a quiet day for a street vendor, so Claude Killeen leaves his cart at the storage unit and takes a walk around Bayfront Park. He is using this free time to scope out the park for the best area to cause the most chaos. He notes the row of palm trees near the end of Chopin Plaza, close to the children's play area that he normally services with his Ice cart, and recalls that there is usually a lot of foot traffic in that area of the park. Believing that this would be the best place to cause the most injury and contamination, he decides to push his cart into that location on New Year's Eve.

Satisfied that he's made the right decision, he walks over to a Starbucks to get a cup of coffee and enjoy the rest of his day off.


When Donnie and Frankie wake up on Christmas morning, they are delighted to see that after the snowfall the previous evening, about three inches of snow cover everything on the ground with a white blanket. Mike and Steve promised the twins that they would help them build a snow fort next to the driveway, but the presents under the Christmas tree quickly take their minds off the snow.

As the boys attack their gifts from "Santa," their proud parents use their cell phones to record the chaotic spectacle of wrapping paper flying in all directions. Jeannie knows that her parents will be arriving later that morning with more gifts for the boys, so in order to keep the Santa mystique alive for them; she tells her sons that Santa dropped off more gifts for them at their grandparents' home.

The family enjoys some time together around the Christmas tree, but soon it's time for breakfast. It takes a bit of coaxing to lure the twins away from their new toys, but before long, the family has eaten a quick breakfast, and Mike and Steve have dressed the boys in their snowsuits and taken them outside. Jeannie and Diane remain inside the house, taking advantage of the relative peace and quiet to begin the preparations for their Christmas dinner of turkey and all the fixin's.

While Jeannie cooks, she keeps an ear out for the arrival of her parents from their condo in Gettysburg, Pennsylvania, about an hour and a half away. She is eager to see them, and she is happy that they will finally be able to meet Diane. Frankie and Donny are also eager to see their grandparents, because they know their arrival will mean more gifts to open.

While Mike is attempting to build a snowman with Frankie and Steve is busy creating a snow fort with Donny, Joe and Mary Russo's SUV slowly pulls into the driveway. The twins squeal with pleasure at the sight of their second set of grandparents, as Steve brushes snow from his knees and approaches the SUV.

"Merry Christmas, you two! Boy, I haven't seen you in a long time. How's everything?" Steve shakes Joe's hand and gives Mary a kiss on the cheek.

Smiling at his grandchildren, Joe responds, "Merry Christmas to you, Steve! Everything's great with us. I retired a few months ago, and we recently sold our house on Long

Island and bought a condo in Gettysburg. We wanted to move closer to the kids, but the taxes in Maryland are too high, so while we were looking around we found a great place in Gettysburg. The cost of living is lower in Pennsylvania than in Maryland, and it's still a lot closer than being on Long Island!"

Mary interrupts her husband to ask, "Steve, the last time we saw *you*, you were on TV, escorting Diane on the red carpet at the Oscars! Where is that beautiful and talented wife of yours?"

"I think she's helping Jeannie in the kitchen. Let's go inside. It's getting cold out here."

Wanting to be helpful, Steve grabs the couples' Christmas presents from the back of the SUV while Joe scoops up Frankie and Mary hugs Donny as she carries him into the house.

When Steve notices that everyone but Mike is carrying something, or *someone*, into the house, he pushes the Christmas packages into his arms, saying, "You're the young one around here; you take them in."

Steve walks into the house ahead of Mike, while behind him, Mike tries to close the front door without dropping anything.

Upon hearing the commotion made by the new arrivals, Diane and Jeannie walk out of the kitchen to shouts of greetings from Jeannie's parents. Mike places the gifts under the tree while the family members greet each other as best they can, since Mary and Joe are still carrying the twins.

When the initial greetings are over, Mary follows Diane into the kitchen and whispers, "You look so much prettier in person than you do on the screen, but I guess you've heard that before."

"You're so kind, thank you. I guess it is sort of a cliché, but I love hearing it, especially now that I'm getting older."

Overhearing Diane's reply, Steve chimes in from the living room, "Not older, but better! Now, who's ready for a cup of coffee?"

# CHAPTER THIRTY-THREE

**Sunday, December 26**

When the day after Christmas dawns, a very busy time begins for Tom and James Moon. Government officials swarm around the brothers, processing them for their transfer to Guantanamo Bay detention camp and prison in Cuba, a two and a half hour flight from Florida's Eglin Air Force Base. CIA interrogation team members are already waiting for them at the prison, having arrived there from Virginia the previous afternoon.

Enhanced interrogation of Tom and James is scheduled to begin the following day, an experience that is certain to establish it as a day of reckoning for the Moon brothers.

With many people off from work and school on this Monday after Christmas, Claude Killeen is already busy in Bayfront Park selling his Ices and blending into the background. He is trying to make himself as inconspicuous as possible while still managing to flirt with the young girls in their halter tops and Daisy Dukes shorts.

On this first day of Mike's vacation week from work, he is looking forward to watching football all day with his father and father-in-law, while their wives and children go shopping for after Christmas sales at the mall in Columbia. The women are happy to leave the "Neanderthals" in their man cave, knowing that they wouldn't enjoy themselves at the mall.

George is also planning to enjoy the day off after the holiday. He anticipates a relaxing day at Duke's Saloon with Frank, watching football on the widescreen TV, and hoping that Colonel Johnson doesn't call him with any bad news.

# CHAPTER THIRTY-FOUR

**Monday, December 27**

The next morning, Steve and Mike drink their morning coffees together in the kitchen, while the Ciccone women get the twins out of bed.

"Mike, I may have to leave here a little early. Geo called; he may need my help. I know, I know, don't do anything stupid."

"Dad, when are you and Geo going to retire and leave the good guy, bad guy stuff to guys half your age?"

"Hey, don't knock experience! I forgot more than some of those young guns will ever know. Besides, I let them do most of the work. But I know you're right. It does get harder, especially when my sciatica acts up." Sensing that Mike is suppressing a snicker, Steve continues, "Oh, don't you laugh now! One day, you'll be getting dressed in the morning, and you'll do something stupid like trying to tie your shoes, and the pain will shoot down from your waist, across your ass and into your knee, for no apparent reason except to piss you off."

"And Diane? What was her reaction, Dad?"

"My reaction to what?" asks Diane as she walks into the kitchen carrying Frankie.

"Mornin' Babe. I was just telling Mike how I may have to leave early to help Geo."

With Jeannie standing behind her, Mike, Diane and Jeannie stare wide-eyed at Steve, and then they respond in unison, "DON'T DO ANYTHING STUPID!"


That morning, Claude wakes up early, and after saying his morning prayers, he goes down to the lobby for his complimentary hotel breakfast, just as he has every day during his stay at the hotel. He eats quickly, then heads to the municipal parking lot to pick up his truck.

This morning, he needs to drives to Hialeah to purchase more Italian Ices. After that, it will be a day as usual — back to the storage company to load the vending cart into the trailer, then stopping to purchase more dry ice before heading over to Bayfront Park.

In the short time that he has been in Miami, Claude has become a normal part of the park's routine. He waves to the local security guards who are stationed near the Intercontinental hotel, and they wave back at him. He has successfully become one with the population of Miami.

George is also at work early today. He and his team are still going through a list of the Intercontinental Hotel's guests and reservations to see if any of them look suspicious.

This week between Christmas and New Year's promises to be a long one for George, Steve, Agent Sansone, and of course, for the Moon brothers, each of whom is on his way to a rendezvous with destiny.


Two CIA operatives are looking over the setup in the interrogation room that has been reserved exclusively for today's special session at the base in Guantanamo. No one at the base has been told the operatives' names in an effort to preserve their anonymity. When they are satisfied that everything is ready, they summon the guards and ask them to bring Tom Moon in first.

Tom enters the room between two muscular guards, who immediately sit him down at the lone table in the room and shackle him to restraints in the floor. He glowers at the CIA interrogators from across the table, then glances leisurely around the room, stopping when he notices the full tank of water in the far corner.

"So, you guys are giving me a bath today?"

"We ask the questions and you answer."

"Look, you are going to blindfold me, strap me to a chair, then put a sack over my head and pour water up my nose, expecting me to answer questions I know nothing about. Go ahead and have fun. I will not talk."

"Mr. Moon, we convinced Aziz to tell us about you that way, and we will find Claude Killeen that way. So, why don't you avoid all that drama and just tell us. Where is he?"

"Claude who?"

"Mr. Moon, we received information about you and Claude from Aziz Zarqawi Aziz. We have surveillance videos of you picking up Claude at the Plattsburgh bus station, and we have credible evidence that something is going down in Philadelphia, Atlanta or Miami on New Year's Eve. We have certain hotels under surveillance, so if we want to, we can shut them down and interview every person who is renting a room there. We will get Claude, so why don't you make this easy on everyone and tell us what you know?"

"Look, I went to a store to drop off a package that had to be shipped by Greyhound freight, and on my way out of the store, I offered some guy a ride. If you don't like that answer, do what you have to do. Besides, I need a shower anyway."

The CIA operatives unshackle Tom and walk him over to the water tank, while in defiance, he starts singing "God Bless America". The two Marine guards standing outside the room hear Tom's rendition and turn to each other with smirks.

Later that day, Director Hollberg calls Agent Sansone into his office and tells him to close the door behind him.

"Robert, they interrogated Tom Moon today for over six hours. The only information they got out of him was that he said, and I quote, 'You will never find Claude. You don't even know what he looks like.' So now we know that he altered his appearance. Get our artist in forensics to make up a composite sketch of Claude without the long hair and beard, and send it to Mooers police. Maybe we'll get a hit."

"I'm on it."

"Robert, before you leave, did Agent Baddour see Claude in the mosque while he was there?"

"Yes, Sir. He ID'd the photo we have of him with the long hair and beard."

"Show him the new composite sketch just in case."

"Will do."

# CHAPTER THIRTY-FIVE

**Tuesday, December 28**

Modified composite drawings of Claude Killeen with short hair and no beard have been sent to civil authorities and FBI offices in San Diego, Philadelphia, Atlanta, and Miami.

FSA offices in Los Angeles, Baltimore, Atlanta, and Fort Lauderdale were also updated with Claude's new look. When George received the composite sketch at the Fort Lauderdale office, he contacted Miami-Dade police and the manager of the Intercontinental Hotel, the location of the city's New Year's Eve party, then sent four of his men to Miami to reconnoiter the area around the hotel. He instructed them to pose as landscapers "working" in Chopin Plaza.

James Moon is now shackled at the table, staring at the tank of water. The CIA interrogators are watching him quietly. After a few minutes, James begins to fidget and sweat profusely. The interrogators continue to wait.

Seconds tick away slowly, then James breaks the silence.

"I guess you are not just going to wash my feet, are you?"

"Well, they may get a little wet, Mr. Moon. Let me tell you what we know so far and let's see if you can fill in the gaps.

You and your brother are responsible for the bombing at Grand Central Station. You received explosives from Khalid al-Mohammed. Claude Killeen is one of your operatives, and he was picked up by your brother at the Plattsburgh bus depot. You bought a white pickup truck, an Italian Ice vending cart, and a trailer, and Claude drove them south out of Champlain, New York. We also have information from a reliable source that another incident is planned for New Year's Eve. So now tell me, James, where is Claude?"

"Look, I have told you people and the FBI that I do not know where Claude is. Tom handled all of that. Ask him."

"We have, but now I'm asking you. We can do this dry, or we can do this wet. Again, James, what do you know? Where is Claude? Atlanta, Philadelphia, Miami?"

Upon hearing the word "Miami," James looks at the floor and replies, "Wet or dry, I do not know."

The interrogation team unshackles James and escorts him to the water tank.


Steve is sleeping late this morning while Diane watches the morning news in the kitchen of the garage apartment at Mike's house. Suddenly, Steve's cell phone rings. Diane takes it off the charger and answers.

"Hello?"

"Diane? This is George Jackson. Merry Christmas."

"George! Merry Christmas to you!" After a slight pause, she asks, "Is this the phone call Steve told me about?"

"I'm afraid so. Is he there?"

"He's still asleep. Hold on."

Diane places the cell phone on the table and walks into the bedroom to awaken Steve. At the sound of her voice he cracks one eye open, then, when he hears that Geo is on the phone, he bolts out of bed, walks into the kitchen in his skivvies, and grabs the phone. Brushing the hair out of his eyes, he asks, "Geo, what's up?"

"Nothing definite yet, but I think you need to get down here. I got a bad feeling about this. There's a ticket waiting for you at the Southwest counter at BWI for an 11:08 a.m. flight. A police escort will come by in thirty minutes to pick you up. I'll meet you in Fort Lauderdale."

"Wow, you're not giving me a whole lotta' time, bud. See you soon."

Steve hangs up the phone, looks at Diane, and sighs.

"I'm going to Fort Lauderdale today and I'm leaving in thirty minutes. There are no details yet, but Geo is worried."

"Go get ready. I'll tell the kids."


Officer Joe Daily of the Mooers police department has been assigned to work with the FBI to assist them in gathering as much information as possible on the Moon brothers. He has been methodically working his way around to every establishment in town, and his latest stop is Sandi's Kuntry Kitchen on Route 11, the town's only restaurant. When he enters the business, he shows the newest composite sketch of Claude to the restaurant's customers and staff, but no one recognizes him. He exits the restaurant and points his cruiser down Route 11.


Leaving himself enough time to spare, George Jackson drives his FSA-issued black Suburban to Fort Lauderdale-Hollywood International Airport to meet Steve's flight from Maryland. He parks directly in front of Terminal One and climbs out of the car, showing his FSA ID to the officer directing traffic. With its official markings, the SUV can be parked in front of the terminals indefinitely. As he enters the building, his cell phone rings. It's Colonel Johnson.

"George, the CIA has finished interrogating James Moon for today. They eliminated the Super Bowl as a target, and narrowed the possible target cities down to Atlanta and Miami. James told them that 'time is running out,' but they were unable to get any additional information from him, and his brother, Tom, is not talking. The CIA doesn't think Tom will crack, but they believe James is on the verge of breaking. They will work on him again tomorrow. On another note, wintertime in the northern part of the country is not the best time to buy Italian Ices, so we suggest that you contact Italian Ice distributors in the south Florida area to see if Claude has been seen there. Concentrate on businesses in Miami-Dade County and Broward County. I also contacted our office in Atlanta, and they will check distributors in their area. We have to find Claude quick. My bet's on Miami."

"Colonel, we're already on it down here. I assigned an undercover team to keep an eye on the area in front of the Intercontinental Hotel near Bayfront Park, and Steve Ciccone is on his way into town to help me."

"How the hell did you get Steve involved? He told me he was out, and he isn't exactly one of my best friends."

"Yeah, well, he's *my* best friend and that's what counts, but this could be the last time. In fact, Colonel, after this, *I'm* out, too. We're both getting too old for this shit."

"George, I'm older than you, but you're right. We *are* getting old. Semper Fi."


George waits at the luggage ramp for Steve to descend from the upper terminal area. It's early in the afternoon and he wants to bring Steve to the office for a quick briefing.

George waves when he spots his friend on the airport escalator.

"Welcome back to Florida, Chic."

The *compadres* give each other a quick hug and handshake while they walk up to the baggage carousel.

"So, Geo, what do we have so far?"

"I'll brief you at your old office. Too many ears here."

While they wait for the flight's luggage to appear on the baggage carousel, it seems to Steve that it's taking longer to retrieve his bags at the airport than it took to fly to Florida. Finally spotting his bags, he grabs them quickly before they can slip past, then follows Geo out of the airport terminal and into his SUV.

Fifteen minutes later, they enter the FSA office in Fort Lauderdale. Steve happily greets his former crew and gives Sandra, now Geo's receptionist, a hug.

George turns away from the commotion when he notices an incoming fax at the office's fax machine. When he picks up the paperwork, he realizes that it's the copy of Claude's updated image that was sent to him by Colonel Johnson.

"Hey, we gotta' break on Claude's disguise! He now has short blonde hair, blue eyes, and is clean-shaven. Sandra, call down to Miami and get our crew on the phone. Pipe the call into my office when you have them on the line."

Steve follows George into his old office and closes the door behind them. He reacts quickly to catch the cold coke that Geo throws at him from the fridge behind the desk, but before he can take a sip, line two rings and Geo answers.

"Guys, we think the target city is Miami. Sandy is scanning a new composite sketch of Claude into her computer so she can email it to your cell phones. Re-check the Intercontinental Hotel at Bayfront Park to see if they've seen Claude or rented him a room. Call me back when you get the sketch."

Geo turns to Steve. "I have an undercover crew working as landscapers in front of the Intercontinental. They'll call me if they uncover anything significant."

Agent Xavier Hernandez approaches the front desk of the Intercontinental Hotel in his landscaper's overalls and flashes his FSA ID, along with the updated composite sketch.

"Hi, I need a minute of your time. I'm with the FSA, and we're looking for this man. Have you seen him?"

"Seen him? Sure. We rented him a room. Give me a minute and I'll check my records."

A few minutes and a string of computer keystrokes later, the hotel clerk announces, "That man is Guido Rivera. He was here for a couple of weeks, but checked out early this morning."

"Do you know what room he was in?"

"Sure do, but it has already been rented."

"Okay, thanks for your help."

Agent Hernandez turns away from the front desk and calls Geo from his cell phone. "Boss, I got good news and bad news."

"Okay, 'X,' hit me."

"Claude was in Miami and he rented a room at the Intercontinental. The bad news is, he checked out this morning."

"Shit! Okay, come in. We gotta' get more boots on the ground."

George hangs up the phone and looks at Steve.

"The shit just hit the fan. Claude was in Miami, but now he's on the run."

Steve glances up from reading Claude's file and responds, "Yeah, and we're still not positive that we know what he looks like—blonde hair, brown hair, blue eyes, brown eyes, beard, no beard. Look, it's Tuesday, late in the afternoon, and New Year's Eve is three days away. Your best chance to stop this guy is to call off the New Year's hoopla."

"Come on, Chic, the Mayor of Miami is *not* going to call off New Year's Eve."

"Then we better get *everyone* on the phone, and quick. We only have seventy-two hours to find this guy."


As Claude sells Italian Ices at his customary spot in Bayfront Park this afternoon, he notices a crew of men working on the landscaping along Chopin Plaza in front of his hotel. As he watches them, he slowly gets the feeling that a few of them look out of place. There is nothing that he can put his finger on, but a couple of them seem to stand out for some reason. Maybe they are a little too tall; maybe they are a little too clean-shaven. They just seem phony, so he decides to end his work day a little early. But before hauling the trailer to the self-storage unit to secure it for the night, he studies the landscaping crew one more time from a secluded place under the Miami Metromover tracks, across the street from Chopin Plaza. After observing them for a while, he feels satisfied that they are legitimate.

After a late afternoon meal in the hotel restaurant, Claude stands in the front lobby, looking out onto Chopin Plaza. He immediately notices the same landscape crew from earlier in the day, and the same men who had made him uneasy. Without hesitation, he walks back to his room and packs his things. Within ten minutes, he is back in the lobby, checking out of the hotel.

After finalizing his bill, he heads into the men's room. There, he waits until he is alone, then removes a wig from his backpack and places it over his dyed short blonde hair. Putting on dark sunglasses and a baseball cap, he exits the hotel and crosses the street to get his truck from the parking lot.

Claude knows that there are other hotels in the area, and that he still has enough cash on hand to cover all his expenses for the remaining few days before he fulfills his mission. He won't let anything stop him now. If he needs to, he will sleep in his truck.

George's undercover men do not notice Claude as he leaves the area.

# CHAPTER THIRTY-SIX

**Wednesday, December 29**

James Moon once again finds himself in front of the CIA interrogators. They will not waste any more time on Tom, because they feel that James is about to crack.

James is more nervous today, and the interrogators know it. They further unsettle him by ordering him to be unshackled and offering him a cup of hot tea. James grudgingly accepts the tea and slowly sips his beverage.

"So tell me, Mr. Moon, where is Claude? We know that he's not in Philadelphia or San Diego, so where is he?"

James smiles. "He is somewhere safe and sound, and you won't find him in time. And *that* will be glorious."

"Glorious, Mr. Moon? How so?"

"Allah will be pleased, and you will not."

The lead interrogator takes out the updated drawing of Claude without his long hair or beard and asks, "Is this what Claude looks like?"

James looks at the sketch and smiles, but says nothing. The interrogator grabs James's arm and escorts him to the water tank, announcing, "Time to get wet, James, over and over again, until you tell us what we need to know."

After a short search, Claude locates a Holiday Inn a few blocks from the Intercontinental Hotel and rents a room there. Once in his room, he works on changing his appearance again, removing his blue contact lenses and donning a dark wig.

When his new appearance is complete, he drives his pickup truck to the storage facility to continue his transformation. He needs to change his routine in order to throw anyone who may be watching him off the track.

After opening the door to his storage unit, he pulls two ramps out of the trailer, then uses them to push the vending cart onto the bed of his pickup truck. After folding the ramps up, he places them in the back of the pickup, along with the vending cart. As part of his new routine, he will leave the trailer in storage and transport the vending cart to Bayfront Part in his truck.

Although Claude is confident that he has altered his appearance enough and changed his routine sufficiently to remain unnoticed, he decides to lay low for a while and not return to Bayfront Park until New Year's Eve.

He parks his pickup truck behind the Holiday Inn, in a special storage area the hotel provides for its guests' RV trailers and boats, and locks the truck inside the fenced lot.

He is looking forward to the morning of New Year's Eve, when he intends to purchase a fresh supply of Italian Ices to restock the vending cart before his date with destiny that evening.

Officer Joe Daily is continuing to visit every business in Mooers, and he is now at the post office, showing Claude's updated composite sketch to the patrons waiting on line, and asking them if they have seen Claude. When the pastor of Saint Anne's Church enters the building and notices the officer and the composite sketch, he walks up to him and says, "Excuse me, Officer. I think I can help you."

"Yes, Reverend?"

"I saw a man like the one on the sketch you're showing around. He was at the coffee shop at the old grist mill. I was there one morning a few weeks ago for breakfast and I saw him walk from the mill area to the food prep area. Never met the man, but that drawing doesn't do him justice. He had bright blue eyes, piercing blue eyes, and very blonde hair, almost white. Does that help you at all, Officer?"

"Yes, Reverend, it does indeed."

Officer Daily makes a note of the Reverend's personal contact information and walks back to his cruiser to call in the lead.

# CHAPTER THIRTY-SEVEN

Claude spends the afternoon relaxing at the hotel pool, drinking iced tea and enjoying the warm December South Florida weather. He has altered his appearance again, now sporting his natural brown eye color and wearing a beret over his dark-colored wig.

After thinking things over, he decides to make another change in his plans. Instead of replenishing his supply of Italian Ices on New Year's Eve, he aims to head out to Hialeah to purchase them later that afternoon. On this trip, he will buy only two tins of Ices instead of his normal four, filling the rest of the vending cart's tub with dry ice. The cart's insulation will keep the dry ice cold for at least seventy-two hours, so that will give him plenty of time to slip back into sales mode at Bayfront Park on Friday afternoon.

Before leaving for the supply store in Hialeah, Claude alters his appearance again by removing his dark wig and re-inserting his blue contact lenses. After making his purchases he will need to transform himself once again, but since he will probably not return to the hotel until later that evening, he will have time to work on his new disguise the following day.

# CHAPTER THIRTY-EIGHT

After sending Sandra home for the evening, George contacts all the law enforcement agencies involved in this operation to an emergency meeting at his office. As the attendees arrive, Steve spots an old acquaintance in the crowd.

"Colonel? What are you doing here?"

"It's been a long time, Steve."

Frowning, Steve replies, "Not long enough. Why are you in town?"

"We got new information out of Gitmo. One of the Moon brothers finally broke, and he's spilling his guts. We should have more info tomorrow."

"Well, then, I guess we should get this show started."

The FSA's situation room is now full with representatives from Miami-Dade police, Homeland Security, the FBI, and the United States Coast Guard. Also in attendance is the assistant mayor of Miami.

George Jackson starts things rolling.

"Ladies and Gentlemen, each of you has in front of you a folder containing all the information we have been updating your offices with since the bombing in Grand Central Station. As you know, intense investigations after the bombing undercovered the existence of an al-Qaida terror cell that was operating in upstate New York, which we were able to shut down. The reason I called this meeting is let you know that through information we obtained from the terror cell members and their seized records, we have uncovered credible evidence of a threat to the city of Miami that they planned for New Year's Eve. We believe that an attack is scheduled to occur at Bayfront Park sometime during the city's New Year's Eve celebrations. At this time, our urgent recommendation is for the City of Miami to cancel this event."

Anticipating the surprised looks from around the conference table, Geo continues.

"Now hold on. Before anyone speaks, we realize that the event will not be cancelled; that's why you're all here. Please open your folders to the composite image and surveillance photos of our suspected terrorist. His name is Claude Killeen, and he's a French National. He is approximately five foot, ten inches tall, and weighs between 125 to 140 pounds. We believe that he has dark hair and that he's posing as a street vendor selling Italian Ices. Our agents have spotted a man by the name of Guido Rivera selling Ices in Bayfront Park. This man fits Claude's general description, except that he has blonde hair and blue eyes. Guido Rivera was registered at the Intercontinental Hotel at Bayfront Park, but he checked out early this morning. We're checking hotels in the area to see if anyone has seen this man or has recently rented him a room, but as of now, there are no records of him reappearing in any of the local hotels. Before I discuss our next steps, I'd like to ask Colonel Johnson to give us an update on the latest information we've obtained. Colonel, you have the floor."

"Thanks, Geo. Tom and James Moon, the brothers who were operating the terror cell in New York, are now at Gitmo, where they are being 'interrogated with prejudice' by the CIA. The agents were able to break James Moon down with enhanced interrogation techniques, enabling us to learn that the brothers planned a New Year's Eve attack in

Miami that would rival their successful bombing of Grand Central Station. We have reason to believe that the suicide bomber assigned to the New Year's attack is a French citizen named Claude Killeen, and that he is using the name Guido Rivera as an alias in Miami. We don't have much information on Killeen, but since we know he's a French national, we contacted Interpol and asked them to send any details they can provide.

"James Moon also let us know that reservations were made at the Hotel Intercontinental in Miami by a mosque in Albany, New York. That same mosque also obtained a vendor license from the City of Miami, and recently purchased Italian Ice supplies from a wholesaler in Hialeah. The FBI obtained a search warrant for Cascade Ices and Gelato Supply Company, the Hialeah supplier, and will serve it in the morning. In the meantime, the CIA is continuing their interrogations, and they are confident that they will be able to provide us with more information soon. Back to you, George."

"Okay, thanks. I suggest that we set up our field operations center at the Intercontinental Hotel. We believe that area will be ground zero, and we're pretty sure that Claude won't be back there anytime soon. Steve, we need to take advantage of your sharpshooting skills, so I've decided to send you to Miami with two sharpshooters from my staff. You can take up positions on the Miami Metromover tracks adjacent to Bayfront Park. We should also assign uniformed officers to patrol the park, along with undercover operatives from Homeland Security and the FBI. This morning, the Department of the Army notified me that they're sending us their Nuclear Accident or Incident Response and Assistance team (NAIRA). They have special portable radiation detection devices that can pick up the radiation signature from yellowcake, the uranium ore that the Moon brothers used in the New York bombing, since they may try to use it again in Miami. The team will be here early Friday, and they'll be on standby in case we're unable to prevent the attack. Remember, unless we can obtain a detailed description of Claude and determine his whereabouts, everyone will need to be extremely vigilant during this entire operation."

After a short pause, George continues. "Are there any questions before we discuss more specific details of the operation?"

"George, we expect over thirty thousand people at Bayfront Park on New Year's Eve," states Assistant Mayor Weinstein. "If a bomb is detonated, it may be the worst attack on this country since 9/11. Failure is not an option, and neither is cancelling the event. If we cancel, I'm afraid the terrorist may bomb something else we don't already know about. At this point, we're pretty confident that we know where he'll be and when, we just don't know what he looks like yet."

After more discussion, the meeting attendees eventually settle on specific courses of action, then each of them departs for their individual assignments. Colonel Johnson and George Jackson remain behind to set up a radio communications link in the FSA office that will be used to keep in touch with each task force member during Friday's operation.

# CHAPTER THIRTY-NINE

**Thursday, December 30**

On the day before Claude's greatest mission, nervous energy wakes him up early. He showers, then shaves his face, legs and underarms, and also removes what little hair he has on his arms and chest. As he eyes himself in the bathroom mirror, he reaches for a bag filled with cosmetic supplies, then carefully applies foundation, eye shadow, and mascara, finally topping all of it off with a light dusting of powder, some pink blush, and a touch of lipstick. To complete the transformation, he dons fake boobs and a long, dark wig before dressing himself in shorts and a low-necked top. When he is finally satisfied that he no longer looks like himself, he leaves his room and becomes a striking, six-foot, "Maria."

Testing his new look, he walks down to Bayfront Park and hangs around there a while to see if anyone recognizes him as the park's Italian Ice vendor. When it seems that he's in the clear, he leaves the park and goes shopping at Bayside Marketplace for a different outfit for Friday.

When Claude checked into the Holiday Inn the day before, he registered as Maria Lopez. He is confident that his constant disguise changes will confound anyone who may be trying to track him.

Steve Ciccone and two Marine snipers are standing on a secluded platform near the elevated tracks of the Miami Metromover people mover, posing as maintenance men. They arrived at their assigned station a day early so they could survey the area while establishing their covers. Armed with the Army's new xm2010 rifles, they are vigilant, constantly surveying their terrain like a pride of lions searching the Serengeti for their next meal.

"Hey, Steve. Take a look at that chic in the halter top. She's a tall one, and her legs go on forever."

Steve turns and looks down from the elevated tracks toward the playground, watching the show.

"Damn, she's a tall one; could be a model. Wonder who she is."

They return to the pretense of working on the people mover tracks as they continue to maintain their surveillance. Below them, undercover agents are entering the park and posing as families in order to blend into the background. Meanwhile, FBI agents, along with Homeland Security officers, gaze intently out of the windows of their fourth floor hotel room overlooking Bayfront Park. Each of the officers is in constant contact with each other via miniature transmitters inserted into their ears. When the agents in the hotel hear Steve's comments, they also spot the tall woman walking toward the retaining wall near the bay.

All communications with local law enforcement and undercover agents will originate from this hotel room at the Intercontinental Hotel. It will serve as an observation point for the New Year's Eve festivities and also as the team's field operations center. Since the raising of the giant orange at midnight will take place on the outside wall of this hotel, they will have a perfect view of the crowd that will gather in Bayfront Park. They hope they will also have a perfect view of the suicide bomber before he strikes.

Keeping his eye on the activity below him, Steve takes a minute to place call to his son, John. During a quiet moment, he suddenly remembered that Diane will be flying in from Maryland today, and he wants to makes sure that arrangements are in place to pick her up.

"Hey, John. It's Dad."

"Hi, GI Joe! What's shakin'?"

"Very funny. You know, you're not too old to be put over my knee. Hey, don't forget to pick up Di, okay?"

"No problem. I'm leaving in about thirty minutes. Hey, where are you? Oh, never mind, I know you can't tell me. Anyway, give 'em hell, Pop. And be careful!"

# CHAPTER FORTY

**Friday, New Year's Eve**

Steve and two of his men have been sleeping in shifts in the field office at the Intercontinental Hotel. Before going down to the lobby for breakfast, he gives Diane a wakeup call at their condo in Fort Lauderdale.

"Morning, Di. Miss me?"

"I told you, don't call me here. What if my husband answers?"

"Di?"

"Hi, Chic. Miss me?"

"Geez, this whole family has become a bunch of comedians. Of course I miss you, and I hope I can be home later today. Gotta' go back to work now, though. Love ya, babe."

"Be careful, Steve. Remember, you're a grandpa. I love you, too."

Steve hangs up and shakes his head, takes a deep breath, and goes downstairs for breakfast. He has not received an update from Gitmo and there have been no leads about Claude's current whereabouts.


Nearby, Claude has just finished his morning prayers. He

intends to remain in his hotel room until later that afternoon, until the size of the crowd around the park increases enough to complete his mission. Aside from wanting to cause harm to as many people as possible, he also hopes that a larger crowd will enable him to blend in easier and remain unnoticed.

The NAIRA decontamination team is on its way to Miami, but they are being held up on I-95 just north of Savannah, Georgia, due to a tanker truck that flipped over and spilled liquid soap all over the highway. That accident could delay their arrival by a couple of hours.

At the same time, two FBI agents at Cascade Ices in Hialeah are reviewing Claude Killeen's purchases with the owner.

"So what you are saying is that Claude was here Wednesday, buying Ices?"

"Yes, it was late in the afternoon, after 5:00. As you can see from the receipt, he only purchased two tins of Ices. He said he wouldn't need any more right now, that business was a little slow and would get worse after the New Year."

"Did he seem nervous or anxious in any way?"

"No, not at all. He was always calm, but cold and distant, not very friendly. I wondered how he sold anything at all. Not a people person."

"How do mean, not a people person?"

"He acted like he thought his shit didn't stink. Do you know what I'm saying?"

The FBI was also busy this morning. They raided a mosque in Albany, New York, based on information obtained by interrogators at Gitmo. They were able to arrest the mosque's Imam, but it was not without a fight. Armed personnel inside the religious compound tried to defend their territory, resulting in two FBI agents being injured and four being killed before the raid was over. FBI agents seized weapons and computers from the mosque and removed them from the premises for further investigation.

The interrogations at Gitmo have so far been very fruitful, resulting in information that has linked together four mosques in plots against the United States. The mosques in Plattsburgh and Albany have already been raided, and the remaining two, located in Montreal and Burlington, Vermont, will be raided within the next few days.

The afternoon is turning out to be a hot one in Miami, even though it's the last day of December. Steve and his crew are already in position at the park, stationed on the overhead platform of the Metromover tracks and scanning the crowd that is gathering for the evening's festivities. The city expects that over thirty thousand people will be in the area by midnight, however, by the looks of the crowd that has already gathered, the final tally could be increased two-fold. So far, there is no sign of an Italian Ice vendor in the park, or in the immediate area. Steve gets on his headset.

"Any word yet from Gitmo about this Claude asshole?"

"Nothing yet, Steve. We have thirty agents in the park, and the Coast Guard is patrolling Biscayne Bay. NAIRA should have been here by now, but they got hung up on I-95."

Steve looks at his watch. It's 4:40 p.m. and it will be dark within an hour and a half. Even with night vision equipment, firing shots into a crowd is not a great scenario.

Steve turns to his crew. "Well, guys, this isn't going to be easy."

"We're screwed, ain't we, Steve?"

"Oh, *yeah*. Screwed, blued, and tattooed."

Claude is getting ready to make his final appearance in Bayfront Park. He has dressed himself in jeans and a red halter top topped off with a baseball cap through which he has pulled a ponytail from his wig. On his way out of the hotel, he stops to fill a black plastic garbage bag with ice from the vending machine, which he takes to the vending cart that has been stored in the lot behind the hotel. He pours the ice into the compartment that is still cold from the dry ice that had been stored inside it.

After verifying that he had everything necessary for his final evening on earth, he pushes the cart out of the parking lot and down Biscayne Boulevard toward Bayfront Park, slowly making his way toward Chopin Plaza. Agents working the crowd take notice of his arrival.

"Steve, can you pick up the woman walking along the bay's north wall with the vending cart?"

"Got her. She was walking around here yesterday. Go buy something."

Steve watches the agent's transaction through his rifle's Leupold scope and waits for a response.

"Her name is Maria Lopez. At least that's what's on her license."

"Okay, but keep tabs on her. So far, she's the only one with a cart selling Ices."

As day turns into night, the crowd continues to grow. The NAIRA crew finally arrives and parks their rig near the American Airlines Arena on Biscayne Boulevard. Jane Kaufman, the lead FBI agent at the hotel, gets on the line.

"Okay, NAIRA has arrived. I sent an agent to pick up the radiation detector. I'll have him walk through the park with it."

It's only 7:00 p.m., but there are already over twenty thousand people in Bayfront Park. Claude is now in Chopin

Plaza, and the agent holding the radiation detector is one hundred feet away from him.

Jane Kaufman begins an urgent transmission to the team.

"Heads up! Colonel Johnson just updated us with new information. Claude is in disguise. Repeat, Claude is in disguise. Costumes and beauty supplies were purchased through a mosque in Albany. He has perfected multiple identities and he's probably disguised as a woman. Repeat, he's probably dressed as a woman."

Steve breaks in. "Get that detection device over to the broad with the cart near the hotel."

Steve and his team train their sights on the woman. Their Remington Xm2010 rifles are equipped with suppressors and night vision scopes to reduce any panic that may result from a loud gunshot.

The agent carrying the radiation detector makes his way over to Claude slowly, trying not to draw attention to himself or to Claude. Other agents approach the cart and wait a short distance away.

Unfortunately, one detail that was overlooked involves the radiation detector. Its silent mode was not activated before being deployed in the crowd, and as the agent approaches the vending cart, the device starts to beep loudly. Upon hearing the beeps, he calls out, "Oh, shit! We got her!"

Everyone in the immediate area turns to look at the agent frantically trying to shut off the incessant beeping, including Claude. Without hesitation, Claude reaches over the cart and begins to open its top, intending to activate the bomb's countdown clock.

As he watches the unfolding drama through his Leupold scope, Steve wrestles with two opposing thoughts—is the vendor about to serve Italian Ices, or is she about to meet Allah?

Reacting swiftly, Steve takes his shot. Claude's head jerks back as he falls to the ground and agents swarm around the vending cart. They immediately notice that a timer has been set to go off in three hours.

Claude was trying to meet his virgins in paradise, but he failed.

As more and more persons in the crowd begin to notice the commotion surrounding the vending cart, a Miami-Dade police officer calls for EMT's and attempts to disperse the crowd.

"Please clear the area, folks. We have a medical emergency here. It looks like she had a stroke." After receiving little response, he repeats, "Break it up, people! Let's go!"

Within seconds, more police arrive at the scene. FBI and Homeland Security personnel examine the cart and determine that it is safe to be moved away from the crowd. They roll it over to the dock area near Biscayne Bay and wait for the bomb squad to deactivate the bomb.

After taking the shot, Steve and his crew stand down. They pack up their gear and head to the Intercontinental Hotel. Meanwhile, the NAIRA crew arrives at the scene and immediately goes into action, skillfully cutting away the duct tape that's holding the yellowcake against the explosives, and carefully removing it from the cart.

With the radioactive uranium ore now safely removed from the bomb, a Miami-Dade Bomb Squad technician approaches the vending cart and cautiously examines the detonation device, quickly noting that the device has been designed to go off if it is tampered with. The technician reports his observation to his superior, who contacts the operations field office with his findings.

"The bomb squad can't get the explosives out of the cart without possible detonation, and there are too many people in the park to try to move them all out of harm's way.

In addition, our bomb containment chamber is too small to accept the vending cart."

When the details of the bomb squad's dilemma reach the operations office, lead FBI agent Jane Kaufman listens to the problem, then has an idea. She contacts the Coast Guard and directs them to tow a flat barge over to the dock area near the vending cart.

Within thirty minutes, a barge pulls up to the dock and the bomb squad members carefully load the cart onboard. Jane's plan is to get the bomb as far away from the population as possible by towing it out to the ocean through Biscayne Bay and leaving it on the empty barge while the countdown clock ticks the time away, allowing the bomb to detonate without harm to anyone.

Everyone is tense while they wait for the remaining minutes to pass. At the appointed time, the bomb explodes in a burst of energy that quickly sinks the barge, making it the newest addition to Miami's artificial reefs.

After hearty sighs of relief and energetic congratulations are passed around the operations center, Jane leaves the room to find Steve and his Marine snipers enjoying rounds of beers in the lobby lounge of the Intercontinental Hotel. She walks up to him and asks, "Who took the shot?"

Steve raises his hand.

"You still got it, old man! But now we need to get you all upstairs for de-briefing. I doubt we'll be done before midnight."

The group downs their beers and makes their way to the elevator. In the hallway outside of the operations room, Steve stops and places a call to Diane.

"Hey, babe! Good guys, one, bad guys, zero!"

As an explosion goes off in the background, Diane asks, "Steve, what was that?"

"New Year's Eve celebration, Miami-style. Di, save my New Year's kiss for me. I'll be home soon. Love ya, Babe."

"I love you, too, Steve, and thanks for not doing anything stupid."

# EPILOGUE

At eight degrees Celsius, it is a fairly warm January day on the Amalfi Coast of Italy as Steve walks into La Stella's Panetteria off *Via dei Rufolo* in downtown Ravello with Diane, Ken Peters, and his wife, Linda.

Vince looks up when the door opens.

"*Buon giorno,* Steve. Oh, my! Ken Peters!"

"Good grief. They know me over here, too!"

Steve laughs. "Vince, I didn't know you watched NASCAR." Turning to Ken, he explains, "Vince lived in New York for years before he returned home to Italy."

"Hey, Steve, when I couldn't get my Formula One in America, I watched NASCAR instead. Not as good, though," Vince adds.

As the group continues to chat, Steve orders cappuccinos for everyone, along with some of Vince's mouth-watering sfogliatelle.


After months of legal maneuvering, the military trial of Tom and James Moon was put on a fast track, and the brothers were eventually convicted of terrorism, murder, and crimes against the United States. Tom was sentenced to death and was executed by a military firing squad, while James was sentenced to a life of solitary confinement. He was able to avoid the death penalty because of the cooperation he provided, however, three months into his sentence, he committed suicide.

For his part in the terrorist plots, Imam Khalid al-Mohammed was tried in a civilian court and sentenced to forty years to life, but while he was waiting to be transferred to a maximum security prison, he was murdered in his cell.

Even during tense times, life goes on. The Ciccone family celebrated two significant events after the tension of the terrorist attacks and the subsequent trials died down. Just before purchasing a larger home along the Intracoastal Waterway in Fort Lauderdale, John and Carla were blessed with the birth of a baby boy they named Steven. And a few months later, Mike and Jeannie found out that they were expecting again, eventually welcoming a beautiful baby girl into their family as a complement to their twin boys.

With the passing of time, Steve's friends have also moved on. True to his word, George "Geo" Jackson resigned from the FSA and went into partnership with his pal, Frank "Angie" Angelo, at Duke's Saloon. They spend many evenings together now, entertaining old friends and new in the relaxing atmosphere of their casual establishment.

Finally, Steve re-retired from the rat race, submitting his resignation to Colonel Johnson after the New Year's Eve operation was put to bed. He still receives occasional queries from the Colonel, but he is determined to live out his remaining years with Diane in peace and quiet, spending most of each year on the Amalfi Coast and visiting family and friends in Florida and Maryland during the winter.

And every winter, Chic and Angie are determined to continue to enjoy a "man day" at Eglin Air Force Base, where Steve can still hit his target 1,000 yards down range.

Some things never change.